"A superb debut by an exciting new voice in the thriller genre. Remember Tom Wilde. In the coming years, you'll be seeing his name a lot on book covers."

—Steve Berry,
New York Times bestselling author of
The Jefferson Key

THE
BLOOD
OF
ALEXANDER

TOM WILDE

TOR®

A TOM DOHERTY ASSOCIATES BOOK
NEW YORK

This is a work of fiction. All of the characters, organizations, and events portrayed in this novel are either products of the author's imagination or are used fictitiously.

THE BLOOD OF ALEXANDER

Copyright © 2014 by Tom Wilde

All rights reserved.

A Tor Book
Published by Tom Doherty Associates, LLC
175 Fifth Avenue
New York, NY 10010

www.tor-forge.com

Tor® is a registered trademark of Tom Doherty Associates, LLC.

ISBN 978-0-7653-6947-5

Tor books may be purchased for educational, business, or promotional use. For information on bulk purchases, please contact the Macmillan Corporate and Premium Sales Department at 1-800-221-7945, extension 5442, or write to specialmarkets@macmillan.com.

First Edition: April 2014
First Mass Market Edition: February 2015

Printed in the United States of America

0 9 8 7 6 5 4 3 2 1

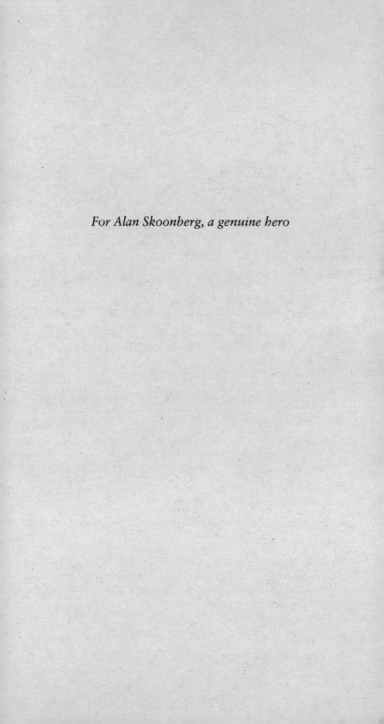

For Alan Skoonberg, a genuine hero

ACKNOWLEDGMENTS

I owe a great debt of gratitude to the people who made this story possible:

My agent, Eleanor Wood, for her belief in me.

Robert Gleason of Tor/Forge for giving me the opportunity.

Christina MacDonald for her superb copyediting; all remaining errors and omissions are my fault alone.

Kelly Quinn for her unceasing diligence.

Denise and Nicole, for all the reasons why.

And for all the men and women of Beta Team—past, present, and future. History wouldn't be the same without you.

THE
BLOOD
OF
ALEXANDER

PART I

I have been called upon to change the face of the world.

—NAPOLEON BONAPARTE

CHAPTER ONE

Bamiyan, Afghanistan

I'd spent the day in the place where the gods used to abide, staring for hours at one of the enormous, empty stone cradles where, nearly two thousand years ago, men carved the gigantic likeness of the Buddha out of the living rock. For hundreds of years, travelers along the Silk Road would come and see and be amazed. No one knows how long it took to create the magnificent images of the Light of the Universe. But it took only minutes for men to destroy them.

The mountainside was sun-bleached and wind-scoured, pockmarked with man-made caves that used to serve as homes for the refugees who were forced to live in them. I'd come to this largely forsaken part of the world along with a convoy of United Nations relief workers—until this morning, when I slipped away from the motorized caravan and kept out of sight until they had left for the return trip to Kabul. The local men and women paid me no attention as they went about the business of scratching out a living, save for the times they would keep their curious children, whose robes and clothes provided the only flecks of color against the timeworn landscape, from looking too long at the stranger near their village.

I stayed until nightfall near the place where a half-blind mullah and his illiterate henchmen had used tank shells and explosives to destroy a sacred and ancient marvel, all because they believed their god would have wanted it that way. At the time it was the best place I could be. The sight of the massive ugly scars where beauty once dwelt burned into my soul the reason I was here, and why I was going to meet with a man who would doubtless try to kill me.

When the moon crested the surrounding mountains and washed the desolate outskirts of Bamiyan in silver and sepia, I made my way to the lonely rendezvous point, wondering if I was going to freeze to death before I made my appointment. Finally, I spotted vehicle headlights cautiously bouncing along the dirt road. I shielded my eyes against the glare as I waited for the Land Rover to grind to a halt. The sound of the four doors opening was followed by the clicks and clacks of automatic rifles being brought to ready and a booming laugh I remembered all too well.

"Jonathan Blake! My good friend!"

"Yusef Mohammad," I called in return, opening my arms in a gesture of greeting and to show that I was the only person around for miles that didn't carry a firearm. The last time I had seen Yusef, he had been dressed in the Western-style suit of an Istanbul businessman, but tonight I saw that he'd donned the traditional headdress with army-style fatigues, complete with a pistol and gun belt as opposed to an automatic rifle, showing that he was in management. "What have you brought for me?" he asked.

"My friendship. And a large amount of money," I replied.

Yusef stepped around to the front of his Land Rover while his three men scoured the roadside with flashlight beams. "I thought we'd agreed to meet alone," I said. "What's with the henchmen?"

Yusef stroked his beard with a pudgy hand. "Henchmen? What henchmen? These men are practically my family. I am quite certain that one of them will marry my sister one day. Now, will you take some tea?"

Yusef Mohammad was an opium smuggler, a small arms dealer, and a trafficker in anything valuable that he could lay his hands on, but he always respected tradition and hospitality. This meant he wouldn't try to poison me until he'd gotten his money. Yusef and I had a history together in this part of the world. The first time we collided was when the Argo Foundation sent me to help smuggle out part of the Bactrian Hoard, a collection of two-thousand-year-old golden artifacts discovered in the 1970s and hidden away by the Afghanistan people in the wake of Russian invasions and the Taliban regime. My job was to see that the treasure didn't fall into the wrong hands. I employed Yusef for his criminal expertise and told him that I'd need to get two shipments out of the country, and that I'd send the first shipment, of less valuable antiquities, as a test to make sure we could pull it off. Sure enough, the first shipment made it safely over the border into Pakistan, but the second one mysteriously vanished.

My only regret was that I couldn't see Yusef Mohammad's face as he broke open the second crate, which he doubtless stole, only to find all the carefully packaged pieces of army tank parts, spent shell casings, and other worthless junk I'd packed instead. Ever since, the knowledge that Yusef would always try and double-cross me was one of the very few constants in my world.

I came up to the hood of the car while Yusef produced a thermos and plastic cups and poured for the two of us. His men stood back in a rough semicircle, ready to kill me when the social pleasantries were concluded.

The tea was sweet though tepid, and a welcome relief to my desert-parched throat. After I had my drink, Yusef rubbed his hands together in anticipation, the universal signal to commence business. "So, my good friend, about this money you have for me, is it American dollars, or euros? I am hoping for euros."

"Gold, actually."

I could see Yusef, underlit by the headlights, wince through his beard. "Gold? What are you, a barbarian? What am I to do with gold?"

I shrugged. "Best I could do at the time. I got ahold of a stash of pre-Apartheid Krugerrands. If it makes you feel better, last time I checked the world market prices, you're getting over ten percent of what we agreed upon."

"Ten percent, eh?" Yusef mused. He looked me up and down. "And just where is this treasure?"

"Close by. I'd like to see what I came for first."

Yusef's eyes flashed, then he remembered to smile. He opened his hands and performed a little bow. "As you wish." I watched as he picked up the thermos and unscrewed the top, carefully removing a hollow cylinder of black plastic. Without making any sudden moves, I brought out a small but potent flashlight of my own and illuminated the hood of the vehicle. With a surprising bit of delicacy, Yusef slowly unrolled the plastic until it revealed the ancient curved birch-bark parchment that I had traveled over half the world to see.

I hardly dared to breathe as I beheld the nearly two-thousand-year-old artifact, as if afraid it would crumble into the dust of history before my eyes. Through the chilled, dry air came a faint scent of something that evoked ashes and old incense. In recent past years, other such scrolls had been unearthed from their hiding places and smuggled out of Afghanistan. Since their discovery they'd been dubbed "The Dead Sea Scrolls of Buddhism," and every fragment was a fragile pearl beyond price. The blood beat in my ears as I matched the faded letters with the photograph Yusef had sent along with a letter inquiring if I wanted to purchase this "little scrap of paper," or should he just blow his nose with it?

I suddenly realized that Yusef had been clearing his throat for my attention. "So," he said finally. "If you are satisfied?"

I was. The experts back at the Argo Foundation had analyzed the writing on the photograph, and I'd memorized the pattern of the characters before leaving New York. I'd personally handled scrolls of this nature before, but never one so old and valuable. I just nodded and carefully rewrapped the scroll, taking great pains not to stress the delicate material. "Was this piece the only one you found?" I asked.

He nodded. "Yes. The man I got it from convinced

me he was not hiding any more. Now, as for my money?"

I slipped the parchment into a stainless steel container brought along for the occasion and placed it into a secured pouch on my thigh. When it was safely packed away I pushed the button on the little remote transmitter I kept out of sight in my pocket. There was a sound like a cricket chirping and off the road to the south a blinking red light appeared, all of which caused Yusef's men to noisily swing their weapons around looking for something to shoot.

Yusef himself gave out a high-pitched shriek as he dropped himself down to a near fetal position. When he realized he wasn't about to meet his demise, he slowly stood up with murder in his eyes. "Ha," he said hollowly. "A joke."

I tried to look innocent. "What? I didn't want to lose all that gold in the dark, did I?"

Yusef kept his glowering expression aimed at me while he hissed some commands at his men. Two of the gunmen ran off across the rock-strewn ground toward the blinking beacon while the third came up and placed himself between his employer/future brother-in-law and me. I noticed the way he kept his ghutra wrapped around his face, concealing everything but his eyes—a certain sign he was expecting to perform some dark deeds tonight. Without taking his eyes from his two running errand boys, Yusef asked, "So, how were you planning to leave here?"

"Me? I was just going to fly away."

"Truly?" Yusef scanned the star-filled sky. "By the way, how did you manage to get gold into this country?"

"Easy. I put it into boxes marked 'rocket-propelled grenades.'"

"Another joke," Yusef said flatly.

"Well, come on. I don't ask you how you smuggle all that opium, do I?" I knew by now Yusef's men would be digging up the box I had placed off the road, and I decided it was time to put the cards on the table. "You're not planning on letting me leave here, are you?"

He had the grace to sigh and pretend to be sad. "No, my friend. I am certain that it was you who caused me to lose my arms shipment outside of Istanbul after you got your precious Babylonian trinkets last year. I lost money on that deal. Besides, if you think this scroll is valuable, then others will too. A good merchant can sell something once, but a great one can sell the same item many times over." From out of the darkness, I heard one of Yusef's men gleefully shout, *"Peroozi!"* That was my signal to turn my head away, shut my eyes, and hit the second button on my remote transmitter.

The magnesium-laced explosive I had set up between the gold stash and the road blew up with a lightning-bright flash, guaranteed to blind anyone looking in that direction. I kept my eyes shut while I rolled to the ground and took Yusef's remaining man off his feet at the knees, dropping him to his back with a satisfying *thump*. Working blind, I slid my hands up his arms; my left one clamped a hold on his trapezius to paralyze his right arm while my free hand found his trigger finger. I shoved his rifle toward the front of the Land Rover and squeezed off a short burst, slamming high-velocity rounds into the engine block and radiator, and was rewarded with hearing a steam-hot hissing sound. I finished him off with a left-hand chop into his carotid sinus, grabbed the forestock of his rifle, and shot off the rest of the magazine out toward the stars, well over the heads of the remaining thugs. Then I got to my feet and ran like hell down the road.

I didn't get five paces away before the idiots behind me opened up with full automatic fire. Instinctively, they were shooting at the source of the blinding explosion, forgetting the fact that they were aiming at their own people and vehicle beyond. Over the shuddering din of the gunshots, I could hear Yusef screaming at them. Pure music to my ears. Only I didn't have the time to enjoy it; I was coming to the really crazy part of my escape plan.

I had to risk using my flashlight, sweeping the ground until I spotted the small rock cairn I'd set up by the side of the road. I ran up to the camouflaged cover where I'd hidden my ticket out. I hadn't lied when I told Yusef I was going to fly out of here. I tore off the tarp where I'd concealed the engine backpack of my powered paraglider, the half parachute, half backpack propeller contraption that I was now betting my life upon. The whole unit fit inside an oversized duffel bag that I'd lugged to the arranged meeting spot outside Bamiyan the night before. The adrenaline surge I'd been running on helped me hoist the eighty-pound motor unit onto my back, but at the same time made my fingers tremble while locking the quick-release straps to my arms and legs. It didn't help to hear Yusef getting his men back under control. Through the clear desert air I could hear the telltale sounds of automatic weapons being reloaded.

I hit the engine starter and took off running away from Yusef and his goons. The lines connected to the parachute snapped taut as the propeller motor roared to life with a sound that seemed to travel over half the world. I dragged the parawing until it caught the air, and I was suddenly in a waking nightmare of running as hard as I could while the parawing grabbed air and slowed me down as the pops and whines of high-velocity bullets whipped through the space around me.

Finally, after struggling through a small eternity in hell, I felt the lines of the chute pull upward and my running feet left the earth once, twice, and then with a throat-clutching moment when my legs dropped and dragged over the rough ground, I was yanked into the air. I opened the throttle full up and took to the star-filled sky like a puppet on a string.

The vibrating roar of the engine filled my head as I left the cold, dusty ground behind me, and all my fear blew out of my body through an uncontrollable fit of laughter—just as it always does in times such as these when I'm surprised to find myself still alive despite my own best efforts.

For now all I had to do was get some distance between me and the men who wanted to kill me, without splattering myself against the jagged, snowcapped Hindu Kush mountains, then take my flying contraption down to the eastbound road, going low and slow until I'd covered the ten miles or so to where a truck with my fellow Argo Foundation compatriots was waiting, and then a leisurely but bumpy ride back to Kabul. With any luck, anyone hearing the whine of my engine would mistake it for a military remote-piloted drone and get under cover as I sailed overhead.

As I flew over the moon-washed rock and scrub tree desert under a blanket of countless Afghan stars, I was happy. Not only because I'd just managed to pull off a coup that left all involved still alive, but mostly because at this time I had no idea how much trouble that damn dried-up piece of parchment was going to cause me.

CHAPTER TWO

New York City

I was late for my appointment, but it was hard to leave one of my favorite places in the entire world. For me, the arms and armor wing of the Metropolitan Museum is far and away the best toy show ever. It has everything from a small army of knights in full armor to a display of the history of firearms and beautiful examples of all sorts of wicked, deadly stuff from throughout time. Not that I don't have a love for all of the other magnificent pieces of art and artifacts the museum holds, but like many a kid I had a fascination with swords and other deadly implements, and mine I never completely outgrew.

I was just about to tear myself away from the late Medieval period, hopefully in time to keep my boss from tearing something personal of mine, when I heard a distinctly feminine voice say from close behind me, "What a shame, it's dented."

The owner of the voice, which had a quixotic blend of warm tone and cool inflection, had a face as pale as ivory and eyes of golden, radiant brown. Her hair was golden as well, falling to her shoulders in waves shot through with molten bronze, and a secretive smile played on her lips. I suddenly remembered why my fascination with swords and such fell into a distant second place during my early teenage years.

"Dented?" I asked. "You referring to me, or my friend here?" The friend in question was a seventeenth-century display of harquebus armor half-plate, forged in London.

The woman gave me a quick but encompassing glance. "I was speaking of your friend, as you call him. You don't look much like the Galahad type."

I made a small bow of acknowledgement, seeing how I was dressed in my habitual black sports coat and slacks. I noted that the woman, in a white tailored jacket and skirt with silver necklace and earrings, made a contrast to me—a White Queen to my Black Knight. "Actually," I said, "that little dent in the breastplate was an important selling point."

"Selling point?"

"Certainly. That piece was made back in the day when firearms were starting to come into fashion. Armorers, when they finished making a breastplate, would shoot a gun at it. If the bullet was deflected, then the armorer declared the plate as bulletproof."

She arched a delicate eyebrow. "And if the bullet happened to go through the plate?"

"Then it was back to the forge, or I suppose the armorer could sell it at a discount: 'On sale, semi-bulletproof,' that sort of thing. By the way, I'm—"

"Late," she interrupted me.

"Excuse me?"

"You're late. For your meeting."

"Okay," I said slowly. "So that makes you . . . ?"

"The woman who was sent to round you up. Are you coming quietly, or do we continue discussing how things get dented?"

I half-raised my hands in surrender, and she gave me the "after you" gesture, which in turn put her diamond wedding ring set on display. Ah, well. The flirtation was fun while it lasted.

We walked together through the grand halls, traveling past the remnants of human history as we made our way up to the Rose Room. As usual for a summoning to the Inner Circle of the Argo Foundation, I hadn't been given any advance information—we just don't trust any modern communication system, not even our own. But whatever the reason that made me drop everything to fly to New York, if the enchanting creature walking beside me was involved, I was glad I came.

The Rose Room is the smallest of the private dining areas in the Metropolitan. The museum lets us have it whenever we need an out-of-the-way place to conduct private business, in consideration of all the "donations" of art and antiques the Argo Foundation has made over the years. The room is appointed with a single long oval table and a slanted floor-to-ceiling window that offered a magnificent view overlooking Central Park on this spring afternoon. A view that was currently eclipsed as Nicholas Riley, the founder of the Argo Foundation, rose to greet me. "Blake!" he roared, the prelude to the traditional bone-crushing hug.

Nicholas Riley is a man of six foot six, compacted down into a globular five-foot-eight body. With the face of a charming, blue-eyed gnome king wreathed with a fringe of snow-white hair, Old Nick looked like he'd be everyone's favorite jolly uncle. Having seen him angry, I knew better. I once again had to marvel at Nick Riley's tailors—making those expensive suits look good on his frame must have been like trying to dress a weather balloon. Standing behind Nick was the ever-present Mr. Singh in his never-varied black Nehru jacket and blue turban, which, along with the circular steel kara bracelet, silently proclaimed his Sikh faith. His razor-sharp Kirpan he kept carefully out of sight. When Nicholas let me up for air he stood back and proclaimed, "Damn, boy! We had to send a search party, but it's good to see you! C'mon over and meet our guests."

The woman in white who'd come for me went up to a man of advanced years, stooped with the weight of time and leaning upon a slender black cane. His face was like old parchment and of a distinctly vulpine cast. He was dressed in an expensive black suit that would have befitted an upscale undertaker, even though he looked more inclined to be a customer of that profession in the very near future. Nicholas did the introductions:

"Mr. Jonas, this here is Jonathan Blake, the young man you're so interested in."

Mr. Jonas nodded his head in a brief bow as Nick finished up by saying, "Mr. Jonas here is with the government intelligence services."

I felt my smile freeze into place at that piece of news and hoped the shock didn't show on my face. Because while to the world at large the Argo Foundation is a nonprofit corporation that champions the cause of preserving the past and expanding the boundaries of man's knowledge of his own history upon planet Earth, there's a secret about us we keep hidden as deeply as the location of Plato's Atlantis.

To put it simply, we're pirates.

But the madness in our method is that we only prey upon the smugglers, tomb robbers, and thieves who traffic in the treasures of the past. So even though our methods are unlawful, our cause is just. The relics that remain of mankind's history on earth are rare and often delicate, and it's an unfortunate fact that criminals will steal and smuggle artifacts with no more thought than they use when smuggling drugs or guns. So we just make like modern-day pirates and steal from the thieves and looters and then make certain that whatever treasures we recover find a good home. Although I can't say we're all that altruistic; we usually make a pretty good dishonest dollar or two on the transaction.

But historically speaking, pirates and governments were deadly enemies of long standing, so I was torn between curiosity and caution in regard to what Mr. Jonas would want with me.

I tried to keep my poker face intact as Mr. Jonas said with a deep, sepulchral voice, "You've already met my associate, Caitlin Street." I just nodded to the woman who was now doubly scratched off my list of potential mates. Married was one thing, but a married government agent? To Jonas, I said, "So what is it I can do for you? And why the interest in little ol' me?"

We all took our seats at the table as Jonas said, "Mr. Blake, we have received information concerning you from an associate of yours. You know Mr. Yusef Mohammad, of course?"

So there it was—after all the trouble I took to keep from having to kill that drug-peddling, motherless little demon, he goes and rats me out to my own government. So much for honor among thieves. I kept myself in neutral as I replied, "So, how is dear old Yusef the Storyteller these days? Doing time in a Turkish prison, I hope?"

Mr. Jonas was unmoved. "Mr. Mohammad is what we call an 'intelligence asset'; he supplies us with information regarding the Middle East."

"Is that all he supplies?" I asked. "You know he's a drug smuggler and illegal arms merchant, right?"

My announcement had no apparent effect on Mr. Jonas's frozen features as he said, "I shall start from the beginning."

"For those who came in late," Nicholas rumbled, looking pointedly at me.

Caitlin Street lifted an armored briefcase from the floor to the table and popped it open, revealing a compact laptop inside. The built-in screen fired up at the touch of a button, and I saw Mr. Singh, Argo's technical guru, lean toward the machine with interest lighting his dark eyes.

The display revealed a close-up photograph of a man's face, broad featured and framed with long, wavy, snow-white hair and beard. In stark contrast, the man's large, dark eyes held a hypnotic stare.

"This is James Phillip Vanya," Mr. Jonas explained. "Almost thirty years ago he was an American citizen living in the San Francisco area, a college student and self-published poet. Shortly after he dropped out of college he ran into some trouble with the law and had arrest warrants for drug possession issued for him. His parents had money, so they shipped him off to Europe to avoid prosecution. No one heard or cared about him until the 1980s. Now, does anyone here know anything about a group called the Children of Cronos?"

"They have any hit singles make it on the charts?" I asked.

Mr. Jonas was not amused, but the lovely Caitlin smiled as she said, "Not that kind of group. The Children of Cronos are a religious cult. And Vanya is their founder and leader."

"Cronos was the father of Zeus, Poseidon, and Pluto, among others in the Greek pantheon," Nicholas added. "Until his children killed him."

Mr. Jonas took back control of the conversation. "In this example, Vanya published some books proclaiming that ages ago, primitive humans were visited by the gods, who were actually visitors from other worlds, and they created modern humans by meddling with our DNA. He cites several examples of ancient texts that he claims are the proof of his theory."

"Wait," I said. "That's the old 'Chariots of the Gods' routine. It's hardly original."

"Agreed," said Jonas. "But be that as it may, today Vanya has a group of followers that number in the hundreds of thousands, with branches in America, Europe, Canada, and Japan. And they're spreading. Vanya's followers believe that they must prepare themselves mentally and physically for the time when the 'Progenitors from the Stars,' as they call them, return to Earth. With one exception, the cult members are expected to abstain from the vices of the physical world."

"What exception is that?" I asked.

Jonas stated, deadpan, "They advocate total sexual freedom."

Nick barked a laugh. "That puts a new spin on the concept of communion. You ever manage to get any of your agents on the inside, so to speak? That must have been a popular assignment."

"One," Jonas said seriously. "He met with a fatal accident, and we couldn't prove otherwise. But what we were able to discover is that Vanya has been quietly investing millions of dollars into genetics research. He's been taking pains to keep his connection to these investments secret. Over the years, the contributions from Vanya's followers, along with the sales of his books and recorded lectures, have made him very wealthy. According to our sources, Vanya's personal financial fortune should be somewhere in the tens of millions, and with that he's bought his own private Greek island in the Ionian Sea and built a complex upon it using Egyptian construction companies and manpower. On top of that he owns a two-hundred-foot motor yacht and a couple of private jets."

I saw Old Nick stir at this last piece of news. The Argo Foundation had a yacht too—the hundred-foot *Queen Neva,* a reconverted military cargo vessel that had been outfitted for exploration, research, and, on occasion, smuggling. Nicholas loved that old boat more than anything in this world, and I think he was feeling a bit of "ship envy" at the moment. I was brought back to the discussion at hand when Caitlin said, "On the face of it, it appears that Vanya's investments in genetics research are in line with his philosophy. He preaches that we humans are the result of genetic engineering and that with scientific research we can prove this theory. But we've found traces of something frightening."

Mr. Jonas took over. "Back in 1995, a Japanese death cult, the Aum Shinrikyo sect, released sarin nerve gas in the Tokyo subways. What was never revealed to the public was a potential connection between the cult in Japan and the Children of Cronos, but it was very shortly after that attack that Vanya became an absolute recluse. Over the last several years, he's only addressed his followers via satellite broadcast and computer webcast. So here we are today, faced with a man who not only has an army of fanatical followers, but also has access to laboratories, via his financial contributions, that could be used to produce deadly chemical and biological weapons."

Mr. Jonas fixed me with a cold stare as he said, "Now here's where you come in, Mr. Blake. In 1990, the Gardner Museum in Boston was robbed of several priceless works of art. Two thieves disguised as policemen overpowered the guards and made off with three Rembrandts, five sketches by Degas, and four other pieces."

"I know that case," Nicholas said. "The thieves also made off with a twelve-hundred-year-old Sheng Dynasty bronze."

Jonas was unfazed by Nick Riley's knowledge of criminal matters. "Yes, exactly. But there was one item that didn't fit in with the rest." He tapped a key on his laptop with a skeletal finger and the picture was replaced by a statue of a gold-colored eagle. "The thieves also took a gilded bronze flag top, from a standard once belonging to the army of Napoleon Bonaparte.

Its intrinsic value, even to a collector of such things, is very small when compared to all the other items stolen. But whoever pulled off the robbery took precious time to steal this item as well. All of the stolen valuables have remained unrecovered, but two days ago we received word that an antiques dealer in Paris may have found the Napoleonic eagle. And more importantly, we learned that James Phillip Vanya wants to buy it. At any cost."

Caitlin then said, "We applied some pressure on the antiques dealer, a man named Marcel Troyon, and he's willing to cooperate with us in exchange for the fact that we keep his involvement with stolen art trafficking a secret. He's been instructed to tell all potential buyers that before he can sell the eagle, he'll need to consult an expert to verify the eagle's authenticity."

I couldn't help but notice the way both Caitlin and Mr. Jonas were focusing on me as Jonas said, "We took the names of people we could use to pose as an expert in rare antiques and ran them through our data sources. Because of your involvement with Mr. Yusef Mohammad, our agency was provided with information about you: Jonathan Blake, an employee of the Argo Foundation and an expert in historical artifacts." Jonas leaned forward like a bird of prey as he said earnestly, "We need you to go to France as our antiques expert. Once you've verified that the eagle is indeed the one stolen from the Gardner Museum, and Vanya or one of his people take possession of it, we can make a move against Vanya on criminal charges of trafficking in international stolen antiquities. Then we'll have him."

"Hah!" Old Nick barked. "Like getting Capone for tax evasion."

"Precisely," Jonas stated. "This may be the only chance we have to get to Vanya. With his resources, he'd be capable of producing a terrorist act that would make the sarin gas attack in Tokyo pale in comparison, and we cannot risk the chance of an event like that."

"And speaking of danger," I said quickly. "Let me get this straight—you want me to go and deal with people who may have stuff like nerve gas?"

Mr. Jonas leaned back in his chair. "Don't concern yourself on that score, Mr. Blake. We've taken steps to see that you'll be protected around the clock on this mission. Which is why you'll be taking your wife to Paris with you."

"Wife? What wife, I don't have a . . ." My words ran as dry as my throat as it hit me, while Caitlin Street slowly raised her left hand, displaying her wedding set.

Before I could utter another word, Nicholas roared with thunderous laughter and slapped his hand to his knee, making a pistol-like report. "Oh, good for you, boy," he laughed. "And here I was afraid I'd never see you walk down the aisle."

CHAPTER THREE

I pushed myself away from the table and stood up before Nicholas's laughter ground to a halt, and said, "Okay, you've told me what you want me to do, but you haven't explained just why I'm the guy who should do it."

Mr. Jonas looked as stern as ever. "Really, Mr. Blake? From what Mr. Mohammad told us, I'd have thought that this kind of deal was right up your alley. Tell me, what is it exactly that you do for the Argo Foundation?"

I was about to reply, but Nicholas beat me to it. "The Argo Foundation is dedicated to the preservation of mankind's history. The foundation arranges for and provides funding for archeological recovery efforts all over the world. I employ Blake here, among others, to go and visit the various sites where the Argo Foundation has provided financial support, to oversee the projects and see how well our money is spent."

"My title is field researcher," I added. Although I always thought that in the interest of truth in advertising my business cards should read "Executive Ninja."

"Field researcher," Jonas repeated with a voice as dry as old leaves. "According to Yusef Mohammad, you are a criminal and terrorist who attacked him and his men with military explosives and then stole a priceless antique scroll that belonged to the Afghani people."

I laughed. "Really? And he gave his word as a drug dealer this was all true? Come on, Jonas; Scheherazade told more believable stories."

If Mr. Jonas was puzzled by my *One Thousand and One Nights* reference, he gave no sign. "But what of the allegation that you removed an artifact from Afghanistan?"

"That, Mr. Jonas, is what we do here," Nicholas Riley proclaimed. "The Argo Foundation is dedicated to saving the past. Had Blake here not recovered the scroll, it most likely could have either been deliberately destroyed as an affront to the current national religion of Afghanistan, or lost like several other treasures, like when the Kabul Museum was all shot to hell in the last brouhaha."

Mr. Singh added, "Not to mention the evidence shows that the scrolls were originally created in India. Therefore, if any country could lay a claim, I would have to say that it would be my own."

I kept my thoughts to myself, knowing that in this particular instance, a certain wealthy popular music icon and recent convert to Buddhism had paid the Argo Foundation handsomely to recover the scroll. I understood that, after the fragile parchment underwent restoration, she intended to present it as a gift to the current Dalai Lama.

Jones bent his head and fixed us with a glare shot from under his wrinkled brow. "This is how it will be: You help your government, and your government promises to not look too closely at what you and your foundation have been doing all around the world."

That got another rise of laughter out of Nicholas. Jonas just sat there, tight-jawed, and waited for Nick to finally wind down. Wiping away the trace of a tear, Nick said, "Forgive me, Mr. Jonas, but your threats don't mean squat to me. You'd have a worldwide uproar on your hands if you made a move on the Argo Foundation. But before you go and get your knickers in a twist, just relax. We're going to help you."

The elderly Mr. Jonas was leaning forward and ready to return fire against Old Nick's verbal broadside when he stopped suddenly and said, "What? You agree you'll help?"

I was as surprised as Jonas. "We will?"

Nicholas swiveled his head toward me. "Yes, you will." Back to Jonas he said, "Blake will be happy to assist in any way. Call it the Argo Foundation's contribution to our patriotic duty."

Mr. Jonas looked more suspicious than relieved. "Indeed? How soon can Mr. Blake be ready to leave for France?"

Never was looking pretty good, but I said instead, "Whenever. I'll need a few things first."

Caitlin appeared to have anticipated my acquiescence, as she reached into an open portfolio briefcase next to her and handed me a large, sealed manila envelope. "Here are certified copies of the Napoleonic eagle's statement of provenance along with the most recent set of photographs." She smiled as she asked innocently, "Was this all you were going to need?"

I walked around the table and took the envelope from her. "Yeah, pretty much."

Mr. Jonas checked his watch. "There's an Air France flight out tonight at 2050 hours. My people will make the arrangements."

I wondered if by "arrangements" Mr. Jonas was including potential funerals as I checked my own watch and saw that it was approaching 3:00 P.M., leaving over seven hours until the flight. Mr. Singh said, "We will have Blake there in plenty of time."

"Whoa, hold it," I interrupted, not caring for the way I was being discussed like I was a commodity. "I've still got some questions. Lots of them, in fact."

Mr. Jonas rose from his chair, leaning on his cane. I caught a glimpse of the gold ring he wore, shaped like a serpent with its tail in its mouth, and wondered what that ominous symbol meant to him as he said, "No doubt, Mr. Blake, but do not concern yourself. We will arrange a briefing for you before your flight. Where can we find you later today?"

"I'm staying at the Algonquin."

Caitlin closed up the armored briefcase as Jonas said, "Good. Go there directly and we will be in touch as soon as we can."

Mr. Jonas turned to leave the room as if we had all just ceased to exist to him. I did my best not to act awkward with my newly acquired wife. She, on the other hand, said her farewell with a smile as unfathomable as the Mona Lisa's. Jonas stopped just shy of the door, then turned to me and said, "Just out of curiosity, Mr. Blake, how did you manage to get that scroll out of Afghanistan?"

"Oh, that was no problem. Once I got to Kabul, I just packaged it up and mailed it home. It was just old birch bark, so there was nothing to trip any security scans."

Mr. Jonas smiled at me. The effect wasn't pleasant and left me feeling like I was some sort of acquisition that he got at a bargain rate. Then Jonas and Caitlin left the room. I could hear the ghost of a laugh trailing him down the hall, a sound like a rusty blade drawn across a rough stone.

When the company had gone, I was finally able to vent my feelings. "What the hell, Nick? Since when do we volunteer to help the government? We don't even pay taxes."

Nick sat back down with a sigh and said to Mr. Singh, "What's the current status of the reward money on the Gardner Museum heist?"

Mr. Singh produced his computer pad and entered some data, then said, "Five million dollars for the recovery of the entire collection, payment for partial recovery will be based on the value of individual items recovered. Actual value of the collection is estimated to be worth three hundred million American dollars."

"There you go, Blake," Nick said. "We got millions of reasons to be helpful."

"Ah. I see," I said. "You're thinking that if we can find one piece, then we might get a line on the rest?"

"Oh, yeah," Nick agreed happily. "Rembrandts, Degas, and Vermeers, oh my. And I get dibs on the Chinese bronze."

By the unwritten law of the Argo Foundation, I get

ten percent of the value of all my recoveries, and half a million bucks made a lot of my hesitation evaporate. Along with that was the certain knowledge that whatever I was able to find and bring back for Nick Riley would be one more piece rescued from the dustbin of history. We may be thieves, but at least our crimes lead to an honorable end.

During my musing, I'd turned and faced out the window toward Central Park. Spring was in evidence, but my eyes were drawn toward the monolithic majesty of the misnamed ancient obelisk of Cleopatra's Needle, dragged here across the Atlantic from Alexandria, Egypt, over a hundred years ago. It was once one of a pair of guardian edifices erected by Tuthmosis the Third in Heliopolis. But in the late 1800s, a greedy Egyptian ruler broke up the family of twins, letting one go to America and her sister to London, all in an effort to curry international political favor. To me, she always looks somewhat sad and forlorn, all alone and far from home. And after the Herculean effort it took to bring her here, we just leave her outside in the cold like some gigantic forgotten toy.

Mr. Singh brought me back to the present by saying, "You had best go and prepare. Doubtless you will want time to ingest some of those poisons you are so fond of."

Nicholas added, "Three things, Blake: One, after you verify that bronze bird for our newfound friends, find out whatever you can on the rest of the art collection. Two, you need to keep all your little special skills under wraps. It wouldn't do for the government to know that I train my people better than they do."

"What if there's trouble?"

"Run like hell," Nick said simply. "Or better yet, let that good-looking bodyguard they're sending you with guard your body."

"And the third thing?"

"Enjoy your honeymoon!" Nicholas roared. He was still laughing as I left the Rose Room and headed for the elevator to the first floor. I resisted the impulse to detour from the Great Hall for a quick visit to either the Greeks and Romans to my right or the Egyptians to my left, and instead walked through the usual gaggle of tourists and art students to go outside. The weather was nice, and I decided to walk the couple of miles to my hotel. I joined the herd on Fifth Avenue and marched down toward Times Square.

The exercise did me good and allowed me to work off a gnawing feeling of aggression that had been building up inside me, a reaction to being railroaded into my current situation. I was in the perfect mood to be mugged, but no one obliged me in the broad daylight. I was feeling slightly less homicidal by the time I got to the Algonquin, the closest thing I have to a regular address. I love the old hotel, with its rich turn-of-the-last-century décor. And here I never have to drink alone, for when all else fails, I can always hoist one with the ghost of Dorothy Parker.

I went to my room for a quick shower and change of shirt, repacked my battered old Samsonite suitcase for travel, then took it and the packet Caitlin gave me down to the lounge, where I picked up an eighteen-year-old Scotch and found a table away from a group of tourists who were loudly discussing at great length what musical show they should see tonight. I took a bracing sip of my drink and opened the envelope, sliding the contents onto the table.

After reviewing the purported history of the bronze eagle, I could see where this was the one item that was different from all the rest of the stolen art. Based on everything I read, the thing just wasn't worth very much. The real value of most artifacts lies in the ability to prove that they were somehow connected to famous deceased persons. The documentation on the history of the eagle was spotty, to say the least. Produced in the year 1813, it was an icon of Napoleon's second coming after escaping from Elba Island, that brief span known as the Hundred Days. This particular eagle was known as a Cent-Jours model, cast in gilt bronze to replace those destroyed during the First Restoration. The eagle was designed to resemble the standard of Imperial Rome, with its beak in profile and wings spread and arched, clutching the thunderbolt of the god Jupiter in its claw. All throughout history, various empires adopted the symbol of the eagle for their standard, the Nazis being just one of many. But to be fair, it should be remembered that Benjamin Franklin was in favor of having the turkey selected to be the national bird of the American Colonies.

Among the documents in the package was information regarding the museum robbery itself. I had just read the part that explained how the thieves simply slashed most of the paintings out of their frames, leaving ragged remnants of precious canvas behind, when I became aware that I was being watched. I looked up and saw Caitlin Street staring at me from across the lobby.

She'd changed into a light gray, comfortable-looking jogging suit and had her dark gold hair pulled back into a ponytail. Her delicate face was composed into a serious mask as she walked toward me from the concierge desk. I rose to meet her. "Hello," I said.

"That's quite a face you were making," she replied. "What were you thinking just now?"

In fact, I had just resolved that should I meet with the men who committed such barbarous atrocities against the art world, I was going to deprive them of the use of their hands. I attempted to throw Caitlin off the subject by indicating the burgundy T-shirt she wore, which displayed the seal of a well-known university. "Harvard?" I inquired.

"Yes," she replied.

"Had I known ahead of time, I would have worn my Miskatonic University shirt."

"Miskatonic? Wasn't that an H. P. Lovecraft invention? What are you drinking?"

Her familiarity with my arcane university reference made my estimation of her intelligence take an upswing. "Glenfiddich. May I offer you one? Or would you prefer a vodka martini, shaken or stirred or something?"

"Martini, with a twist, as long as it comes with dinner. That would be lovely."

It was early enough that we were able to get a small table in the Oak Room. I ordered a grilled fillet of beef, having learned in my business to eat well when I could, and she decided on fettuccini with wild mushroom ragout along with the martini.

Caitlin looked around the gorgeous old Oak Room, the site of the historic Round Table's fetes, with an appreciative eye, taking in the dark wood paneling and stained glass. "Hard to see how you can afford this on your salary," she mentioned causally.

"I have an Argo Foundation expense account. But don't think that entitles you to the really expensive martini."

"Oh? Which martini is that?"

"Specialty of the house. They take an actual diamond and put it in the glass. It goes for around ten thousand bucks."

"What a lovely wedding present that would make."

"Did I mention company expense account?"

She gave me her mysterious smile. "Oh, dear. I seem to have married another cheapskate."

"Another? You've been married before?"

"Yes," she said seriously. "I'm a widow."

"Oh. Sorry."

"Yes. It was rather sudden."

"What happened?"

"He didn't buy me the martini I wanted."

The waiter intervened with the salads, and when he left I asked, "So while we're on the subject of dead husbands, just what else do you know about me?"

"Not much," Caitlin replied. "From your tax returns we saw that you list the Argo Foundation's office as your home address, and that appears to be the only job you've ever had. What did you do before you joined the foundation?"

"Oh, you know, the usual. Went off in search of myself."

"And did you? Find yourself?"

"Sure. Turns out I was playing poker in Atlantic City. That's when I decided I needed a job. Seems I can't play cards worth a damn." I needed to get Caitlin off the subject of my past, especially since it was all a fabrication, but I couldn't help but ask, "So, what else did you discover about me?"

"Only that you have no living relatives, and that you've never been married. Until now, of course."

"Okay, now it's your turn," I said. "What's with your Mr. Jonas? I swear I've seen younger-looking mummies."

"Now, that's not a kind thing to say about Grandfather."

"Grandfather?" Grandfather of Assassins, maybe, I thought.

"Yes. Although around my department, there's a rumor that he used to be presidential advisor to Roosevelt. Both of them."

I laughed. "You never said which department you work for."

"That's true," she said agreeably. "By the way, this will be our last opportunity to speak openly. The moment we leave here, we've got to act our parts and stay in character until this is all over with."

"So we're to act as a married couple?"

"Within reason," she said slyly.

"Last chance for questions, eh? So, is your name really Caitlin Street?"

"Not anymore," she said blithely. "It's Mrs. Caitlin Blake now. Says so right on my passport. That reminds me." She retrieved her purse, and after a moment of perusing inside she said, "Give me your left hand."

I did. That's when she slipped a platinum-colored

ring on my finger. "There," she said. "Now you look like a married man."

"Did I suddenly develop a trapped-animal look?" I asked as I stared at the matrimonial band that felt locked on my finger.

"Not like the look you had when I came in tonight. What were you thinking about then?"

The woman's curiosity was unshakable. I settled on giving her a different truth. "This whole museum robbery doesn't make sense," I complained. "The thieves made quite a haul, but they missed stealing the very valuable *Rape of Europa* by Titian, and instead took the time and trouble to steal this relatively worthless bronze bird. I thought I spotted a pattern to the whole thing, but my theory falls apart."

"What pattern?"

"Mythology," I explained. "The name 'Children of Cronos' refers to an ancient Greek world creation myth. Zeus, or Jupiter if you prefer, was the primary child of Cronos, and the eagle was one of his symbols. His throne in Olympus was supposed to be a giant eagle. Which ties in with the bronze eagle Napoleon Bonaparte adopted for his battle standard, right down to the 'thunderbolt of Jupiter' the eagle holds in its claws."

"So where does this pattern break down?"

"Right at the Titian painting I mentioned. It depicts the god Zeus, uh, 'plighting his troth' with a mortal woman. So if a fascination with all things Zeus was the motive, then why would that painting be left behind in favor of some old bronze bird? What are you smiling about?"

"I was just thinking that this could be like the 'Maltese Falcon'."

"Oh, that old thing. Forget it; we found that ages ago. Nick Riley uses it for a paperweight."

I finally made her laugh, a lovely sound. "I almost hate to tell you," she said, "but it was actually mythology that led our department to you."

"How's that?"

"We ran a deep computer scan on the Children of Cronos. The computer made a connection with the Argo Foundation, based on the Argonaut myth. And that cross-checked with your file and the information Mr. Mohammad gave us about you, and so now here we are, happily married. So you think you can identify the real bronze eagle when you see it?" she asked.

"Probably. The photographs show enough distinctive nicks and scratches, and it helps that all the bronze eagles were individually numbered with their military unit designations. Our bird happens to be Number One, for the emperor's First Brigade. Problem is, this thing in France could easily be a forgery."

"Forgery?"

"Sure. Art forgery is the world's third oldest profession. I've got a friend of mine over in Hong Kong who could knock out a perfect copy of this thing. At a discount."

Caitlin narrowed her eyes and said in a quiet, serious tone, "Then let's make this simple for you. As long as whoever Vanya sends to collect the bronze thinks it's genuine, then a charge of attempting to buy stolen artwork can still apply."

"Even if it's a fake? That hardly sounds fair."

"We're dealing with much bigger issues. Like the

possibility of weapons of mass destruction in the hands of fanatics."

"I'll try to keep that in mind," I said dryly.

"Good. You know, I was a little worried about you at first."

"Why?"

"I was afraid you'd actually turn out to be some kind of tomb-robbing crook. It's nice to see that you're really a professional antiquarian. I also see you have a real passion for your work. But frankly, you don't look at all like an antiques kind of guy."

"Oh? Then what do I look like?"

"A pirate."

I flatly refuse to believe in things like psychic abilities, but this woman was starting to shake my lack of faith.

Over dinner, we discussed and created our fictitious past together. Turns out we met at the Metropolitan Museum, fell in love, and had a mostly long-distance relationship, since I was out of the country so often. Caitlin then brought our tale of romance to a sad turn. "And here is where the love of a good woman drove you to a life of crime," she said.

"It did?"

"Oh, yes, definitely. You were contacted by Marcel Troyon, who has offered you ten thousand dollars under the table to come to Paris and authenticate a piece of stolen artwork. You've agreed because you love your wife and feel we need the money. Either that, or you wanted to buy me a really expensive martini."

"Wow. What a nice guy I am. What do we know about this Troyon character?"

"He's an art thief and fence. He also doesn't mind

making money from informing on other crooks, as long as he doesn't get caught at it. He'll be acting as the middleman in this deal. My people are arranging the time for the meeting after we get to Paris. One last thing," Caitlin said seriously. "This could turn out to be dangerous. But no matter what happens, stick to the cover story and leave everything else to me."

"And what will you be doing?"

"My job is to try to identify the people who want to buy the eagle, and hopefully use that information to tie all this in to Phillip Vanya. It's also my responsibility to keep you as safe as possible."

"Thanks."

"Think nothing of it," she said with a smile. "It's what any good wife would do. Your part is simple, really. We'll meet with the buyers at Marcel Troyon's apartment in Paris, you authenticate the bronze eagle as the one from the museum robbery, and then just leave the rest to me."

It was too bad, really. The chances were better than even that Caitlin and I were going to wind up at crossed swords. She had her mission, and I had mine, and I had a bad feeling that we were going to collide over them. I held no illusions; the two of us were being pleasant with each other, but underneath it all we were like a pair of gamblers in the Old West, keeping our cards close and derringers ready while we bluffed and cheated each other. Still, at the moment, she was lovely to look at in the candlelight.

We finished with dinner, retrieved our luggage from the concierge, and called for a cab to take us to the airport. Once outside, I lit up one of my Shermans, and in the process caught the sideways glance from Caitlin. "I didn't know you smoked," she said.

"I don't very often. Although there are quite a few places in the world where people would question the masculinity of a man who didn't smoke."

"I noticed you didn't offer your wife one."

"Sorry," I said as I held the box out to her. She turned away, offering a haughty profile. "I don't smoke," she said simply. "And neither should you. What's the point of keeping you alive if you're just going to commit slow suicide?"

"You know, ever since we've been married, it's just been nag, nag, nag." I closed the box and put my cigarettes and battered old Zippo inside my suitcase. The lighter was etched with the outline of a Chinese dragon, and there was a small dent in one of the lower corners, matching a dent in the skull of the man I took the lighter from while I was working in the jungle west of Angkor Wat. I later used the lighter to set fire to his truck, after I removed a set of stolen tenth-century bas-relief pieces that the man had chiseled off ancient temple walls. "Still," I said to Caitlin as I straightened up from my suitcase, "it's nice to know you'll be protecting me."

The cab arrived and I said my silent good-bye to the Great Electric Babylon of the West as we set off for JFK International. When we reached the airport, it was in its usual state of semi-controlled chaos, but we managed to run the gauntlet of high-tech security that ultimately let me board the Air France Boeing jet, armed with only the 112 weapons that nature has provided me with. After takeoff, we settled in for our in-flight seven-hour nap and I felt fortunate that we had a row all to ourselves, though I suspected Caitlin's elderly boss may have arranged for this small luxury. Caitlin, near the window, kicked off her athletic shoes and snuggled in with a pillow and blanket after wishing me a good night. But I was feeling too wired up to even try to sleep just then. During all of my other jobs, by the time I was in transit to whatever corner of the world I was going to raid, I'd have already planned and schemed and prepared. But this time around I was flying blind, and as I watched the stars sail by in the night sky, I thought back to how my life had brought me to this point.

And how it all began just as my first life ended.

CHAPTER FOUR

Looking back now, I see my first life was like it was an old, half-remembered movie, and not a very interesting one at that. Until I discovered that hell is a very real place and could be found right here on earth. The final night of my first life began when I was dragged out of my filthy, festering prison cell, tied with rope and blinded by a stinking burlap sack pulled over my head, then shoved into the back of a truck. I remember thinking, as I was half-choked unconscious by the toxic fumes of the exhaust and hammered by the jarring, bumpy ride over dirt roads, that I had a faint hope that I was being taken off to a place where I'd finally be allowed to die. Ultimately, the truck skidded to a halt and I was shoved out to the ground by a final kick on my back. I could hear the truck grinding its way back down the road as strong arms lifted my body and placed me in a sitting position against a tree, then the sack was pulled from my head.

I took in a shuddering breath, full of the thick jungle

air that to me, after my timeless stay in a disease-ridden hellhole, was sweeter than any wine. My eye, the one I could still see out of, found a cluster of bright stars burning through a hole in the dense tropical forest canopy—stars so bright they almost hurt after all the time I'd spent in the dark. In the next instant I had to clamp my good eye shut against a sputtering glare that came from a match struck nearby. I felt the flicker of the flame through my eyelid as a deep, rough voice said in English, "Mother of God, they really did a number on you, kid."

I squinted a look out and saw a rounded, silver-wreathed face and a pair of blue eyes reflecting the match flame. "My name's Nick Riley," the man said. "Just sit still awhile. I'm getting you out of here."

I didn't say a word as the match guttered itself out and the world turned back to black. I'd had many, many lessons pounded into me during my incarceration, and the first lesson you learn is never to talk back.

In the starlit darkness, I heard Nick grunt as he stood back up. With the noise of the truck receding in the distance, I could now hear the sounds of the nighttime jungle coming back to life. As for me, I was like a wounded crab in a broken shell as I scuttled back and pressed against the rough bark of the tree behind me.

"It's all right now, boy," Nick rumbled gently from above me. "You're safe now. I just bought your way out of prison. Even though the crooked cops I bribed will have to say that you escaped."

I tried to swallow around a tongue and throat as dry as leather before I spoke through my broken teeth. "Escaped?"

"Yeah," Nick sighed like an old bellows. "It was the

quickest way. I wasn't sure how long you were going to last locked up in there. But for what it's worth, I know that you're no drug smuggler."

I didn't dare believe what I heard. "You . . . you know?" I mumbled.

"I know," Nick said with a heavy voice, "that you were nothing but an innocent dupe. You thought you'd signed up for a legitimate archeology field dig with a certain Professor Wainwright. What you didn't know was that the guy who calls himself Wainwright is actually a thief and a relic smuggler. He must have thought you were onto him; that's why he slipped the drugs into your luggage and tipped off the local cops about you."

My head was swimming with Nick Riley's words. I'd lost track of how long I'd been trapped in an absolute nightmare, far from home in a foreign country where no one believed me, cast into prison to rot.

But now, I was pulled out of that abyss and was listening to a man tell me in my own language that I was free. Free. I barely noticed the fact that he had bent down and had cut the rough ropes binding my hands. "We'll be getting out of here soon," Nick explained. "There's a plane coming. Then we'll get you to a hospital. Can you stand?"

I reached up with the hand that still worked and felt Nick's strong grip as he hoisted me upright and then steadied me on my shaky feet. As I leaned on him, I could feel hard muscle buried beneath a soft padding of fat. I forced out the words, "Thank you."

Nick made a growling sound, and then said, "I wouldn't be so quick to do that, boy. In a way, it's my fault all this happened to you."

Nick sensed the question I wanted to ask, and said to me, "Professor Wainwright used to work for me. But I had no idea he was going to do anything like this. Especially to an innocent like you."

"Wainwright worked for you," I whispered out of a tight throat.

"Past tense. I fired the bastard. If I'd known he'd go and do something like this, I'd have seen him sent to hell."

Everything was happening so fast, I couldn't be sure I wasn't hallucinating. I kept sucking in breaths as if the world were going to run out of air. Then I realized Nick Riley was speaking again, in a low, gravelly voice, almost as if he was speaking to himself.

"Listen, you're going to have to face some facts. I'm going to see that you get to a doctor and get fixed up when I get you out of here. But I'm afraid your life is ruined. Everyone is going to think you're an escaped prison convict and drug smuggler. But I can offer you another option."

I was seeing the truth in Nick Riley's words, knowing that I'd never get completely free of hell, no matter how far away I got. Then Nick's next words changed everything.

"I can give you a new life."

I didn't speak; I couldn't speak. Nick continued, "I figure I owe you that much—a new name and a blank slate. After all you've been through, it's the least I can do for you."

I was trying to grasp the thoughts Nicholas Riley floated before me. They hummed around my head along with the mosquitoes as Nick said, "And I can see to it that you would never, ever have to be afraid of anyone, ever again."

That's when all the small, broken bits inside me struck together like flint and steel, sparking a flame that burned away the last traces of the person I used to be. I pulled my arm back from Nick, feeling my legs take hold, and then I was standing on my own. I didn't know who Nick Riley was at that time, and I didn't know what he'd want me for. But in exchange for what he offered me, at that moment I'd have signed a pact with Faust's pen and my own blood.

My second life began after I was taken to a private clinic in the Caribbean, where Nicholas Riley's Argo Foundation kept a staff of doctors who, for reasons both varied and criminal, had lost their licenses to practice in their respective countries of origin. It was here where my body was treated and repaired. It was also here that I had written my final letters to the people I had to leave behind: a sister and a niece that I would never see grow up, a couple of close friends, and a girl I thought I had a future with. I wrote and explained the simple truth about how I was wrongly accused, and that I had escaped prison and for the rest of my life I couldn't risk the chance of letting them know where I was. I hoped they believed me. But I would never know. And nothing could change the fact that there was an international warrant issued for my arrest due to my "prison break."

It was during this hospital stay that Nick came and visited me for the first time since he rescued me. We were sitting on wooden chairs in the shade of the clinic's veranda, overlooking a sandy beach so pure and white it hurt my eyes to look at it in the sunlight and the blue ocean beyond, savoring a clean salt breeze. After the hell I'd been rescued from, I could almost believe this was heaven. Nick, wearing a wrinkled white Panama suit, was opening the first of a case of Red Stripe he'd brought for the occasion as he said, "From what I hear from these quacks on my payroll, you're expected to live. Happy birthday."

"Thanks," I said after taking the offered beer. "But it's not my birthday."

"It is now," Nick said as he handed over a manila envelope. I set my drink down and slid the contents of the envelope out. I looked at the birth certificate and other documents, reading the name they bore out loud. "Jonathan Blake?"

"That's you," Nick said agreeably. "I promised you a new life, didn't I? And there you go, a blank slate. Blank slate. Blake. Get it?"

I spoke the name again, trying to get a feel for it. It was as strange to me as my own face had become. It wasn't just that my nose and jawline would never be the same, or even the scars I now had, but I swore that when I looked in the mirror, my eyes were those of a stranger as well. "So what am I supposed to do now?" I asked.

Nick took a long swallow, and then said, "Since the docs tell me you're expected to make a good recovery, I'm thinking it's time you quit malingering and decide what you want to do with this new life of yours. I can offer you a job with the Argo Foundation."

"Doing what?"

Nick smiled. It was an expression I was going to learn to both love and hate. "Well, that all depends on you now," he drawled. "I've seen where you were a pretty promising archeology student. Now, I can always use people for everyday research and such, but what I really need is a good criminal."

"Excuse me?"

"Criminal," Nick said deliberately.

I felt a cold dagger of fear stab me in the gut. "Uh, in case you've forgotten, I just got out of prison."

"Yep," Nick said agreeably. "And that proves to me just how tough you are. I need tough people for what the Argo Foundation really does."

Nick stood up, eclipsing the sun as he turned and said to me, "In case you haven't heard, there's bastards like Wainwright all over the world who steal what's left of mankind's past just to sell it for money. They take priceless, irreplaceable artifacts out of sheer greed. Governments and private agencies do what they can to stop them, but it's never enough. That's where I come in. The only good way to stop a thief is to use a thief against them. That's what I can use you for."

"And you want me to become a thief. Just like Professor Wainwright." I felt my new teeth grind together when I spoke the name of the man who had torn my life apart.

"No," Nick said seriously. "Not like Wainwright. He stole relics for his own profit. What I do with the Argo Foundation is to steal from bastards like him, so we can save and preserve what little we have left from our own history. But we do manage to make a little money off it, too," he added slyly.

"But I'm not really a criminal. I was framed, remember?"

Nick barked out a laugh. "Crime is just a trade, like

anything else, boy. I can see to it that you learn that trade from the masters of the craft." Nick was quiet for a moment, then said in a serious tone, "I won't lie to you. If you come in with me, it'll be a hard, dangerous life. But I'll see to it that you'll be equipped to survive. Not only survive, but get back at bastards like Wainwright and all the others like him. And truth be told, you'll be doing a service to the world, even though no one will ever know. Unless you screw up," he added as an afterthought.

I took a long look out over the ocean, watching the tides roll in and out as I thought about Nick's offer. "What would I have to do?" I asked.

Nick sighed, as if in satisfaction. "All you have to do now is make it through Nick Riley's School for Artful Dodgers. I've got people who can teach you all you'll ever need to know. And not just how to steal, but how to fight and to survive anything. When my people are done with you, you'll be a dangerous man to mess with. You'll never have to be afraid of anyone, ever again."

That cold knot of fear I had suddenly broke up and melted as Nick's words wove their spell around me. I took a drink before I replied, "Call me Jonathan."

The next phase of my rebirth took the form of brutal physical regimens that hammered and strained my body as if it were steel being forged, until I was stronger and faster than I ever thought I could be. When I was ready, I was sent all over the world to train with men, and in some cases, women, who taught me all the skills that I would come to rely upon. It was like being initiated into an arcane school of black arts. I was taught how to fight, and even maim and kill my fellow man, with not only my bare hands, but also by utilizing common, everyday things, transforming the innocuous into dangerous weapons. I learned how to transmute the chemistry of harmless commercial products into the alchemy of explosives and incendiaries, and how to use the sciences of electronics and mechanics to create detonators or neutralize security systems and bypass locks with tools made from simple, ordinary items. In fact, if there was one overriding theme to my education, it was learning the art of improvisation. Or as Nick Riley himself put it, "By the time my people are done with you, you'll be able to do anything with nothing."

And so my education in matters most criminal went on for nearly a year, amidst the more mundane aspects of learning things like rock-climbing, scuba diving, shooting, and other commonplace pursuits. But during this time I found out that Nicholas Riley was dead wrong about one thing. While it was true that through my training I had lost my fear of others, it was replaced by a new and different fear. I had come to fear myself. More specifically, I'd come to fear what I could do with all the deadly and dangerous abilities I now possessed. Then came the day I had to face this final, ultimate fear.

In a small bungalow house in Southern California, near the border of Mexico, there lived a man who used to call himself Professor Wainwright. He came home one night to find a stranger sitting in one of the guest chairs in his small and untidy office. He was fatter than I remembered, and had grown a brown beard that was flecked with gray. But I was certain it was he when he turned and found me sitting there after he turned on the lights.

"What! What are you doing here? Who are you?"

I just smiled, savoring the moment. "Good evening, Professor Wainwright."

His face flushed with a ruddy red color as he sucked in air. "How dare you! How did you get in here?" His eyes darted around the room like an animal looking for an escape.

I didn't answer his question, and in truth the locks on his doors were no challenge to me at all. I just sat there with my gloved hands tented, waiting to see if he would remember me after all.

"I've a good mind to . . ." His voice trailed off as the color left his face, and I saw his mouth move silently, framing the name that used to be mine.

"Come now, Professor," I said gently. "Surely that man was left to die down in Central America. You don't believe in ghosts, do you?"

"Oh my God," Wainwright wheezed hoarsely. He stumbled and more or less fell into his chair behind the desk. "What . . . what do you want?"

My heart was pounding in my chest and my pulse throbbed in my temples as my mind flashed through all the lovely ways I could hurt this man. Nick Riley had taken me out of the jungle prison a broken shell of a human and had transformed me into a creature that was more of a biological weapon than a man. And after my training was completed, Nick had told me where to find Wainwright, to go and do whatever I wanted, like it was some macabre graduation day present.

Looking across the table at Wainwright, I was almost surprised that my voice remained steady as I answered him, saying, "What do I want? It's really very simple, Wainwright; you took a life, now you owe one. I'm here to collect."

Wainwright stared at me like his eyes were frozen open as he pawed around his cluttered desk. "Money," he croaked. "I can give you money."

I was about to reply when I saw his hands disappear from the desk with a clatter as he jerked open a drawer. He rammed his hands inside, yanking out an old pistol and shoving it toward my face. It took an almost physical restraint on my part not to move as Wainwright, teeth clenched and breath hissing, snapped the trigger over and over.

Only nothing happened.

Wainwright inhaled, making a sound like water going down a rusty pipe, as I slowly stood up, then let my hand snatch the gun away from him, fast as a magician's trick. I'd already found Wainwright's old German P-38 shortly after I let myself into the house, and had removed all the ammunition. Wainwright's eyes bugged out as he watched me materialize a single 9mm cartridge and load it directly into the pistol's chamber. His eyes locked onto the unblinking gaze of the gun's barrel as I lined it up, aiming at his forehead.

Wainwright suddenly began pleading for his life, only his words were all tied together and spilling out of his mouth in an almost incomprehensible stream. With one simple squeeze, I was going to blow Wainwright straight to hell and then walk away into the night. But the hand that held the gun, the hand that had been tortured and mangled back in Central America, didn't move the fraction of an inch it would take to splatter the man's brains across the wall.

That's when I discovered I truly had nothing to fear. Even though I'd been made over into a dangerous creature by Nick Riley and his people, my will was still my own. I'd come to Wainwright's house fully expecting to take some justice for myself by taking his life, but in the end I wound up giving him mercy instead, knowing the choice was mine to make. And if I could keep myself from destroying the one man I hated most in the world, then I need not be afraid for the sake of others. I could keep my inner monster under control.

So in the end, I let the man I knew as Wainwright live. But before I left, I at least made certain that his penmanship would never be the same.

"You're making that face again."

With a start, I was snapped back from my past into the metal belly of the jetliner, surrounded by the pervasive roar of the engines. I looked over at Caitlin, who was staring at me like a cat patiently waiting for a mouse to appear. "What?" I asked.

"That face. The one I saw back at the Algonquin. The one that makes you look like a pirate. You're doing it again. What are you thinking?"

I tried to make a smile. "Sorry. I guess I'm just worried about Paris," I lied.

Caitlin reached over and took my hand, giving it a warm press. "Don't worry," she said in a low, lovely tone. "I'll take care of you. Now try to get some sleep." Giving my hand a final firm squeeze, she turned back and faced the window and the blackness outside.

I looked down at my scarred right hand, and thought about how good Caitlin's touch made me feel just now.

"I'll take care of you, too," I said, too quietly for her to hear.

CHAPTER FIVE

Paris, France

I was in Paris in the springtime. And it was raining. The morose gray sky was a perfect reflection of my mood as I pondered the thought that if water was the only thing that hit my head during this job, I'd be a lucky man indeed. The trip to the city had not begun auspiciously. My overused and much abused passport drew its usual attention from the customs agents, not to mention the fact that I've got a face that inspires policemen to go and check their "Wanted" posters. I was treated to a "routine" interview in one of the small, sterile offices while a dour customs official questioned me in regard to my honeymoon vacation plans, all the while flipping through the ragged and colorfully stamped pages that told the tale of my travels around the world. Minus all the countries I had to sneak in and out of, of course.

Finally, I was given leave to depart, and I found my new wife waiting for me with my old-fashioned suit-case. No doubt my luggage had been given a far more intimate inspection than I, but I was confident that my weapons, along with my burglary and escape tools, went undiscovered. The case itself was a Stone Age throwback—a big, tough, dark brown suitcase that one had to actually carry with one hand. I'm always amused to see so many of my fellow travelers who obviously spend time in a gym rely on those ubiquitous black pull-types with wheels, rather than have an opportunity to exercise their arm muscles. I've seen those same workout aficionados drive around a crowded parking lot rather than walk an extra few steps.

I took a moment in the busy, crowded concourse to retrieve my new cell phone. I hadn't completely familiarized myself with my latest techno-toy. Like its predecessors, it could send and receive data, take photographs, advise me of my current global position, store tons of information, and even make a telephone call if it had to. I tend to break or lose these things with regularity. As Mr. Singh puts it, "They can make phones foolproof, but not Blake-proof." I saw that Mr. Singh had electronically sent me a file on Napoleonic-era flag tops, along with a searchable map of Paris and a personal note from Nicholas Riley, requesting me to send back lots of photos from the honeymoon. After I had updated myself, Caitlin and I visited the currency exchange, where I bought a fat, colorful stack of euros that I split up into three sets for easier concealment.

It was during the drive into Paris that my mood really took a downward turn. Sometime before our jet had even touched down, the cool, calculating Caitlin had transformed herself into the very model of the happy young bride on her first trip to Paris. It was an effort not to ask her who she was and what had she done with the woman I left New York with. So, as she smiled and laughed, I found myself acting the part of the curmudgeonly husband who had allowed his wife to drag him off to parts unknown. But the thoughts beneath my dark demeanor were much more sinister. I was used to being in control of the dangerous stunts I pulled off in my line of work, and more importantly, only being responsible for myself if everything went to hell. Now, I was working blind in someone else's shadowy game with a woman I didn't know and couldn't trust. Probably not the best way to start a marriage, I reflected.

I'd decided to be generous with the Argo Foundation's money, so Caitlin and I took a taxi into the city. Our *anglais*-speaking driver was a young, cheerful North African named Paul Mahomet, and he insisted that we young lovers should have an automotive tour of the glorious City of Lights. Since our plane landed around noon local time and our meeting with Marcel Troyon wasn't scheduled until that evening, we had time to kill, and so agreed to the impromptu road trip.

I was used to the thrill of the New York cab ride, but Paul apparently wanted his American guests to feel safe as he brought his little blue taxi into the city streets of Paris, and he promptly slowed down as our car merged with the great, noisy, mechanized parade. Despite myself, I fell under the spell of this corner of the world. From the massive Greco-Roman palace of the Opéra Garnier (I wondered aloud if The Phantom was buried somewhere nearby; Caitlin corrected me in that his actual title was The Opera Ghost) to the Champs Élysées and around the massive and magnificent Arc de Triomphe (the immense size of which almost gave me a grasp of the ego of the emperor who ordered its construction) to the Place de la Concorde, where Marie Antoinette and her royal kin were put to death (and also home to the Obelisk of Luxor—I mentioned that the Egyptians must have just been giving those things away at one point in time), to a neck-craning view of the Eiffel Tower. I'd never given much thought to the great iron monstrosity before, but to see it now, against a majestic, cloud-painted sky, made me realize what a true wonder it really is. Or maybe it was the scent of Caitlin's perfume and the press of her body against mine as we squeezed together like school kids on a field trip that heightened my appreciation.

Finally, Caitlin and I told Paul that we should be taken to our hotel; his answering grin stated plainly that he thought he knew the reason for our desire to take our leave from his excellent company. Caitlin directed him to the Saint Michel, and our driver-cum–tour guide took us there, albeit in a circuitous route, while he pointed out the bridge to the Cathedral of Notre Dame. We parted company with Paul and I parted company with a wad of the foundation's money, and in return Paul offered his card and a promise to come with all speed should we call for him again—taxi meter running, no doubt.

After all the examples of European old-world charm I'd viewed that afternoon, the Saint Michel Hotel was a bit of a disappointment. The façade was a classic reflection of the beautiful, carved limestone of Le Belle Époque, as was the rest of the neighborhood, but the interior was all new, wood-paneled and modern. Our room could have belonged in any four-star hotel from here to Singapore, with the only touches that spoke of Paris being the framed black-and-white photographs of city scenes from the late 1800s and the bottle of complementary wine. I couldn't help but notice the twin beds were snuggled close side by side. When Caitlin and I were finally left alone, I uttered the words that must have been spoken by countless bridegrooms across the ages.

"I'm hungry. That 'petit-dejeuner' at the airport was ages ago. I could eat a horse."

"I understand that can be arranged," Caitlin replied as she checked her watch. "Have courage. There's a place near Troyon's apartment where we can have some dinner before the meeting tonight. Why don't you take a shower, or go out for a smoke or something in the meantime?"

"If I didn't know any better, I'd say you were trying to get rid of me."

She was back in her inscrutable mode, and I found I missed the woman I had just shared a taxi with. It made me wonder which of the two was the real Caitlin—if that really was her name, I thought ruefully. "Fine," I said. "I'll retreat to the bathroom. But no peeking."

I washed and shaved and did my best to make myself presentable, then realized that I'd forgotten to bring a change of clothes in with me. I wrapped a towel around myself and announced my entrance. "Avert thine eyes," I warned.

Caitlin turned from the closet, where she'd been in the process of hanging up my clothes. Her face became still, and then she asked quietly, "What happened?"

Some people collect souvenirs and trinkets as they travel around the world. I, on the other hand, just amass scar tissue. "What? Oh, you mean me? Nothing, really. I'm just clumsy as hell."

Caitlin came toward me slowly, her eyes tracking all the divots and gouges on the map of my body. "That," she said as she pointed to my left shoulder, "looks like a gunshot wound. And what's this across your rib cage? Looks like someone cut you up good, and not too long ago. I see now why you've got military wound dressings in that first-aid kit of yours."

"You went through my luggage?"

"Of course," she replied, matter-of-fact. "It's one of the many Wifely Duties. By the way, if we have time after the job, I should take you shopping. All your clothes are boring."

My working attire all came from the same company, guaranteed to be rugged and survive all extremes. But they didn't have my lifestyle in mind and I have to replace my wardrobe frequently. All my clothes were plain, solid colors, more camouflage fashion. "How would you like it if I went and pawed through your things?" I asked.

She just shook her head and looked sad. "That's what happened to my second husband," she sighed.

"Well, I'm not the curious type anyway."

"That's good. It will do wonders for your life expectancy. Although from where I'm standing, I'm wondering if your job of 'field researcher' isn't a little more hazardous than I was led to believe."

"The only hazard I'm facing now is whether I'm going to freeze to death first, or die of starvation."

Caitlin raised an ironic eyebrow. "Let me freshen up and change, and I'll save your life. I've managed to get us a reservation for dinner."

"Where?" I asked as she gathered up some clothes and a handbag.

"Someplace historical," she replied. When the bathroom door shut, I started to dress myself, noticing that Caitlin had had ample opportunity to take inventory of my luggage. I put on dark slacks and a pullover, and gathered up a couple of weapons and a handful of useful things. In the process, I noticed a crumpled-up wad of plain brown paper and some string in the wastebasket. I unfolded the paper, but it didn't have any markings or writing on it. The wrapping looked just large enough to have contained a medium-sized handgun at one point in time, and I wondered if Caitlin had received a special delivery while I was in the bath.

I wandered over to the half balcony, opened it up to the accompanying sound of the traffic below, and had a cigarette while I waited for Caitlin. The dark clouds overhead were slowly breaking up, and a dying sun was washing the gothic spires and carved stone façades of the rooftops across the boulevard Saint Michel with a crimson stain. Only the blaring horns and tire squeals from the street broke the spell of the view. I thought about Caitlin's reference to dining "someplace historic" and wondered what she meant. The whole city was a mosaic of the ages.

I really don't know how long I leaned against the

wall near the balcony, watching as the night crept over the venerable rooftops, but all at once I was aware of Caitlin standing behind me. I also don't know how long a time it was that I just stood there and stared at the woman. She was attired in a simple black cocktail dress, with her wavy, dark gold hair bound into a crown a princess of Troy would have cause to envy. "I think I like being married," I heard myself say.

"Really? I couldn't tell. You've forgotten your wedding ring," she said as she held up the item in question.

"Sorry," I replied, taking the ring from her.

"Just be thankful I'm not the kind of girl who'd insist on having your finger tattooed."

We got our coats and left the hotel, then hailed a taxi. I heard Caitlin give our dreadlocked and bespectacled driver an address on the boulevard du Montparnasse. While we were driving past the Luxembourg Gardens, I took a minute to review the data on my phone. Caitlin gave me a sideways glance, but said nothing as I scrolled and gleaned information on Napoleon's choice of decorative flag tops, cramming for my upcoming test tonight. The trip was over sooner than I expected as we pulled over in front of a single-story Art Deco–style restaurant with the name "La Rotonde."

I paid the driver and escorted Caitlin inside, immediately taken by the rich, wine-colored furnishings and dark paneled wood, softly lit by the glow of gold-shaded lamps. The main room was, as the name implied, rounded and curved, and with its small tables draped in white linen it evoked an intimate mood that matched the illuminated Impressionist paintings that adorned the walls. We were early for Continental dining and had the restaurant mostly to ourselves.

I wasn't quite up for sampling the escargot and was pleased to see that the specialty was beef dishes. I ordered a filet with béarnaise while Caitlin requested sole meunière. The fact that we didn't order any wine or other alcohol didn't seem to faze our waiter in the least. "I thought you said you were taking me somewhere historical?" I asked when our waiter departed.

"I have. Don't you know where you are?"

"Sure. I'm in Paris. That big iron radio antenna we saw this afternoon was a dead giveaway."

"And this is your first time here? Hard to believe, especially when I caught a look at that passport of yours."

"Yeah," I sighed. "I never get to go anywhere nice."

"We're on the Left Bank," Caitlin said in a patient tone. "This is where artists like Pablo Picasso and Max Jacob used to hang out."

"Ah, so we're on *that* Left Bank."

"Not to mention writers such as Henry Miller and Anaïs Nin."

"Never read them."

Caitlin gave me her look of amused irony. "You're quite certain you went to college?"

"Yep."

"How about Karl Marx or Leon Trotsky? Ever hear of them? They used to come here too."

I looked around the expensive environs. "Oh, yeah,

I can see them now: 'Down with the capitalist over-lords! Right after they serve the chateaubriand!' "

Caitlin laughed, a lovely sound that complemented the candlelight reflected in her golden eyes. "Well," she admitted, "perhaps things have changed around here a bit since then."

The rest of the dinner was excellent food and small talk, spoiled just a little by the way Caitlin checked her watch, until she said at last that we should call for the waiter and leave.

Outside the restaurant, the sky was awash with clouds that allowed a three-quarter moon to sail in between the patches of darkness. The street was alive with people, walking with a slower tempo than the focused, on-a-mission feel of the pedestrians of New York. The parade of small cars pursued their paths of perpetual motion while motorcycles and scooters wove through the traffic, honking like metallic geese, and there was just enough of a breeze to keep the burned-petrol fumes from annoying the senses. "We're close to Troyon's place. You ready?" Caitlin asked.

I took a moment to look at the city. The only thing that spoiled the view of the Old-World landscape was the sight of a giant, monolithic skyscraper that dominated the background off to the east. I decided that I wanted to return to Paris someday, and hoped tonight's escapade didn't result in me having one more Place I Can't Go Back to Ever added to my list. "Ready?" I echoed. "No. But let's do it anyway."

Caitlin took me along the Montparnasse until we came to the rue de la Grande-Chaumière, where we approached a small alcove of a four-story, white-brick building. Caitlin pressed a buzzer for the second floor, and from the intercom we heard, " 'Allo?"

Caitlin motioned me to speak with a nod of her head. "It's Jonathan Blake."

"Excellent!" the voice from the speaker effused. "Come up!" There was a muted *click*, and the black outer door unlocked. Once inside the foyer, I could see a steep, narrow set of stairs lit by a pale orange overhead light. Caitlin and I ascended on steps that squeaked and sharply turned at the landing. A tall, hawk-faced man with heavy-lidded eyes and dark, almost black hair, wearing a rumpled suit, was holding open a door. *"Bonsoir!"* he greeted us jovially. "I am Marcel. Come in. You are the last to arrive."

He stepped back from the doorway and Caitlin and I squeezed in, the apartment being filled almost to capacity with an amazing collection of bric-a-brac of every description. We had to walk single file behind our host, between precariously stacked boxes overflowing with what might be politely described as "stuff." The place looked like an entire secondhand store had been crammed into a closet.

We emerged from the man-made tunnel into a room that appeared to be surrounded by junk. In the clearing there was a round card table covered in dark plastic. Past the center of the room I could make out a kitchenette, half-buried under stacks of God knows what. To the left was a small hallway, narrowed like a clogged artery with boxes of mostly books, and to the right there was a window, shrouded in dark, dusty curtains. The whole place looked to be in imminent danger of an internal avalanche.

In the central clearing around the table, lit by a yellowish overhead lamp, were four individuals, two seated and two standing. For a group of people gathered to commit the crime of receiving valuable stolen property, they were an intriguing-looking bunch. Marcel Troyon made the introductions. "Our party is complete," he said. "This is Monsieur Blake, the American expert I was telling you about, and his wife. Monsieur Blake, may I present Mademoiselle Rhea."

Mademoiselle Rhea was a stunning example of Eurasian beauty. She was seated at the table to my left and attired in an expensively tailored business suit and coat, with a wealth of lustrous, raven-black hair, exquisitely coifed. She brought to mind a female version of the enterprising business sharks I'd seen cruising the financial districts of New York or Tokyo. She was a woman of mature years, but on her it was the age of perfection. She just gave me an impatient nod of greeting. "And her companion, Mr. Ajax." Mr. Ajax looked like he could be stunning, too. Literally. He was well over six feet tall and looked like he'd been chiseled out of bronze. He also wore expensive-looking business attire, but he didn't look comfortable in it. We got the silent nod from him as well.

Marcel continued. "And next we have Monsieur Ombra." A small, spare man dressed in Continental class rose from his seat and shook my hand, taking it in both of his. He looked to be somewhere in his late fifties, with a pale, smiling face, well-groomed gray hair and beard, and sharp blue eyes behind rimless glasses. "Hello," he said warmly, with traces of an accent I couldn't place. "It's a pleasure. And this is your wife?"

"Caitlin," she replied. I was a bit surprised that he didn't kiss her hand. As Mr. Ombra took his seat, he indicated the tall, slender man standing by the curtains. "And this is my associate, Mr. DeWinter." DeWinter was dressed in a long, black coat and held a matching hat in his hand, in stark contrast with his white hair, combed back away from a narrow, hatchet-like face. He didn't even offer a nod of greeting; he just stared.

Marcel had Caitlin and me take the two remaining chairs. "It appears we have a small change of circumstance," he announced. "Mr. Ombra contacted me very recently. He also wishes to make a bid on our rara avis."

I smiled at Marcel's Latin title for the bronze eagle flag top, and hoped my expression covered my concern over this last-minute change of plan. Rhea wasn't so concerned with hiding her feelings. "This wasn't our deal," she said sharply.

That identified the beautiful Ms. Rhea and the monolithic Mr. Ajax as emissaries of the mysterious James Phillip Vanya. Marcel shrugged expansively and said, "What am I to say, mademoiselle? I was surprised myself when Monsieur Ombra contacted me and told me he also wished to purchase the item in question. So I am thinking that we will have an auction, yes?"

Mademoiselle Rhea indicated me with a slight toss of her head as she said to Troyon, "And just what is Mr. Blake's part in all of this?"

Troyon held a hand up as he explained, "Monsieur Blake is an expert in antiquities from the Argo Foundation. He will be able to ascertain that the article is genuine."

"Actually," I added quickly, "the foundation doesn't know I'm doing this, considering the, ah, questionable provenance of the artifact. Namely that it's stolen merchandise. So I'm acting on my own here."

Everyone grew quiet in response to my statement, like I'd just made a huge social blunder. I deliberately put all the cards on the table for Caitlin's sake. Anyone who stayed in the room now was patently tied into the conspiracy to acquire stolen goods. Mademoiselle Rhea started the ball rolling again. "Let us see what we came for."

Marcel nodded. "*Bon*. Give me a moment." He disappeared into the narrow, darkened hallway. Rhea, Ajax, and DeWinter kept their eyes on the spot while Mr. Ombra said to me, "So, Mr. Blake, you are an expert on Le Petit Caporal?"

"The Little Corporal?" I translated, smiling at the use of one of Napoleon Bonaparte's nicknames. "Not specifically. I'm more of a generalist than an expert on the general. But he was one of the greats."

"One of the greats?" Ombra asked dryly.

"Sure, right up there with Temujin Genghis Kahn, or Julius Caesar."

Ombra looked like he was just about to engage me in spirited debate when Marcel Troyon returned and set a small, inexpensive-looking plaster casting of a cherubic angel on the table, along with a short ball peen hammer and large flat-head screwdriver. All eyes were on Marcel as he chipped away at the statuette with the delicacy of a sculptor, slowly revealing a form wrapped in an old, faded newspaper. He carefully peeled the paper away, exposing the dully gleaming gilded eagle, wings spread, perched among the shards of plaster as if it'd just been hatched.

Ombra was smiling with quiet reserve, while Rhea was gazing at the eagle with razor-sharp intensity. I felt a touch of admiration for Troyon's simple but brilliant method of hiding stolen property. No one would ever find such a treasure amidst the mounds of trash crammed into the apartment, and it made me wonder if he had any more genuine artifacts squirreled away nearby.

I reached out and picked up the eagle, feeling all eyes on me. It was cold to the touch and surprisingly light in weight, and it gave me that familiar thrill I feel whenever I get to hold an actual relic from the ages in my hand. I estimated it to be about ten inches from base to top and roughly the same width across the wingspan, with a circular hollow joint at the base where the eagle would be attached to a flagpole. But frankly, the old bird had seen better days. Most of the patina of gold plate had been worn away down to the bronze, and based on the marks and scars it carried I could easily believe this military icon had been involved in numerous battles. I asked quietly, "I understand that there were other items taken from the Boston museum at the same time as this one?"

Marcel nodded. "Yes. I was in the process of making a deal with an Irish friend of mine, and he offered me the eagle as proof he had a connection to the rest of the artworks taken during the robbery. Unfortunately, he died suddenly."

"Oh," was all I could say. Damn. So much for getting a line on that Chinese bronze for Nick Riley. I brought out my small pocket monocular, took out the magnifying lens, and made a show of examining the eagle, turning it this way and that and holding it up to the light. The more I looked, the more I started to feel like I could be holding the genuine article. But overall, it was still a relatively ugly piece of gilded bronze, and in no way could it compare with the masterpieces that were also taken during the Boston museum robbery. Caitlin silently interrupted my chain of thought by delicately but firmly grinding the heel of her shoe into my ankle under the table, a certain signal to get on with it. I reluctantly set the eagle down and announced, "This is the one. I'd stake my reputation on it."

Mr. Ombra said, "Then it is my intention to purchase it. At any price," he added with a polite nod to Rhea.

Rhea acted like she didn't hear what Ombra said. "I need to make a test of my own," she stated as Ajax bent down and picked up a small but heavy-looking hard-sided case. As Ajax opened it up, I caught a glimpse of a panel with a small screen inside.

"What do you mean, test?" Marcel asked.

"It's not invasive," Rhea said dismissively. "We have a machine here that works like a portable ultrasound. I just need to make a quick scan of the eagle. This will only take a moment."

Mr. Ombra looked down, almost sadly, when he heard what Rhea said, then he stood up from the table and stepped aside. That's when I saw that Mr. DeWinter had drawn a long-barreled pistol.

Everyone froze as Ombra announced, "I'm sorry, but now I must insist—" Before Ombra could finish, Ajax lurched up from his chair, his large hands diving under his jacket.

That's when DeWinter shot Ajax twice in the chest.

CHAPTER SIX

I should have been dead by now.

The only reason I was still alive was that DeWinter thought Ajax was the biggest threat in the room and shot him first, even though I was closest to him. Though the pistol was silenced, the concussion of the blast as the bullet exploded out of the barrel was like having a heavy book slammed shut a millimeter from my face as fiery pinpricks of burnt gunpowder peppered my head. I made DeWinter pay for his mistake by grabbing his gun hand and his elbow as I launched myself as hard as I could out of my chair, breaking his arm in the process.

The long pistol spun away and I made a grab for it as Ajax fell back like a sack of sand into a tall cupboard of crockery, pulling it down with him in a crashing avalanche, but Rhea, quick as a snake, snatched the gun out of the air. Faster than a blink, she pumped three shots into DeWinter, cutting off his scream as he collapsed onto the table.

The next thing I knew I was violently yanked backwards by the collar of my coat and my legs were swept out from under me. I curled up to turn my backwards fall into a rolling somersault and saw it was Caitlin who pulled me down, getting me out of the line of fire. I glimpsed a flash of Caitlin's arm as it chopped the pistol from Rhea's grasp just as Rhea grabbed the eagle with her free hand and rammed it into Caitlin's stomach.

Caitlin fell back and slammed down on top of me, and instantly it felt like I had an armful of angry jungle tiger. She fought her way upright and launched herself after Rhea, who was already heading for the door with the eagle. I swear I heard Caitlin growl as she pounced.

I scrambled to my feet just in time to see Ombra pull a gun from his coat and turn to aim it toward the running women. My hand found the large screwdriver Marcel had used to crack open the eagle's plaster nesting place. I swept it off the table and threw it hard, slamming the blade of the screwdriver into Ombra's back, high, near his right shoulder. His diminutive body seized up like he'd been hit by electricity as the pistol spun away from his hand and he fell into a pile of books.

I glanced back and saw that Marcel Troyon had raced over to the kitchenette, where he was wrestling with another door at the back of the room, off to the right. I heard a crash, and turned to see that Rhea had managed to get the front door open. I watched as she and Caitlin, wrapped together in snarling combat, tumbled out into the hall. I vaulted over Ombra, and as I made it to the doorway I saw the bronze eagle fly from between the women, who both rolled off the landing and down the stairs.

I made a grab for the eagle and scooped it up, just in time to see Caitlin and Rhea collide with a pair of dark-coated men wearing black ski masks. The whole human avalanche crashed down to the first floor, and one of the men managed to raise a pistol in my direction, squeezing off a muffled shot before I could pull back and slam Troyon's door shut. My fingers were shaking from the adrenaline charge as I fumbled one-handed with the latches on the heavy door, locking it shut, and I could hear a woman's scream from outside calling out in French for the police.

Caitlin was trapped out there, and for a split second I froze, locked between my training and a sudden, unbidden desire to try to save the woman. But the rapid, thudding sound of booted feet and the impact on the locked door as someone tried to crash their way inside snapped me back to the fact that there were at least two armed men out there and I had to be smart, not suicidal.

Turning back toward the room, I was just in time to see Ombra, eyes mad with pain, lunge at me with the bloody screwdriver that he had managed to extract from his back. I smacked the impromptu weapon out of his hand with an upward slash of the bronze eagle I held, and finished up with a looping, backhanded blow to the side of his head, dropping him like a stone. That's when I saw Troyon across the room as he managed to yank the side door open. For the briefest instant, I saw a flickering green spark flutter across Troyon's chest, then he got kicked backwards and landed on the floor in a boneless heap. There was a sniper outside, armed with a laser-sighted gun.

I felt like a piece of porcelain perched between a hammer and an anvil with the sound of the gunmen slamming themselves into the door behind me and the sight of the lethal, bright green spark as it fluttered through the kitchenette, looking for something else to kill as it blocked the only other way out of this junkyard killing floor.

I leapt over the moaning body of Ombra and looked over to the curtained windows on the right; it was the only chance left. There was a cracking sound behind me as the front door started to give way, telling me it was time to get the hell out of here. I couldn't see the switch for the overhead light, so I just grabbed an old metal alarm clock close to hand and threw it upward; there was a pop and flash and the tinkling sound of glass falling to the table in the sudden darkness. I tucked the eagle under my arm, grabbed ahold of a standing metal lamp that was close to the window, then swung it through the curtains, blasting a hole through the glass and frame. The curtain broke away from its mooring and dropped, revealing a moonlit landscape of sharply angled rooftops and the blazing lights of the city beyond.

Racing against the sniper outside, I rolled out of the window and crouched on the deck of a narrow wooden balcony. I blindly reached for the edge and got a grip while I slid my body off the deck and swung into space. I tried to keep my hold on the rough wood, but my own weight yanked me down and I broke free, flailing my arms on the way down. Muffled bullets slapped the air over my head in the brief flash of free fall, then my feet collided with hard pavement and I instinctively tried to roll with the fall as if from a bad parachute landing, bringing my hands up to guard my head as I was slammed onto hard stone and kicked in the side as if by a raging bull.

I don't know if I went unconscious or not; my first semi-cogent thought was that I'd been shot in the chest. I grew aware that I was lying on cold, wet, hard cobblestone, and that there were dogs barking somewhere in the distance. My eyes started to bring lights into focus, coming from a jumble of windows above me, along with the bright beam of a high-powered flashlight that quested from one of the angled rooftops. My arms and legs started to move like they were coming back to life on their own and my numbed left hand fumbled across my chest until it found the cause of my agony: the bronze eagle. I must have landed on the damn thing.

I managed to pull myself up with the help of a nearby brick wall, noticing my right leg didn't want to cooperate at all. Through the diffused lights from above, I saw I was now in a narrow brick cul-de-sac surrounded by six different doors. There was a small decorative fountain in the middle of the tiny courtyard, and I was grateful that I hadn't impaled myself on it when I fell to earth. The first two doors I tried were locked, but the third opened to reveal a narrow hallway with stairs running up one side and another door directly ahead, and I was glad to see that I didn't stumble right back into the apartment building I'd just escaped from. I hobbled to the door and pushed through, finding myself outside in a narrow, crooked alleyway lined with small shops packed closely together, leading to a brighter street beyond. I silently cursed my lagging body and stumbled down the path, hoping I wasn't heading right back toward the enemy.

I emerged from the mouth of the alley and into the lights and sounds of a busy street. I ducked back around the corner and slipped off my overcoat, noticing how it had taken the brunt of the damage of my escape, and wrapped the eagle up into a bundle. I heard the high-pitched, two-tone whine of a French police vehicle, the direction of the siren giving me a bearing on the location of the recent disaster. Keeping my head down, I joined the small parade of people and walked away from the trouble as best as I could manage. Making my way along the sidewalk, I was hoping my mere appearance and limping gait weren't frightening the people as I forced myself to adopt the lingering stride of the Parisian pedestrian, hoping to blend in with everyone and glad I was in a populated, cosmopolitan city. The lights of the giant rectangular skyscraper I'd spotted earlier gave me a general bearing as I made my way north.

I was struck by a sharp edge of fear and suddenly felt trapped on the cobblestone street that was too narrow, wedged between white stone buildings with too many darkened windows, amidst too many people and noisy vehicles to watch all at once. I was tempted to duck down into the Paris Métro subway, but decided against the risk of getting caught underground. Instead, when I figured I'd hiked my way out of the immediate danger zone, I looked for a hiding place off the street among the restaurants, which included Greek and Chinese places, and chose a small, cozy-looking bistro that wasn't overly populated. I wove through the tables that crowded the outside sidewalk and made for the bar, where I ordered a small, expensive brandy with a large tumbler of water, happy to note that the young man bartending didn't give me a second glance. I took a little table toward the rear that afforded a view of the front door. Marking my territory with my drinks, I headed for the back of the place, spotted a possible rear exit, and then found the toilet and went to check myself over for any obvious signs of damage. The pale, wild-eyed face in the mirror was a familiar sight as I smoothed my hair back into a semblance of normality. My ribs on the right side hurt like hell and felt like they'd been cracked again, a feeling I was far too familiar with. My lower pant legs and shoes were wet and smudged, but it didn't show much against the dark material. I rewrapped the eagle in my overcoat so as not to display the obvious damage to the coat. I was mildly surprised to see I wasn't leaking any bodily fluids this time.

I washed my hands and my face to cool down, then went back to my table, scanning the room to see if anyone was paying any particular attention to me. All the patrons were clustered together in small groups and engaged with each other. I drank my water, then took a sip of brandy, letting the liquid fire burn away the ashen taste in my mouth. I leaned back and let the tension pour out of me as I listened to the sound of a violinist hacking away at Vivaldi's "La Primavera" somewhere nearby on the street. My left hand rested on the wrapped bundle in my lap—a treasure so valuable that men were willing to kill for it. And I had no idea why.

I had to pull myself together and make a plan. My

battered old Seamaster watch told me that it was slightly after ten o'clock—just after four in the afternoon back in New York. I pulled out my phone and checked to see if it was still operational, but the display screen was just a bright mass of swimming pixels. Chalk up another piece of high tech that I managed to convert into useless junk. But while my electronic device failed me, my internal radar was working just fine as I spotted a large, dark-skinned man in a tan overcoat and cap coming into the café. The new arrival scanned the room and set his eyes on me. He gave a dazzling smile and called out as he walked straight toward me. "Hey, Johnny!"

My left hand came up to the brandy glass as my right brought out and palmed my lighter, ready to ignite the alcohol and send it flying as a flaming distraction, while my legs braced themselves to move. The man kept his hands in view as he approached. "It's me, Sam Smith. From New York," he said. "Your wife said I'd find you around here."

My mind raced to change gears, but my keenly honed sense of paranoia stayed in the lead. "Sam Smith," I repeated. "From New York."

He laughed. "Yeah. Grandfather wanted me to look you up. Come on, I've got a taxi waiting outside."

If it was a trap, it was a damn good setup. The guy said all the right things to lead me to believe he was one of Caitlin's people. I decided against the impromptu fireworks display and just nodded my head as I got up to go with him. As we walked to the door, the man said, "You okay, man? You're not walking so good."

"Old football injury," I replied shortly. As I stepped outside, I paused and looked up over the rooftops to see a geyser of black smoke, lit in flickering red from below, pour out across the sky, while more sirens wailed in the distance. "Looks like someone started a fire," Sam said from beside me. I just nodded, coldly acknowledging the ruthless efficiency of it all. The police wouldn't discover the real cause of so many deaths at Troyon's apartment for a while yet.

The man who called himself Sam Smith led me to a taxi, and as he joined me in the backseat, I got a better look at him. He was easily six foot two, and moved like an athlete. When he took off his cap, I saw that he kept his head clean-shaven; it dully reflected the marquis lights from the street. Sam gave the driver an address on the boulevard du Montparnasse. We drove in silence through the busy, narrow streets until we arrived, and as I got out of the taxi I saw one of those familiar signs that are so jarring to see in other parts of the world. I couldn't help but ask, "You come all the way to Paris, and then stay at a Comfort Inn?"

Sam said as he paid the driver, "Hey, we can't all have fat expense accounts."

I followed him into the hotel, where he led me to the door of a room on the second floor. Smith pulled out a phone, checked it, and then opened the door. The man turned on the lights as he waved the phone in a circle around the room. Closing the door after me, he said, "Okay, Blake, I hope you've got your passport with you, because we're going to be leaving soon."

I looked around the room and saw a large black luggage bag, as well as an open laptop computer on the single desk near the double beds. "Where's Caitlin?" I asked.

"She's making her way on her own, and the rest of

the team is already moving out. I stayed behind to get you."

"How in the hell did you find me?"

"You've been tagged since before you left New York."

"Tagged?"

"That wedding ring Caitlin gave you," Sam explained. "It's got built-in circuitry. I'll need that back, by the way."

I slipped the ring off and held it up to the light, remembering how Caitlin was always making sure I was wearing it. "She's not coming back, is she?" I heard myself saying.

Sam stopped halfway over to the desk. "No," he said quietly, not looking at me. "Someone got her."

"Wait, you found me, right? Can't you find Caitlin the same way?"

He turned back to me, and I could see he was holding back anger as he said in a growl, "It doesn't work that way. In case it's slipped your mind, we were here to do a job, namely catch Vanya's people in the act of buying stolen merchandise. But that job got blown big time, didn't it? I suppose that's the bird in question you got wrapped up there?"

I nodded, then said, "So that's it? You're leaving Caitlin behind?"

Sam looked away, speaking toward the wall. "Yes. Yes, I am. Because that's the way this works. Just so you know, Mr. Blake, people in my business get left behind all over the world. People you never hear about, doing things no one ever gets to see, just to protect people like you." He took a step closer, looming over me as he said through gritted teeth, "So yes, I'm leaving her behind, just like I've left other people behind and just like I'll do again until someday, somebody has to do the same thing to me. So now you can just shut the hell up and do as you're told, and I'll get us out of here."

That's when I hit him.

CHAPTER SEVEN

Smith really didn't give me any choice. There was no way I was going off and leaving Caitlin behind. The edge of my hand slammed into the side of his neck and he dropped like a stone. I used my bandanna to tie his hands, and Smith's own shoelaces to bind his ankles together. With the time I had left before he started to regain consciousness, I turned his pockets inside out and was tossing the contents onto the bed when he groaned and mumbled, "What . . . stupid!"

"No need to call names," I said, looking over my inventory. Along with his phone and wallet he carried a passport that stated his name was actually Samuel Quincy Smith, a Casio G-Shock watch, and a wicked-looking Kershaw folding knife with a blackened blade.

"Not you, me," Sam said as he tested his bonds. "Damn. I saw what you did back at Troyon's apartment."

I froze. "You did?"

"Hell, yes. We had the place wired. Audio and visual. I saw you in action. I haven't seen moves like that since I saw a Russian Spetsnaz dude take out three guys. Before someone iced him, anyway," Sam added, then said quietly, "So just who are you, man?"

I was trying to cover up the cold, sinking feeling that I'd exposed myself and my special talents badly, and to a government agent no less. But I wasn't surprised at the comparison Sam Smith made, as one of my many instructors was former Russian Special Forces. "You tell me," I said. "You're the guys who hired me."

Sam laughed darkly. "We thought we were hiring an antiques geek we could pass off as an expert during the sting operation. But you're obviously something else. And unless I miss my guess, I'm not the first dude you've tied up in your lifetime."

I tried to shake Smith off the subject. "What ever happened to 'don't ask, don't tell'? And just who were those other guys, Ombra and DeWinter? Where the hell did they come from?"

Smith sighed. "Can I sit up or something? I'm getting a kink in my neck."

"Sure." I helped him up, which did my damaged ribs no good at all, and then guided him as he hopped to one of the beds, where I set a pillow up and let him sit with his back to the headboard. "So who are those guys?" I asked again.

Smith looked away, then said, "We don't know. They came out of nowhere. I figure Troyon was working some kind of side deal on his own. I got people in Washington trying to identify them now."

I picked up my bundle from where I'd dropped it when I put Sam down, and unwrapped the eagle. I could see now that one of its wings was bent and there was a bad scuff mark on its beak, and I heard the voice of Nick Riley in my head, telling me, not for the first time, "That's coming out of your salary." I held the eagle up for Smith to see. "So what do Vanya the cult leader and Ombra want with a Napoleonic icon?"

Smith shook his head. "We have no idea. So just what do you think you're going to do now?"

I looked down at the eagle and sighed, knowing what I had to do. I thought of the countless men who, hundreds of years ago, faced fire and steel to protect this symbol of their emperor. "It's obvious," I said. "The killing didn't start tonight until Ombra knew that Rhea woman wanted to get a look inside this thing. It's not the eagle that's valuable, it's whatever is concealed inside of it."

"So?"

"So I'm going to crack this bird open and see what's so goddammed important. And when I find out, I'll use whatever it is to get Caitlin back."

"Blake, we don't even know if she's still alive."

"Shut up," I said. In the single desk I found a telephone directory to use as a makeshift operating table, and laid the eagle on top of it. I held the eagle to the light and peered inside the hollow shaft at the base where the icon would be joined to a flagpole, but the cavity was featureless. I took Sam's knife and snapped it open, seeing the blade was serrated halfway up its length. Trying not to feel sick as if I was desecrating a sacred object, I used the knife to chip and saw open the softer bronze of the eagle. It was hard work, but I eventually was able to pry the eagle's head off, and was rewarded by the sight of a dull gray cylinder nestled inside.

I freed the cylinder from the remains of the eagle and cleared the bronze shavings off the table. The metal felt light, and there was a crimped cap on one end. I slowly put pressure to the top, until it gave way and unscrewed. With a final small *pop,* the top came free, and I caught a brief scent of old parchment. I could see a flattened roll of paper inside, and I coaxed it out until I saw the pale red wax seal affixed to the side. Turning it toward the desk lamp, I saw the impressed eagle—the coat of arms of Napoleon.

I tried to disengage the seal while keeping it intact, but it broke apart and crumbled to pieces. I steadied my hands and unrolled the parchment, seeing it was actually three papers stacked together. The first was handwritten in French, with a date of the sixteenth of April in the year 1815. I focused on the spidery and faded script, blessing all the Latin language courses I had in college and cursing the fact that I should have studied harder as I labored to translate the letter, which began: "In the name of His Majesty, by the Grace of God and the Constitution of the Republic, the Emperor Napoleon of France."

As I parsed out the words, I learned that the letter directed the reader to go forthwith to Le Chapelle du Val de Grâce, and present this Warrant to Baron Dominique-Jean Larrey, and secure the property of his Majesty, the Emperor Napoleon. The bottom of the letter was signed: J. Fouché, Minister of Police, Duke of Otranto.

I felt that electric, tingling sensation I always got

when I was on the trail of something big. The second paper was a portion of an age-browned and sepia-toned street map of Paris, dated 1814, marked with a circle in the southeast corner. From the notations on the map showing the River Seine, the indicated area was well south from my current location. The third page was an exacting, hand-drawn floor plan of the Chapel du Val de Grâce, with written notations on the side, indicating directions of two hundred yards south and two hundred yards west. On the floor plan itself there was a circle drawn around the eastern portion of the church, indicating the "Sacristie Interieure." I thought briefly that there should have been an X to mark the spot.

If I was reading this right, I was holding in my hand a map to a lost treasure of Napoleon Bonaparte.

The brittle paper rattled as my hands began to shake at the enormity of the thoughts crashing inside my head. Napoleon not only conquered half of Europe, he looted it as well. The wily old bastard must have set up a secret cache, like an emergency war chest, and kept the knowledge of it among a few trusted men. But now, with such a treasure of historical significance, the value of whatever was locked away in his private vault would be multiplied countless times. No wonder people were willing to kill for this. I was dimly aware of Sam Smith when he asked, "What did you say? What's a 'Fouché'?"

I must have spoken out loud. I swallowed with a dry throat and tried to get a grip on my runaway emotions. "Not what, who," I said, glad my voice wasn't shaking. "Fouché was Napoleon's minister of police. More likely he was His Majesty's spymaster."

"Thanks for the history lesson," Smith said flatly. "Now just what the hell did you find inside that thing?"

I started to speak, and then realized I should just keep my mouth shut about my treasure map. "How do I find Caitlin?" I asked instead.

"You're really going to try and find her?"

"Yes."

"Why?"

The simple question stopped me for a moment. The smart thing to do would be to get the hell out, but I knew for a gut-deep certainty my conscience would never allow it.

"Because she said she'd protect me," I answered. "I believed her. If I was the one who got captured, she'd come for me."

"Then untie me. I want to help."

I was sorely tempted, but I realized that Sam Smith was probably too good a soldier. "Sorry. I can't trust you."

"But I should trust you?"

"Hey, you're the one who was all set to leave without her," I said as I carefully rolled up the letter and map, placing them back inside the tin cylinder, wishing my phone hadn't been busted so I could at least get a photograph of the documents. I looked sadly for a moment at the wreck of the eagle and the broken bits of wax from the Napoleonic seal. I glanced around the room and found a plastic garment bag. As I placed the pieces of the eagle into the bag, Sam said, "Caitlin had a tracer that she was supposed to attach to the eagle, so we could follow whoever it was that bought the thing, and hopefully it would lead us straight to Vanya. Only it looks like Caitlin never got the chance to put the device on the eagle and she still has it with her. I've been monitoring her movements. From what I've seen, Caitlin's being driven around the city and they're circling your hotel. You head back there, and I guarantee whoever kidnapped her will find you."

I suddenly realized why Caitlin had attacked Rhea back at the apartment when Rhea made her mad dash with the eagle. Caitlin was obviously making a last-ditch attempt to plant the bug on the bird before Rhea ran off with it. I grabbed my topcoat and regarded my borrowed knife for a moment; I'd pretty much trashed the blade when I took apart the eagle. "You got a gun around here?" I asked.

"Hell, no."

"What kind of secret agent are you, anyway? Look, just give me thirty minutes, and then you can make a racket and get someone from the hotel to let you out."

"Great, I get seen going into a hotel room with another man, and then I get found like this?"

"Sorry," I said from the doorway.

"Hey, Blake?"

"What?"

Sam Smith didn't look at me as he sat on the bed, and just said softly, "Bring her back, man. Bring her back." I just nodded, checked the hallway, and left the room.

It was only eleven at night according to the bells I heard as I flagged a cab and took the short drive back to the Saint Michel Hotel. When I paid the driver and walked through the wood-paneled lobby, it felt like I'd been gone for years. I made it to the door to the room I'd shared so briefly with Caitlin, then braced myself and entered quickly. There was no one waiting for me, and I only had the blinking message light on the phone to greet me. I played back the recorded call, and heard the voice of Mr. Ombra as he recited a telephone number to call. I punched the numbers in, and he picked up right away.

"Where's Caitlin?" I demanded.

"She's safe," Ombra said. "I assume you know what we want?"

"Yes. I have it. Let me talk to Caitlin."

"No," he said simply. "You'll see her as soon as we have the item in our possession."

I had a sudden idea. "Fine. Meet me at Notre Dame. Bring Caitlin." I hung up the phone. At least now I was the one who chose the location for the meeting, instead of using a place Ombra would know and be able to set up a trap in ahead of time. I took a few moments to prepare myself, then left the hotel and headed north to the stone bridge over the Seine. It was raining again, and I kept moving as fast as my injured leg would allow, hoping Ombra's men wouldn't spot me before I arrived.

I crossed the ornate bridge, too well lit with streetlamps for comfort, and saw how the man-made stone banks of the island ahead made for a sheer drop into the night-black river below. Downstream, I saw a boat lit up like a constellation of stars slowly motor away. Once on the other side, I had a clear view of the Notre Dame Cathedral, but even with my recent experience with the Eiffel Tower and Arc de Triomph, my sense of scale and distance weren't equal to the task of appreciating the enormity of the structure. I found myself standing before a football-field length of open concrete square, staring up through the falling rain at the mountainous gothic cathedral. It was nearly a thousand years old, and encompassed all the grace that mortal man could invest into a monument to God. But the beauty in my vision quickly faded as I realized I was in the absolute worst possible position—a wide-open area with no cover whatsoever. Even at this hour and in the rain I could see people over by the front of the cathedral. What I needed now was the best spot I could find for an ambush.

I walked through the main square, feeling with every step that I'd made a fatal mistake in choosing this place, until I saw over to my right a chance to salvage the situation. I hurried over toward the right side of the square until I was standing before a massive statue of Charlemagne, king of the Franks and emperor of Rome, astride his horse and flanked by two of his paladins. I figured the paladin to Charlemagne's right, the one holding a horn, was supposed to be Roland, and it made me hope that this stunt I was about to try wouldn't turn out to be my own personal Battle of Roncevaux. It was fortunate that Paris, the City of Lights, was also the City of Trees; I saw that on the side of the statue facing away from the square was a darkened area that offered a shadowy, tree-clustered refuge. It was a perfect spot for someone to try and sneak up on me. I gratefully sat down on the wet stone base of the monument, facing the night-shrouded foliage, glad that I had one of the greatest warrior kings of the world to guard my back.

As I sat there, I realized that for the first time in my professional life I was actually hiding in a spot where I hoped to be found. I decided to help out anyone looking for me and took out a cigarette from my flattened box and lit up a smoke, cupping the cigarette in my hands to keep it dry. I was tempted to hold on to the lighter as a last-ditch close-combat weapon, but reluctantly chose to put it away.

My cigarette was long gone and I was starting to think that I was hiding a little too well when I finally heard a quiet, melodious voice from behind me and to my left that said, "May I see your hands, please?" I slowly raised my hands to my shoulders as Mr. Ombra stepped out from behind the base of the statue. Even in the poorly reflected light I could see the damage on his face, and he seemed to have lost his glasses somewhere during the evening. He didn't have a weapon I could see, though I was pleased to notice that he held his right arm stiffly, the result of the screwdriver I had plowed into his back earlier in the evening.

"Where's Caitlin?"

"She is nearby."

"Where?"

Ombra just shook his head, then came and sat next to me. He held out his hand and said, "The eagle, if you please."

I reached into my coat and removed the plastic bag I carried. Ombra received it from my hand and gently hefted the bag a few times, causing the broken contents to clink together, then he slowly tipped the bag over and poured the bronze bits out and watched as they bounced on the concrete ground.

"I forgot to mention," I said, "there was a little damage in transit."

Ombra said nothing; he just sighed and held his

hand out again. This time I gave him the tin cylinder. "So you have seen what was inside," Ombra said, almost sadly. I was just about to answer when a spark of bright green light began to dance on the front of my coat.

My chest exploded.

CHAPTER EIGHT

The bullet hit my chest and slammed me back into the stone base, cracking my head before I tumbled to the hard, wet ground. I don't know if I went completely unconscious or not; all I could see was a black pond filled with frantically swimming electric-bright minnows. I didn't hear Ombra leave the area through the trip-hammer drumbeat of blood pounding in my ears. I stayed still, forcing myself to breathe in slow, openmouthed draughts while my heart beat against the walls of my chest until I thought I was going to pass out from the lack of oxygen. My efforts to imitate the dead were rewarded, first by the fact that no one shot me again, and secondly when I heard the sound of shoe heels as they came running toward me on the concrete.

Hands grabbed me and rolled me over, and I opened my eyes as I croaked out, "Hi, honey, miss me?" Only to see the beautiful, half-shadowed face of Rhea staring down at me. "Damn it!" I uttered. "Sorry, wrong damsel. Where's Caitlin?"

Rhea let go of me, and I almost hit my head on the ground. "Caitlin? Your wife? They still have her."

I cursed, then cursed again when I tried to sit up and couldn't. It felt like my chest was a bag of broken glass. I tore open my overcoat and let my makeshift armor slide off my overheated body and onto the ground. I owed my life to all the people and places in Paris who thoughtfully included themselves in the Parisian telephone directory that I'd taken from my hotel room and packed around my torso. I also owed a debt to the Chinese Tang Dynasty armor smiths who first purportedly used layers of paper as cheap protection for some of their troops. Back during my survival training I'd seen the effect of handgun rounds after they'd been fired into phone books. The exercise then was to show me how some bullets expand on impact, but I noticed how those old books managed to absorb shots fired from guns as big as a .44 Special. I'd gambled on the fact that the guns Ombra's men had been using were silenced and probably loaded with slow, subsonic rounds that didn't give themselves away with the tell-tale whip-crack sound as they traveled through the air. With the phone directory in my coat, I'd looked fairly pregnant on my walk over, but sitting down I was able to hunch forward and conceal the bulk under my overcoat. This was why I'd had to find some solid cover for my back and hope no one would try to take me down with a headshot.

I pulled myself mostly upright with the help of Charlemagne's pedestal, looking up toward the glistening towers of Notre Dame and offering a silent thanks to any saints who may have helped me survive. Rhea was still on her knees. Her raven-black hair had come undone and lay across her shoulders, and her dark gray business suit was soaked through. She was holding the eagle, its head in one hand and winged body in the other. "What happened?" she asked quietly.

"Ombra happened, that's what. Now you tell me—where's Caitlin?"

Rhea didn't speak for a moment, then she looked up and into my eyes with a stare that was both deep and implacable. "You know what was inside the eagle," she stated.

I pushed off from the pedestal and forced myself to stand, feeling a spike of fire shoot through my right side. Of course, it would have to be the right side of my chest again, I thought. "Look, just tell me what you know about Ombra and his men, and then you're free to go. All I ask is that you don't call for the police, at least not for a little while."

"Police?" she said disdainfully as she rose. "I have no intention of calling the police. You know what was inside the eagle. I'm going with you."

"Like hell, lady."

"Then perhaps I should start screaming now?"

Her smile was haughty and disdainful; she knew she'd won. "Look," I said, "I'm going after Ombra and his crew. At least I think I know where they're headed. It's going to be too dangerous to take you with me."

"You're going after Ombra? Look at yourself. You can hardly stand. You look like you belong up there in the bell tower. You're wasting time. I'm coming with you."

A flash of memory replayed the quick and deadly

way that this woman had grabbed DeWinter's own gun out of thin air and shot him to pieces with it. I knew I wasn't going to win this standoff. "All right," I conceded. "Let's go. But don't come crying to me if you get yourself killed over this."

I almost thought I saw a twinge of a smile on her glistening features. From force of habit, I looked around the area for incriminating evidence. I couldn't quite stifle the moan I made as I bent down and retrieved the phone directory. There was a small, ragged hole in the front and a thumb-sized protrusion in the back, and I peeled open the pages, dislodging specks of paper confetti until I found the bullet, lodged almost all the way through the book. I pried out the round and saw how it looked like some deadly, copper-plated insect that got smashed against an impervious windscreen. Rhea had picked up the plastic garment bag and was placing the pieces of the broken eagle inside. I took the bag from her, added the phone directory, placed the bullet in my overcoat pocket, and nodded my head in the direction of the nearest bridge.

Rhea surprised me by coming to my side, placing my arm around her shoulders, and circling my waist with her free hand, assisting me to walk and giving anyone who might see us the impression that we were lovers, out for a rainy Parisian stroll. I could feel the smooth, hard muscles of her body as we moved together. "So where are we going?" she asked.

"You first," I countered. "What happened at Troyon's apartment?"

"You were there. You saw how they killed . . . my companion."

"Yeah. I also saw you avenge him."

Rhea ignored my statement as if it meant nothing and continued, "I tried to get the eagle out of the apartment, but that wife of yours grabbed me. Why did she do that?"

"She's always been impulsive," I responded. "What came next?"

"I almost killed her," Rhea said, as if we were discussing the weather, "but we both wound up falling down the stairs and into those men. They had guns."

"How many men does Ombra have?"

"I think there are five, altogether. We were dragged out and thrown into a large, white Mercedes van, then tied and blindfolded. They spoke French, and must have thought that your wife and I did not, or they just didn't care. When Ombra came down to the van, we left in a hurry. He seemed quite annoyed. I suppose that's when you got away with the eagle?"

I just nodded, and Rhea continued. "Ombra and his men kept the van moving, and it felt like they were driving in a big circle. I heard him place a call and leave a message for you. It seemed like a long time before you called Ombra back."

"I was busy. Then what?"

"Ombra told his men to go to the cathedral, but then he had trouble finding you. I heard him send his men out on foot. They have radios, and I heard one call in that he had you spotted, over by the statue of Charlemagne. I heard Ombra tell your wife that she would see you soon, and he got out of the van. He wasn't gone long when he came back. The next thing I know, his men are cutting my ropes and pulling me outside the van. I was told to go and warn my people to stay out of this business, and that was the only reason they let me live. The last thing I heard was Ombra telling your wife that there had been a change of plans, but that she would still be with you soon. They drove off and left me, so I went looking for you."

I really didn't like the sound of Ombra's last words. "Why'd they let you go and keep Caitlin?"

"I don't know," Rhea replied. "Perhaps, since Ombra thought he had killed you, he didn't want your wife to find out so soon?"

"Those ruthless bastards? Not likely."

"Regardless, that was very clever of you, letting them think you are dead," Rhea said with a tinge of admiration in her voice. "And far too clever for someone who is supposed to be a simple expert in antiquities. Who are you, really?"

"Just a guy who's going to get his wife back," I said through gritted teeth. We'd arrived at the bridge, the Pont au Double, and when we stared across I saw a sparkling pillar of light off to my right over the top of the city skyline as the sound of a bell tolled. The Eiffel Tower had lit up and signaled that it was midnight in Paris. At the halfway point of the stone bridge, in between the pools of light cast by the streetlamps, I looked around to see that Rhea and I were unobserved, then held up the bag containing the broken bronze eagle and the phone book. I could think of no useful purpose for the ruined icon. "Do you want the consolation prize?"

She shook her head, and with a sigh I tossed two hundred years of history down into the River Seine. All throughout my career working for Nicholas Riley, I'd done my best to save and salvage such treasure. Now I felt the ghosts of all the men who died following that gilded icon into battle weighing on whatever was left of my soul as I dropped the wreckage into the water, adding the smashed-up bullet as an afterthought. As I leaned over the bridge and stared down into the black water bordered by reflected columns of shimmering light, I heard Rhea beside me ask, "What are you thinking?" For a brief moment, her question took me back to my time with Caitlin, when she asked me the same question, an eon or two ago. Without taking my eyes off the river, I said, "I was just wondering if you could swim."

Rhea laughed, like she'd heard the best joke in the world. "Like a seal," she replied, almost happily. "And even if you could toss me in, Mr. Blake, I'm betting I could make it to the other side of the water before you could cross this old bridge. Now, where are we going?"

I didn't answer, and asked instead as we resumed walking, "So how did you know there was something inside that old bronze bird?"

"My patron would not want me to answer that question. What is your interest in all of this?"

"I'm just going to get my wife back."

Rhea stopped and turned to face me. Her night-black eyes stared steadily into mine as she said, "If you help me find what I need tonight, I will see to it that you are rewarded. Very well rewarded."

I opened my mouth, and then remembered the part I was supposed to be playing. "Deal," I said. "Now what is it you're looking for?"

"You don't know?"

"No. I know where Ombra is headed, but I don't know why," I lied.

"I see," she breathed. "Well, then. Lead the way, and then we both shall see."

I nodded acquiescence to her command, and we resumed our trek. Despite my concern for Caitlin, I felt that old, burning desire I got whenever I was on the hunt for treasure. Rhea was still playing cagey, as was I, and I silently promised her a good old-fashioned double cross. Just as soon as I got Caitlin back.

I'd been keeping a lookout for a taxi the whole time we'd been walking, and finally spotted a small white one on the other side of the bridge. Rhea and I hurried over and almost raced to see who could get into the backseat first. I pulled out a pair of hundred-euro notes and waved them at the driver, a tall, attenuated elder who looked like an adult crammed into a child's toy car. With a rueful glance at Rhea, I told the driver the destination: "Val de Grâce."

Our driver first held up the money to the overhead light, then grunted and nodded and shot the car out into the boulevard to the accompanying sounds of blaring horns on all sides of us. I couldn't really see what was happening outside the cab; the fact that Rhea and I were completely soaked soon had the windows of the small car fogged over, and the world outside seemed to melt into shifting blobs of color. Our driver cranked up the defroster until he had a narrow view of the street ahead through the rapid beats of the windshield wipers, beating counter-time to some French female crooner wailing a song of desperation from the tinny car radio.

I leaned back into the seat of the car and then Rhea grabbed me by the coat and smothered me in a deep, cold-lipped, hot-mouthed kiss that I instinctively responded to. When she pulled away, she planted a smaller kiss on my lips and whispered, "I wanted to say thank you, in case there isn't time later."

"Okay," was all I could manage to say as she settled back in her seat, looking like a satisfied cat. I was coming to the conclusion that I was sitting next to a dangerous woman of unknown capability and questionable sanity, and that I was probably going to regret not throwing her into the river when I had the chance.

I took the time to make a mental inventory. My bandanna and pocket monocular were gone, but I still had a button-sized flashlight and a small but accurate compass that was about the same size. I'd kept my pocket tool with the short blade and screwdriver attachments and a waterproof aluminum tube with a few strike-anywhere matches, along with a couple of safety pins and a paper clip that could be pressed into service as improvised lock picks. I still had a good wad of cash and my lighter, and a couple other items that I could employ to deadly effect. On the downside, I was hurting, but it was only pain, and I've learned to deal with that over the years.

I'd noticed the lights outside my fogged-up window had been growing dimmer and farther apart, and then the driver stopped the car and announced, "Val de Grâce, monsieur." I mentally kicked myself and told the driver to head up one more block. No sense in delivering yourself to your enemy's doorstep, idiot, I chastised myself. The driver took us a short distance and pulled over as I rolled down the window to get a look at the terrain.

I was sorry to see that the rain had let up and the clouds were breaking apart, letting moonlight shine

through. Not that it mattered; the streets were woe-
fully bright around the neighborhood, made up of tall,
pale-colored structures crowded together. I paid off the
driver and sent him on his way.

I scanned the area, noting the multitude of vehicles lining the street, but didn't spot any large white
vans. My eyes were drawn to the domed basilica-like
structure of the church. "Let's take a stroll," I said to
Rhea.

I led my army of one around the block to a street
named rue Pierre-Nicole and down the avenue, walking slowly to take it easy on my leg and letting my
senses roam. The traffic was light and the neighborhood relatively quiet with no signs of danger. Until
we reached the rue du Val de Grâce. When we rounded
the corner, the sight of the church's façade was revealed,
as if framed between the cream-colored rectangular
buildings of the street. The baroque-domed edifice
looked like a fairy-tale fusion of a Greco-Roman temple melded with a Saracen mosque. Then I spotted the
back end of a white van, parked at the end of the street
on the left.

I pulled Rhea back around the corner with me. "See
it?" I whispered.

She nodded. "Now what?"

Good question, I almost said aloud. I was hoping
that Caitlin would still be alive inside the van, and if
she was, there'd doubtless be at least one armed guard.
"From here on out it's risky. Here's your last chance
to walk away," I said.

"Forget it. How do you want to proceed?"

I looked back at Rhea, her face set into a mask of
fierce determination, and for a moment, I could have

been looking at an incarnation of an "onna bugeisha," a female Samurai. "All right," I said. "Give me five minutes to get around the block to the nearest corner of the van. Then, come down the street and get yourself noticed by whoever may be inside. But whatever you do, you've got to get their attention away from where I'll be. Got it?"

"Yes. Then what will you do?"

"As a friend of mine is fond of saying, I'll be practicing some premeditated self-defense."

I crossed the street and headed around the next block, angling toward my goal as fast as my leg would allow until I was just around the corner from where the van was parked. I resisted the temptation to try and get a look around the corner as I readied my weapon, sliding my belt free and holding the ends close to my body. The ballistic-grade material of the belt is affixed to a plain-looking buckle forged out of five and a half ounces of stainless steel, and it is the most versatile weapon in my personal armory. It can be employed as not only a weighted flail or a garrote, but it can also block attacks and entrap opponents. All I had to do now was get close enough to use it.

The wait seemed to take forever and was punctuated by the arrival of a motorcycle rider who just had to be driving down the street at that moment, but as the whine of the bike's engine receded, I heard the sound of a car door opening up around the corner. I slipped around the edge of the building and caught a flash of a man in a blue jumpsuit stepping out on the street with his back to me. I also got a glimpse of Rhea standing on the sidewalk, smiling like the Cheshire cat. The man in the blue suit was raising something black in his hands as I spun my belt in a scything uppercut that smashed into his forearm.

Something the size and shape of a small rifle popped up in the air as I slid my free hand up the belt and looped it over the man's head, jerking it into a flat garrote. I cranked on the torque, clamping his arteries shut to black out his brain. The lancing pain in my side was converted into angry strength as I pulled him in close to keep him from flailing around. That's when I heard a muffled shot as the man's back slammed into my chest, and he collapsed, dead weight in my hands.

As his body fell, I saw Rhea, the smile frozen on her face as she held the gun in her hands and the spent brass cartridge bounced on the sidewalk. "Hurry," she hissed. "Get him inside the van."

By combat-trained habit I scanned the area for witnesses as I bent down. With an effort that felt like it was tearing me in two, I lifted up the lifeless body as Rhea opened the side of the van. It was all I could manage to drag the corpse inside until I had him flat on the back floorboards. Meanwhile Rhea climbed in, shut the door, and moved to the driver's section. The interior of the vehicle was dark and the widows frosted with condensation. I was on my knees on the back bench seat, and it didn't take but a moment to look around and see that Caitlin wasn't here.

I closed my eyes and struggled to get my heart rate down to close to human levels. The hope that had kept me moving sank inside me like a stone, and I suddenly realized that I didn't give a damn about the treasure anymore. All I wanted was to find Caitlin and get her out of all this, and then everyone else, every single one of these murdering bastards, could all go to hell together for all I cared. I was dimly aware that Rhea had been exploring the map box in the front seat, and I heard soft, electronic beeping sounds. "What are you doing up there?" I whispered.

"I found my phone. I'm letting my people know where I am. Now let's go; we've got to get moving," she said softly.

I didn't like the sound of that—one of her was more than I wanted to contend with, lethal as she was. "You didn't have to kill this man," I said.

Rhea made a small sound of surprise. "Is this a joke? I thought you were in the process of strangling him; I just thought I'd save you the trouble. Besides, these men are killers, or have you forgotten what they did to my poor Ajax?"

"No. But there's been enough killing. It should end now."

"What about your wife?"

Lights from a passing car rolled through the van, diffused by the frosted glass. "What do you mean?" I asked.

"I think she's alive. Look." Rhea held up a small black purse, the one Caitlin had carried with her. "If they had killed her, I doubt they'd be holding on to this," Rhea explained. "I think they took her with them, possibly to use as a hostage. So now you need to take me where they are."

"And just what do I need you for?"

"I have the gun."

I laughed, quietly and darkly. "So what? All those things are good for is killing people. Or was that a threat, is that it? You're just going to add me to the collection in here?"

"No," she said almost pleasantly. "No threat. But you'd be a fool not to take me with you. I'll do whatever needs to be done for us to win, my dearest."

I was glad it was dark, so Rhea couldn't see me shudder from the chill she gave me with her deadly, seductive voice. "All right," I said, glad to hear my voice sounding steadier than I was. "Let's get going."

"Where?"

"It's high time we went to church."

CHAPTER NINE

R hea and I didn't leave right away. Mindful of
blood and fingerprints, we checked out the van
and the corpse inside. I couldn't help but notice how
young the dark-haired man looked. The body was
dressed in the blue jumpsuit of a Paris sanitation
worker, and we found a hard hat to complete the dis-
guise. I didn't risk going through the pockets. Using
the red beam of my button-sized flashlight, I checked
out the rest of the van, finding a tarp in the back that
I used to cover the body. I took charge of Caitlin's small
purse and checked the contents, placing her pen, sunglasses, comb, lipstick, passport, and wallet into my
various pockets, along with the purse itself, stuffing the
shoulder chain into the now-empty bag, hoping I
wouldn't make noise now when I moved, and then replaced my belt.

The carbine Rhea had commandeered was a real
oddity. I held my flashlight while she checked it over.
Essentially, it was a Glock 9mm pistol, but someone

had attached a barrel extension/silencer and a skeletal stock to it, along with a laser sight and flashlight that damn near blinded me when Rhea activated it for a split second. Rhea expertly disengaged the stock to shorten the weapon, then nodded to me that she was ready to go. I'd considered taking her out of the picture at this point, knowing her now for a cold-blooded killer who'd doubtless murder me as soon as she felt I was no longer convenient to her plans. But since she was content to fight our mutual enemies for now, I decided to keep her with me. Although, as far as I was concerned, she was no longer an attractive woman; she was to me an "oni," a Japanese demon hidden inside a beautiful human form.

We got out of the coffin on wheels and closed it up. The rain-washed air was a relief from the death reek of the vehicle. I skidded the keys of the van under the car parked behind it as I checked out the streets. The ornate, black iron lampposts put out far too much light, illuminating both the landscape and us in the process. "Follow me across," I said. "And if we get caught by anyone outside the church, be prepared to play the part of Stupid American Tourist."

"I'm half British," Rhea said with a quiet laugh as she tucked the pistol into the top of her skirt and covered it with her suit jacket. "I'm sure I can manage."

We checked for traffic, then crossed the cobblestone street toward the front of the Chapel du Val de Grâce. We walked quickly across an open area on the other side of the street that offered no cover, other than a short, square font with running water off to the left. There was a black iron portcullis gate separating us from the front courtyard, but I could clearly see the Greco-Roman façade of the domed church beyond. Like every other building in the crowded, jigsaw city of Paris, the church was attached to other buildings that ran from its sides, like wings, but I was happy to see that the chapel itself appeared to be darkened within. As we got closer, I was less pleased with the gate and fence—tall and crowned with gold-colored spear points flanking the golden-wreathed apex of the gate itself—and I doubted that my damaged body was equal to the task of climbing over, until I saw the broken lock on the gate. It looked like Ombra and his crew had just cut themselves a way in.

With a last look over my shoulders to the countless windows of the buildings across the street, I muscled the gate open, gritting my teeth at the loud way it groaned, until Rhea and I could slip through. Over to the left was a statue and pedestal, an island of cover in the open courtyard, and I motioned Rhea in that direction. I had to admire the way the woman moved, gliding toward the statue on the balls of her feet, making almost no noise. We didn't draw any fire, which was especially good since I suddenly came to a dead stop when my eyes lit upon the name on the base plate of the monument: Larrey, the man mentioned in the letter hidden inside the eagle, the man who Napoleon trusted to be the guardian of his secret treasure. "What is it?" Rhea hissed. "What do you see?"

I wasn't about to share any more information than I had to, and other than seeing Larrey's name in Fouché's letter, I didn't know a thing about him. I just nodded at the full-figured bronze above us and whispered, "I love fine art."

Rhea gave her head a small shake, an eloquent statement that she thought she was in the presence of insanity. "What's the next move?" she asked impatiently.

I took a quick look around the pedestal toward the church as I recalled the map from the eagle. The main doors of the church were up a set of steps past the Ionic columns, but the map I'd seen had indicated additional doors on either side at ground level, and I could see one set from where Rhea and I crouched behind the marble base of the statue. "Head for the steps, get close to the building. What we want is on the other side of the main entrance." Without a word, Rhea raced off to the stairs. When she was under the carved image of the Virgin Mary, I smiled at the dichotomy of the sight and then took off after her. Once we were up the stone steps, we could see that the large, ornate double doors had already been forced open. I could feel my anger rising at seeing all this casual destruction by Ombra and his men. I really wanted to make someone pay for these acts of sacrilege.

Rhea got her pistol out, and I followed her inside, pulling the damaged door closed behind me. It was dimly lit inside, and all of a sudden the chasm-like enormity of the Baroque edifice enfolded my senses as the heady aroma of aged incense evoked memories of childish whispered prayers. Rhea and I crept up the grand hall, scanning for movement in the shadowed, arched recesses along the sides. Another black metal gate separated the entry hall from the main domed interior; it too had already been forced open. As I crossed into the expanse of the heart of the cathedral, I looked up and into an enormous, rounded sky filled with frozen, painted images—a reflected God's-eye view of heaven. Below and ahead I could see the main altar, designed and adorned in a way that reminded me of the Ark of the Covenant, and I promised myself then and there that someday I would return to this place, if no one killed me in the meantime.

Pulling the image of the secret map from my memory, I motioned Rhea to head toward the archway off the rotunda to the right. The inlaid marble floor caught the slightest sound of our movements and sent them echoing off through the cathedral until we found ourselves in a smaller, circular room. The dark wooden door with the splintered lock ahead of us left no doubt as to the path we needed to follow.

We crept up to the doorway, and I shined the beam of my small red flashlight inside. The crimson glow revealed the large rectangular sacristy, and across from us were a pair of open doors near a pile of broken tile. Crossing over, I could see that a jagged, man-sized hole had been chopped through the marble floor, revealing a narrow set of steep, rough-carved stone steps heading downward. I took the lead, crouching low as I slowly descended, until I reached the bottom and my little flashlight illuminated a low-ceilinged cavern. A cavern whose walls were lined with thousands upon thousands of human bones.

I knew then where we had found ourselves—we were in the guts of the Catacombs of Paris. Hundreds of miles of Roman-era limestone quarries had been converted into convenient tombs back in the 1800s, and millions of human remains had been placed below the streets of the growing, expanding city. As far as I knew, no one had ever mapped all the vast expanse of the underworld here. It was as if Rhea and I had just been cast out of the realm of heaven above and pitched onto the doorsteps of hell.

Everything was different down here in the depths. The temperature had dropped drastically during the descent, turning my wet clothes into a clammy shroud. The aroma of incense was gone, replaced by a dank, acidic smell, and the limestone walls of the narrow tunnel seemed to absorb any sound. I'd been in places underground before, from the Catacombs of Rome to the ancient cisterns of Istanbul to the buried cites of Cappadocia and the Valley of the Kings, but this macabre monument to the dead was like nothing I had ever encountered before. Still, to be fair, it was probably the way my deadly companion seemed to take the sights in stride that chilled me more than the air.

The bones lay in slanted piles against the wall, like occlusions inside a monstrous artery, leaving only a narrow path in between. Here and there, a time-aged skull stared blankly back amidst the human rubble. This branch of the Parisian catacombs must have been sealed up and neglected for uncounted years, an undisturbed tomb. Until now.

But it was the narrow path between the bones that proved the most interesting. Ancient dust had settled on the ground, and now displayed the recent footprints impressed upon it. My heart leapt when I saw the smallest set of prints that had to be Caitlin's.

By force of habit, I found my button-sized compass and checked our bearings. The needle told me the tunnel was running to the south. The red glow of my little light was swallowed up in the blackness beyond the narrow, low-arched tunnel lined with human bones. I crouched and moved ahead into the confined passage,

feeling Rhea's presence as she followed in my shadow.
I was counting steps as we quietly progressed, careful
to avoid treading upon the ossified remains, and scanning ahead as we followed the trail of footprints in the
dust—until I dimly saw an area beyond that opened
up into an enclosed crossroads. The footprints in the
area ahead formed a confused pattern, with one set
leading off to the left and the main group to the right.
The moment I saw that, I started running.

My move wasn't as crazy as it sounds. The single
set of prints told me that Ombra had left a guard behind and I was now caught in a trap, stuck inside a
narrow killing zone with no cover. All I had with me
now was my small flashlight and my other close-
combat weapon: my pen. Now, in the purely physical
sense, the pen is by no means mightier than the sword,
but if you haven't got a sword handy and know what
to do with it, a pen can be just as deadly, multiplying
the power of your strikes into the nerve centers and
vulnerable spots of an opponent's body. The one I carried was an oversized model made from aircraft-
grade aluminum, and I had been trained to use it with
telling effect. I charged ahead, needing to get to the intersection before any gun-wielding opponent could
come around the edge of the tunnel and kill us both,
and I barely won the race.

A shadow leapt around the corner to my left and I
was painfully blinded by a flash of light, but it was too
late to stop me. I crashed into the man and swept his
gun aside with my left arm as I rammed the end of
my pen in a powerful thrust to his stomach, forcibly
bending him over so that all the air in his lungs coughed
out explosively. I couldn't see if he still held the gun;

I just knew I had to take him down now or die. I wrenched my hand free of his folded-up midsection and ran my other hand blindly up his spine until I reached his head, knocking off his plastic hard hat. I swung my pen down in an ice-pick hammer blow that concentrated all the force of my strike into a keyhole-sized pile driver slamming into his skull.

I felt the man's body collapse and drop like a sack of rocks onto the ground, blowing up a small cloud of dust. A brief bolt of light burned my eyes again as the concussive sound of the silenced shot slapped my ears—Rhea delivering a coup de grace, spraying the air with the smell of burnt gunpowder. Everything went black and I leaned back until I was crouched against the stacked bones of the wall. I kept my eyes closed, struggling to control my breathing and my reawakened pain while straining to listen for any sounds of approaching danger. But everything stayed as black and silent as a deeply buried grave.

"Blake?" I heard Rhea whisper. I didn't respond, and instead pulled out my lighter, having lost my button flashlight during the encounter. The light from the flame revealed yet another dead man in another blue jumpsuit, facedown in the dust. Before I could bend down, I saw Rhea's hand snatch up the man's pistol. I recovered my flashlight and exchanged its light for the open flame. I kept the red light cupped in my hand as I looked at the wild and terrible vision of Rhea standing there, surrounded by countless human bones and holding both pistols. I silently held out my free hand, and she smiled, handing one of the guns to me with a gracious gesture.

I took a moment to check out the weapon, another Glock outfitted with a silencer. I wiped off the powdery dust and then checked the magazine and chamber, seeing the weapon was ready to fire. It was about time I got my hands on a firearm, I thought, seeing how everyone else in the world seemed to have one. In the red glow of my light I nodded to Rhea, indicating the tunnel to the right that bore the signs of Ombra's group, diminished by one set now, but still including Caitlin's footprints.

Buried below the ground, I had lost all sense of time, and our journey down the claustrophobic mausoleum seemed endless, until I heard a faint, flat metallic sound. I extinguished my flashlight, and through the absolute blackness saw a glimmer of light ahead. Step by slow step, Rhea and I crouched and shuffled our way along as I kept one hand on my gun and the other touching the rough, cold bones of the wall next to me. The slight sounds and brief flicker of light appeared to be a thousand miles away. Moving like lost souls sneaking out of hell, we finally crept up to a jagged, man-sized hole broken into the tunnel wall to the right, among strewn, discarded bones.

I got down on hands and knees and took a cautious look around the edge of the cut-away entrance. I was looking down into a large vaulted chamber below me at the bottom of a narrow set of stone stairs. The room was lit up by the greenish glow from a chemical light stick that was set on top of an old wooden box. Through the dim, surreal lighting I could see the chamber was crowded with dark, time-stained wooden chests. A pair of shadowed figures crouched among the boxes, bent to the task of forcing them open. Then my eyes fell upon Caitlin, sitting on the ground as still as a statue. Her black evening dress was now almost white with limestone dust and I could see she was bound hands and feet and gagged with metallic-looking tape.

Rhea's warm body was up close with mine, and I felt her shiver slightly in the cold, dank air. Although I seriously doubted it was the chill that made her tremble; it was more like the anticipating moves of a cat about to pounce upon prey. I brought my head to her ear and mouthed the words, "Stay quiet, no matter what I do." I then shifted over to the other side of the entrance to the vaulted chamber below. I fired up my gun's flashlight, illuminating the room as I called out, "Ombra! Game's up, you bastard!"

In the glare of the light I saw Ombra's pale and neatly bearded face briefly as he looked up and then shielded his eyes from the beam. He and the man next to him were dressed in identical blue jumpsuits, now covered in bone-pale dust, and as they both stood, I was happy to see that neither man held a gun at the moment. In the bright beam of my light, I now saw that most of the chests had been broken open, exposing glittering contents within. It was an act of will to keep my focus on my enemies and not glance at the treasures revealed within the chamber, but I kept Ombra dead in my sights.

The bastard was smiling.

CHAPTER TEN

Ombra's voice echoed through the chamber, amusement lightening the tone of his words as he said, "Monsieur Blake? Is that truly you? I would think that you would be dead by now."

I tried out a laugh of my own. I didn't sound entirely sane. "I was," I replied. "Turns out the devil didn't want me, so he sent me back to get you instead. Now, you and your boy there need to come up here slowly, hands in sight."

"Where are the rest of my men?" Ombra asked.

"Sorry," I called back. "They won't be joining us."

Ombra bowed his head. "I see," he said, so low I almost didn't hear it. Ombra's confederate, a dark-haired young man with a beard, grimaced at this news, flashing a look of hatred in my direction. Ombra lifted his head, and I saw where the right side of his face was bruising up from where I'd smacked him with the bronze eagle hours before. He said to me, "I did not take you for such a killer, Mr. Blake. My mistake. One I will not make again. We have your wife, as you see."

"And I've got a gun. Your move," I called back.

Ombra nodded. He didn't seem to be able to hold his right arm up as high as his left, a souvenir from the screwdriver I'd planted into his back. "So, Mr. Blake," Ombra said. "How do you propose we resolve this impasse, eh?"

Ombra was acting way too calm, and it was making my hackles rise. "You and your boy there come up the stairs, hands raised. We'll sort it out after that."

Ombra tilted his head slightly to one side, and then said with a smile, "I do not think so, Mr. Blake."

I didn't like the tone of his voice; Ombra was playing like a man who had all the time in the world. I spared a glance at Caitlin, bound and sitting against a chest on the floor. Even at this distance, I could see the look in her large, expressive eyes as she flashed me a silent message, tilting her head toward Ombra and his man once, twice, thrice. Three—she was trying to tell me there were three of them.

The realization came right on the heels of the muted shots that were fired up from the darkness to the right of Ombra. I ducked back behind the edge of the opening as bullets cracked into the bones behind me, spraying me with sharp fragments. I heard Rhea swear, softly and venomously, in Japanese. Probably at me, I thought. Everything had gone dark when my finger left the button of my pistol's flashlight, leaving nothing but the pale green glow from the chamber below. "Now what?" Rhea hissed.

As if in answer, the room below us exploded with a flash of light and a thunder that slapped my whole body, as if the jagged entrance was suddenly turned into the mouth of a giant cannon. I fell back, covering my head as a small rain of debris came down.

The ringing in my ears told me I wasn't dead yet as I picked myself up and snapped the light of my gun back on, sweeping the inner room and seeing nothing but a cloud of ash-white fog reflected back. I rolled out onto the steep steps, almost sliding down to the ground while keeping my gun trained on the area where Ombra's man had been when he fired at me. My eyes burned and my throat caught bitter motes out of the choking air. I heard the sounds of suppressed coughs coming from the ground behind me. My light found Caitlin huddled on the floor, ghost pale from the blast of powdery dust. Above me, I saw Rhea's gun light send questing beams throughout the vaulted chamber, which even through the smoke I could now see was much larger than I first thought.

I took Caitlin's arm and pulled her to a sitting position. Quick as I could, I pulled the tape from her mouth, which caused her to finally give vent to a series of heaving coughs. Rhea flew down the steps, her light shooting ahead as she moved into the end of the chamber where Ombra and his man had fled. "Stay down," I told Caitlin, then followed up behind Rhea.

I could now see that the walls of this chamber were made of large, ash-white bricks, and had been sealed into a dead end. Rhea had made her way over to the far wall, where a hole large enough for a man to squeeze through had been blasted through the masonry. The bitter air in this end was thick with the smell of burnt explosives. Rhea flashed her light along the breach, then pulled back and announced,

"They're gone." She stood up and played her light around the rounded chamber, her beam leaping from chest to chest as I heard her mutter to herself in Japanese.

"Blake!" Caitlin coughed. I did an about-face and came back to her, leaving Rhea on her own. "Hi, honey," I said.

Her golden eyes flashed fire and she fiercely whispered, "You idiot! Are you trying to get yourself killed?"

I couldn't have been more surprised at my greeting if she kicked me. "I thought I was rescuing you," I quietly replied.

"We've got to get out of here, now!" she shot back. Just then, the light from Rhea's gun locked on to Caitlin, and I froze; wherever the beam of light was aimed, so was the barrel of the pistol.

"You!" Rhea called out. "What did Ombra take from here?"

Caitlin's eyes narrowed as she tried to see beyond the light splashed on her face. "What the hell is she doing here, Blake?" Caitlin said in a near growl.

"Temporary alliance," I shot back from the side of my mouth, then I said more loudly, "Hey, point that thing somewhere else."

From behind the glare I saw Rhea stalking toward us, the deadly beam of light never wavering from Caitlin as Rhea said, "Tell me now, what did Ombra and his men take from here?"

"They didn't take anything," Caitlin shouted back. "They never intended to take anything."

Rhea's voice was angry and dangerous as she said, "What are you talking about?"

In response, Caitlin pointed with her bound hands toward the center of the room. Rhea's light flashed over and found a small, silver-colored briefcase, lying closed next to a discarded pry bar. "What's that?" Rhea asked.

With a voice charged with quiet intensity, Caitlin announced, "It's a bomb. And Ombra already set it to explode. If we don't get out of here now, we're dead."

Everything froze for a moment in time, then without another word, Rhea turned and raced up the stairs and out of the chamber. "Blake," Caitlin said. "Come on! We've got to move!"

I shook myself out of my shock-induced paralysis and went through my pockets for my utility tool, first finding Caitlin's lipstick case instead. I handed my gun to Caitlin and she held the light pointing up as I fumbled the blade of my tool free and cut through the gummy tape binding her wrists and ankles. Caitlin then grabbed my hand. "Let's go!" she commanded.

She led me as far as the stairs, and then I stopped cold, pulling my hand free of hers. "What are you doing?" she gasped. Most of the dust had settled, and through the greenish illumination from the light stick, now lying on the floor, I saw I was standing among all the open, inviting chests, filled with glistening treasure. I was inside a veritable Cave of Wonders, filled with unimaginable riches. Guarded by the silver dragon's egg of a bomb.

"No goddamn fair!" I shouted. I was well trained in the area of explosives, mostly on how to make them from scratch, and I knew enough to realize that the most dangerous thing I could attempt would be to try and disarm the damn thing. There was nothing left to do but run for our lives. I just couldn't force myself to leave empty-handed.

Caitlin kept calling my name as I raced over to the nearest chest and scooped up a handful of golden coins, dropping them into my pocket. I turned to run for the stairs, but spotted a small, rectangular wooden case on the floor, about the size of a thermos. It was the only box that looked small enough to carry. I almost stumbled as I grabbed it up, then ran toward Caitlin's beckoning light. "Let's go!" I shouted.

I banged the top of my head on the low tunnel entrance, blinded by the sudden lack of illumination when Caitlin turned away, then caught myself and hurried down the tunnel after her. In the bright beam of the handgun's light the skulls in the corridor appeared to be grinning at me as I ran, mocking my attempts to escape the world of the dead.

We made it to the crossroads and saw the body of the man Rhea shot; his arm was outstretched and pointing in the direction we needed to go. We didn't make it more than a dozen steps before the world exploded behind us, knocking us both flat to the dusty earth. I clapped my hands to my ears as a pile of old bones suddenly covered me, just as a powerful wind sucked all the air out of the tunnel. For a heartbeat, there was nothing, then the world turned red as a dragon blew its flaming breath overhead, the terrible heat scorching my back.

I couldn't see, couldn't hear, and couldn't breathe. I was coughing in a vacuum until I felt the wind roar through the tunnel again. It took all the strength I had to raise myself up and out of the clinking pile of human rubble. There was an overpowering stench in the air, and my throat wanted to close itself up against the reek of burning human bones. My ears were ringing like they never had before, and my voice sounded distant as I called out for Caitlin. It was a shock to suddenly realize I could see down here. I turned my head back down the tunnel and saw a bright, flickering light coming from the crossroads, like the doorway to hell had just opened up around the corner.

As I stared into the flaming light, I thought of Ombra. The bitter, ashen taste in my mouth was nothing as I thought of how badly I had screwed up. All night long I'd thought I was in a winner-takes-all race for treasure, and never in a million years could I have imagined that Ombra and his men were out to utterly destroy what had been buried down here for the last two centuries. Except for the paltry few items I'd salvaged, the world would now never know just what my failure had cost.

I turned away and felt a cold, steady breeze against my face as I plowed through the scattered bones, looking for Caitlin. I found her just ahead of me, her arms and legs stirring as if she was waking from a nightmare. I tossed aside the bones that covered her like a brittle pile of sticks and helped her turn over. I found my lighter, and in the guttering flame Caitlin's face was as pale as a frosted ghost. But she smiled. "Are we dead yet?" she whispered.

"I don't think so," I said, my own voice hollow in my ringing ears.

"What did you think you were doing back there?"

"Sorry. Treasure fever. You didn't have to wait for me, you know."

"Sure I did. Part of my job was to keep you alive.

But do something like that again, and I'll kill you myself." Then she smiled again, and her hand ran gently down the side of my face. "Thank you. For coming after me. Now, help me up."

I pulled us both free of the bone pile while my injured side kicked me a shot of pain in the process. I shielded the flame of my lighter from the air current and took a look around. Most of the bones had broken loose from the walls, and Caitlin and I were now calf-deep in ancient, brittle remains. Caitlin came up with the gun, and we had light again. I snapped my lighter shut and said, "Let's get the hell out of here."

I dug my wooden prize free and Caitlin and I headed back down the tunnel. It was slow going, shuffling along through the skeletal remnants. The air current through the narrow tunnel made a mournful moaning sound as Caitlin said, "Blake, I need to know something."

"What?"

Without looking back at me, Caitlin said, "You're not just a mild-mannered antiques expert, are you?"

I was about to give one of my standard, nonsensical answers, until I recalled how Caitlin's associate, the Sam Smith I met in Paris earlier that night, told me that he had filmed me during all the excitement at Troyon's apartment, an event that seemed like another lifetime ago. Caitlin was bound to see that for herself. "No," I replied.

As quickly as I uttered the word, Caitlin swung the gun around until the light was squarely centered on my chest. "No more games, Blake, I need to know everything about you. Now."

"Or?"

"Or I might be forced to kill you. We can't take chances in my business. So talk, and tell me who you are, and who you really work for. Please."

Her "please" sounded starkly sincere. I sighed, knowing that whatever came after this, my life would be changed forever. Again.

"Remember how you said you were happy I wasn't a crook? Well, I'm afraid I've got disappointing news. I am."

Caitlin's voice was colder then the bone-strewn cave as she said, "Go on."

"I'm not a drug smuggler, or a bank robber, or anything like that. But I am a thief. However, I only steal from people who've been dead at least a couple of hundred years."

"So you're a tomb robber?"

"That's a polite way of putting it."

"So that means the Argo Foundation—"

"Is exactly what they say they are," I shot back quickly. "I use Nick Riley and his foundation as a cover. They don't know what I do on the side, so to speak."

"But that doesn't explain—"

I interrupted her again, but this time by kicking up a pile of bones as I dove in for the gun. Taking on an armed opponent is all a matter of time and distance. It only takes a split second for a human brain to command a finger to pull a trigger, but in that time I can cover over twenty feet of space. Anyone who gets within my personal sphere of danger, if they don't shoot me outright, will pay for their mistake.

I rushed Caitlin, sweeping my right arm down and my left hand up, catching her gun hand by the wrist and snapping the barrel up as I struck her elbow to bend her arm. The move tied us together, face-to-face in the darkness as the light on the pistol went out. "Wait," I breathed.

Her reactions were good too. She stopped her attack response as she realized I'd stopped mine. I was wrapped in the most curiously intimate moment of my life, holding this woman close to me with a deadly weapon poised near both our heads. Even through the choking dust in the air, I could breathe in her scent. I could have stood there with her forever.

I slowly unclamped my hand from her wrist and eased back as the light from the gun flashed on, and then centered back on my chest. I held my hands out, palms upward as I said, "Trust has to start somewhere. I could have taken you out just now. But whatever else you may think of me, know this: I am never going to harm you. No matter what."

The light on my chest wavered, reflecting the indecision on Caitlin's part. She knew that I could have disarmed her, or worse, just now. Instead I returned the balance of power to her favor. Finally, she said, "All right, Blake. Truce for now. But when we get out of here, we're going to have to talk."

I let out a breath I didn't know I was holding in as I replied, "Why is it that whenever a woman says that, nothing good ever follows?"

"Funny," she said as she turned and continued through the claustrophobic tunnel, "my third husband said the very same thing."

I smiled. I knew that turning her back to me was her unspoken way of saying, "I'll trust you, too." For the moment, anyway. I followed behind her, our feet occasionally crunching the dry, brittle bones as if they were oversized autumn leaves. My thoughts were as black as the tunnel behind me as I thought over this day. I'd not only lost an unimaginable hidden treasure, but I blew my cover, to a government agent, no less. At least I was able to keep Nick Riley and Argo in the clear. For now.

As we picked our way through the narrow bone field, I asked, "So, do all of your government missions wind up like this?"

"No. Sometimes, they're actually dangerous."

I laughed, then had to stop to cough out a lungful of lime dust. When I could breathe again, Caitlin said, "The last thing Ombra said to me was: 'Madame Rhea's people are known to us, but yours are not. Therefore, you are to witness a most regrettable necessity. When we have finished, you will go and tell your people the treasure of Val de Grâce is no more, and that its destruction is on their heads.' Do you know what he meant by that?"

I clutched my salvaged box tighter as I said, "The eagle contained a map to this place, a map of lost Napoleonic treasure. That's the reason everyone died tonight. To keep whatever was buried down here a secret."

Caitlin was silent for a moment, then said softly, "That's horrible."

Welcome to my world, I thought bitterly. We finally found our way to the narrow stone stairway leading out of the underworld catacombs. Caitlin and I stole up the steps, emerging from the broken marble floor into the sacristy. In the dim light as we escaped the tomb, Caitlin's dust-covered figure looked like a marble statue of the goddess Athena come to life. We dusted ourselves off as best we could, but the limestone powder clung to our still-damp clothes like glue. I nodded to Caitlin and then pointed to the floor, which bore the ash-colored footprints from Rhea's recent passage.

Caitlin and I moved through the enormous cathedral, hurrying under the magnificent dome and down the grand hallway to the large black double doors, which Rhea had left ajar. We could now hear the two-tone sounds of multiple emergency sirens. Once outside and into the clean, rain-washed air, I spotted a dense plume of black smoke, lit underneath in a baleful red, billowing over the neighboring buildings while blue-flashing police cars blocked off the street.

Caitlin and I exchanged rueful glances—under the streetlights we were going to appear like escapees from Pompeii—but it looked like all the local attention was being drawn up the street away from the church. Caitlin offered me the gun; she obviously had nowhere to conceal it. I let my belt out a notch and stuck the pistol in my waistband, hoping all its internal safety devices were in good working order. I then tucked the old wooden box under one arm and offered Caitlin my other. She smiled, in that secretive way of hers, and accepted. The two of us crossed the courtyard of Val de Grâce like tourists out for a stroll. "Think we'll find a taxi this late at night?" I asked quietly.

"No need," she answered. "Just get me to a phone, and I'll make contact with someone who can get us out of here."

"Would that someone be your Mr. Smith?"

Caitlin nodded. "Yes, how did you know?"

"Well . . . I had a little run-in with him earlier. He was all set to leave without you, so I had to convince him otherwise."

"Convince him how?"

"Let's just say he was tied up for a bit tonight. But he's fine. Really."

"You did that to Smith? Damn, boy. You really are good," she said with a small shake of her head. I scanned the area ahead and saw Ombra's van hadn't moved. I hoped he'd just abandoned it, as I didn't think I could handle one more strenuous encounter tonight. As Caitlin and I slipped through the front gate and started walking up the street away from the fire, a wave of exhaustion washed over me. Just a little while longer, I promised myself, until you can go roll up in a ball somewhere. That's when a long black limousine passed us, unusual in this city full of tiny toy vehicles. I felt a slapping sting as something hit me on my back and spread like liquid ice up to my brain.

I didn't even care when the ground leapt up and hit me.

PART II

I know how, when it is necessary, to leave the
skin of the lion and take that of the fox.

—NAPOLEON BONAPARTE

CHAPTER ELEVEN

Terra Incognita

I was trapped in a nightmare world of shifting lights and riotous noise, suffused with scents that ranged from jet fuel to jasmine, until I finally fell out of the kaleidoscope and calliope world and down into a dark hole. After a measureless span of fractured time, the world turned a deep, soft blue.

My senses seemed to come back online one at a time. My eyes still couldn't focus, but I was definitely seeing a diffuse aqua-colored glow around the edge of my vision. Close by, I could hear the sound of water, like a small stream falling over stones, and a familiar scent of jasmine was strong in the warm, humid atmosphere. Eventually I was able to move my head a bit, only to find that I was on a cushioned couch, bound with thick leather straps. Worse, I was naked.

The rising panic helped clear my mind. I rolled my head to the left, fighting a wave of nausea, and I could see I was near a small pool of water that had its own running waterfall. It was like being in a cross between a Japanese bathhouse and an underground grotto. "Mr. Blake," I heard a musical, feminine voice say. "Whatever am I to do with you?"

It was Rhea.

I turned my head to the right, slowly so as not to shake my soggy brains loose, and saw her standing there. She had transformed herself into a vision of a Greek goddess, with her raven-black hair piled high, and wearing a long, white gown, falling from one shoulder and belted in silver. In the blue lighting she appeared to glow.

"Where am I?" I managed to whisper from a desiccated throat and a mouth that tasted of old ashes.

She seemed to float as she came toward me. She smiled as she said softly, "You are now where no one will ever find you."

"What do you want? And where's Caitlin?"

She didn't reply, and instead started walking down the length of the couch, slowly shaking her head as she surveyed my body like a suspicious buyer of dubious merchandise. As she circled the couch, her hand reached out and with the nail of her forefinger she began tracing the paths of my scars, sending electric trills running through me. She said, almost absently, "We know your secret. We know who you really are."

I closed my eyes and let my head fall back down; it was almost too much effort to hold it up. I then felt Rhea's face close to mine as she whispered, "I have a secret too, Mr. Blake." Before I could respond, Rhea placed her finger to my dried lips and said more loudly, "Vanya wants to see you. But we can't have you looking like this, now, can we?"

I opened my eyes, but Rhea had moved out of view.

I tried to get a better look at my surroundings, but the blue light from above acted like a curtain, rendering everything beyond a few feet opaque blackness. The pool and waterfall close by looked like they had been cut into native rock. There was a small rattling sound behind my head, and Rhea's hands came in from behind and started massaging a warm, sweet-smelling substance on my cheek and neck. "There," she cooed. "Doesn't that feel better?"

Despite myself, I felt my muscles start to unkink; I'd been chafing and straining against the straps that confined me. Rhea continued to massage my face and neck, and I actually closed my eyes. Even through the silky liquid, I could feel how strong her hands were—hands that were capable of dangerous deeds. Her hands went away, and when I opened my eyes, I suddenly wished I hadn't. Rhea was leaning down close to my face, holding a thin, deadly knife that caught a spark of blue light on its razor edge. Her large black eyes narrowed as her smile grew wider, and she brought the edge of the blade delicately against my throat. "You wouldn't lie to me at a time like this, would you?" she said with a low, throaty laugh.

My head involuntarily arched back and my breath caught in my throat. Then she smoothly ran the razor's edge up my neck in a slow stroke. When the blade came away, I whispered, "I could probably manage to shave myself, you know."

"But where would the fun in that be?" she replied with mock petulance. "Does your wife know about your secret life?"

Rhea was making no sense, but her words made me feel like I was treading in deep, dangerous water. With a knife to my throat, no less. I just made a small shake of my head before Rhea started moving the knife down my left cheek. "Do you ever get lonely?" she asked. "Having to keep all those secrets locked up inside yourself all the time?"

Rhea finished her stroke, then she slid herself on top of me, straddling my body. I could feel the heat of her. She brought her mouth and the razor close to my head and whispered, "There are cameras and microphones everywhere. I'm an operative also. Koancho. Department Two. I'm on your side."

Except for the fact that she told me we were under surveillance, I had no idea what the hell Rhea was talking about, but at the moment, my traitorous body didn't care. Rhea felt my involuntary response, and she gave a little laugh of pleasure, or maybe it was satisfaction of conquest. "We're two of a kind, you and I," she whispered hotly in my ear. "We should join together. Tell Vanya everything he wants to hear, and we'll get through all this together."

I wasn't about to disagree with a woman who could kill me with the flick of her wrist, until she said in my ear, "I was sent to seduce you."

Everything stopped for a moment, and Rhea rose up until I could see her face. She wore the same smile I saw right after I had seen her kill two men. "I want to see Caitlin," I said, loud enough for anyone listening to hear.

Rhea's breath went in with a hiss, and for a flash of time, I saw her lip curl, then her mask of self-possession slipped back into place and she said, "Are you certain that's what you want?" I just nodded, once. Rhea regarded me from above, with an almost pitying look, then she brought the knife to my face and finished the job of shaving me like a surgeon performing a routine operation. All I could do was try to not flinch as the razor slid across my skin. When she finished and dismounted the couch, the breath I didn't realize I'd been holding in came out all at once.

Rhea brought a warm, moist towel and ran it across my face, whispering as she did so, "Be careful when you meet Vanya, and you and that wife of yours just may make it out alive. But don't even think you'll be able to escape from here without my help." She then moved along the side of the couch and I felt the bands restricting me loosen. Louder, she said, "Good-bye, Mr. Blake. I trust you can manage on your own for a while." And with that, she was gone.

I tried to sit up and leave the couch, but mostly I just rolled off, catching myself before I fell all the way to the floor. I was still dazed and confused from the drugs. Now that I could move my head freely, I saw that I was inside a cave of dark rock that had been furnished like a spa. When my legs regained some mobility, I lurched over to the nearest wall and used the rough stone as support to move around the confines. I turned a corner into a tiled enclosure big enough to park a full-sized truck in. The moment I took another step, brilliant white light poured down from above, making me squeeze my eyes shut in self-defense. When my flash blindness cleared, I saw I was standing in front of a bathroom arrangement that'd be the envy of your common-variety millionaire.

The place was lined with mirrors, and I almost jumped when I saw the guy whose upper face, head, and hands looked like they'd been cast in dirty plaster.

I headed straight for a shower area that was large enough to accommodate a party of four comfortably, and as soon as I puzzled out the plumbing, was basking in the middle of a barrage of blessedly warm, clean water. For a guy like me who spends a lot of his working life in deserts, jungles, or stuck on crowded boats at sea with limited water, this was paradise on earth. I massaged the strained muscles of my right leg and carefully probed my damaged ribs. I now sported a pair of roughly circular bruises on my side, one from where I'd landed on the bronze eagle on my trip off the roof at Troyon's apartment, and the other where I'd caught the bullet. My ribs weren't broken, but they felt as cracked as a cheap mirror.

I'd have been content to spend the day under the water, but I caught a scent of overpowering attractiveness: coffee. I reluctantly shut off the water and found a set of white, luxuriously made towels along with a full-sized bathrobe and a selection of slippers. I followed my nose out of the bathroom and back into the blue-lit cave, where I saw someone had placed a selection of meats, cheeses, and breads along with carafes of coffee and water on a marble table. I drained the lemon-flavored water, and savored the rich Sumatra coffee. My stomach told me that it probably wouldn't send any offerings back, and I tried a selection of the foods, noticing that someone had neglected to provide any tableware.

I had just finished with refueling when I heard a masculine and oddly accented voice from behind me say, "Mr. Blake? Please come with me." The owner of the voice was a young, dark-skinned man wearing an outfit of short-sleeved shirt and knee-length pants that looked like a tropical military uniform, an impression fortified by the black nylon gun belt that supported a large, holstered pistol and the sturdy-looking hiking shoes he wore. The man himself had a broad-featured face and jet-black hair cut close to his skull. In the bluish light his smile was as dazzling as his uniform. I placed my coffee cup down and said, "I'm not quite dressed for company."

His smile stayed fixed and frozen on his face as he held out an ushering arm. I belted my robe more tightly and walked in the indicated direction. The cave wall had a tunnel carved through that took an abrupt right-hand turn, finally terminating about twenty feet ahead at a door that retracted into the wall when I approached, flooding the tunnel with bright sunshine. I had to guard my eyes as I stepped outside, but when I could see again, I had to wonder if I wasn't hallucinating.

I was near the mouth of a much larger cave, one the size of a commercial airplane hangar, that had a waterfall pouring down like a curtain. Within the cave there were an assortment of pools set into a marble floor—a working, semi-enclosed Roman bath. I was busy gawking at the architecture when the guide, or guard, took me by the arm and gently pulled me away to a set of steps cut out of the rock that led around the waterfall to the outside, where I was treated to another impressive vista. I found myself in daylight and standing before an enclosed courtyard, bordered on three sides by ivory-colored six-story buildings that all had balconies spaced at regular intervals. The courtyard itself was a garden adorned with marble statuary that gave the appearance of a giant-sized chess set. The sun was low in the sky, hovering over the structure to my right, bathing the garden in a reddish hue, and the air was warm and rich with the scent of unseen olive and pine trees. In the center of the garden was a long, marble table set beneath a white stone roof supported by Ionic columns, with a dais and throne at the center. My thoughts flew back to New York, where Caitlin had told me about Vanya's own private island. I don't think you're in Paris anymore, I thought. My escort took my arm and guided me to the table, toward the man sitting upon the throne.

He was dressed in a snow-white robe that matched his long hair and beard and contrasted with his strong-featured, bronze-tanned face. Rhea was standing to his right with her arm on the high back of the throne, and on the other side was a tall, muscular African who looked like he was carved out of obsidian, dressed in a uniform that matched my escort's, right down to the pistol belt. The man on the throne rose to his feet as I approached, and with a deep, rich, orator's voice he said, "Mr. Blake, welcome to Cronos Island. My name is Vanya. Please be seated. We have much to discuss."

On my side of the table was a backless marble chair with a cushion, and I sat down while trying to keep my robe decorously closed. I said, "You can start by explaining what I'm doing here. And telling me where Caitlin is."

Vanya regained his throne, a Zeus upon his Olympus. "Your wife is here, Mr. Blake," he said. "And in good health, although she's been quite worried about you. You will see her soon, I assure you."

"Great. How about now?"

Vanya held up his hand. "Not so fast. There are a few things we need to talk about first."

"Such as?"

Vanya leaned forward, fixing me with his deep, dark eyes. "Such as why the United States government sent an agent against me. Was it to assassinate me?"

"What are you talking about? I'm not a government agent."

And with that, Vanya laughed.

It was written that they whom the gods destroy, they first make mad. So here I was sitting in an Olympian garden with a man who fashioned himself into the likeness of a god, with the power to back it up. And gods could be capricious, destructive creatures at best. "So you think I'm some kind of spy?" I asked.

"We know it," Vanya intoned. "My consort here saw you in action. Also, that passport of yours reads like an itinerary of every trouble spot in the world. Besides all that, my technicians took apart those little toys you were carrying." Vanya shook his head in amusement. "Quite ingenious, actually."

"What toys?" I said, then shut my mouth with a wince as it hit me: Caitlin. I'd been carrying all the stuff from her purse in my own pockets, and I remembered that mysterious small package she received back at our hotel. There must have been some hidden spy gear in the collection of innocuous-looking items she was carrying, and now Vanya thought that stuff was mine. This is why I never carry a gun or any other obvious weapon while traveling in foreign and hostile countries—at the very least, it makes it hard to pretend innocence if you get caught in the act of carrying out a criminal enterprise while armed.

Fortunately, Vanya was still looking amused at my denials. "All right, so you think I'm a spy," I said. "So now what?"

"Relax, Mr. Blake," Vanya said warmly. "I'm not your enemy. You have nothing to fear from me. But I do want to know what the United States government thought it was doing by sending you to Paris."

"Something to do with you receiving stolen property, as I recall."

"They sent a government operative all the way to Europe on account of some suspected petty thievery? That doesn't seem very likely, now, does it?"

"It might also have something to do with the fact that you're a big cult leader and all."

"Cult leader? Is that what they say? Whatever happened to the concept of freedom of religion?"

"I don't know. Why don't we ask all those followers of Jim Jones down in Guyana? Or how about those people in the subway in Tokyo who got hit with nerve gas by group called Aum Shinrikyo?"

I kept the corner of my eye on Rhea as I said this, but her smile remained fixed and unfathomable, and I tried to keep my own poker face intact as I wondered just what she had to do to become Vanya's "consort." I also realized that if Rhea was an agent of the Japanese government, then the probable reason she'd be here would be the connection between Vanya and the terrorist cult in her country. I glanced at the guard on the other side of Vanya, but he just looked as impassive as the statuary in the garden.

Vanya leaned back on his throne and sighed. "A fair point, I suppose," he mused. "Given that my former country could not grasp the concept of what I'm trying to accomplish here." Vanya looked over my shoulder and made a beckoning gesture. A young Hispanic woman wearing a short white toga seemed to materialize on my right with a silver tray bearing my flattened box of cigarettes along with my battered old Zippo lighter. I took a look at Vanya as he said, "Please, avail yourself. Is there anything else you'd like? Something to drink, perhaps?"

I just shook my head as I reached for my cigarettes and lighter. The cigarettes themselves had been crushed into oval shapes during my recent exertions, but none were broken. I fired one up with a nod of thanks to my host as the young woman placed a silver ashtray before me. "You treat all your captives this well?" I inquired. "For some reason, I get the distinct impression that we should be having this discussion while you have me dangled over an active volcano or something."

Vanya smiled. "Sorry, we're fresh out of volcanoes. As I said before, Mr. Blake, I'm not your enemy. Although you don't realize it yet, you've done me a great service. But before we proceed any further, I need to know something else. Are you a government operative pretending to be an expert in antiquities? Or an actual antiquarian who happens to work for the government?"

I took a drag of my cigarette to buy some time. Despite the exotic surroundings and veneer of civilized behavior, I was trapped in as dangerous a place as I had ever been, and I'd have to tread carefully through this potential minefield by using a tissue of lies within a fragile framework of truth.

"A little of both, I suppose," I replied. "But in truth, I'm a thief."

"A thief? You admit to this?"

"Hey, between being accused of being a government spy or a thief, I'll admit to being an honest crook any day."

Vanya looked dangerously skeptical. "You have identification that claims you work for an entity called the Argo Foundation. Is this part of your cover?"

"No, that part is real. I've worked for Argo for years. The foundation sends me all over the world to collect artifacts. What they don't know is that for every collection I retrieve, I've been stealing and selling a few choice pieces for myself."

"So when did you start working for the government?"

"Right after they caught me in the act. I screwed up and got arrested in Central America. The guys from the government gave me a choice; I could either work for them or go to prison. Although I'm starting to think now I made a bad deal."

Vanya leaned back against his throne, his brows furrowed in thought. "So," he said almost casually, "as an actual antiquarian, you would probably know where I would find the Spear of Destiny?"

"The Spear of Destiny? Which one? There's like, four or five of those things floating around."

"What about the location of the tomb of Genghis Kahn?"

"Go to China and start digging. Good luck. No one's found it yet."

"And the city of Troy?"

"You mean Illium? That hack Schliemann stumbled on it in Turkey back in the 1800s."

Vanya leaned forward, his dark eyes boring into mine. "So tell me, Mr. Blake, how would you recognize the mummy of Alexander the Great?"

"Alexander?" I scratched around my memory. "Well, for one, I'd look to see if the nose was broken off."

"Really?" Vanya asked silkily.

"Yes. If I remember correctly, one of the Roman emperors made a pilgrimage to Alexander's tomb. The emperor tripped over himself and busted the nose off Alexander's mummy. One of history's better pieces of slapstick."

Vanya just stared and smiled at me, in a way that reminded me of how Caitlin's ancient boss, Mr. Jonas, had looked at me after he finished railroading me into this job. "So," Vanya said at last, "you really are a trained historian and an admitted thief, and became an agent of the government afterwards? How long have you worked for them?"

"Would you believe you're my first job?"

"No."

I shrugged. So much for telling the truth. "Oh, well. Now I've got some questions for you. Just how did you get Caitlin and me out of Paris? Speaking of that, just where the hell am I anyway?"

"Oh, it's much easier to sneak someone out of a country than into one, especially if you have a private jet," Vanya said easily. "And as I mentioned before, you're a guest in my home. Now, what were your orders concerning the operation in Paris?"

I took in some smoke to buy a bit more time. Rhea had warned me to tell Vanya what he wanted to hear. I decided to try some simple truth. "I was told that you were in the market for a piece of stolen property. A Napoleonic bronze eagle finial, to be precise. I was sent to watch the transaction and see if you or one of your people was actually going to take possession of the thing. Then you'd be caught in the act of receiving stolen antiquities."

"And you brought your wife along with you? Didn't you think that'd be dangerous for her?"

"Hell, yeah. It certainly wasn't my idea to bring her along," I said with sincerity. "But some government idiot back home thought it'd be good cover to show up with my wife. Besides, I was told the job wasn't going to be dangerous. I was just supposed to observe the transaction go down."

"You sound angry."

"I am. She should never have been there."

"So you've been forced to work for the United States? Tell me, what would you say if I offered you an alternative?"

The light from the sky was darkening, filling the courtyard with indigo-tinted twilight. "What do you mean?" I asked quietly.

Vanya didn't reply, and instead stood up and strode off the dais, walking along the length of the table with Rhea and the guard falling in behind. I put out my cigarette and stood as well, putting my pack and lighter into the pocket of my robe. It felt good to have a weapon again, even a diminutive, last-ditch knuckle-duster like my lighter. I matched their course on my side of the table, with my own armed escort falling in line behind me. As he walked, I noticed that Vanya was well over six feet tall, and broad through the shoulders and chest, and that the robe he wore didn't quite conceal the swell of his stomach. We met at the end of the table and Vanya proceeded toward a large, life-sized marble statue on a raised pedestal, framed against the fading sunlight. I saw the statue was of a man clad in ancient Grecian armor, with an angelic alabaster face. There was no inscription, but the visage was familiar to me. Vanya spoke toward the statue as he said to me, "So what do you know about the men who attacked you and kidnapped your wife?"

"You mean Ombra and his group? They weren't supposed to be at the meeting, and I don't know a damn thing about them, other than the fact that they're completely ruthless killers. Worse than that, Ombra and his men were organized, and prepared for every contingency. Whatever treasure was down in that underground chamber must be melted into unrecognizable slag by now. But who in the hell would go through all that trouble to find such a treasure, only to destroy it?"

Vanya sighed. "I've dealt with their kind before. They are like an unseen plague, lurking in the shadows like venomous spiders. Twice before now, I almost had Napoleon's eagle in my hands, only to have these assassins attack and ruin it all. Until now."

"What do you mean? And just what is your interest

in Napoleon and his treasure anyway? It doesn't look like you need the money."

In the fading light, Vanya seemed surprised. He turned to face me and said, "Napoleon? I have no interest in that failed, would-be conqueror, save one."

Vanya looked away, as if weighing a matter of deep importance. Finally he said to me, "Mr. Blake, what do you know of Napoleon's Egyptian campaign?"

I searched my memory. "Not much," I admitted. "If I remember right, it was a failure. On the other hand, that's where the Rosetta Stone was discovered."

"Yes, but do you recall where Napoleon and his troops first landed when they reached Egypt?"

"No."

"Alexandria," Vanya stated. "Napoleon took control of Alexandria first, before he did anything else, even though his ultimate destination was Cairo. And do you know why he did that?"

I just shook my head. "Because," Vanya explained, "he was looking for something. Or to be precise, someone."

That's when it all came together for me. I didn't have to ask Vanya who Napoleon was looking for as I finally recognized why the face of the statue seemed so familiar. Vanya and I were standing together under the marble avatar of Alexander of Macedonia, known in some parts of the world as Alexander the Great, and in others as Alexander the Scourge. I was staring up into the twilight-shadowed face of the Conqueror of the World as Vanya said, almost in a whisper, "And he found him."

I broke the spell of the moment as I said, "You're kidding."

Vanya seemed to come out of a half dream, shaking his head and saying, "No, Mr. Blake, I'm not. As a matter of fact, you yourself have provided me with the best proof to date."

"Me? What are you talking about?"

Vanya looked around and said, "We need some light." I heard a series of hisses and pops, and then the courtyard was illuminated in dancing firelight from a series of torches. This bit of common magic reminded me that everything I said was probably being recorded and could be used against me later. Vanya headed back to his elevated chair at the table and I returned to my place on the other side as our retinues followed. Rhea and the guard silently assumed their stations by Vanya's side. From his throne, Vanya stared down at me, the torchlight sending flickering shadows warring across his face as he said, "I've spent years of my life and a fortune hunting for the tomb of Alexander."

"You and just about every other archeologist in the world. What makes you think Napoleon Bonaparte is the key to it all?"

Vanya held up a hand. "Let me start from the beginning. When Alexander died in 323 BC, his body became a bone of contention, as it were. Since Alexander's succession was unsure, the leaders at the time knew that the body and sarcophagus of Alexander could be a powerful symbol. His sarcophagus was taken first to Babylon, then Memphis, and finally to Alexandria. And there it remained."

Vanya's recitation was stirring my own memories. I said, "Right. As I recall, Ptolemy was the guy who first stole Alexander's mummy and gold sarcophagus. If I remember right, one of Ptolemy's descendants took the gold sarcophagus and had it melted down for the precious metal."

Vanya nodded and stroked his long white beard. "Ptolemy the Ninth," he affirmed. "He then had Alexander's body placed inside a casket made of glass. And so he remained in the tomb that Ptolemy prepared for him. Finally in 200 AD, the Roman emperor Septimius Severus made his visit to Alexandria, and according to the historian Lucius Cassius Dio, ordered the tomb to be sealed after he placed some books of Egyptian magic inside. Some believe these may have been the Lost Books of Thoth. The last recorded visitor to Alexander's tomb was Septimius's son, Caracalla. There is where the story seems to end."

"Not quite," I countered. "Alexandria was razed to the ground by a war or two since then, not to mention a giant earthquake. No one knows what could be buried under the ground there anymore."

Vanya smiled. "No," he said as if to a child. "I said the story seemed to end. In 1517 Leo Africanus wrote that the tomb of Alexander was in 'a small house in the form of a chapel,' and later, in 1575, the map of Alexandria prepared by the Europeans Braun and Hogenberg indicates a place with the notation 'Domus Alexandri Magni.'"

"Latin for the house of Alexander the Great," I translated.

"Correct. Then in 1798, when Napoleon set off on his Egyptian campaign, he publicly stated that he was 'following in the footsteps of Alexander the Great,' and he doubtless had the Braun and Hogenberg map in his possession. After conquering Alexandria, Napoleon set up a fortification in Kom el Dikka, in the very heart of the city. And there, I have cause to believe, Napoleon took possession of the tomb of Alexander."

I shook my head. "Hold it. If Napoleon found Alexander's tomb, why didn't he tell the world?"

Vanya's eyes seemed to catch the fire of the torches as he said, "You forget, Mr. Blake, Napoleon was defeated in Egypt. The British Lord Nelson destroyed most of Napoleon's invasion fleet, and later Napoleon was forced to flee with only a small contingent of men and ships. With the British in control of Alexandria, Napoleon would be forced to first hide his Egyptian treasures, and then he would have had to smuggle them away without the British knowing they were taken out of Egypt."

"Just how do you know all this?"

"Because some years ago my people discovered a document written by Joseph Fouché, head of Napoleon's secret police, that contained clues to the secret locations of Napoleon's hidden treasures. The plan included the use of the bronze eagles that were the keys to the treasures' location. This document also makes mention of a secret expedition to Alexandria in the year 1815, the year Napoleon was exiled to the island of Elba. Using the Fouché document, I began to hunt for one of the eagles that held the key information inside. But it was you, Mr. Blake, who provided me with the vital evidence that all but proves my theory."

"Me? What evidence?"

Vanya stood again, and this time he walked toward the center of the garden. Rhea and the guard stayed put near the throne chair, and I stood up and joined Vanya, though not so close as to spook anyone who may have had a restless trigger finger. Vanya himself seemed almost oblivious to me as he held his head back and looked straight up into a darkening, star-filled sky. At last, Vanya spoke, almost as if he was speaking to himself.

"Tell me," he said softly, "what made you risk your own life to pick up that wooden box you found down in the catacombs of Paris, right before the bomb exploded?"

My mind flashed back to that moment of mad chaos. "I had to try to save something. It was the only thing I saw at the moment that I could carry. So what was in the box?"

"I think you'll be very interested to know that you managed to rescue a pair of papyrus scrolls, inscribed with Egyptian hieroglyphics and possibly thousands of years old. They will need much more study, of course, and very careful handling, but I believe them to be the books of magic that Septimius Severus placed inside the tomb of Alexander. The first physical proof that Alexander's remains are within my grasp."

I made the mistake of looking up when I heard this news, and I felt dizzy as the implications pounded into my brain. I focused on Vanya as he stood with closed eyes, his head surrounded by stars.

"And because of what you've found," he whispered, "the very course of the world may change."

CHAPTER THIRTEEN

"You mind telling me how finding one old broken-nosed mummy is going to change the world?"

Vanya, wrapped up in a vision only he could see, opened his eyes, and I caught a flash of regal annoyance. I reminded myself it's not smart to antagonize someone who can have you killed, by his own minions no less. Vanya walked back to his throne and seated himself with a sigh. With Rhea perched over his shoulder like one of Odin's ravens, he spoke to me in the manner of a teacher addressing a not particularly bright student. "Millennia ago," he began, "our ancestors knew where the home of the gods lay. In their imperfect understanding, they referred to that place as heaven, but when they looked up, they were all looking toward the stars."

"Well, sure they were," I said. "They were also looking at the sun and the moon, not to mention that the sky was the source of all sorts of phenomena, like thunder and lightning. Early mythology was their only way to explain such things."

Vanya's deep voice held amusement. "Mr. Blake, you don't give your forebears nearly enough credit. Our ancestors not only experienced those commonplace events, they were also witnesses to the actions of the gods themselves. Tell me, are you familiar with the theory of Clarke's law?"

"No."

"Arthur C. Clarke postulated that any advanced technology, if seen by a primitive people, would appear to be magic," Vanya said, leaning forward from his throne. "This, I believe, is the basis for every religion on the face of our planet. Elaborate rituals created in response to witnessing the actions of gods—technologically advanced visitors from distant worlds."

I kept my poker face on as I said, "Well, like most religions, your theory lacks proof."

Vanya's dark eyes flashed. "Proof!" he roared. "The proof is everywhere! It's been recorded in every religious text ever written! The Bible, the Quran, the ancient Sumerian tablets, and all the innumerable surviving scraps of knowledge from all over the world describe, in specific detail, acts and events which now can be explained by our so-called modern science. And according to that passport of yours, you've been to many of the ancient lands and must have seen these wonders for yourself."

Rhea silently reached down to the table and came up with a silver goblet. Vanya suddenly seemed to become aware of her presence, accepted the goblet from her, and took a drink. Vanya was right about my having been to many of the Lands of Antiquity, but I never had time for sight-seeing, and the last time I was in Alexandria I spent my final night running through garbage-strewn back alleys with a Twenty-sixth Dynasty statuette of the Egyptian cat goddess Bast in my backpack, escaping from the looters I stole it from. I was in no hurry to go back there.

Handing the goblet back to Rhea, Vanya sighed, closed his eyes, and said, "We as a species have finally ascended to the doorstep of those ancient astronauts that came to our primitive planet all those centuries ago. Only somewhere along the way, we perverted our memories into the religious beliefs that we have killed each other over since recorded history."

Vanya opened his deep, dark eyes and said, "If we had but time enough, Mr. Blake, I would show you the passages written by those first observers. The descriptions of Elijah's 'fiery chariot,' the likes of which are also recorded in Buddhist and Hindu writings. These same events are mirrored in the writings about the Egyptian king Pepi, who ascended to the sky, and the god Quetzalcoatl, the 'plumed serpent' who, whenever he flew, was accompanied by a 'great wind.' All the comings and goings of the gods of our ancestors, the ascents into heaven on pillars of fire, are described in ways that are exact observations of rockets and jet engines."

Vanya's mood shifted again, and now he seemed almost sad as he said, "It's not just those writings. It's the uncannily accurate descriptions of events our primitive ancestors could not possibly have known anything about."

"Like what?" I asked.

"Nuclear war."

Despite the warm, almost heavy night air, laden with the pleasant scent of nearby olive trees, I felt a chill course through me. I reminded myself it's not a good idea to argue with a fanatic who has his own private army. Vanya leaned back and tented his fingers, regarding me through half-closed eyes. "You don't believe me?" he asked with apparent gentleness.

"Let's just say I don't know what you know."

Vanya closed his eyes and leaned his head back, and then he began to recite: "An incandescent column of smoke and flame, as bright as a thousand suns, rose in all its splendor. It was an unknown weapon, an iron thunderbolt, a gigantic messenger of death, which reduced to ashes the entire race of the Vrishnis and the Andhakas." Vanya paused, opened his eyes, and said to me, "Do you know what that is from?"

I shook my head, and Vanya said, "That comes from the translation of the Indian Mahabharata. A story written four thousand years ago."

While I was trying to wrap my mind around the concept, Vanya continued, "And it doesn't end there. The ancient texts go on to describe in vivid and perfect detail the results of radiation sickness and contamination, everything from the hair and nails of the surviving victims falling out to the poisoning of the crops and the land. I submit to you, Mr. Blake, that if you read the verses in the Christian Bible regarding Sodom and Gomorrah, you would find them indistinguishable from the historical records of Hiroshima and Nagasaki."

"*Deus vult,*" I muttered, but not so softly that Vanya missed it. I saw a scowl gather on his face and figured he was unfamiliar with the Latin slogan of the Crusaders: "God wills it."

"Proof," Vanya barked in a contemptuous half-laugh. "Men like you couldn't see the proof if it fell on them. So you tell me, how do you account for the massive monuments of engineering constructed by our primitive ancestors? There are the Standing Stones in the Nubian Desert, erected a thousand years before Stonehenge. Or the pyramids of Giza that are precisely aligned with the stars in the Belt of Orion. Or the geometric precision of the design of the great Mayan city of Teotihuacán. Do you honestly believe these and all the other fantastic structures that have lasted thousands of years were made with stone chisels and reed ropes?"

"All very fascinating," I said, trying to keep an edge out of my voice. "But how does all of this relate to Alexander the Great?"

Vanya seemed to relax some, and the firelight softened his features. "How indeed," he murmured. "Now we find the question at the very heart of the matter: Where do we come from?"

"I'm afraid my study of history didn't go quite that far back."

I earned a small bark of a laugh from him. Then he quoted, "'And God created Man in his own image.' Only, the gods did not actually create man, rather they found him here among the rest of the beasts of the earth and modified him into a better servant."

"Modified?" I asked.

"Through genetic engineering," Vanya answered. "A process that we humans are now beginning to use. We have now almost attained the status of gods ourselves in our ability to modify the very foundation of life, the DNA of living creatures." Vanya tilted his head and asked slyly, "Have you never considered the ancient symbol of the caduceus? The twin snakes encircling the Staff of Life are a perfect representation of a DNA double helix. Our ancestors were leaving us clues, Mr. Blake."

"So you're saying that we humans are the result of some alien meddling with our genes?"

"Exactly," Vanya said complacently. "When you look at the situation scientifically, there really is no other explanation. Consider our genetic similarity with apes, and then ask yourself: Where is the so-called Missing Link between us and the apes? The answer is simple. We didn't evolve, Mr. Blake, we were genetically improved by an outside agency, the gods who descended to earth from the heavens of space. And it didn't end there. Every religious text, every mythological epic includes stories of the gods breeding with humans to create demigods, the *Homo sapiens* who are superior models. All the ancient heroes of Grecian mythology had divine origins—Achilles, Jason, Heracles."

Vanya paused, waiting for his words to sink in, then said, "And one of the last of these demigods was Alexander."

I tried to hold my poker face intact as Vanya said, "Consider the evidence—not tales and legends, but documented writings from true historians such as Arrian and Plutarch. It was Plutarch who wrote that Alexander was not truly the son of Phillip of Macedonia, but rather the son of Zeus Ammon, the son of a god. And Olympius, Alexander's mother, had promised Alexander that she would reveal to him a great secret about his birth upon his return. Only Alexander died before Olympius would ever see him again."

"You're still talking legends," I said, too caught up in the argument for caution.

But Vanya now seemed to relish my skepticism and his words took on heat of their own. "History has already judged Alexander as one of the greatest men who ever lived. In every aspect of mind and body, Alexander was light-years ahead of any other mortal man of his time."

"He also had more advantages than any other man," I countered. "Namely, he was a prince of a successful warrior clan. Not to mention he was educated by Aristotle himself."

Vanya waved away my observations as inconsequential. "Not even Aristotle could have helped an idiot," he said. "Alexander's accomplishments were entirely his own."

"That makes him a demigod?"

"One of many," Vanya answered with certainty. "But the only one whose earthly remains are known to still be in existence."

"Well, up to a point," I admitted.

Vanya rose from his throne and stretched. The evening air was starting to cool. He turned toward the life-sized statue of Alexander. "Did you know that when Alexander died, his generals did not know what to do without their leader, and they argued amongst themselves for days. When they returned to Alexander's tent on the sixth day, they were amazed to see that his body had not even begun to decay. More proof, as if any were needed, of Alexander's superior physicality."

As Vanya turned back to face me, the torchlight behind him gave his hair a glowing corona. "When Alexander's body is found, the proof of his unearthly origins will be discovered in his very bones. We now have the technology to read the genetic map, and I will have undeniable, incontrovertible scientific evidence that all the religions of the world that man has killed and died for are nothing but ignorant superstitions."

"Speaking of bones, there's a good chance that after all this time, whatever was left of Alexander may be nothing but dust."

Vanya waved my words aside. "There are writings that state Alexander's body was entombed in honey, almost as good as preserving him in amber. But regardless of his body's state, one intact bone will be all that's required for the truth of the matter to be known."

I was starting to feel the weight of Vanya's words as I saw in my mind's eye all the world's crusades, jihads, and inquisitions stretched out before me like an endless scroll of the Bayeux tapestry. I shook my head. "It doesn't matter what proof you have. True Believers will never be swayed from their faith. But they will kill for it," I added, thinking of Ombra and his men. That's when it hit me. "It all makes sense now."

"Go on," Vanya said softly, regarding me in the same manner as one of my old college professors when I finally got something through my thick skull.

"Ever since Ombra and his men blew up the Napoleonic treasure in the catacombs, it's been driving me crazy, because it looked like an absolutely senseless act. I kept asking myself who on earth would do such a thing?"

"Religious fanatics," Vanya assented. I nodded,

thinking back to the ugly, empty gouges in the sand-stone mountains of Afghanistan where the gigantic images of the Buddha had been blasted to pieces by a band of moronic zealots. I felt a slow, cold fire in my guts as I thought of Ombra and his men utterly destroying all those utterly irreplaceable relics.

Rhea, who'd been as silent as the statues in the garden, surprised me when she spoke. "What are you thinking, Mr. Blake?"

"At the moment, I was thinking about Ombra and his men."

Rhea tilted her head. "And what would you do if you met up with him again?"

I didn't reply. I let my expression speak for me, reflecting the anger I felt burning inside me as I recalled the absolute wanton destruction of the treasures in the Parisian catacombs. Rhea just nodded, apparently satisfied. I looked over to Vanya. "Well, for what it's worth, it looks like Ombra believes you're on to something."

"Hence the need for absolute secrecy," Vanya said. "It's bad enough I've got one group of fanatical terrorists trying to stop me. I can only imagine the storm I'd invite if word got out to the world at large of what I was attempting to do here. My poor little island would be besieged by the armies of almost every religion. So now tell me, Mr. Blake, have I satisfied your curiosity? More importantly, are you now willing to join me on my quest?"

"What?"

"You're a man of unique talents. I could use someone like you. Moreover, I can offer you a sanctuary away from that prison sentence that the United States government has dangling over your head. So what do you say?"

It was the biggest surprise in a night filled with them. I'd gambled that if I could convince Vanya I was a crook and a thief, that he'd feel more comfortable with me, since I first judged him to be a con man using religion as his dodge. What I didn't count on was that Vanya was insanely fanatical in his own unique way and that he'd want to recruit me into his personal Holy War.

But on the other hand, if there were a chance in hell that the tomb of Alexander could be found, then to hell I would go. It would be the absolute archeological find of the century. I looked past Vanya to the armored marble figure of Alexander, who was staring down at me with sightless eyes that reflected the firelight. It was to the stone monument that I said: "I'm in. All the way."

CHAPTER FOURTEEN

At the sound of my assent, Vanya nodded once. "Good," was all he said, then he bowed his head, hiding his face in shadow. Rhea stole up beside me and took my arm, leading me away. Vanya was oblivious to our departure. Rhea took me along a winding path through the garden toward the central building, and as we approached I saw that over half of the windows on the concrete six-story structure were lit, giving the appearance that we were in the courtyard of a tropical hotel. We passed between a pair of freestanding Corinthian columns on a walkway of flagstones that led to a double-wide set of glass doors and into a lobby area. The overhead fluorescent lighting made me blink after my time in the firelit darkness. The interior was air-conditioned and felt almost chilly in contrast to the balmy atmosphere outside.

Straight ahead I could see a glass wall, and past that was an expanse of sandy beach, sugar colored under a brilliant three-quarter moon that rendered the ocean beyond an oil-black mass, featureless except for a tiny constellation of light coming from a ship out to sea. Rhea gave me no time for sightseeing. She took my arm and drew me into an elevator with stainless steel walls. She pushed the button for the sixth and topmost floor, and I noticed that there was also a level below ground indicated on the control panel. I also observed that the buttons were actually biometric security mechanisms, designed to operate only when they recognized a particular user's fingerprint and biological signature. The doors closed silently and we began our ascent. "So now what?" I asked.

Rhea didn't face me as she said, "Now you should rest. In the morning you'll begin working on finding the location of Alexander."

"That's asking a lot. I haven't the faintest clue where we go from here."

Rhea smiled, not looking at me. "We may have some new developments for you by tomorrow. Until then, I suggest you try and keep your strength up."

The elevator stopped and the doors opened to an identical lobby. Rhea took me to a hallway at the intersection, lined with numbered wooden doors on either side. After a short walk, she stopped before one of the doors. "Good night, Mr. Blake. Remember what I said about you needing your rest." Rhea gave me a smile, one that concealed a secret significance, and then she opened the door and stepped aside.

There was Caitlin, standing in a small room and dressed in a Grecian gown like Rhea's, with her hair loose and spilling down across her shoulders, looking like an ivory and gold avatar of a goddess.

"Jonathan!" she cried as she ran into my arms, giving

me a hug that sent a spear of pain through my injured side. A pain that I forgot completely when she kissed me as a long-lost lover would. Caitlin broke the kiss and the spell of it all at once then stroked my cheek and said with quiet urgency, "Oh, baby, I was afraid I'd never see you again. Are you okay? And what were you doing with that woman?"

I was feeling confused, to say the least; my head was still swimming from Caitlin's kiss as her large, golden-brown eyes searched my face. I realized belatedly that Rhea must have closed the door behind me while my attention was completely captivated by the woman in my arms. Caitlin had transformed again, and was now portraying a frightened and confused wife who'd been kidnapped and taken away from her husband. Now I had to play the part with her as though our very lives depended upon it. Which, it occurred to me with a chill, they did. "Whoa," I said, "one thing at a time. But you, are you okay? What happened?"

Caitlin backed up a step and I looked back to the door and saw that there was no doorknob on this side, just a plain bronze plate where the handle would be. I brought my attention back to Caitlin, whose words were coming out all in a rush. "What happened? I woke up somewhere near here; I thought I was in a hospital, only no one would tell me anything. People just came and kept asking me questions about you. I told them everything I knew, about how these horrible people kidnapped me. Were they terrorists? And, oh my God, Jonathan, I didn't know what had happened to you. I mean, one minute we're in Paris, and then the bomb exploded, and now I don't know where we are. I thought I'd never see you again. Who are all these people? Where are we? And why won't they let us go home?"

While Caitlin's words washed over me like an ocean wave, I saw that we were in a small apartment that looked like a college dorm room, furnished simply with a single bed and a table with a couple of chairs. Across the way was a sliding glass door that led to a balcony and a view of the sea beyond. "Let's sit down," I suggested. Caitlin held on to me as if afraid I would disappear as we sat close together on the edge of the bed.

I took in a breath as Caitlin looked at me, wearing an expression of anxious anticipation. I had to remember that everything I said was going to be relayed to Vanya. "Honey," I began, "I'm afraid I haven't been entirely truthful with you."

Caitlin's expression shifted from nervousness to suspicion in a flash. "Does it have to do with that Rhea woman?"

"Sort of," I replied. "But mostly it has to do with why we were in Paris in the first place."

"What do you mean?"

My next words came out like I was confessing to an affair. "I'm a kind of government agent."

Caitlin's eyes widened in surprise. "Government agent? You mean, like a spy or something? Jonathan, what are you talking about? You said you were a research assistant. For the Argo Foundation."

"I am; primarily, anyway. I just do occasional jobs for the government."

Caitlin shook her head and stood up, turning her back to me and hugging herself as she said, "Oh my God. And you never told me any of this? Jonathan, I'm your wife!"

"I'm sorry," I said quietly. "I couldn't tell you. Believe me, I couldn't tell anyone."

Caitlin turned to face me, shaking her head slowly, her eyes shining with unshed tears. "Jonathan, I'm sorry, but I don't know what to say. I feel like I don't know anything anymore."

I stood and went to her, and she melted into my arms. I just held her for a while, taking in her warmth and breathing in the wonderful scent of her hair. "It's going to be all right, I promise you," I whispered to her. "You're just going to have to trust me for a little while longer."

"Trust you?" she said, her voice muffled in my chest. "I'm not even sure I know you anymore." She pulled her head back and looked up into my face, her eyes searching. "What's going to happen to us?"

"These people here, they want my help. And if it turns out like I think it will, then everything will be all right," I said for the benefit of our unseen audience.

"Your help? Your help with what?"

I shrugged, helplessly. "I can't tell you. Not yet."

Her head on my chest, Caitlin made a sound that was half laugh, half sob. "You can't tell me," she said with soft bitterness. "I'm just supposed to go along with this?"

"Yes."

"How can you ask me to do that?"

"Because I love you."

Just like that, with words that I had not uttered in years too long to count, it felt like my entire world had stopped in its orbit. The blood beat in my ears and my chest felt too small to contain my heart. Caitlin raised her face up toward mine, and her deep brown eyes were shining like they held a universe of stars. "Do you?"

I didn't reply, caught up in acting the part of a man in love and suddenly surprised to find a depth of true feeling. But Caitlin answered without words as she took my hand and led me back to the bed. She left me there as she went and turned off the lights, plunging the room into darkness that slowly became etched in silver as my eyes adjusted to the moonlight streaming from the balcony. I heard the slightest of sounds as the robe Caitlin wore slithered to the floor, and then she took my hand again and drew me down beside her. Soon there was no one in the world but her. And then nothing but us.

Afterwards, when the primal, driving need had passed and we had separated, a feeling of loneliness struck me before I could catch my breath and slow the beating of my heart. The pains of my injuries returned, making me wonder where they'd disappeared to during our lovemaking. My melancholy was evoked by the thought that what I'd just shared with her took us out beyond this place and time. Only the spell couldn't last, and we were back, trapped inside a gilded prison.

As my body slowed, my mind began to function, and I felt a bitterness twist my lips at the thought that Caitlin certainly went above and beyond the call of duty to convince any unseen observers of our marital relationship. I had gotten lost in the lie myself, and now felt the shame of a slave forced to perform for the debased pleasure of a soulless master.

Caitlin and I had shifted our bodies; I was on my back and she was entwined at my side. She reached for the single sheet to cover us, then laid her hand on my chest under the sheet and tapped gently three times. Then she traced the letters of the word "HI."

I almost laughed with surprise and admiration. Covered by the sheet, Caitlin was communicating with me in the only way that would be completely undetected. No doubt about it, I thought, Caitlin had brains and beauty. My thoughts came back into sharp focus as I reached my left hand down to her side and traced the letters to spell out HI.

Caitlin traced a question mark, and I wrote in response: V WANTS ME TO JOIN HIM.

Caitlin next traced WMDS? on my chest. Ah, the weapons of mass destruction, the biological warfare material that Caitlin and her boss spoke of back in New York. I sketched the circle and slash for NO on her thigh.

GO ALONG, Caitlin wrote, and then added: NEED MORE INFO.

I remembered the words Rhea had whispered to me while running a knife along my neck and I wrote: RHEA SAID SHE IS ON OUR SIDE.

Caitlin sketched a fast reply of: DON'T TRUST HER, adding a sharp jab of her fingernail for emphasis. I just patted her side in silent acquiescence.

All was still for a while, and I lay there with Caitlin and just listened to her softly breathing as the moonlight cut the small room into shapes of silver and sable. Then Caitlin wrote the letters that asked: CAN YOU DO THIS?

I just wrote in reply: YES. Then added a single number and a letter—a shorthand text message telling her that I would do it "4 U."

Caitlin gave me a gentle hug, and then rolled over

to her other side. I followed suit and snuggled in close beside her, cradling her back and breathing in the scent of her hair. I'd been with other women throughout my life, but with one exception all of my relationships were fleeting, ephemeral things. I could never be honest about my life and my work to begin with, and the long separations while I was sent off across the world invariably caused those relationships to fade and fail. And in truth, all the women I had known seemed to be pampered, protected creatures, cloistered within their comfortable, artificial shell of civilization. I had journeyed for so long and done so much that I no longer felt like I belonged in their protected and insulated world.

Then there was Caitlin. Where all the other women I had known were like expensive yet fragile crystal, Caitlin was as strong and resilient as a cut diamond. She was the only woman I'd ever known who knew at least part of the truth about my life, and it made me wonder if there perhaps could be a future with her.

But given our current situation, I wasn't sure there was going to be a future. We were cut off from the rest of the world on Vanya's private island, and subject to his whim. And Vanya himself was of questionable sanity. But there was no doubting the man had charisma. He exuded an attraction that would draw lesser-willed people into his orbit like a Jovian planet capturing meteors. Rhea, on the other hand, was as cold and deadly as they come, and I've had the extreme displeasure of meeting some dangerous people in my line of work. Then there was Ombra and his men. Who they were and how they figured into all of this was a deep and vexing mystery, and I recalled Vanya's words from earlier that night when he said they were like a plague. It made me wonder if all the sins they committed had been done in the name of a god. And there's nothing more implacable than a religious fanatic on a mission.

Now Caitlin and I were stuck in the game with all of them: Vanya, Rhea, and Ombra. But if there was even the slightest chance of finding the tomb of Alexander the Great, then it would be the find of this or any other century. One that would put Howard's discovery of Tutankhamen to shame.

But that particular treasure had been cursed as well.

❦ CHAPTER FIFTEEN ❦

I awoke to streams of sunlight pouring through the sliding glass doors of the room. Caitlin was sitting next to the small table, limned in an aura of light that turned her hair into molten gold. She was wrapped in the robe I had been wearing the night before. "Good morning, sleepyhead," she greeted. "I wasn't sure you'd be waking up today."

I held up a hand to ward off the light. "Good morning yourself," I replied. "What time is it?"

"Daytime," she said, holding up a bare wrist to indicate the lack of a timepiece. I was lacking things too, namely clothes. The dress Caitlin had been wearing was draped across the other chair, and all I had between me and the world was the sheet I was under. "Why don't you take a shower," she suggested. "You'll feel better." Caitlin then rose and opened the sliding glass door to the balcony, allowing a warm breeze into the room. She stepped outside and turned her attention to the sea. It was a seemingly casual maneuver that granted me a moment of privacy to make it to the bathroom, and it didn't escape me how odd it was that two people could share the ultimate intimacy and yet retain the innate shyness of strangers.

I didn't get up all at once. I did a quick inventory of my biological machine. The right side of my chest still wanted to go on strike, but my right leg was better, with the exception of a lingering stiffness. I also had a small collection of seldom-used muscles that were reminding me that I don't get nearly enough exercise in the act of human interaction. My eyes were drawn to Caitlin, leaning against the balcony with the breeze caressing her hair, and I wanted nothing more than to come up behind her and cradle her in my arms. Until my brain gave my emotions a solid kick and told them to get back down under, where they belonged. I quit wasting time and got up.

The bathroom was a compact unit with a single shower stall, toilet, and sink, as Spartan and functional as the rest of the room. The man in the mirror sported a pair of diffused circular rainbow bruises on his side, but other than that he appeared functional as well. Not decorative, but functional. There was a selection of small guest supplies, but nothing like a shaving razor. I ran my hand over my face and felt grudging admiration for the close shave Rhea gave me the night before, the memory of which left me with a tinge of fear. I tried to drown out that memory with a hot shower.

It felt good to be within the warm cocoon of the running water, and I reluctantly emerged after too short a time, but once again I was captivated by the aroma of coffee nearby. I wrapped one of the heavy towels around my waist and came back to the bedroom to find Caitlin, dressed in a white short-sleeved shirt and matching shorts, sitting near the table, now with a wheeled tray of food and drinks parked beside it. What caught my eye was the sight of my clothes and belongings arranged on the bed. "That woman came by," Caitlin explained. The cold emphasis on the word "woman" told me she was referring to Rhea. "And she brought room and laundry service with her. I was waiting for you."

I was torn between wanting to inventory my belongings or dive into the food, but I figured my clothes weren't going anywhere without me, so I sat down with Caitlin as she poured the coffee. Judging from the eclectic selection of edible delicacies, it appeared that our host was going out of his way to pamper us, but the lack of tableware on the service cart reminded me of our status as prisoners. As I reached over to help myself, Caitlin said, "The baklava's all mine. I won't fight you over the rest of it."

My hand changed direction and I selected a slice of salmon arranged on a wedge of bread. Caitlin was acting subdued yet tense. "Are you all right, love?" I asked.

She took a sip of coffee, then said, "As long as you tell me we're going to get out of all this, I am." She looked directly into my eyes. "I'm still trying to get over everything you told me last night. Right now, it all seems like some kind of bad dream."

I kept in mind that we were doubtless still under surveillance. "We'll be fine," I said convincingly. "Like I said, the people here want my help. Also, I'm quitting the government spy business. The pay was lousy anyway."

"I didn't marry you for your money."

"Good thing, considering what that skinflint Nick Riley pays me at Argo." There, I thought, now Vanya might get the reassuring message that my services were definitely for sale.

We ate and drank in silence for a while. Until the sound of automatic-weapons fire intruded into the room.

Caitlin's golden brown eyes narrowed, then she opened them wide as she said with apparent alarm, "What was that?"

I got up and went out to the balcony, searching for the source of the gunfire, but from my sixth-floor vantage point, all I could see was a vast expanse of water and the ship I'd spotted the night before, still at anchor. The sunlight dancing off the waves made it hard to make out at a distance, but I could now see the ship was a modern motor yacht, and a big one at that. The rapid popping drumbeat of the guns ceased for a bit, then commenced again. The noise appeared to be coming from somewhere on the other side of the building Caitlin and I were in. "Sounds like a small army on maneuvers," I said.

I took a look around the balcony. The outside of the building was constructed of featureless concrete, and I could see matching balcony areas below and on both sides. There was a straight drop down to the sandy beach, which was flanked by rough black rocks where the waves ebbed and flowed. The building looked as solid as a fortress. So much for a potential escape out the window, I thought. Not that heading in the direction that gunfire was coming from was an attractive proposition. There were three more sets of automatic-weapon barrages, and then the guns went silent. "What do you think that was?" Caitlin asked.

She probably knew better than I did, but she was playing her part to perfection. I tried to sound reassuring as I said, "Probably just someone practicing their target shooting. And if they need guns like that, they're probably bad shots."

Caitlin gave me a small smile. I missed seeing her ironic raised-eyebrow look, but that wouldn't have been in character, I suppose. I cinched my towel tighter and turned my attention toward the clothes and other items stacked neatly on the bed. I'd really missed wearing pants. I nearly did a double take as I spotted among my belongings the short stack of gold coins I'd rescued. I picked them up, feeling their weight as I held one up to the light. The face of the coin was impressed with a profile of a man in late Restoration Period wig with the name "Manoel De Vilhena" surrounding the head. The reverse of the coin had the heraldry of Malta along with a date of 1724. All six golden coins were of the same vintage.

I glanced over my shoulder and saw that Caitlin remained at the balcony, her attention out to the sea. I dropped my towel and quickly slipped into my clothes, which had obviously been thoroughly cleaned, removing all traces of our recent expeditions through the Catacombs of Paris. I wouldn't be wearing my jacket in this climate, which was just as well, as it sported a ragged bullet hole.

I inventoried my other belongings. I had my watch, wallet, passport, and money, including the bills I had tucked away inside my formerly secret pockets. My button-sized compass and flashlight were present, along with my waterproof metal tube of matches and my pocket tool. They even kept the safety pins. Best of all, my belt and pen had been returned. It felt good to be armed again. As I finished dressing, Caitlin returned inside. "Did you get all of your things back?" I asked.

"I didn't see my phone," she replied casually. I tried to summon a mental inventory of all of the items I had removed from Caitlin's purse and carried in my pockets, and wondered which ones were the "toys" Vanya had referred to. Whatever Caitlin's devices were, they were gone now. Caitlin retrieved the bathrobe I'd worn the night before and went into the pockets, coming out with my lighter and cigarettes. She took a moment to examine the etched dragon motif on the lighter before she handed it over. "Gift from an old flame?" she asked.

"More like an old enemy," I replied as I stashed the lighter and cigarette box away in my pockets.

"You'll have to tell me that story someday. Come to think of it, you're going to have to tell me a lot of things I should have known before we got married," she said seriously. "Jonathan, where's your wedding ring?" she asked suddenly.

My mind flashed back to when Caitlin's fellow agent Sam Smith and I met in Paris and he asked for the ring back, explaining it had a homing beacon built inside. "Uh, I'm sorry, honey," I offered. "I must have lost it somewhere in Paris."

Caitlin looked hurt, but didn't reply. If she was counting on the ring's electronic properties to help her people to locate us, then we were well and truly lost. Which underscored another reason I hate to trust my life to any modern, infernal devices—the damn things can fail you. I held out my handful of gold coins to her. "Here," I said.

Caitlin approached, curiosity playing on her lovely face. "What's this?"

"Belated wedding present. Although you're worth far more to me than mere gold."

She gave me a sly, mock-disbelieving look as she accepted the treasure from me. Caitlin held up a coin and said, "So this is what you risked your life for back in Paris?"

"When you put it that way, you make me sound idiotic."

She just gave me a sideways glance more expressive than any words. "What are they?" she asked, pointedly returning to the subject.

"Maltese treasure. Must be part of the loot that Napoleon collected as he rampaged throughout the world."

"Are they worth anything? Like the price of your life?"

"Depends on who you talk to. But if you don't want them—"

Caitlin swiftly turned and picked up her small black handbag from the bed, dropping all the coins inside and snapping the purse shut. "Don't think this gets you off the hook for anything that's happened, like losing your wedding ring," she said with finality.

I was saved from making a rejoinder by a knock at our door. Without waiting for an invitation, Rhea entered the room. "Good morning," she greeted us pleasantly. She was no longer attired as a Grecian goddess, and instead was dressed in a tight pair of black shorts and a matching short top that displayed her smooth musculature to good effect. Her glossy black hair was wrapped tightly to her head. She also wore a pair of black athletic shoes and came in looking like she was ready to run a marathon. "Vanya would like to see you now, Mr. Blake."

Caitlin tossed her purse on the bed. "Let's not keep our host waiting, shall we?"

Rhea kept her pleasant demeanor as she said, "You were not invited, Mrs. Blake."

"I'll forgive the oversight," Caitlin replied. "But I go where my husband goes."

Rhea's smile stayed fixed, albeit a little strained. Caitlin remained impassive and immovable, and I had just enough brains to stay the hell out of the staring contest. Finally, Rhea gave a small nod of acquiescence and ushered us toward the door. I'm certain I only imagined the feline hiss Rhea made as we passed by her.

As Rhea shut the door and led us to the elevator, I said, "I heard gunfire this morning."

"Really?" Rhea replied casually. "You must have heard our security people practicing."

"Your security people have automatic weapons?"

"Certainly," Rhea said. "Rest assured, Mr. Blake, you will be very well protected as long as you are a guest here."

Rhea's statement did nothing to bolster my own sense of security, but Caitlin helped immensely by the simple act of taking my hand as we walked. The three of us remained silent as we took the elevator to the ground-floor lobby and then walked toward the central courtyard. The sun hadn't crested the eastern building yet and the garden area was shaded, but the air felt warm and heavy, promising real heat for the coming day. Then I heard a most unexpected sound: laughter, and coming from multiple voices.

We followed Rhea through the winding path past the carved stone columns and statuary, until we came to the long, covered marble table and I saw the source of the laughter. There were women, all young, at least a dozen of them of various nationalities, and they all appeared to be talking at once. Every one was a handsome, healthy specimen of the female gender, all dressed alike in short-sleeved white tops and shorts such as Caitlin was now wearing. It looked as if the United Nations were fielding an all-girl Olympic sports team. With all the lovely women in the Garden of the Gods setting, I was reminded of the Samuel Coleridge poem: "In Xanadu did Kublai Khan a stately pleasure dome decree." Of course, old Coleridge was just coming down from an opium high when he concocted that one. When we came within sight, several of the girls called out Rhea's name and waved in happy greeting.

As we approached, Vanya himself came into view, still dressed for playing the part of Zeus and resting on his high-backed throne, smiling beneficently over the assembly. Rhea clapped her hands together and called out, "Ladies! Come. It is time for your lessons." There was a general, good-natured chorus of groaning as the girls got up from the table and filed out toward the west-side building complex, all the while casting curious glances at Caitlin and me and whispering among themselves as they sauntered past.

Vanya raised a languid hand from the arm of his

chair. "Welcome, Mr. Blake, Mrs. Blake. I trust you spent a pleasant night?"

As if you didn't know, I thought to myself. I summoned a smile and said, "Yes, thank you. Who were all those young ladies?"

Vanya smiled and stroked his long white beard. "Ah, they are my daughters, the true Children of Cronos," he announced.

I glanced after the departing crowd. "Really?"

Rhea, finished herding her flock of girls, returned to her accustomed place beside Vanya and said, "They are our foundlings, Mr. Blake. They are orphans from all over the world. Vanya has taken them in, and we raise and care for them together."

"Surely, Mr. Blake," Vanya added, "you have seen the plight of the children in the places you have traveled to?"

I had. It was the worst part of my job, really. Wherever I went, from Africa to the Middle East, from India to Central and South America and throughout Asia and the Pacific Rim, I'd seen the wretched refuse of humanity, suffering from abject poverty and cruelty. And everywhere I went, there were the children. I'd use whatever time and resources I could spare during my missions to help out where I could, but it was always like putting a Band-Aid on a gaping, bleeding wound. In the end, I always got to go back home to the States, where I'd try to drown the memories of the sights, sounds, and smells in alcohol.

Caitlin pulled me out of my dark reminiscence by saying, "That seems very commendable."

Vanya's smile took a deprecating downward turn. "Children are the future," he said simply.

I had a sudden thought that chilled me. "So, what about those guards I saw last night? Are they also considered your children?"

"Of course," Vanya replied reasonably. "They have been raised here on Cronos and have chosen to devote their lives to our cause."

I could only hope my face didn't betray the emotions that churned up inside me. I'd also seen children in war-torn countries lugging around automatic weapons and grenade launchers that were almost bigger than they were, desperate to fight and prove themselves as men, and utterly devoted to whatever cause the adults in their world created for them. Vanya didn't just have a private army; he had his own cadre of religious worshipers, no doubt ready to both kill and die for him.

Vanya snapped me out of my waking nightmare by saying, "So tell me, Mr. Blake: Are you still resolved to join me in my quest?"

"I am. But I also have my price."

Vanya looked pleased, though not surprised. "Of course. You have but to name it."

"Two things," I said. "First, the Egyptian scrolls. Caitlin and I almost died down in the catacombs, and since I found them, by rights they're mine."

Rhea's placid smile remained fixed and frozen, but Vanya's face started to darken like a coming storm. "That's . . . an expensive proposition," he answered slowly. "Those scrolls could be extremely valuable."

"What do you care as long as I help you dig up Alexander?"

Vanya appeared on the verge of releasing some pent-up anger, but then Rhea laid a hand on his shoulder. He snapped his head up, and the two of them exchanged some deep, silent communication. Vanya visibly relaxed, then turned back to me and said in an agreeable tone, "Very well, Mr. Blake; the scrolls are yours. But only after you've completed your work here."

And just like that, I knew Caitlin and I were as good as dead. Vanya would now agree to anything I asked for, knowing he'd never have to pay me off. I had one last gambit to try. "Second thing," I said, "is that you send my wife home."

Vanya started to speak, denial clearly written on his face, but Caitlin beat him to it. Her eyes flashed with real heat as she said, "Jonathan Blake! How dare you? I told you last night, we're in this together. I'm not leaving you, and that's final."

Rhea looked faintly amused over Caitlin's outburst, while Vanya simply traded a look with me that men have shared ever since time immemorial. "Well, there you have it, Mr. Blake," he said. "What are mere mortals to do?"

I didn't think for an instant that Vanya was about to let any of us leave his fortress paradise, but it would have been out of character not to try.

Vanya rubbed his hands together. "Then it's settled, and we have work for you, Mr. Blake. Rhea will take you to meet with our resident researcher. As for you, Mrs. Blake, may I take this opportunity to show you my island? I'm certain we can find some diversions for you while your husband toils for our cause."

Caitlin smiled. "Thank you. I'd like that." Turning to me, she laid her hand on mine. "Well, so now this is where I say: Have a nice day, dear?"

Rhea held out a hand, indicating I should follow her.

Caitlin shot a small, poisonous look toward her, then smiled toward our host as Vanya said to her, "Come sit by me, Mrs. Blake." I gave Caitlin's hand a squeeze, then followed Rhea back toward the central building. When we passed by the large garden fountain, I took a look into the water, slightly surprised I didn't see any piranha, or a least a venomous lionfish or two. Once back in the ground-floor lobby, the cool, air-conditioned atmosphere was refreshing compared with the sultry air outside. Rhea led me to the elevators, and once inside the steel-lined box she hit the button for the bottom floor. The descent seemed to take longer than it should have, and when the doors opened I saw we were now in a fluorescent-lit concrete bunker that looked like it could have survived a hit from a nuclear weapon.

The only thing missing was a sign advising all who enter to abandon hope.

CHAPTER SIXTEEN

As Rhea led me around the corner of the elevator alcove and down a hall to the left, I saw that the below-ground complex was built like a grid, with hallways branching off to our right. Every intersection had a mirrored hemisphere in the ceiling that allowed a glimpse around the corners and doubtless also had cameras concealed within. All the doors were made of heavy metal and looked airtight, like the hatches on a submarine, and were marked with letters and numbers. The prefix for each was "L1," which made me wonder if there were levels yet below us. Every door I saw had a biometric locking mechanism installed.

Rhea and I had to walk single file in the narrow confines to pass an oncoming couple, an older Caucasian male and a short, rounded Asian woman, both dressed in what looked like hospital surgical garb. They smiled and nodded to Rhea, though somewhat nervously, while paying no attention me. We then took a right turn, and unless my sense of direction failed me, we were walking beneath the central courtyard and heading toward the Roman-style baths that were dug into the hillside above us. Rhea stopped in front of a door marked L1-4, pressed her finger to the lock, and then opened the hatch, calling as she did, "Peter! I've brought company!"

My first impression of the room beyond was that I'd been led to a library repository. Stacks upon stacks of books were everywhere, along with piles of paper. Buried under the mounds I could make out shapes of small square tables and some chairs. Every wall was covered with large-scale maps and displays. From near the center of the room a man stood up, like a gopher popping out of its hole.

He was tall and slender, with a large forehead crowned with dark hair that fell in careless waves above an angular, bony face. He had blue eyes behind the lenses of a pair of horn-rimmed glasses, and he was dressed in a denim shirt and pants, along with a tooled leather belt. I placed his age at somewhere in his mid-forties. As he navigated the stacked–book obstacle course he smiled and held out a hand. "Hi. Pete Weir. Welcome to the bunkhouse."

His long-fingered hand gave a firm grip. "Blake. Jon Blake," I replied.

"Ah, fellow American, I see," Weir said.

"Mr. Blake is our newest recruit," Rhea explained. "He's the one who found the Egyptian scrolls."

"Really?" Weir said with admiration. "Excellent. You know, that's the first piece of real evidence we've found on this scavenger hunt."

Rhea made a small bow. "I'll leave you two to get

acquainted. Please bring Mr. Blake up to speed on all the developments."

"Sure thing, Rhea honey," Weir replied. He had an American Southwestern accent that went with the belt and cowboy boots I could now see. As Rhea left, he watched with unabashed appreciation, then asked me, "So where do you hail from?"

"Well, before I got spirited away to Never-Never Land, I worked for the Argo Foundation."

"Argo? Nick Riley's outfit? Is that old pirate still aboveground? I haven't seen him since he took fifty bucks off me playing poker at a conference."

I nodded, not surprised. Nick Riley has friends all over the world. "So it's Dr. Weir?" I inquired. "And Nick only took fifty bucks off you? You must be good. He usually gets me for half my paycheck. But yeah, I just saw him earlier this week." And half a lifetime ago, I thought to myself. I took a look around the room. "So what do we have here? Other than a fire hazard?"

Weir gave an easy laugh. "Hey, this here is my office, son. And since it sounds like we'll be bunking here together we can leave that 'Doctor' stuff to the guys that make us turn our heads and cough. But I'm forgetting my manners; let me find you a chair."

As it turned out, finding the chair was easy. Digging it out of the paper shell it had accumulated was the tricky part. "You know," I said as I sat down, "they have these new devices called computers. They're like fancy file cabinets with a built-in TV. You'd kill a lot fewer trees if you used one."

Weir sat down in a high-backed leather chair and swung his booted feet up on a nearby table next to a monitor and keyboard that were almost obscured by a pile of books. "Those technological tinker toys are fine in their place," Weir said. "But I like to hold the results in my hand. Besides, I think I'm addicted to printer's ink."

"So how did you get caught up in the Alexander quest?" I asked. "You don't seem to fit in with the rest of Vanya's true believers."

Weir raised his glasses to the top of his head. "I'm not," he said simply. "I'm really just an academic mercenary. That, and I can't resist a good challenge." He made a lazy gesture toward a large full-color poster taped to the wall. It was a copy of one of Napoleon's portraits, and it depicted the emperor of France in full military regalia astride a rearing white steed, one hand pointing toward the sky. "Our job is simple," Weir said. "All we have to do is outfox one of the greatest geniuses the world ever produced." Weir wagged a finger at Napoleon's image. "Yes, I mean you, you sawed-off little bastard."

Turning back to me, he said, "Of course, it's a little difficult being cut off from the outside world here. Vanya's terms are pretty strict about all the total secrecy stuff."

"Well, at least you must feel pretty secure. This place reminds me of one of Saddam Hussein's old bunkers."

"Sounds like you've actually seen one."

I had. But since no one was supposed to know about those forays, I said instead, "So how long have you been down here?"

"I joined up about six months back. Couldn't tell a soul. But when Vanya showed me the Fouché document and said he had a line on one of the eagles that supposedly had a genuine treasure map inside, I just couldn't resist. Still, as indentured servitudes go, it does have its side benefits."

"Side benefits?"

"Oho! You mean you haven't seen the recreational facilities? Son, you are in for a treat. It's like an Arabian paradise around here. Complete with houris."

Houris were the female virgins that were promised to the Islamic faithful in their particular version of paradise. Faithful men, anyway. "So you're saying that there're, shall we say, women of easy virtue on the payroll here?"

Weir rolled his eyes. "I'll say. This here island is Vanya's personal recreation park. Those of his flock that can afford to pay the honorarium get to fly out here and enjoy an earthly communion. Us working stiffs, too, of course."

"Actually, I'm here with my wife."

Weir's face froze for an instant. "Okay," he said slowly. "So, getting back to the subject, what do you need to know?"

I looked around the room. "Well, everything, I guess. From what I gather, the theory is that Napoleon actually discovered the tomb of Alexander the Great, and now all we have to do is figure out what he did with the body."

"Right." Weir nodded. "History tells us that after Napoleon's first major defeat, he was exiled to the island of Elba, right next door to his home island of Corsica, then he escaped, took over the French government again, got his ass kicked by Wellington at Waterloo, and was later exiled to the island of Saint Helena, where he eventually died."

I raised my hand. "Teacher? Should I be taking notes?" I asked pointedly.

Weir looked sheepish. "Sorry. I haven't had a lot of conversation lately. I'm not allowed to discuss my work with anyone except Vanya and Rhea. Until now, anyway. I didn't mean to come off all academic on you. Let's try again—what do you need to know?"

"What's the story on this Fouché document that I've been hearing about?"

Weir kicked his booted feet off the table and swung his chair around, pointing to the wall opposite the Napoleon portrait. Hanging there was a copy of a painting depicting a man with wispy gray hair and a gentle-looking, almost effeminate face with wide-apart, dark eyes and a cryptic smile playing on a small mouth. "Fouché," Weir said as one would speak a curse, "was one of the most wily, conniving snakes ever produced by the bloody French Revolution. He was also a survivor par excellence. He was physically too weak to be a sailor like his daddy intended, and instead got educated to be a priest, of all things. But by the time the French Revolution got under way, he got himself into power, always willing to play both sides against the middle. And talk about ruthless—he's the guy who started off the White Terror and got ol' Robespierre guillotined. The most amazing thing was how Napoleon kept him around. Bonaparte's on record as saying one of his few regrets was that he didn't have Fouché shot when he had that chance. Fouché fell out of favor a time or two, but always managed to weasel himself back into power. Makes me wonder if he didn't have some kind of blackmail material squirreled away. But there's no doubt about it, his secret police force was probably the best espionage outfit the world had seen up to that time."

"So you think Fouché was the guy who came up with the idea to hide the map of Napoleon's treasure inside the bronze eagle?"

"Probably. It sounds like his style. Although Napoleon himself gave us a clue about that."

"What was that?"

Weir grinned. "Right before Bonaparte was sent off to his first exile, on the island of Elba, he gave a speech to his troops, the Old Guard, telling them: 'I wish I could press every single one of you to my heart, but I will at least press your eagle.' So you really did find the map to Napoleon's hidden stash?"

"Oh, yeah. Down in the catacombs under the Val de Grâce church."

"Perfect," Weir said, as if extremely pleased with himself.

"How so?"

"It fits another piece of the puzzle. Here, I'll show you." Weir got up and made his way through the columns of books to the wall nearest the steel door. I followed him to a display on the wall. One side was a blown-up photograph of a handwritten letter in French, with a typewritten translation placed next to it. As I ran my eyes over the words, I flashed back to the letter that was hidden inside the eagle—at first glance they looked identical.

Weir placed his glasses back on his face and tapped the copy of the letter. "This here's a copy of the Fouché document, written in code. And right here is the translation."

I looked at the poster-sized typewritten blowup next to the French letter, and instantly did a double take when I read the first line. "The letter was addressed to the Duke of Wellington? What the hell would Napoleon's minister of police be doing writing to the enemy?"

Weir laughed. "I told you Fouché was a double-dealer. Right up to the time of Waterloo, Fouché was sending secret letters not only to Wellington and the British, but also to agents of the Bourbon royalists, just in case they should ever get back into power, which, of course, they did."

"Damn. Looks like I should have paid more attention in school." I turned back to the translation of the letter and read:

Your Grace,

I take upon myself the duty to warn Your Grace of certain plans and machinations of the followers and servants of Napoleon Bonaparte, former Emperor of France. It has come to my attention that specific orders, coming directly from Napoleon himself and conveyed in secret by his Agents, are even now in motion with the goal of liberating Napoleon from his period of exile on the Island of Saint Helena.

The means by which to accomplish this task are thus: An American ship is now at berth in a secret island harbor in the Mediterranean Sea. The Captain of this ship, who at this time shall be Nameless, is even now in preparation for the voyage. It was this same ship that spirited away Napoleon from his place of exile on the Island of Elba, and then eluded the British Navy when it was

*sent to retrieve the treasure of Alexander from the city
that bears that conqueror's name. It is by the means of
this vessel that Napoleon will be rescued from the Island
of Saint Helena, and then by the means afforded by the
Egyptian treasure will he finance his return to France
with the ultimate goal of regaining the Throne Itself.*

*This treasure, which includes items that are most won-
drous from the Ancient World, remains in part on the
secret island. The other half of the treasure has been entrusted to the care of he who shall be referred to for now
as The Doctor. As a measure of faith and trust between
us, I now inform Your Grace that the key to the location of the second treasure will be found inside the
Golden Eagle of the First Regiment.*

*It is my most sincere hope that Your Grace and I will
be able to come to an accord upon the terms of my future service to Your Grace, at which time I shall most
expediently provide the information that must, for now,
be withheld from this missive.*

*Your Expectant Servant,
Joseph Fouché*

"Damn," I breathed. "So Fouché was planning to rat
out Napoleon's escape plan?"

"Yep," Weir replied. "Just as soon as Wellington
agreed to his terms. Fouché was smart enough to provide proof to Wellington, but held back the crucial information, no doubt thinking Wellington would pay
a lot for the full story."

"So where did this letter come from?"

"Trieste, Italy. It's where Fouché was exiled to when

the French Royalists got back into power and everyone decided they'd had enough of the old boy. You'll note the letter's dated 1820, which is the same year Fouché died and a year before Napoleon kicked the bucket. For all we know, Fouché may have been secretly killed to keep from spilling the beans about the escape plan."

"But Napoleon never did escape from Saint Helena Island."

"Not for lack of trying. This little conspiracy wasn't the only escape plot cooking, by a long shot. The British intercepted other plans similar to this one. One of my favorites, from the British Library, described a plan for Napoleon to use a 'boat shaped like a wine cask and painted the colour of the sea' to sneak past the British ships."

Weir paused, then said in a doubtful tone, "You know, there's still a lot about Napoleon's death that's screwy. The latest buzz is that he died of stomach cancer."

"So I've heard. What's so screwy about that?"

Weir gave a knowing grin. "Check this out: Napoleon had his own physician on Saint Helena, a fellow Corsican named Antommarchi. But just a couple of months before he dies, he calls for one of the British contingent, one Dr. Archibald Arnott, to see him."

"Maybe he wanted a second opinion?"

"Hold that thought," Weir said as he turned and went for one of the precariously piled stack of books. He yanked one out like a magician pulling a laden tablecloth off a table and flipped it open to a marked page, then read aloud: "'The room was perfectly dark and he could barely distinguish the form of Napoleon as he lay on his camp bed.'" Weir shut the book with a clap. "That was on April 1st, 1821, the month before Napoleon died. Helluva way for your new doctor to first examine his patient. Then, on May third, Napoleon gives the order that no English physician is to touch him except for Dr. Arnott."

Weir began to pace the room, avoiding the pillars of books. "Now, Napoleon was buried on Saint Helena and then exhumed nineteen years later and taken to France, even though he stated he wanted to be buried back on his Corsican homeland. Oddly enough, Napoleon's body was perfectly preserved when they dug him up. And that brings us to the teeth."

"Teeth?"

"Yep. The account of his exhumation mentions the Corsican corpse had 'perfectly white teeth.'"

"So?"

"So according to Sir Henry Bunburg, the man who gave Napoleon the bad news that the British were shipping him off to exile in Saint Helena, Napoleon's teeth were 'bad and dirty.' That was written in 1815, just six years prior to his death."

"Just what are you saying here, Sherlock?"

Weir stopped his pacing and folded his arms. "Let's just say there's still some mystery here. Turns out that a couple of years before Napoleon supposedly died, his majordomo and constant companion, Franceschi Cipriani, also died. Only no one's ever been able to find his body. It flat-out disappeared."

"Go on."

"So here we have a pile of inconsistencies and some outright bizarre circumstances along with two deaths and only one body. Who's to say they buried the right one?"

I let the swirl of information rattle around my head for a bit until I said, "You're kidding. Are you trying to tell me that wasn't Napoleon Bonaparte they buried?"

Weir shrugged. "Think about it—just how many discrepancies does it take before it adds up to something? And if the best independent witness to Napoleon's death is the good Dr. Arnott, my question is this: How reliable would his identification be if the first time he met Napoleon, he couldn't even see who he was talking to? For that matter, why would Napoleon call for any British physician, even though Arnott was actually Scottish. Unfortunately, even modern science might not help in a positive identification."

"How so?"

"There's some evidence to suggest that Cipriani was Napoleon's half brother. Even a DNA test might not be conclusive proof to tell the two apart."

I followed Weir's argument like I was tracking a particular leaf in a windstorm, then gave up and shook my head. "You know what I think? I think you've been kept underground too long. Can we leave the Murder Mystery of the Century for a while and get back to this letter?" I pointed to the translated Fouché document. "What's this here about an American ship that supposedly Napoleon used to escape from Elba? I never heard of anything like that before."

Weir grumbled "Philistine" under his breath, and then grinned and said, "Your guess is as good as mine. The best historical record we have of Napoleon's escape from Elba comes from the man himself, in his memoirs that he dictated, but were actually written by Louis Antoine Fauvelet while he was stuck on Saint Helena with the former emperor. Fauvelet wasn't actually at Elba, but he wrote that Napoleon left the island with about a thousand men on a ship named the *Inconstant,* along with 'six small craft.' No one else has ever recorded actually seeing Napoleon leave the island, but there's no question he arrived at the port of Frejus on the French coast. Coincidently, this is the same port he retuned to after his Egyptian campaign. But as far as any American ship helping Napoleon escape from Elba, there has never been any mention anywhere. The United States kept their Mediterranean squadron in the area from 1801 forward, and there were countless American merchant vessels in the sea, but I've never found any evidence that any of them got involved with Napoleon."

"So there was no American connection at all?"

"Actually, there were a few," Weir said. "Right before Napoleon got shipped off to Saint Helena, his brother, Joseph Bonaparte, was trying to get him to America, and when that failed, Joseph went to live in the U.S. from 1815 until 1830 or so. And Napoleon's brother Jerome actually married an American woman, Elizabeth Patterson, the daughter of a wealthy American merchant, although Napoleon disapproved and had their marriage annulled. Still, Jerome was an experienced naval commander and is a prime suspect to be the ship captain referred to in the Fouché document."

"Great. So in regard to Captain Nameless and the Secret Island, are there any other clues?"

Weir laughed. "When you say it like that, you make

it sound like Jules Verne. But no, unfortunately, we've got nothing. But thanks to you we do know now that 'The Doctor' who Fouché referred to is none other than Dominique Jean Larrey. Now there was a real hero. He was one of Napoleon's military surgeons and accompanied the army from the Italian campaigns to the Egyptian expeditions and all the way until Waterloo. He not only pioneered medical advances in wound treatment, but he also designed the forerunners of the modern ambulance. Napoleon himself once said that if they ever started putting up statues, that Larrey was the man who deserved one the most."

I thought back to the dark, dangerous night in Paris. "They did," I said. "He's got a big monument right in the courtyard of the church of Val de Grâce."

"It makes sense," Weir said. "If Napoleon was going to trust anyone outside his own family, it'd be a man like Larrey."

The memory of the catacombs brought something else to mind. "Wait a minute. The only other thing I was able to get out of the catacombs was a handful of Maltese coins. That's not Egyptian treasure by a long shot."

Weir's eyes brightened. "Maltese coins? Really? Perfect!" He sprang to a map of the Mediterranean Sea that took up half a wall. "Look at this," he beckoned.

I came over and watched as he traced lines on the map written in red felt pen. "See? Napoleon departs for Egypt from the south of France here, then his first stop is the island of Malta. He took over the island, reorganized their government, then raided the treasury right before he took off and landed in Alexandria, Egypt, in 1798. Then from that point, Admiral Horatio Nelson blows the crap out of the French fleet, and in August of 1799 Napoleon leaves most of his troops behind in Egypt and sails away, making a brief stop home in Corsica, and then returns to France. So those Maltese coins you found are a direct connection to the Egyptian campaign."

"Could be," I admitted. "But I still haven't seen any evidence that states Alexander's tomb is part of the treasure that Fouché wrote about."

"What do you want? A map with an X to mark the spot? Thanks to you, we know that Alexander's sarcophagus wasn't among the treasure hidden in the Parisian catacombs, so this here mysterious island would be the next most likely place."

"You really think so?"

"Well," Weir said slowly, "Napoleon is on record as saying that one of his wishes was to be buried in the sarcophagus of Alexander the Great."

"So how many islands are there in the Mediterranean Sea?"

"Hundreds. But I'm sure we can narrow it down some."

I was studying the path of the lines on the wall map when I heard the heavy door open up and turned my head to see Rhea. She looked weary as she said to me, "You have to come with me, Mr. Blake."

"Why?"

She didn't answer at once, then she tilted her head slightly as she said, "Remember when I asked you what you would do if you ever saw Ombra again?"

I felt my gut tighten. "Yes," I said slowly.

"Now is your chance. We've had him here on the island since we collected you from Paris."

I felt the shock of the news course through me like electricity, and then Rhea said, "And he's been asking to see you."

CHAPTER SEVENTEEN

My hand itched.

I've got a small star-shaped scar on the back of my right hand. There's a matching mark on my palm. That's where I had a nail pounded into my skin, transfixing my hand to an old wooden chair in a squalid shack in the outback of a Central American country, where I had the bad fortune to be taken and "questioned" about my involvement with illegal drugs. I never knew if my captors were actually policemen or drug smugglers or both. I also never knew the name of the man who nailed my hand to the chair, but I remember with vivid clarity his bored, brutish face; his guttural, phlegm-muted voice; and the acrid stink of his breath and body. The only time he showed anything close to a human emotion was after he pried the nail out of my hand, right before I was dragged away to rot in a festering pit of a third-world prison. I remember him running his fingers over the blood-soaked arm of the chair, shaking his head over the damage to the wood.

My days as a prisoner are like fragments of a fever dream now, one that I woke out of after Nicholas Riley came and rescued me. One of the doctors I met with during my recovery period told me how lucky I was that I still retained full use of my hand, despite the partial nerve damage. For years afterward, I would scratch the palm of my hand and feel shooting sparks of pain fired by the damaged nerves, and I would remember the man who did it to me. All through my early combat training, I would recall the man with the old hammer and corroded nail, and I'd focus that much harder on learning my lethal lessons. Sometime along the way, I don't recall exactly when, I stopped planning to go back to that little shack near the jungle and find the man, and then show him all the painful, maiming techniques I had learned. But every once in a while, I trip over that memory. And when that happens, my hand starts to itch.

Rhea had led me through the concrete maze to a room marked L1-3. It was mostly dark inside, but with pale light that came from wall-sized glass panels separating it from the next room. On the other side of the glass was a fully equipped operating theater, painted a stark white and filled with stainless steel accoutrements. The operating table in the center of the room held a human body, looking at first glance like a subject of a pending autopsy. It was Ombra.

He was strapped naked to the table, and his small, wiry frame looked pale beneath the bright overhead lights. The closer I got to the glass separating us, the more I could see the welts and dark discolorations inflicted on his body. Ombra's eyes were closed and his breathing was labored. I could feel my own respiration kicking up a notch, a combination of the memory of my own torture mixed with revulsion of what I was witnessing now.

And my hand itched.

Rhea, standing close behind me, spoke up. "He's been very difficult to work with, but I was finally able to reason with him."

I kept my eyes on the small, beaten body. "Reason? Looks like you've damn near killed him."

"Oh, he's strong enough," Rhea said, almost absently. "And very stubborn. What was surprising was the fact that he wants to speak with you directly."

"About what?"

Rhea came and stood next to me, and I was aware once again of the scent of jasmine. "I've been asking him about the Fouché document, and where we can find the secret island the document refers to. He's finally ready to tell us. Or rather, he specifically said he would tell only you."

"Why me?"

"I have no idea," Rhea said softly.

I kept my eyes on the slender man strapped to the table as I asked, "So who is he?"

"I'm still not certain," Rhea replied. "According to the papers and pocket lint he carried, his name is Simon Ombra, and he's an antiques dealer living in Paris, but it's probably all false information."

"Pocket lint?"

"Pocket lint," Rhea repeated. "You know, incidental papers and business cards used to bolster a false identity. You don't know the phrase?"

"It's a new one to me."

"Really?" she said with interest. "It comes from your own American intelligence services. How long have you worked as an operative of your government?"

I shrugged to cover a wince. "I must have cut school that day," I said quickly, then nodded toward Ombra. "So what did you do to him?"

"What I had to," she replied simply. "Are you ready?"

Hell, no, I was tempted to say. I wanted nothing to do with this cold, clinical obscenity. But I couldn't escape the fact that if I didn't play along, it could just as easily be me strapped down on that operating table. Or worse, Caitlin. I just nodded acquiescence and hoped my face didn't reveal even a fraction of what I was feeling.

"Good," Rhea said. She took my hand and led me back into the concrete-lined hallway and one door down. She activated the lock and the heavy metal door popped open slightly with an audible hissing sound. The hatch opened to reveal a small, airtight chamber. Ahead was a matching metal door with a small window built in. Rhea gave me a gentle push, and I heard the hatch shut and lock behind me, then the door ahead buzzed and slid open, revealing the white tile-lined area beyond.

It was the smell that hit me first. There was a tang of burnt flesh that the antiseptic hospital overlay couldn't quite mask. Ombra was flat on the operating table, strapped down and wired up to monitors that reported the fact that he was alive. Close by was a stainless steel table on wheels that held a collection of medicine bottles and hypodermics, and a pair of heavy, insulated gloves. On a steel pedestal next to the table was a square electronic device connected to a pair of insulated wires that terminated in slim needles—obviously the source of all the burns that pockmarked Ombra's body.

I moved the tables and torture devices out of the way. Ombra appeared to be in a deep sleep. "You wanted to see me?" I asked.

His eyes opened and blinked in the bright overhead lights. His mouth worked, but nothing came out. I spotted a plastic water bottle with a bent straw, and I took the bottle and placed it near his cracked lips. The bruise I had given him on his face had purpled, and I saw that he obviously hadn't gotten the same close, personal shaving job Rhea gave me. He managed to draw some water in, but then started sputtering and choking. I put the bottle down and located a set of handles on the side of the table, and managed to tilt it upward. Ombra's head lolled forward to his slender chest, but he managed to quit coughing. "*Merci,*" he mouthed.

"*Je vous en prie,*" I replied.

Ombra wheezed and rolled his head back against the table, almost forcing a smile from his desiccated mouth. "Please," he said with effort. "Your attempt at speaking *français* is more than I can bear."

I blinked, stopped dead in my tracks for a moment in pure amazement. After everything the guy had been through, he could still make a joke. "Well, '*excusez le mot*' all to hell," I said. Then before I knew what I was saying, I added, "I'm sorry."

Ombra didn't reply, but he tried to focus his eyes on me. "*Pour quoi?*" he wheezed, then said, "For what?"

"For everything that brought us both here today," I said. "Look, I don't know what you think you're protecting, but trust me, nothing can be worth dying for."

Ombra's watery blue eyes narrowed, then he said in a hoarse whisper, "Nothing? You truly believe that?" His eyes searched my face, and then closed as he let his head fall back against the stainless steel table and said, "Then I feel sorry for you, monsieur."

I couldn't help it—I got angry. "Look, damn it, in case you haven't noticed, these people here aren't screwing around. Whatever it is you've got that they want, they're going to drag it out of you piece by piece. Now let's just put a stop to all this and tell me what they want to know. Please?"

Ombra didn't respond to my outburst at first. Finally, he sighed, opened his eyes, and said in a low voice, "You said 'these people.' You are not one of them?"

"Let's just say I've been drafted into their cause."

Ombra's eyes took on a faraway look, as if he could see something beyond the sterile, white-painted walls. "If I name a place where you could find what you seek, you would go there yourself?"

"Sure," I said, hoping I sounded sincere.

Ombra closed his eyes again, and then said, "Château de Joux." His head rolled forward, as if he was under a weight too heavy to bear. "You will find what you want at Château de Joux."

I was about to ask what he meant, but I saw his eyes were tightly shut, though not so tightly as to prevent tears from leaking out. I heard the door behind me hiss open—obviously my summons to leave. I didn't make it out before I heard Ombra say ever so faintly, "I am sorry as well."

Coming through the double-doors was like being released from a decompression chamber. Rhea was waiting for me in the hall. She was smiling. "Well done, Mr. Blake. For a moment, I was afraid Ombra wasn't going to talk to you after all."

"It's a trap," I said flatly.

Rhea's smile twitched slightly. "Really? What makes you so certain?"

"The last time Ombra told me he was sorry, I got shot in the chest. His apologies are a danger alarm. So what are you going to do with him now?"

"We'll have to keep him around, of course, in the event the information he gave us doesn't produce results," she said as casually as if discussing a family pet.

"And then?"

Rhea's smile never wavered, but her eyes looked as hard as polished obsidian. "And then there should be no more reason to keep him around."

"No," I said.

"No what?"

"I meant every word I said to Ombra. So from now on, no more torture. We keep him alive, and when all of this is over, we let him go. End of story."

Rhea laughed. "Oh, really? Just like that? What if the tables were turned, as you Americans like to say? Do you think a dedicated religious fanatic like Ombra would do the same for you? He's tried to kill you at least twice already."

"Big deal. That's not exactly a unique occurrence in my world."

"Are you as forgiving with all your other enemies?"

"No," I admitted. "But there is one thing that makes Ombra different from all the rest."

"What's that?"

"He's the only one who ever apologized for trying to kill me."

CHAPTER EIGHTEEN

Rhea took me to another room, one that was deeper under the mountain by my reckoning, and left me there. This new area also had the now-familiar armored doors and was a large rectangle shape, dominated by an oval conference table made of richly inlaid wood surrounded by comfortable, leather-upholstered chairs. On one of the long side walls was a large flat-screen television monitor, while the other held a framed, recently produced map of the world. Besides the metal entrance door the room had three others: one was locked, one opened up to an executive-style washroom, and the last admitted me into a small but well-stocked bar. Both furnishings were well appreciated, especially as I was left alone for over four hours.

My watch was still on Paris time, but it kept good track of my solitary confinement. The only other thing that vexed me was the presence of a telephone, set at the head of the table. I had no illusions about trying to call up the outside world; I knew for a fact that there was no way something like that would go undetected in Vanya's kingdom. And I really didn't want to find myself strapped to a table next to Ombra.

Finally, my solitude was interrupted by the arrival of Rhea, still clad in her shorts and tight, abbreviated top, and Pete Weir, who came in the room with an armload of long rolls of paper, nodding a greeting to me. A few moments later, the previously locked inner door opened and admitted Vanya, who was accompanied by a large, tough-looking man decked out in desert camouflage and a gun belt. Vanya made the introductions for the newcomer. "Mr. Blake, this is Commander Vandervecken, our head of security."

Vandervecken looked to be a very fit man in his forties, with a bronzed, craggy face, ghostly blue eyes, and a thatch of nearly pure-white hair mostly covered by his military-style beret. His gun belt sported a worn-looking Beretta 9mm and a knife that looked too big for a bowie but was not quite a scimitar. The commander smiled and nodded at me, no doubt thinking to himself that he could take me on in a fight. I smiled and nodded back, knowing he couldn't.

Vanya still wore his white robes, though now he had his snow-colored hair tied back, and I caught a glimpse of something that looked like a hearing aid in one ear. I was certain that this was actually a radio receiver, one of the devices Vanya used to keep up the appearance of omnipotence over his island paradise. Vanya made a gracious gesture, indicating we should all be seated (I had stood up at the arrival of Rhea, but not because I considered her a lady), and settled in his own chair with a practiced flourish of his robes. Vanya opened the meeting by saying, "Dr. Weir, tell us all about this Château du Joux."

Weir grinned and selected one of the long paper maps he carried, unrolling it like a rug merchant displaying his wares. "This here's fresh off the printer," he announced. "The chateau is in fact a castle, and it's a beauty!"

I looked at the black-and-white overview with a baleful eye. "Castle" was a deceiving term for the melded cluster of structures depicted on the blueprint. It looked like something Escher would have come up with if he went in for medieval military designs.

"Actually," Weir continued, "it's more of a collection of fortifications built over time. The chateau itself is situated in the Jura Mountains of France, right near the Swiss border." Weir consulted another paper he held in his hand. "The first fort was built in the eleventh and twelfth centuries, and there've been a succession of improvements and additions over the years. Even the famous military engineer Vauban designed some of the later fortifications in the 1700s. But mostly, the place was used as a prison."

I couldn't help myself from saying, "Prison?"

"Yeah," Weir enthusiastically confirmed. "Matter of fact, this is the very spot Napoleon had Toussaint L'Ouverture confined after he was captured in Haiti. Poor bastard died here, too."

Rhea must have caught a look on my face. "Is something wrong, Mr. Blake?"

Not that I'd confide anything to the present company, but besides my early bad experience with prisons of the Central American variety, I had all my romantic illusions regarding castles crushed out of me during my very first field trip for the Argo Foundation. I was sent to the rough and rugged mountains of central Romania and the crumbling ruins of Poenari Castle, once a residence of Vlad Tepes, also known as Vlad Dracul. The mission was to follow up on a nebulous lead as to the location of the famous Golden Cup of Vlad Dracul, and it turned out to be a complete failure. A failure compounded by the fact that all my local experts who were guiding me through the woods that night demonstrated their survival expertise by running away the moment trouble arrived in the form of renegade ex-Romanian army troops, who mistakenly believed we'd found treasure. I wound up getting away on my own, running through the moonlit, steep, wooded mountainside with only the howls of the wolves for company.

My bad trip down memory lane was interrupted when I realized I had all eyes in the room on me. I indicated the picture of the castle on the table. "I was just wondering what kind of shape the château was in. I'm not overly fond of going through unstable ruins."

"It's in great shape," Weir confirmed happily. "It hasn't been used as an active fort since the First World War, and these days it's used as a military history museum. It's supposed to house a collection of over six hundred weapons. And get this—the museum displays mostly Napoleonic-era stuff."

Oh, just great, I thought to myself: a combination

castle and prison with its own armory. I had a bad premonition that I was looking at a map of my future, short as it may be.

Vanya spoke up. "So it's now a public museum?"

"Yeah," Weir answered. "Although it's closed throughout the winter months. As a matter of fact, it's not scheduled to be reopened to the public until this July. There've been active reconstruction projects going on for the last few years. Someone's been pouring a lot of money into the old place."

"Interesting," Vanya murmured. "Thank you, Dr. Weir. This is most helpful."

Weir looked around the table, surprised at being dismissed. "Oh, okay. Well, here're the printouts I got, and some overhead satellite photos, so, I guess if there's nothing else?" Weir shrugged and laid his other papers down on the table. "Adios," he said as he left the room.

When the main door shut, Vanya said, "This must be it; I can feel it."

"What?" I asked.

Vanya stood up and tapped the printed sketch of Château de Joux. "Think about it. Where else would Napoleon choose to hide one of his greatest treasures, except in a well-defended location?"

I looked at the castle plans, wondering how much of the fortified edifice would be hidden from view. "You think the sarcophagus of Alexander could be here?"

"Why not?" Vanya said, his dark eyes gleaming. "It's perfect."

Vandervecken had unrolled one of the satellite photographs. "It's perfectly bad," he said in a lilting Afrikaans accent. "I am thinking it is a place that will be hard to get inside of."

Vanya waved away Vandervecken's concern. "We'll need more information, of course. Rhea? Do you think our guest could be persuaded to talk some more?"

By "guest," Vanya was no doubt referring to Ombra. Rhea gave a weary shrug. "Maybe," she said doubtfully. "He's exhausted, and so am I. The problem is that his associates know he is missing, and time may not be on our side."

Vanya leaned back and tented his fingers. "Of course," he said absently. Then he smiled and looked at me. "Do you know why Ombra decided to reveal this location to you?"

"Sure. Like I told Rhea already, it's got to be a trap. Ombra wants me dead."

Vanya traded looks with Rhea, and then said to me, "Then I believe it will be necessary to proceed with caution, Mr. Blake. Rhea, when can you and Mr. Blake be ready to go?"

"Go?" I asked. "Go where?" But I already knew the answer to that.

"In the morning," Rhea replied. "I've been working almost all night already." The sight of Ombra's tortured, abused body sprang unbidden into my mind.

"Whoa," I said. "Just what do you expect me to do once I get to the chateau?"

It was Vandervecken who supplied the answer. "We'll need information on the layout. Someone needs to do a reconnaissance mission."

"Reconnaissance," I echoed. "So now I'm expected to be on the scouting party?"

Rhea smiled, and said in a voice that was almost a purr, "I'll be there to hold your hand, Mr. Blake."

"Thanks, I feel so much better now."

"There is another concern," Vanya stated to me. "Do you think that your former government agency will be actively trying to find you?"

I shrugged. "Probably. Things got pretty noisy back in Paris. Somebody must be looking into everything that happened that night."

Rhea returned to her chair. "According to the Parisian news reports, the fire at Troyon's apartment and the bodies that were found there are being attributed to an organized crime assassination. The most recent news about the explosion near the church of Val de Grâce is that it occurred due to an underground gas main accident."

Which meant that someone, somewhere was covering up the real reasons for all the murder and mayhem, I thought. "Well," I said. "In that case, I'd say we were in the clear for now. I don't think the G-men will waste too much time looking for me, but I'm toast if they ever catch me."

Vanya rubbed his hands together. "Very well. For now, I suggest you get some rest. Tomorrow may be a very interesting day. Rhea? Please escort Mr. Blake to his quarters, then come back quickly. We have more planning to do."

I cast a bitter look at the plans of the castle on the table as I got up to leave, letting Rhea lead the way. Once we were back in the concrete tunnels, she led me back toward the elevators, where we passed a figure exiting one of the armored air lock doors, dressed in what looked like a blue plastic spacesuit. Rhea showed no reaction to the sight, so I made no comment, and asked instead when we reached the elevators, "So now what?"

Rhea punched the button. "So now you get some rest, as will I. I believe we'll have an early start tomorrow."

"To go and storm the castle? Seems a tall order for just the two of us."

The elevator doors opened, and as we entered, Rhea activated the control for the topmost floor. As she turned, I caught a glimpse of an earpiece receiver like the one Vanya wore, hidden within her raven-black hair. "I'm certain we'll manage together," she replied casually.

We rode in silence until the elevator stopped and the doors admitted us into the topmost lobby. Rhea led the way to the room Caitlin and I shared, and then took me farther down the hall to a set of double doors nearer the corner. "Your new rooms," Rhea explained. "I strongly suggest you get some rest tonight. Also, say nothing of our plans to your wife." She gave me a conspiratorial smile, opened the doors, and then walked away without another word.

I entered the room and found myself inside a large, penthouse-style suite that looked fit for visiting royalty. Caitlin launched herself off an enormous sofa and came to me. "Jonathan! Check this place out! Looks like we've moved up in the world."

She wasn't kidding. The room was L shaped, taking up the whole corner of the building, and everything inside, from the bed that could accommodate a party of eight to the huge entertainment center, was pure luxury.

Caitlin was smiling and playing the part of the bubbly newlywed. We hugged and exchanged perfunctory kisses. "They just brought dinner up," she said, indicating a wheeled cart loaded with silver-domed trays. "Let's take it out on the balcony."

As I went to get the cart, I saw that the enormous flat-screen television was on and showing a picture of Vanya, looking for all intents like Zeus Almighty himself, while behind him was a moving panorama of stars and the planet Saturn. Vanya was saying something about "the Universal Brotherhood of Man," and in the background I heard the strident musical strains of Holst's "Mars, Bringer of War."

"Good-looking special effects," I commented, "but what else is on?"

Caitlin picked up a remote from the sofa and flicked the television off. "It's closed-circuit TV," she said. "It's like the all-Vanya-all-the-time network. Although he really is a fascinating man."

"Is that all there is to watch?"

"No," Caitlin said flatly. "There's another channel. One we won't be watching."

"Why's that?"

"It's just pornography."

"Pornography?" I asked. "Really?" I caught the look in Caitlin's eye and was suddenly certain what caused the death of her fourth husband. Or were we up to her fifth? "Right," I said as smoothly as I could. "I mean, who'd want to watch that sort of thing? So, what's for dinner?"

Dinner turned out to be braised and roasted lamb

kabob with Greek salad and a bottle of Syrah. The French wine just served to remind me of my pending journey in the morning and sour my disposition, despite my lovely dinner companion and the exquisite view of the sun as it slowly melted into the calm, dark blue sea.

Throughout the meal, Caitlin chatted away about her tour of the island with Vanya as her guide, and in the process managed to inform me that (1) there was another complex east of here that looked "like a cross between a Greek amphitheater and a miniature Roman colosseum" where she saw "about a hundred" young men going through military-style drills and training; (2) to the west was a boat harbor; and (3) Vanya's yacht, the *Phaeton,* was fully crewed and always ready to sail, although Vanya himself rarely left his island.

When I'd digested this unpleasant set of facts, I said to her, "I have to go away for a while, starting tomorrow."

Caitlin smoothed back an errant strand of her hair. "Where are you going?"

"I can't say. And I'm not sure when I'll be back. Like Odysseus, I've been drafted into Vanya's version of the Trojan War."

"You still can't tell me what you're doing for Vanya, or where you're going?"

"Right. But I promise, when I'm done, we'll be set for life," I said for the benefit of any unseen eavesdroppers. I'm convinced Vanya would agree with my statement, considering that I was certain that "set for life" translated to "deceased" in his dictionary.

"I see," Caitlin said quietly, looking out over the sea. "What am I supposed to do while you're gone?"

"Well, Odysseus's wife Penelope spent her time weaving. And fighting off suitors."

Caitlin's golden-brown eyes locked on to mine. "Penelope sounds like an idiot. Didn't it take Odysseus twenty years to get home from the war?"

"Well, yeah. There were some unavoidable detours, like Cyclopes, Sirens, and stuff."

"Not to mention the witch Circe, as I recall. And speaking of witches, is the Rhea woman going with you?"

"Um, yeah," I admitted. "I think that's the case. So in any event, I should probably get some rest tonight."

Caitlin, her hair set aglow in the rays of the setting sun, looked at me with her unfathomable eyes. Then she stood and came to me and simply held out her hand, and as I took it she said, "Even though I don't know what's going on here, I know this: You saved my life in Paris. You came back for me. And when I think of that, I think that maybe you really do love me."

I was about to make an off-hand reply, but the look in her eyes stopped me. Her face told me everything she was feeling at the moment, and I didn't dare to break the spell with my clumsy words.

"So tell me," she said, in a voice low and husky. "How would Penelope send her man off to sail beyond the sunset?"

Later, when our private storm subsided and we were left entwined together in the warm, gentle night, I wrote on her skin the name of the French castle. With her head resting on my arm, she nodded to tell me she understood the message, then she pressed my hand to her thigh and I drifted off to sleep.

Sometime in the depth of the night, I was woken by the harsh, beating staccato drone of a helicopter lifting off from somewhere close by. After that, my dreams were a collage of dark, ruined castles and the sound of wolves in the distance.

CHAPTER NINETEEN

"We have company."

Caitlin's voice made me open my eyes, blinking away sleep. I slowly raised my head and saw Rhea standing near the foot of the large bed, backlit by the early morning light from the balcony. She was dressed in comfortable-looking jeans and a dark blouse, and she was holding a flat bundle in her hands. One of Vanya's uniformed guards pushed in a cart loaded with silver-domed trays that exuded an inviting aroma of food and coffee. Bowing with the affectation of a geisha, Rhea said, "Forgive the intrusion, but it's time for Mr. Blake to prepare to leave."

"Thank you," Caitlin said in a fair imitation of graciousness, then added, "Now get out."

Rhea smiled and bowed. "Please be ready in sixty minutes, Mr. Blake." She placed her bundle at the foot of the bed and then silently left the room.

When the coast was clear, I regretfully left Caitlin, took the bundle of clothes that Rhea had left, and retreated into the bathroom. I hurried through a quick routine of shaving and showering, sorry that I couldn't relax and enjoy the luxury of the decadently appointed furnishings. I saw that my damaged ribs had picked up an extra layer of color, like a pair of circular rainbows, but they hurt less than before. Marginally, anyway.

The clothes Rhea brought were a pair of tan pants and a shirt that had a distinctly military styling, and I suspected that they were donated by Commander Vandervecken. I dressed and left the bathroom, picked up my meager collection of pocket gear, and found Caitlin sitting up in bed with the sheets gathered about her. As I went toward the breakfast trays, I had an unwelcome feeling I was being fattened up for the kill. I asked Caitlin, "Join me?"

She shook her head. "No. You go ahead." So I just went about the business of refueling my body as Caitlin kept silent and watched, and I would have given any of the treasures I've found over the years to know what she was thinking about.

When I finished, I stood at the foot of the bed. Caitlin and I shared a look for a time, and then I said, "Well, I guess I've got to go to work."

"Just make sure to come back in less than twenty years. I'm not nearly as patient as Penelope. Come here."

I did. And she gave me a long, warm reminder to return. Soon.

When I left the suite, Rhea was waiting for me in the hall with a black leather shoulder bag that had a matching jacket folded over it. She consulted a gold Lady Rolex. "Close enough," she said, then her dark eyes narrowed as she asked, "Is something wrong?"

I just dumbly shook my head while I fought an impulse to back away from her. In the hallway light I saw the thin chain-link belt she wore, loosely tied in the front, each end of the chain terminating in a teardrop-shaped metal weight, and her midnight-black hair, pulled back sleek and tight with a pair of long, silver-colored metallic pins the size of chopsticks woven in. These decorative accoutrements were nothing less than potentially lethal weapons, ones that would be invisible to the untrained eye, and I had seen first-hand how dangerous this woman could be. She was a venomous predator hidden within perfect camouflage, a creature you'd never see coming for you until it was way too late. In short, she was a creature very much like me. And that scared me.

I realized she was awaiting some reply, so I murmured, "Sorry. Didn't have time for a second cup of coffee."

She nodded understandingly. "No need to apologize, but I'm afraid we must hurry."

I nodded and followed her to the elevators and down to the main lobby. She brought me out to the seaside front of the building, where I saw the sandy beach bracketed by the dark rock clefts. The morning was warm and bright, which made me envious of the sunglasses Rhea placed on her face as she walked to an electric-powered, open-topped Jeep parked in front. Rhea tossed her bag and jacket in the back and took the wheel, driving us down a bumpy, unpaved road that wound along the island's coastline. I cast a look back and saw that Vanya's complex looked like a fortress in its own right from the outside.

After a short, winding drive I got my first bad surprise of the day. Rhea had driven us to a cove with a boat dock, where I got a tantalizing glimpse of a pair of fast-looking inboard motorboats and a cleared area where a white Sikorsky helicopter rested on a concrete landing pad. I've had more than a passing fancy with the history of transportation and an undying love of ships, from Phoenician triremes to Spanish galleons to the last great passenger liners of the mid-twentieth century. As for aviation, I've always been sorry I missed the chance to travel the skies in a Zeppelin airship. But as far as I'm concerned, the idea of the damn helicopter should have been abandoned right after the first autogiro. Unfortunately in my line of work, I have to ride in the noisy, cantankerous contraptions far too often for my liking.

Rhea brought the little Jeep to the edge of the landing pad and waved to the pilot, a dark-skinned man in a dazzlingly white uniform, who smiled and waved back as he stood by the open side hatch to the passenger compartment. Rhea grabbed her bag and jacket and I followed her, climbing up the stairway and into the helicopter. I had to admit the fact that this was the most luxurious example of flying deathtrap I'd ever been inside, furnished with a pair of soft leather bench seats facing each other. I took the forward-facing starboard side and Rhea sat opposite. We strapped in while the pilot closed and locked the hatch, and before long I felt the engines start up, scattering a flock of seagulls near the water. I was just admiring the sound-reduction systems when we took off, dropping my stomach into my lap.

Rhea sat across from me, and smiled as she said, "You don't like to fly?"

"Flying's fine. It's the falling I hate."

"Funny, you didn't seem to mind that last time you were a passenger here."

She was obviously alluding to when Caitlin and I were brought to the island while unconscious. "If I'd known we were flying in one of these things, I'd have asked to be knocked out again," I said.

Once we leveled out, I looked out the windows and tried to get my bearings. I got a quick aerial view of Vanya's complex—roughly U-shaped against a scrubby tree-covered hillside, with the garden in the middle. I also saw, on the other side of the living quarters, the oblong shape of the combination amphitheater/colosseum Caitlin told me about. The apex of the little island sported a series of antennas and radio dishes at the highest point.

We were traveling north across dazzling water with the rising sun on our starboard side, and within ten minutes I could see green, hilly land out the port-side window. Thirty minutes later the chopper veered to port and I spotted more terra firma and signs of civilization nestled within rolling green hills as we shed some altitude, flying over a small, square-shaped, tree-studded island. The helicopter flew in a circular vector, and I caught a glimpse of commercial airplanes arrayed on a tarmac as we came in for a landing.

I decided it couldn't hurt to ask my hostess, "Where are we?"

Her eyes were unfathomable behind her smoke-dark glasses. Finally, she answered, "Corfu."

Ah, the major island west of the Grecian mainland. Which put Vanya's private island well to the south in

the Ionian Sea. Not that the information was helpful—
it was still far beyond swimming distance—but it did
bring to mind those powerboats I saw at Vanya's dock.
It also brought to mind an old and honorable enemy
of mine, Niko Konstantinopoulos, a member of the
Greek police. Although I couldn't be sure that he'd be
willing to help me in my current predicament, even if
I could get word to him somehow. Niko was convinced that I was some kind of artifact looter, which I
suppose is one way of looking at my profession. He
and I clashed a few times, and I once sent him a peace
offering in the form of a small headpiece from a marble frieze looted from Greece by the British Earl of El-
gin in the early 1800s. Niko wrote back and said while
he appreciated the head, the one he really wanted was
mine. Still, at the moment, I missed the sight of his big,
mustachioed face smiling at me over a cup of Turkish
coffee while we talked about history, art, and how he
was going to send me to prison someday.

When we exited the Sikorsky, I saw that Corfu Airport was a small, 1960s-style terminal, and I noticed
a twin-engine Olympic Airline plane in the distance.
Rhea, with her leather bag over one shoulder, led me
away toward a smaller section of hangars, where I saw
a sleek-looking private jet was waiting. We walked
over and climbed aboard, and once again, I was in
the lap of airborne luxury. The twin-engine jet was
plain white on the outside, but the interior space was
plushly carpeted, with ten individual light brown
leather seats, and the cabin was richly inlaid with
dark wood paneling. "Strap in," Rhea advised. "We're
leaving as soon as we get clearance."

I selected one of the forward-facing chairs, and Rhea strapped in right across from me, despite all the available room we had. Her jasmine scent washed over me, and I was starting to wonder if the smell would now and forever be associated with poison somewhere in the back of my mind. One of the uniformed crew, another Mediterranean type, though younger than our helicopter pilot, gave Rhea a brief nod and smile of welcome as he secured the passenger hatch, then went and locked himself into the pilot's compartment. The engine noise was far less than I would have expected in a small craft, and after a brief time taxiing into position, we accelerated smoothly and leapt off into the blue Grecian sky.

The cabin was pressurized, but my ears were still getting quite the workout from all the air travel. Once we leveled off, Rhea unbuckled her belt and said, "There's a small galley up front. I take it you can make your own coffee?"

"Yeah. It was part of my survival training. You want some?"

Rhea moved over to a wood-topped table that had a flat-screen monitor attached. "No," she said as she plugged her smartphone to a connecting wire. "I don't drink coffee."

That settled it, I thought as I made my way forward, the woman just wasn't human. The pocket-sized galley had way better accommodations than my hotel room back in New York, and I was tempted to sample some of the exotic snacks in the tiny refrigerator, but I decided to keep things simple for my stomach as I braced myself against the roll and pitch of the flight while I brewed up some Sumatra and used one of the thick ceramic mugs secured in the rack.

With coffee in hand, I joined Rhea at the table. She swung the monitor screen so we could both see it, displaying a reproduction of the French castle. "We came up with a plan after you left us last night," she said.

I stared at the castle's outline, shaking my head again at the haphazard montage of fortifications. "A plan," I echoed. "Something tells me I'm really going to hate whatever it is you have in store for me."

Her beautiful golden-hued face lit up with a smile. "Well, we do expect fair service in return for that Egyptian scroll you want."

"With my luck, that scroll is probably nothing more than Cleopatra's shopping list, but do go on."

Rhea tapped her phone, and the image was replaced by a photograph of Ombra. It almost looked like a postmortem shot. "Simply put," Rhea said in a matter-of-fact tone, "we want you to approach whoever is in charge at the castle and tell them that we are willing to exchange Ombra for all the information they have in relation to the Fouché document. Specifically, all information relating to Egyptian treasure Fouché refers to in his letter."

"The treasure you assume will also contain the remains of Alexander," I said. "Great. Except for the fact that Ombra's people appear to be total religious fanatics. For all we know, Ombra's already considered a martyr to the cause. What's to stop them from just killing me? After they laugh themselves silly, of course."

Rhea shrugged. "They probably don't have that much sense of humor. But we do have contingency plans, of course."

"Like what? Something that doesn't include me getting killed?"

"As a former agent of your government, I'm sure you're familiar with things being on a 'need to know' basis. What you don't know, you can't reveal to the enemy."

My right hand tingled, like it had a memory of its own. "I think it's only fair to tell you," I said, "that I don't do well in captivity."

"All the more reason to not let you know all of the plans. But I think you underestimate your resilience. You were certainly able to resist my attempts at persuasion, as I recall. Or is it that you don't care for older women?"

"*Au contraire,* I adore older women. Cleopatra, Boudicca of the Iceni, Zenobia, the list of my former crushes is almost endless. So, see? You're just too young for me."

"I'm not as young as that wife of yours."

"Well, let's just say she's a remarkable woman."

Rhea's dark eyes took on a speculative cast. "Yes, she must be. She's being remarkably calm about all this. Far more so than I'd expect a pampered American princess to be."

It was high time to get Caitlin off of Rhea's radar. "Well, that's why I married her. So, where are we going now?"

"I see," Rhea said, with just a hint of suspicion. She glanced at her watch. "We'll be landing in Geneva in less than three hours. I suggest we try to rest. We'll have a long day ahead of us."

Resting was far more easily said than done. I couldn't keep the vision of the castle from looming in my imagination. I occupied myself by checking out the jet, and noted the fact that I was flying in a Dassault Falcon 2000EX, just in case the Argo Foundation ever decided to invest in some decent aerial transportation, then spent the balance of the flight cursing my fate and longing for the days when I was a simple thief and smuggler of antiquities. Throughout all this time, Rhea sat still with eyes closed, apparently oblivious to the world.

Sooner than I would have liked, the jet began its descent. I saw the airport laid out below us, looking like a giant aircraft carrier set near the waters of Lake Geneva. The pilot was skilled and the landing smooth. Just as smooth as the reception we received from the guys at customs. The uniformed officers practically fell all over themselves to be accommodating to Rhea, barely giving my beat-up old passport a second glance. This was a novel experience for me, as I was used to either sullen suspicion or outright bribe pandering from the border guards I usually had dealings with. Rhea, who chatted with the uniformed officials in conversational French, was receiving the majority of the attention, and I speculated that the Swiss agents probably believed she was some kind of Japanese movie star. I also tried to get a look at her red-and-gold passport to see what name she was traveling under, but I wasn't quick enough or close enough.

We were escorted to a courtesy van and whisked

away to a small, private automobile garage, where I was introduced to our latest conveyance—a sleek gray BMW Z-4 Coupe. I checked my watch, which was now back in synch with the current time zone, and saw that it was just a little after 11:30, Sunday morning. I'd been flung halfway across Europe before lunchtime. Rhea opened the driver's side door, activated the rear hatch release, then tossed her bag in and slammed the trunk lid shut. "Can you drive?" she inquired.

"I'm American. Driving is our sacred birthright."

She grinned. "Then here's to hoping you drive better than James Dean. Get in, I'll tell you where to go."

"Most women do," I muttered. I slid behind the wheel, and fell in love even before I engaged the engine. Nick Riley had the forethought to send me to an evasive driving school in Colorado, a place that catered to professional bodyguards and diplomatic security agents, and I wondered what I could really do with a machine like this. Hopefully, I wouldn't have to find out in a hurry.

Rhea directed me out via a gated security point and onto a street that merged with the regular airport traffic. She kept busy between consulting her cell phone and waving me off in various directions as I tried to speed-read the traffic signs, until we hit a major roadway that was designated A-1. When we finally got to the point where I wasn't avoiding playing bumper cars with my fellow motorists, Rhea seemed to visibly relax as she said, "Try to keep it at one hundred kilometers per hour. And keep an eye out for the route toward Bern. We'll be staying on the Swiss side of the border for a while."

"Aye, aye. How far to the castle?"

"Not far. We should be there in an hour and a half or so."

I began to relax a bit and appreciate the magnificent view of the snowcapped Alps in the distance. Just over an hour and a couple of tollbooths later we were waved across the French border and we climbed into the lush green Jura Mountains. Rhea pointed ahead to a turn-out. "Pull over there."

I did as directed, easing the car over next to a fence that bordered a green meadow where some oddly colored red-and-white cows lounged about, probably some special breed of bovine bred to produce overpriced French cheese, I thought to myself. Rhea opened the door and got out, putting on her leather coat in the process. I joined her, and then regretted it—I wasn't dressed for the spring Alpine weather. Rhea apparently noticed my discomfort. "Open the trunk," she said.

I reached back in and activated the release. Before I pulled my head out of the interior, I heard the lid slam shut. Rhea walked toward me bearing a black leather jacket. "Here," she said. I took the coat, slipped it on, and nodded thanks. The coat felt a little stiff around the torso, and I could feel it had a heavy interior lining. "There's a layer of Kevlar inside," Rhea explained. "It should protect you from most handgun rounds."

"Really? Damn. Thanks. This makes me feel warm in more ways than one."

Rhea bowed, then graced me with a beautiful smile. "And now, Mr. Blake, I think it's time for proper introductions. My true name is Suzume Saito."

This new tack took me by surprise. "Well, hello, Ms. Saito."

"There was no way for us to speak candidly until now," she said. "It is time for you to know the truth."

"The truth about what?"

The woman's face became a rigid mask as she said, "About how Vanya intends to destroy the world."

CHAPTER TWENTY

Château du Joux, France

So there I was, staring at the green rolling hills and tall snowcapped mountains. The sun was bright, the air was fresh, and my world had just taken a decidedly screwed-up turn for the worse. I didn't respond to Rhea—or Suzume—immediately. Instead, I took out my flattened box of cigarettes and lighter, lit one up, and took in a deep, poisonous breath. I let the smoke out all at once as I said, "Please tell me you're just making the worst joke in the world."

Rhea came over beside me and leaned against the car. She didn't look at me as she said, "No. Phillip Vanya may be the most dangerous man alive. It is now within his power to murder millions."

"So you really are a Japanese secret agent?"

"Operative," Rhea corrected, "and yes, I have been sent by my government to infiltrate Vanya's operation and stop his plans."

"So what has all this to do with finding the body of Alexander the Great?"

She stared across the distance as she said, "Vanya's dream is, in his own twisted way, to save the world. To accomplish that, he's willing to kill over half the people on the planet."

I felt my head drop to my chest. "Okay, let's take this from the top. Just how is he planning to do this?"

"Vanya doesn't want to use Alexander's DNA to prove any radical religious theories. He wants to use the genetic material to create a brood of children. Children who will be raised to believe they're the natural rulers of the earth."

"Genetic material? From a mummy? That's insane."

Rhea shook her head. "No. We have the science to do this. Geneticists now have the ability to harvest the genetic material of the deceased and fuse that material to a viable human female's egg. The technique is called somatic cell nuclear transfer. The only reason it hasn't been accomplished yet is because of all the ethical restrictions in the international scientific community. But putting moral objections aside, it can be done. At least Vanya believes this to be true."

I was dimly aware of a car passing by on the road, carrying ordinary people to an ordinary destination. "But even if Vanya can use Alexander's DNA, what good will it do him?"

"Imagine a whole family of Alexander's progeny. You've seen the girls Vanya keeps in the compound? They're his potential brood mothers for his new master race. The children they will produce will all be raised to be conquerors of the world."

My mind flashed back to all the young, beautiful girls I met in Vanya's courtyard, and Vanya's own seemingly off-hand comment, "Children are the future."

"Wait," I said. "So what's the hurry? Sounds like this is one long-range pipe dream."

Rhea shook her head, almost imperceptibly. "The danger lies in the fact that Vanya knows that if word of his plans ever got out, the governments of the world would stop him, and he would be attacked. And he has already armed himself with weapons of mass retribution."

I felt an icicle sink into my guts as I asked, "Weapons?"

"Plague virus."

I felt my jaw clench as Rhea explained, "Vanya has had his scientists, some of whom are virtual prisoners on the island, create an enhanced, highly contagious and lethal plague virus. This virus is already in the hands of Vanya's more fanatical followers throughout the world. Vanya calls this his Pandora's Box, and his plan is to decimate the world population so that by the time his 'children' are ready, they will inherit a planet with a vastly reduced population and weakened governmental infrastructures."

I began to automatically take in some more smoke, then dropped the cigarette and crushed it out. I was going to need something a lot stronger than tobacco to assimilate all this. "So why don't you just kill him? You certainly didn't mind killing those men of Ombra's back in Paris."

Rhea's tone was almost wistful. "If it were that simple, I would have done it long ago. Vanya is a highly paranoid man. He's told me more than once that if he were to die suddenly, he's taking the world with him. His death will be a sign for all his worldwide followers to trigger the plague weapons they have. And hard as I've worked to prove myself to him, he still doesn't trust me completely, and I don't have the list of his followers who are already armed with the plague."

"So he's got an army of biological suicide bombers? Where'd he find that many crazy people?"

"They're innocent true believers," Rhea said with cold clarity. "They don't know they're holding biological weapons of mass destruction. They believe they are Vanya's Chosen Few, and that the devices they've been entrusted with are actually signaling devices to be activated during the Second Coming of our Brethren from Space. But Vanya's plan need not rely entirely on his followers—he can trigger all the devices remotely via worldwide broadcast as well."

The weight of her words was as heavy as if the surrounding mountains had just fallen on top of me. "Now what? We just go along with this plan to dig up Alexander's corpse? How's that supposed to help stop Vanya?"

Rhea stepped away from the car and stood right in front of me, close enough for a kiss. "Yes," she said with low-voiced intensity. "We go along with it. Because the only hope is to make Vanya believe that we are on his side, until we can find his list of agents and neutralize them. Hopefully before it's all too late."

"We've got to tell people about this."

She shook her head, almost imperceptibly. "That is not a good idea. I believe Vanya and his people have already infiltrated your own government. Just last year, an American agent tried to join the Children of Cronos under cover. Vanya found out his identity and had him murdered."

I felt my jaws clench as I remembered hearing about

an agent getting killed during my briefing back in New York, and it pumped up my own paranoia to a heightened state of awareness. "So you're saying we're all alone on this?"

"Yes. Although now there are two of us." She looked downward and said, almost shyly, "I am very glad you are here. I have been all alone, living with the enemy, for a very long time. But now we have to prepare to deal with what may lie ahead and keep our secret between the two of us."

"How many more will you kill just to prove you're Vanya's pet?"

"As many as I have to," she said simply. "What I do, I do for my country and the people of Japan. The question is, what are you willing to do for your people?"

I didn't answer. All I knew at that moment was that she was standing way too close, and it felt like she was suffocating me. Finally, she shook her head, slowly. "You Americans; you lack the will and the strength to do what's necessary, even to defend your own people. If you understood the Japanese way, your path would be clear."

"And your way is better?"

"My way is simply efficient; Vanya is a threat, a threat my government has sent me to eliminate."

"So Vanya really was responsible for the nerve gas attack on the Tokyo subway?"

"Not directly," she said. "But there were enough connections that I was assigned to the case. This is where the trail has led me."

I thought back to what Mr. Jonas had told me about Vanya's potential ability in regard to biological warfare, but he'd never mentioned the possibility of Vanya creating his own army of New Age Alexanders. However, it was Rhea's words about Japan that brought everything into focus for me. I'd been sent to her country during my early Argo training. I was the guest of a family living on the outskirts of the Koga prefecture, where I was a student of a man who taught me many useful and dangerous techniques. The fragile-appearing elderly man who trained me didn't speak a word of English, so his fourteen-year-old granddaughter would translate. I never forgot how she would cover her face and giggle when the old man would throw me around the dojo, or twist me up into interesting and painful positions. But when the old man would speak, the girl would become completely serious as she looked downward and translated things like: "Grandfather says you are hopelessly clumsy, and he is afraid you will be here for a very long time."

So if Rhea was willing to do whatever was necessary to stop Vanya from wrecking the world for the sake of her people, then well and good. As for me, I knew I'd do it just for the memory of a young girl I'd never see again. Besides, the world was screwed up enough without having a horde of egomaniacal, psychopathic Alexanders loosed upon it.

My eyes refocused to find Rhea still standing too close to me. "What are you thinking?" she asked gently.

"I was thinking that even if your story is half true, Vanya needs to be stopped."

She nodded. "Good. Then we are partners?"

I remembered something I'd said to Vanya. "I'm in. All the way. So now what?"

"We should get a look at this castle. I believe we are very close now."

We got back inside the German road rocket and I let Rhea direct me while she consulted her phone. I zipped along the winding mountain pass until Rhea held up her hand. "Stop. We're here."

I pulled over to the side and shut the engine down. From the car's interior, I saw an abundance of green trees on the hillsides, past low, red-roofed, white-walled houses near the crossroads. I got out of the car, looked around, and then up. And up.

It looked like someone had planted a castle at the very peak of a narrow mountain, crowning the top. The mountain itself was clad in bright green foliage, offset by the dusty red tiles of the roofs of the castle fortifications, set in irregular shapes atop the gray granite walls and turrets. Even at this great distance, the fortress looked as impregnable as any I've ever seen.

I was aware through my peripheral vision that Rhea had gone to the trunk of the car. She came and stood beside me, handing me a pair of Steiner 10×50 binoculars. When I focused on the castle, the magnified view made me feel that many times worse, and I felt a chill that had nothing to do with the cold mountain air. "You have got to be kidding me," I murmured.

Rhea tapped my arm. "What's that over there?"

I swung the glasses in the indicated direction and saw, across a deep divide, another stone fortification, smaller and not as elaborately eccentric in design. "Great. Which one are we supposed to go and get ourselves killed in?"

I heard Rhea tapping on her cell phone. "Ah. The smaller one must be one called Fort du Larmont. We want the big one."

"The big one," I echoed. "Naturally. Want to bet they have a functional dungeon?"

"Why not? The place was supposed to be a prison at one time."

Rhea took a quick but careful look around. "Open the trunk," she said. This was the first time I'd gotten a look inside the luggage area. Besides Rhea's black leather shoulder bag, I saw two large, silver-colored metal cases. Rhea tripped the combination lock on one of the cases. I caught a quick glimpse of electronic gear nestled inside protective foam. Rhea picked up a small, black plastic rectangle the size of a pack of playing cards. She thumbed a switch, and I saw a tiny green light activate. "Here," she said, "put this in your inside coat pocket."

I did as asked, then said, "What is it?"

"It's a tracking device. So I can find you again." She took another quick look around then said in a conspiratorial tone, "Now, do you want a gun?"

That remark made me look around in a guilty manner. "A gun?" I whispered. Rhea gave me a serious nod. "No," I replied. "It might make me look like I had dishonorable intentions. I'm supposed to be a diplomatic go-between, right?" I truly was tempted by the offer of a real weapon, but I figured anything less than a rocket-propelled grenade launcher wouldn't help much with storming my way into, or especially out of, a fortified castle.

Rhea shut the trunk lid and held out her hands for

the car keys, which I reluctantly handed over. I was really getting to love driving the little German beast. I took my place in the passenger seat and Rhea expertly drove us toward the castle. In all too short a time, she pulled into a turnoff at a sign that informed us we were heading to the town of La Cluse et Mijoux, a small village of provincial cream-colored buildings with red-tiled roofs. Rhea pulled up at the base of a steep drive marked with a sign for the Château de Joux. She kept the engine purring as she said to me, "Remember, the deal is we will release Ombra to them in return for the Fouché letter, or any information they have on the location of Alexander's tomb." She handed me a slip of paper and a digital photograph of Ombra. I glanced at the photo—it was the same one I saw in the private jet, and he didn't look good in the picture at all. "Once they agree, have them call that number on the paper for further arrangements."

"Is that deal contingent on them letting me get out alive?"

She smiled. "Don't worry. I have some emergency plans of my own. I'm not about to lose you now." And before I could move, she grabbed the back of my neck and pulled me to her, kissing me with strength and passion, a kiss I automatically responded to for the wild, heady moment it lasted.

When she broke her hold, she leaned back and laughed, a pleasant, crystalline sound. "Sorry," she said insincerely. "Call that the sealing of our partnership. Come back to me, and together we'll figure a way to stop Vanya once and for all."

I just nodded like an idiot and fumbled my way out

of the car. Once I shut the door, she took off, burning the road in a wide, swinging one-eighty, and roared off back through the town, earning a raised fist from an elderly man riding an old, shaky bicycle. I took in a deep, cleansing breath of Alpine air mixed with a tincture of burnt tire and petrol, and let it all out. But I didn't shake the lingering warmth of Rhea's kiss.

I started my hike up along the steep climbing path toward the castle, setting myself an easy pace, as I wasn't used to the altitude yet. And truth be told, I wasn't in any hurry to deliver myself to the enemy. "Killing the Messenger" was an age-old tradition throughout the world, and I started to wonder what Odysseus would do in my situation. That got me thinking about the old adage in regard to accepting gifts from Greeks.

I stopped my trek and caught my breath in the cold air, feeling along the sides of the leather coat Rhea gave me. The Kevlar lining was built into the vest, leaving the arms of the jacket more supple. I took out the black box from my inside coat pocket. The box was coated in some kind of flat black material, and it didn't weigh much at all. It was featureless with the exception of a small sliding switch and the green light on one of the sides. Rhea said it was a tracking device, and apparently Vanya's technology was way behind the U.S. government's, if you compared this thing to the wedding ring Caitlin gave me that performed the same function.

Out of curiosity, I snapped the switch, and the green light extinguished. I then got my pocket tool and went to work on four small screws that held one side in place. I popped the lid off and saw the expected array of transistors and diodes. Along with a one-ounce square of plastic explosive nestled within the device.

The bitch was planning to kill me.

I felt a freezing trill run along my spine that had nothing to do with the chill air, and my hands began to tremble. Then I laughed, glad I didn't have an audience, since I didn't sound entirely sane in the process. Rhea had slipped me a perfect one-shot murder device. With the box in my jacket pocket next to my heart, Rhea could explosively pulverize my chest while standing right next to me, since the Kevlar lining would contain the shrapnel. It was murderously ingenious.

I carefully peeled the plastique out of its hardwire nest and closed up the box, losing one of the screws in the process due to my unsteady fingers. I switched the box back on and replaced the device back inside my jacket. I then took a couple of other precautions, and finally rewarded myself with one of my dwindling supply of cigarettes, letting the smoke smooth over my nerves.

I looked out over the postcard-perfect green hills and valley, as if seeing it all for the first time, while recalling the words of Winston Churchill, who maintained that there was no more exhilarating feeling in the world than to be shot at and missed. It was a feeling that I certainly never tired of. But the euphoria was fleeting as I realized my world had once again taken an enormous downward turn for the worse: On the path ahead of me was a fortified castle containing ruthless enemies, while behind me was a treacherous assassin and the worldwide army of a maniacal madman who had Caitlin in his clutches. And here I was, all alone in the world, trapped between the two, caught betwixt the hammer and the anvil.

It was high time to even up the odds.

CHAPTER TWENTY-ONE

I finished the rest of the winding uphill climb, all the while keeping my eyes on the looming presence of the Castle Joux. The cold air and all the trees were somewhat alien to me. Usually when I was surrounded by this much greenery it meant that I was in the midst of sweltering jungle growth. But the view of the castle itself was almost majestic enough to make me forget I was walking straight into a double-sided trap.

As I reached the apex, I saw an empty parking lot and a tunnel ahead cut through a low green hill. The chateau, with its collage of styles and designs, looked like it was grown right from the limestone rocks at the base of the plateau, which were then cut into roughly rectangular bricks in varying shades of gray, crowned in slanted roof tiles of faded, rust-colored terra cotta, with numerous gray stone chimneys sprouting forth. The path led to a stone tunnel that curved to the right. A sign affixed to the wall announced in French that I was at the Château de Joux, originally built in AD

1034. The sign also mentioned three of the chateau's distinguished prisoners: Mirabeau, Kleist, and Toussaint L'Ouverture. I hoped I wouldn't add my name to the list.

The tunnel opened up to the massive outer wall of the castle, with the words "Fort de Joux" chiseled above the stone portal. All of the ancient stonework of the castle was weathered with the weight of centuries, brightened here and there with tufts of mossy green that sprouted through the cracks. Once through the outer wall and under a raised iron portcullis I was greeted by another tunnel, which brought me to an actual drawbridge with a pointed archway. Here I spotted some modern touches in the metal guardrails and the inactive floodlights at the base, along with metal grates laid down on the path to accommodate vehicle traffic, but the archway itself was adorned with bas-relief carvings of late-medieval-era arms and armor. The beauty of the drawbridge portal was stolen by the long, ugly drop to the rocky bottom of the chasm it spanned. Just across I could see a rounded castle turret on the right that was married to a solid, rectangular wall—different centuries of fortifications mated together. I was surprised to see actual windows in evidence; I was still expecting to be greeted by arrow slits.

The archway led to another bridge that spanned a dry moat filled with green grass. I crossed the bridge and entered a narrower stone tunnel built through the inner defensive wall of the castle. I hurried through this somewhat claustrophobic artery with visions of old-fashioned murder holes and other historical castle defenses dancing in my head. Once back into the sunlight, I was now at the threshold of an irregular-shaped inner courtyard with tall Renaissance-era walls set with a plethora of windows and doors on one side, across from medieval fortifications on the other. Straight ahead was a melded mix that looked like a brick house was half-swallowed into the defensive wall with a rough-planked wooden door and a narrow single window. The nearest turret sported arrow slits that would accommodate modern rifle fire far too well for my comfort. Near this door I saw a black Volvo sedan parked next to a small white van. It looked like someone was at home.

I crossed the courtyard, feeling like I was under the gun from the numerous paned windows in the tall, gray stone walls, took a breath, then pounded on the door. The minute or so I stood awaiting a reply seemed to stretch into eternity, until one wing of the doors opened a fraction and revealed the half-shadowed face of a woman. "The museum is closed, monsieur," she said.

"I'm here on behalf of Mr. Ombra," I replied. "He sent me here."

The woman hesitated for a fraction of a second. "Ombra? I'm sorry, monsieur; there is no one by that name here."

I held up the photograph of Ombra, level with the woman's eyes. "This man," I said firmly. "And while we're speaking, would you tell me why you decided to address me in English?"

Her eyes, which were a pale, almost colorless blue, wrinkled in what may have been a smile. "A moment, please," she said as she closed the portal. I heard the sound of metal clanking behind the door, and then the right-side wing opened with a creaking groan. "Come in," I heard.

I walked through the entryway, noting the solid thickness of the walls, and took a step to the side as the door was pushed closed. My eyes tried to adjust from the transition of late-afternoon sunshine to the gloomy interior. In the half-darkness, my hostess turned toward me and I saw I was standing in front of a tall, slender woman with long, silver-gray hair that spilled over the full-length black coat she wore. Her face was the color of parchment and etched with fine lines of age on small, delicate features. "Thank you, madame," I said. "I have news of the utmost importance."

She smiled, and said in a lilting accent, "I do not believe you should be thanking me quite yet, Monsieur Blake. But you are correct; we do have business."

"Wait, how do you know my name?" The words were no sooner out of my mouth than I heard a series of metallic clicking sounds coming from behind me as an overhead electric light came on. I turned, slowly, while keeping my hands in plain view, and saw a sight that dropped my heart down to my guts. A youngish, bearded man was standing in the darkened recesses of the room, dressed in casual denim clothes with a dark woolen cap—the last time I saw his face we were both deep under the Paris catacombs, inside Napoleon's hidden treasure chamber. He was armed, of course, and at first I thought I was being covered by a sawed-off shotgun, but as my eyes adjusted, I saw the man was pointing an antique twin-barreled flintlock pistol at me. The orifices of the gun looked like they were about .70 caliber, a numbed, detached part of my brain reported to me. The man's dark eyes flashed in angry recognition as he half-whispered, *"Merde! C'est l'homme!"*

I slowly raised my hands. "I'm not armed. I'm here to talk."

The woman, who had stepped away from me and out of the line of fire, nodded and smiled, only the smile didn't seem to be so pleasant now. "So you shall, Monsieur Blake. So you shall." She gestured to her companion as he came down the stairs, his eyes as unblinking as the barrels of the gun. He motioned toward the castle interior, the gun twitching in time with his head, like they were connected by invisible string. *"Après vous,"* he said.

"Look, we don't have time for this," I began.

"Mr. Blake," the woman interrupted. "My young man there would be more than happy to shoot you in your legs and drag you along. The choice is up to you."

The man with the elderly hand cannon understood enough English to grin at the thought, but not enough to completely follow directions as he lowered the gun to point at my groin. I did as told and moved from the antechamber into a passage with a low, arched ceiling, but my attention was on my captors behind me. "We're running out of time," I said over my shoulder, my voice sounding hollow in the stonework hall. "I've reason to believe this place will be attacked at any moment. You're in danger."

The woman's voice held a musical, if slightly contemptuous quality as she said, "I would not be concerned with that, Mr. Blake. I believe you will find we are most secure in here. Now, no more talking."

I shut up and let my guards direct me through a confusing series of twists and turns among the shadowed halls. We'd left the lighted area and moved into the interior, and one of my captors turned on a flashlight behind me. The odds just weren't good enough that I could take them both out under these conditions; what I needed to do was start talking my way out of this. But I wasn't going to get the chance until they had me where they wanted me, and at the moment I was busy mentally counting steps and turns in the event I was able to run out of here. I was directed to an old wooden bookcase that had been moved aside to reveal a man-sized archway cut into the stonework. Once through the arch, I was inside a circular, vertical tunnel built like a well, with stairs coiling around the walls and leading straight down. A damn long way down. As we descended, it felt like I was being swallowed by a gigantic snake of mythic proportions.

When we finally reached the bottom of the circular staircase, we arrived at another opening. It felt much colder down here than in the air outside, and I realized I must be in the heart of the mountain. At the base of the stairwell was a chamber that opened to three low tunnels, cut out of the rock like mine shafts. I was directed toward one, and saw that it terminated at an open, rusty iron door with a large, old-fashioned key left in the lock. It was this final chamber that manifested my worst fears as the weaving light from behind me exposed the iron bars and chains riveted to the solid rock wall. They had taken me to the dungeon.

I turned around and saw the woman place a large, handheld lantern on a low wooden table. She switched the light from a white spotlight to a red area lamp, illuminating the chamber in blood-colored light. The man handed the big pistol to the woman, and then pushed me back against a wall. I could have taken him out right then and there, but not before the woman could have blown my head off from across the room. He raised my hands and I felt him clamp cold irons around my wrists. When he had my hands locked up, he unzipped my jacket and ran his hands across my body in all the obvious places a gun could be hidden while missing the flat black box in my inside jacket pocket. He then stepped back and placed a key on the table, taking the gun back from the woman. I pulled at my restraints and heard chains rattle while feeling a small shower of rust particles fall on the back of my neck.

My insistent hosts spoke in low, fast French with their heads together. Finally, the man placed the pistol on the table and with a final hateful look toward me, he took out a flashlight and left the room. The woman seated herself on a plain wooden chair, the red lamp bathing her face the color of burning coal. "Well, now that we are comfortable, tell me all about this danger we are supposedly in."

There was something in her pleasant-sounding, matter-of-fact speech that turned my guts colder than the stone wall I was chained to. "Listen," I said urgently, "I don't know what you've been told, but right now a man named Philip Vanya, who has his own private army, believes you're holding something he wants, something he's willing to kill for."

"And what would that something be?"

"He's looking for the lost sarcophagus of Alexander the Great, and he believes that Joseph Fouché knew where it was hidden by Napoleon Bonaparte."

I almost held my breath waiting for her reply to my

fantastic claim, but I only heard her make a small sigh as she said, "Ah, Fouché. Dead all these years, and still he causes trouble."

She was speaking as if she were discussing a slightly unruly child. "So," I said, "it's true?"

She ignored my question. "Tell me, Mr. Blake, what is your part in all of this? And why are you betraying your own people to me?"

"They're not my people. I've been forced to work for Vanya."

"Forced?" she replied in a disbelieving tone. "You were seen in Paris, and I was told how you ruthlessly killed our men while pursuing one of Fouché's little trinkets. No, you are no innocent at all."

I rattled my chains. "I'm in no position to argue," I said. "But you've got to believe me when I say none of this is going to matter when Vanya's men come crashing in here."

She was as unmoved by my voice as a glacier. "Mr. Blake, do you know what the word 'oubliette' means?"

"It means 'place of forgetting'; it's where people used to toss prisoners."

"It's was the end of the world for some," she said. "And you, I'm afraid, are now in your own personal oubliette. This is but one of many secret places hidden within the castle's walls, like the needle in the haystack. You should feel honored—when the tourists come, they only get to see a, how do you say? A mockup of a dungeon. No one will ever find you here. As for an army coming to attack us? I think you will find our fortifications adequate."

I nodded to the firearm on the table. "What, you're going to repel attacking boarders with antique muzzleloaders? I told you, Vanya has an army, with automatic weapons and plastic explosives. Probably nerve gas, too."

"Now you are just trying to frighten an old woman," she calmly replied.

"Fine. If you have all the answers, then why are you keeping me around?"

She looked away, her face falling into shadow. "I would like for you to tell me the truth," she said. "The man you know as Ombra, he is alive?"

"Yes. The last time I saw him, anyway, about twenty-four hours ago."

"And he was in good health?"

I hesitated. "No."

"I see," she said slowly. She looked toward me again, and now the lantern showed her face looking as hard as carved amber. "Then it may interest you to know that your fate and Ombra's are linked. For your sake, it is hoped he is still alive."

"At least you have concern for your men."

"He is my husband," she replied simply.

"Oh," was all I could say, feeling my hope sink like a rock in a pond. "Wait, I was told there was going to be a trade—you get Ombra back in exchange for Fouché's document."

"Truly?" she asked, her face a blood-colored mask. "I was told something quite different."

"What?"

"I was told that the man who was responsible for my husband's imprisonment would be delivered to me, and I could do with him what I will."

"The man who . . ." I didn't believe my predicament could get any worse, and just then I discovered how enormously wrong I could be. "Wait a goddamn minute," I said. "Whatever you've been told, I am not the man responsible."

"So someone is lying, yes? No matter. I will have the truth soon enough. As for being responsible, consider this: We would never have had to destroy the hidden chamber of Val de Grâce, except for you. I assure you, monsieur, that I and my people will go to any lengths to perform our duty."

"What do you mean by that? What duty?"

She leaned back on her chair. "You'll see."

"What exactly was the deal you made?"

"It won't matter to you," she said with cold indifference. Then she laughed softly, shaking her head. "So you believe that Fouché's paper will lead you to the body of Alexander the Great? Ah, well. You are not the first man to seek after secrets best kept buried. I can promise you this: Whatever else may come, no one who comes here will get their hands on any of Fouché's records, no matter what."

"So that means the document is here? In this castle?"

"For now," she admitted slowly. "But it will soon be gone and safe for another hundred years at least."

"Then what the hell are you waiting for? Get out now, while you still can."

Madame Ombra tilted her head to one side, studying me like I was a specimen pinned to a board. "You appear concerned for me? Even now?"

"Look, lady, I don't know what you're guarding here that's so important you're willing to kill for it, but unless your particular religion encourages martyrdom, you're going to wind up dying for the cause."

For the first time, she looked genuinely surprised.

"Religion? What does religion have to do with anything?"

"What? Wait ... Vanya said that your people are trying to stop him from finding the body of Alexander because he could cause a worldwide crisis of faith, changing the foundations of the world's religions. But if you don't care about that, then what ... ?"

She gave me an almost pitying look. "Mr. Blake, I am very afraid you have involved yourself with something that has caused the death of many men, and women, before you for hundreds of years. For what it is worth, I am sorry if it comes to that for you. I only wish I could tell you why."

I rattled my chains a bit. "Why not? Sounds like I'm already condemned. Whatever happened to the tradition of the last request?"

She shook her head slowly. "No. My people have been entrusted with the task of keeping secrets, and we have faithfully done so for hundreds of years. And we have not become as old as we have without learning to be cautious. The only question you need to concern yourself with is will there be daylight for you tomorrow? You must forget everything else."

"Like I told you before, lady. I'm not the one in trouble here. You're the one facing an imminent invasion."

She didn't speak for a moment, and silently regarded me with narrowed eyes. "You are not lying?"

"Hell, no. I just figured it out myself. I was sent in here as a diversion, like a Trojan horse's ass. An expendable one at that."

The woman in black held up her hand for silence. "I believe we may both have our answers now," she said. I heard the sounds of footsteps approaching and the creak of the iron prison door.

Rhea was smiling as she entered the red-lit ante-chamber of hell. "Hello, Jonathan," she purred. "Have you missed me?"

"Like a plague," I replied. "What are you doing here? Wait, let me guess—you cut a side deal with our hostess here."

Madame Ombra remained seated when Rhea entered, followed by the young bearded man who'd escorted me down here. He was holding a modern pistol now, and he looked flushed and winded from climbing up and down the long, circular staircase.

Madame Ombra stood and said sternly to Rhea, "You were not to send Monsieur Blake to me until midnight. That was our arrangement."

"Sorry," Rhea replied insincerely. "Change of plan."

I rattled my chains, getting another shower of itchy rust particles down the back of my neck. "Would this be a good time for me to say 'I told you so' about this being a trap?"

Rhea replied, "Don't be upset, Jonathan. I got a good price for delivering you here. We've had Ombra's cell phone since we picked him up in Paris—that's how we contacted his organization. So sorry if we gave you the impression that you were actually joining us." Rhea faced the woman in black and said, "As you see, I've kept my end of the bargain."

"So it appears," the woman replied coolly. "However, I have some questions."

"Oh?" Rhea said silkily. "Has Blake been telling stories again?"

"Indeed. But more to the point, I believe we need to

alter our agreement. You said you'd deliver Monsieur Blake to me in exchange for a certain document. I agreed at the time, but I'm sorry to inform you that I never intended to keep to that bargain. Now, you and Monsieur Blake will remain here with us until the man you call Ombra is released."

"A double cross?" Rhea said, nodding as if in agreement. "I see."

In the blink of an eye, Rhea took a fast side step and hurled Madame Ombra into the wall, then she raised her hand and pointed toward Ombra's bodyguard, all the while smiling like the maniacal Cheshire cat. Madame Ombra's boy was fast, and he had the gun aimed at Rhea and was pulling the trigger in rapid staccato snaps; only the gun wasn't firing. Then came the ear-splitting *crack* and flash from Rhea's hand, and the man's head snapped back as he collapsed to the ground like all of his bones had disconnected at once.

Rhea glided in behind the table, reached down, and pulled Madame Ombra to her feet. Rhea's hand was under the older woman's chin, and in the red light I caught the faintest glimmer from a sliver of steel. "Now," Rhea purred, "about our agreement?"

Madame Ombra, her voice strained by holding her neck away from Rhea's blade, said, "I will never give you what you seek."

Rhea laughed. "You don't need to. I already know the location of your hidden library."

Madame Ombra's eyes betrayed her surprise as Rhea continued, "Don't blame your husband. He stood up very well to the physical torture. It was the drugs that got to him. By the time I was done, he truly believed everything I was telling him. And he wanted one more thing: He wanted you to know how much he loved you."

Madame Ombra didn't have time to reply as Rhea, fast as a snake, dropped her hand down the woman's back and with a hiss, made a vicious strike. I saw Madame Ombra's body arch in pain, and then she slowly slid down to the floor. Rhea had used her blade on the woman's kidneys, a professional, lethal stab. Madame Ombra could have been dead before she hit the ground.

Rhea made a contended sigh, then said, "Well, Jonathan, it's just you and me now."

Rhea didn't make a sound as she crossed the floor to me, the red light now behind her, hiding her face. She was like a Shadow of Death, taking its time in coming for me.

CHAPTER TWENTY-TWO

As Rhea approached, the scent of her jasmine perfume mingled with the smell of burnt gunpowder and fresh blood. I suddenly felt the pain in my wrists, caused by my unconscious act of impotently lunging against my iron restraints as Rhea murdered Madame Ombra and her man. As she reached up for my face, my jaws clenched in fear and revulsion. Her leather-clad hand stroked my cheek as she said in a soft and soothing voice, "I'm sorry things didn't work out differently between us."

"Did you have to kill them?"

"I told you I was willing to do whatever is necessary."

"So everything you said about Vanya, all that talk about his unleashing a plague—"

"Is all true," she said calmly. "And I am going to change the world with him."

With the red light behind her, I couldn't see her face. "Now what?" I asked, trying to keep my voice calm.

"The plan remains the same. Only you are no longer a part of it. I convinced Vanya that you were just too dangerous to keep around." Rhea ran her hands down my chest, her fingers lingering over the flat box she had given me, which still rested in my jacket pocket. "Do you have any final messages for that wife of yours?" she asked.

I felt my teeth clench. "If you're smart, you'll keep Caitlin alive."

"Oh? Why?"

"Because the way you're going, sooner or later, you'll need a hostage."

"What makes her so special?"

I couldn't think of anything more creative than the truth. "Because she's a government agent."

Rhea laughed, softly. "Oh, really? Well, if she is, then I would say that America is in very sad shape indeed."

Rhea turned and went back to the table. She picked up the flintlock pistol and examined it curiously, then carefully set it back down. Then she picked up the electric lantern and switched the light from the gentle red glow to the bright white spotlight that fired directly in my face. I screwed my eyes shut against the painful glare, waiting for God knows what to happen. Then I finally heard Rhea say, "I think I want to remember you, just as you are now."

The light slid off my face and I blinked my eyes, trying to coax them back to work as I heard the groan of the iron door, along with Rhea's pleasant-sounding laughter. I heard a muted clanging sound, and as the afterburn of the light cleared from my eyes, I realized I'd been left alone in the dark with the dead. Moments later I heard a sizzling, crackling sound coming from inside my jacket and the faint smell of burnt insulation mingled with the dank, blood-soaked odor of the dungeon. Rhea had triggered the explosive killing device near my heart. If I hadn't removed the C-4 charge first, I'd now be the third corpse in this tomb.

So there I was, chained to a wall in an ancient dungeon and left for dead in utter darkness. It was time to get the hell out of here.

The key to the manacles around my wrists was over on the table. It may as well have been on the dark side of the moon. But I'd learned a long time ago all about locks and how to defeat them, even locks as old as the ones restraining me now. All I needed was a thin length of metal, narrow enough to fit into the keyway, soft enough to be bent at an angle, yet strong enough not to break as I manipulated the internal levers. I was carrying something that just might do the trick—the ink cartridge inside my pen.

The first problem was that I had my pen clipped to the inside of my front pants pocket, and my hands were chained so that I couldn't drop my arms below shoulder height. The second problem was that my hands were going numb. My scarred right hand was tingling, and I tried to tell myself that feeling was just all in my head, but my left was practically dead from the wrist up due to the fact that the manacle was clamped around my watch, and the tight fit had been squeezing the life out of my hand ever since. I took a deep breath, reached up for a grip on the chains, and with a jump pulled myself straight up. When I was as high as I could manage, I slowly released my right hand, holding myself up with my quivering left arm alone, and felt around my pocket for my pen. I grabbed it just as my overstrained left arm failed and dropped me. My feet hit the floor and my knees buckled as my arms snapped up just as the back of my head banged against the wall, sending electric shooting stars through the darkness. But I kept a grip on that pen like it held my very life.

Pulling myself up, I sent my near-lifeless fingers to work stripping the cartridge out of the pen, letting the metal shell fall and bounce on the stone floor. I felt my way to the keyhole on the manacle on my left wrist, and then inserted the slender tip of the ink cartridge, forcing it down until I had bent it into a curved piece of metal to work with. I used my improvised lock pick to probe the innards of the manacle, feeling for a piece that moved to the touch. The internal mechanics seemed to be rusted solid. Fearing I'd break my make-shift tool, I managed to put enough pressure to bear until I felt the mechanism finally give way.

I yanked my left hand free, shaking the life back into it, then went to work on the other lock. I was getting impatient, and felt something go *snap* all at once, but fortunately it was the locking lever and not my pen cartridge that gave way. I pulled my hand free, hearing the chains rattle and clink together im-potently as I rubbed the gritty rust particles off my wrists.

I'd had enough of working in the dark and I was glad my little button-sized flashlight still functioned, illuminating the chamber in its now-familiar red hue. I saw the young bearded man sprawled on the floor, his sightless eyes turned up toward the glistening, ragged hole in his forehead. I picked up the pistol that he'd dropped, then let it fall clattering to the floor. I had no doubt that this was the same gun that Rhea had offered to give me earlier, and she had obviously rigged it to be useless.

My light caught a couple of other items discarded on the floor. The first was a metal pen that I recognized as the one that belonged to Caitlin, only the tip of the pen was missing and I could smell a faint scent of gunpowder. It was some kind of concealed one-shot pistol, and Rhea had used it to kill Madame Ombra's guard. The other thing I saw was Caitlin's dark-framed sunglasses, only one of the earpieces was now missing. I curiously pulled on the remaining earpiece, and it popped free of the frame. I was now holding a slim hilt with a thin, razor-sharp blade attached. Rhea must have used the mate of this knife to murder Madame Ombra. Rhea had come prepared with Caitlin's own deadly government issue toys, and it made me wonder what else was in the collection of innocuous-looking items I had briefly been carrying.

Ahead of me I saw the table that held the manacle key and the large antique double-barreled pistol. I went over behind the table and knelt down beside the still form of Madame Ombra. She was lying on her side, and my flashlight revealed a wet, shiny patch on the lower back of her long black coat. What was almost invisible was the thin black stem of the needle-like blade protruding from her like a stinger from some monstrous insect. There was no doubt she was dead. Which is why when her eyes suddenly opened and she groaned, I damn near fell over from the shock.

"*Mon Dieu,*" she hissed.

"Stay still," I stammered. "You shouldn't move." Hell, I thought, you shouldn't be able the move at all.

She started to reach behind her with a trembling hand, then stopped. "*Ques* . . . What is wrong?"

"You've been stabbed. In the kidney. Now try to lie completely still."

For a moment, I thought she was having a seizure, and then I realized she was quietly laughing. Just as I was thinking she was falling into shock and hysteria, she whispered, "I haven't got a kidney there. I gave it to my daughter years ago. Help me up."

I did my best to gently lift her to the chair, setting her in the seat sideways and making sure the slender hilt of the knife didn't bump into anything. The knife was plugging the wound and I didn't want to disturb it. Madame Ombra leaned on the wooden table, breathing in short, shallow gasps. "Where . . . is that woman?"

"Gone. Left us both for dead. She said she knew where your library was hidden. She's no doubt going to get the Fouché document."

That squeezed another rusty laugh out of Madame Ombra. "Then she is to be . . . disappointed. Old Fouché didn't leave enough clues to matter." She focused her pale eyes on me. "I was, how you say? Stalling for time. You were not supposed to arrive here until midnight, and the rest of my men are still on their way."

"So we're all alone here?"

"*Oui,*" she wheezed. "And now you are the only one who can stop her."

"You said Fouché's document wouldn't help her."

She reached out and grabbed my sleeve with a trembling hand. "But she knows about the library! And if she finds that, she may find out what Byron knew . . . and Shelley. It's why he had to die, you see."

Her eyes filmed over and her hand dropped to the table. I was losing her. "Byron? Shelley? Wait, you mean Lord Byron? And Percy Shelley, the poets?"

Her head slowly fell forward, as if she was going to sleep. "Keep her away from . . . the Tower Mirabeau," she whispered.

I came around the table just in time to keep her from falling to the floor, and I eased her down as gently as I could, laying her on her left side. Her pulse was weak, almost fleeting, and I didn't think she'd be alive much longer. There was nothing more I could do for her here. I grabbed the heavy flintlock pistol and went for the iron door. Rhea had taken no chances; the damn thing was locked, and there was no keyhole on this side of the dungeon. But my clever little assassin had provided me with a key of a different type when she arranged to murder me.

I went back to the table and set the pistol and flashlight down, then retrieved the small square of C-4 explosive that I'd kept after I disarmed the pocket-sized bomb Rhea gave to me. I've worked with this grade of explosive before, and I knew how stable it was, but it was still a relief to quit carrying it concealed so close to my reproductive organs. I rolled the malleable explosive into a thin snake and then got out my survival matches and made up a miniature warhead to use as a detonator.

I packed the plastic explosive into the doorjamb. Now the only questions were whether the cluster of match heads would be enough to kick off a detonation, and if so, could I get my hand the hell out of the way before I got it blown off? Only one to way to find out, I thought grimly. I went back to the table and set

it on its side as a shield for the supine Madame Ombra, put the flintlock pistol on the far side of the room,
then went back to the door and readied my lighter. I
briefly wondered who the Patron Saint of Explosions
was, and then I lit the C-4 and jumped for the corner,
covering my ears and averting my eyes.

I was there long enough to feel like a dismal failure,
when suddenly the concussive thunderclap knocked me
stupid. I had to take a moment to reorient my blinded
eyes and ringing ears. My flashlight showed the
heavy iron door had buckled near the keyway, and it
still resisted my efforts to open it. I had to slam my
body against the door three times, feeling like I was
being speared in my previously wounded ribs with every attempt, until I forced a narrow passage open. I
retrieved the antique pistol, and took one last look at
the woman in black, holding a fleeting hope that she
was still alive. I took the black box remote-control killing device out of my jacket and tossed it across the
room—it may have held more nasty surprises that I
didn't need. I squeezed myself out through the door
and into the passage of the tunnel.

I took to the winding stairway like a lost soul stealing out of hell, and I was ready, willing, and able to
deal out some lethal payback to anyone who'd try to
stop me. It felt like it took forever to ascend to the top
of the tunnel, and when I reached the top I saw that
Rhea had moved the wooden bookcase back into
place, inadvertently giving me some cover. I gave myself a few moments to get my breath back, using the
time to examine the old-fashioned hand cannon. During my long course of combat and survival training
I'd been taught to shoot everything from a tiny, five-

shot derringer small enough to be hidden inside a pack
of cigarettes to a .50 caliber tank-killing rifle, but I'd
never actually fired anything this antiquated. It was because of my fascination with weapons of historical
value that I knew theoretically just how to operate this
big, two-shot horse pistol.

I carefully opened the priming pans on both sides
and made sure they held a charge of gunpowder, then
closed them up. The twin hammers were already pulled
back into firing position. I was as ready as I was going to be. Pushing the bookcase open as quietly as I
could, I slipped out into darkness, straining my abused
ears and questing for a sound. I heard nothing through
the concussion-wrought ringing in my head.

I had no idea where the Tower Mirabeau was located
in this enormous maze of fortifications, so I crept back
along the way I was brought in. I stayed close to the
walls, feeling like the confines of the rounded stone
passages made me an easy target. But before too long,
my nose gave me my heading—I could smell a current
of fresh air from ahead of me. I reached the foyer where
I'd first met Madame Ombra and saw that the overhead electric lights had been doused and the heavy
wooden door was left ajar. The slight breeze carried
something else along with it: the unmistakable staccato beating sound of an approaching helicopter.

I stepped into the foyer just as a pair of shadowed
figures emerged from a darkened side hallway. I raised
the heavy pistol and shouted: "Hold it!" just as a jet
of fire spit and my chest took a sledgehammer blow.
The gun in my hand snapped and flashed, then a split
second later a double shock of thunder erupted as a
gout of flame lit up the room, nearly breaking my wrist

and giving me a snapshot of a darkly dressed man being slammed into the stone wall.

My knees buckled from the hit I took, and I dropped to the floor. Gritting my teeth against the pain, I forced myself to stand, blinded now by darkness wreathed in the gunfire afterburn as I made my way to the door. Reaching the portal, I caught a glimpse of a running figure crossing the courtyard and headed for the open maw of the tunnel that led to the front gate. There was no doubt it was Rhea, making a hasty retreat. As I started to give chase, there was a heavy-sounding *thunk* over my shoulder. I spun around and saw the man I'd shot, now in the act of prying a large knife out of the door where my head had been a moment before.

I backed out to the open courtyard as the man freed the weapon and came stalking toward me. Moonlight caught on the blade in his hand as he crouched in a professional knife fighter's stance. My heart was hammering in my chest and my legs were shaky, aftereffects of the bullet that slammed into my chest; I'd have been dead if not for the Kevlar-lined jacket Rhea had given me. Unfortunately, the man I shot was obviously wearing the same kind of jacket.

"Blake? Rhea said that she killed you."

Though his face was shrouded in darkness, the lilting accent identified my opponent: Vandervecken, Vanya's personal mercenary. "Yeah," I panted in reply. "Want to sit down and talk about it?"

"I would," he said with a barked laugh, "but I have to fly."

Vandervecken closed in for the kill, holding the knife low. Both barrels of my gun had discharged, but the pistol itself made a good, heavy club and we circled each other like ancient warriors under the looming castle walls. I tried to keep my mind off the deepening roar of the approaching helicopter as I studied my opponent in the moonlight, searching for an opening.

He didn't give me time to find one; he came at me with a slashing, scything attack that had me backing up across the courtyard. I grabbed the barrels of my gun with my free hand and made a sweeping, upward block, then had to throw myself back to keep from having my gut slashed open when he countered with a wicked horizontal backhand swipe. I knew all at once he was too good with a knife for me to beat him in a stand-up fight. I either had to get creative or get cut to pieces.

I went for the unconventional move and threw my pistol at his head, bouncing the gun off his skull with a glancing blow as he ducked. It didn't drop him, and that was my cue to turn and run like hell. I launched myself into the tunnel, which echoed with the sound of the helicopter blades. Even so, I could still hear Vandervecken's footsteps racing up behind and gaining on me. I was slowed by the fact that my hands were busy readying my next weapon for attack. I cleared the tunnel and made for the bridge. The instant I was out of the mouth of the arch I spun and threw myself sideways, whipping my belt free and sending the heavy buckle crashing into Vandervecken's midsection.

It was his turn to back up as I swung my weighted weapon and slashed at him, missing a head strike. I kept up a flailing attack, the heavy buckle thudding into his arms as he covered up from the blows, until I had him backed up against the metal guardrail of the bridge. I dropped down and whipped the belt around his legs, grabbing the free end and pulling up with all my strength, flipping him over the railing and dropping him out into space. I lurched over to the rail and watched as Vandervecken vainly fought against the lethal pull of gravity. He didn't make a sound until he crashed into the jagged rocky bottom of the moat.

I didn't even have time to catch a breath before I was buffeted by the wind whipping from the helicopter blades. I was painfully speared by an overhead searchlight as I heard and felt the stones around me crack from an onslaught of high-velocity rifle slugs. I dove for the cover of the tunnel and kept moving blindly for the other end. If I was caught in here while they shot into the tunnel, I could get chewed up by ricochets. I had to make my way with one hand on the wall, and once I cleared the tunnel I dashed as fast as I could across the courtyard, throwing myself through the open wooden portal. I hit and rolled, then scrambled back and shoved the heavy door shut.

I reached up and threw the big iron bolt, locking myself in, then collapsed to the cold stone floor, every breath I gulped giving me a lancet of pain in my chest. Flashes of bright light that shot through the high windows and arced around the room lit the inner chamber. Then it all went dark and I heard the blessed sound of the helicopter beating a retreat across the sky. But as I lay there panting in the darkness, I was aware of a new sensation. Somewhere in the castle, something was burning.

Rhea must have found the library.

As I lay there on the ground, I briefly reflected on the fact that since I'd woken up that morning, I'd been betrayed, chained to a wall, and damn near killed half a dozen times, and now this. It was just no god-dammed fair, I thought as I pried myself off the floor and fumbled in the dark for the light switch. I blinded myself with my success, and as I blinked my eyes clear I could see a thin haze of smoke wafting out of the corridor from which Rhea and her now-deceased companion had emerged. I also spotted a black pistol with an attached silencer and a small flashlight that Vandervecken must have dropped when my antique bullets crashed into him.

I quickly replaced my belt and picked up the pistol and flashlight, using the latter to light my way as I fol-lowed the thin trail of smoke along the arched corri-dors of the castle. I was led to a larger, rounded tower room with stairs that led down to the darkened depths. My light showed me that the smoke was emanating from below, and the rounded tower was now like a giant chimney drawing up plumes. I could see flickers of fire through the obscuring clouds below.

I squinted my eyes as I went down the stairway, choking from the fumes, until I came to an enormous black iron door. The door was open, and for an instant I thought I was in front of a giant furnace. I crouched low and used my hand to shield my face from the heat as I looked inside the flaming chamber.

I was kneeling before a large room, lined with old wooden cabinets on either side. Most of the cabinets had been opened, their drawers pulled out and droop-ing from the weight of their contents. In the heart of the room was a crucible of flames, fed by a pile of pa-pers and documents heaped in a lump. Through the stinging smoke I could make out shapes within the fire: a bundle of scrolls burning like fireplace logs, a wooden box filled with old wax recording cylinders lit up like candles, the torn-out plates of an illuminated manuscript curling and blackening from the heat.

My chest was heaving with the strain of holding my breath. I had to get out quick or die here. But my anger at the sight of the destruction of all the irreplaceable historical artifacts burned hotter than the fire forcing me back. I'd be damned if I was going to let Rhea get away with destroying all of it. And with the memory of Rhea came another, a memory of what Madame Ombra had said: "Byron knew."

I lurched up and reached into the burning room, grabbing the nearest drawer to me and wrenching it free. It broke loose all at once and I fell back, kicking myself away from the fuming furnace. By the flickering light of the fire I squinted and pawed my way through the files and papers in the drawer, blessing the fact that everything was labeled alphabetically. I frantically went through to the documents starting with Bs, seeing almost all of the files were labeled "Balsamo." I was afraid I'd have to try another dive in for the next cabinet when I grabbed a small packet that felt like old oilskin. Through the pall of smoke I read the hand-printed title: "Byron, George Gordon."

I quickly stood up and rammed my shoulder into the heavy iron door, putting all my weight into it and forcing it closed behind me, then I threw myself toward the curving staircase, going up as fast as I could on shaky legs until I sprawled out through the tower's entrance, savoring the cool air near the floor that didn't try to kill me with every breath. But I didn't allow myself a respite. With every moment that passed, Rhea was getting farther away, and I knew that Madame Ombra's men were on their way to the castle. I had to keep moving. And I was going to make Rhea pay for her mistake in leaving me alive.

PART III

History is a pack of lies that others have agreed to.

—NAPOLEON BONAPARTE

The first thing I needed to do was get the hell out and find a place to hide. I hurried out of the confines of the castle, deciding not to steal one of the vehicles in the courtyard—if Madame Ombra's people were on the way, they'd spot one of their own in an instant, and I needed to leave no trace of my escape. From the vantage point outside of the chateau, I spotted a cluster of lights from a town that appeared to be only a few miles away. I checked my bearings with my little compass and verified that my destination lay northward. I made it down off the mountain in the dark, pausing only once to look back at the Castle Joux as it loomed above me, bathed in the light of a fat half-moon and wreathed in stars. I was glad to see there wasn't any smoke issuing from the towers. The steep, winding path brought me down to the two-lane road, and I quickly walked through La Cluse et Mijoux, keeping a nervous eye on the few cars that were out driving this time of night. Marching on the grassy shoulder of the highway, I managed to arrive at the town of Pontarlier before I froze to death in the cold Alpine night. If you took away the electric lights and parked cars from the old European city, you'd think you had traveled back a couple of centuries in time.

I walked the main street of the rue de la République until I could see a tall, arched clock tower toward the center of town. I was tempted to duck into the first hotel I saw, but I wanted to get off the main drag. A helpful sign along the way informed me that the local police station was located off to my left, so I instinctively turned right and found an avenue named rue Jeanne d'Arc. I put my faith in the warrior saint and she rewarded me almost instantly, as I came to a large, whitewashed, barnlike structure that proclaimed itself the Hôtel de Morteau. My Seamaster watch had picked up more occluding scars in its crystal, but as I entered the blessedly warm French provincial lobby of the hotel I could see that it was just after eleven o'clock, Sunday night.

I put on my best smile and rubbed my chilled hands together as I approached a long-faced concierge who greeted me with a lugubrious expression. His countenance brightened as I produced a wad of euros and a rambling story about losing my traveling companions and luggage, and we came to the agreement that there was a room for me at the inn. Could I make a telephone call to the United States from my room? *Oui,* I was told, if I would be so kind as to give him a *carte bancaire?* I produced my Argo Foundation credit card and passport with a bit of awkward juggling, as

I was holding the oilskin packet I took from the castle under my arm to keep the bullet hole in my jacket covered up. He laboriously took my information from my passport as I struggled to keep my frozen smile from melting off my face until he finally gave me my room key. I left a financial *merci* with the innkeeper and went to find my lodging.

My room was a small single on the second floor, painted in an unattractive salmon color, with vintage wood furnishings. I went for the bathroom, and when I caught a look at my face in the mirror, I was retroactively surprised that the concierge didn't automatically call for the gendarmes. I washed up, letting the warm water thaw out my hands, then I drank my fill to ease my ragged, smoke-burned throat. I dried off and took my salvaged package to the single table in the room.

I took off my armored leather jacket, then removed the pistol I'd recovered from the castle from the small of my back, where it had been grinding a hole in my flesh throughout my evening walk. The gun was another one of those Glock 9mms that kept turning up, and I was starting to wonder if I shouldn't buy stock in the company based on their evident popularity. I took the silencer from my pocket and rethreaded it to the barrel, then popped out the magazine and checked the load—the pistol had seven rounds left, plus one in the chamber. Quite enough to raise a lot of hell if you knew what you were doing.

I wrapped the gun in my jacket and left it at the foot of the bed on the flowered quilt, and then I turned my attention to my prize. I carefully untied the leather thong of the oilskin envelope, and gently shook the contents out onto the table. For all of the death and destruction I'd endured that night, my reward was a single sheet of paper. It was old, folded into four squares, and wrinkled as if left out in the rain once long ago. On one side of the paper was an offset paragraph in old-fashioned typeset print, so faint that it took me a moment to perceive that it was printed backwards. The thick, marbled paper was browned with age, and oddly darkened toward the center with uneven blemishes. I carefully unfolded the foolscap stationery and saw a handwritten missive in black ink that left tangible impressions from a quill pen. The ink had bled on every line, giving the cursive writing a shadow, like an aura. I held the letter to the light from the table lamp and saw that six of the words were underscored with yellowish-brown lines. I read:

To Percy Bysshe Shelley
Villa Dupuy, Leghorn
June 8th, 1822

There is nothing to prevent your coming to-morrow, and I regret to say my anticipations were well founded. It is lucky that I am of a temper not to be easily turned aside though by no means difficult to irritate when my blood is up. But I am writing a letter, instead of making a dissertation. I write to you from the Villa Dupuy, near Leghorn, with the islands of Elba and Corsica visible from my balcony and my old friend the Mediterranean rolling blue at my feet.

I have lately had some anxiety, rather than trouble, about an awkward affair here, which on its face would be beneath the dignity of Gentlemen. Some other English

*and Scots, and myself, had a brawl with a Dragoon, who
had insulted one of the party. He called out the guard of
the watch to arrest us (we being unarmed), but I and another (an Italian) rode through said guard. I rode to my
house and dispatched my secretary to give an account
of the attempted and illegal arrest to the Tuscan authorities. But through the intervention of some unknown
agent, this Dragoon, who at first was taken for an offi-
cer, having acted in the manner of an assassin was himself wounded severely not forty paces from where I stood
and well within sight of the tower. Who wounded him,
though it was done before thousands of people, they have
never been able to ascertain, or prove, nor even the
weapon; some said a pistol, an air gun, a stiletto, and
what not. The authorities have arrested people and servants of all descriptions, but can make out nothing.*

*Therefore, and in light of the not inconsiderable trou-
bles of your own, I would press upon you the necessity
of a postponement of our planned excursion, until such
time as the local weather is more salubrious.*

*Yours ever,
N.B.*

But it was the six underlined words of the letter that
seemed to leap from the page as they spelled out
"Blood-Islands-Corsica-Beneath-Watch-Tower."

I felt the hammering of my heart within my battered
chest and my hands started to shake as I realized this
fragile scrap of paper might hold the key to everything.
I gently folded the letter back, squinting at the
backwards-typeset words on the other side as I slowly
read:

To goodley vessels; many a sail of pride,
And golden keeled, is left unlaunch'd and dry
But wherefore this? What care, though owls did fly
About the great Athenian admiral's mast?
What care, though striding Alexander past
The Indus with his Macedonian numbers?
Though old Ulysses tortured from his slumbers

I let the letter drop gently to the table, as if the paper were in danger of crumbling to dust at my touch. The shock and excitement I felt as I discovered the words naming Alexander so prominently made me want to shout, but I restrained myself to the betterment of my smoke-singed throat, not to mention my fellow travelers at the hotel. I gave myself a minute to swallow my emotions, and then returned to the letter with a critical eye.

The ink that underscored the six telling words was a faint brown color, as opposed to the faded and water-bled black of the writing. It was possible that the different-colored underlines could have been a form of invisible ink, which had been in use as far back as the American Revolutionary War. The uneven browning of the paper could have come from the letter's recipient using heat to expose the secret writing. The backwards poetry on the reverse side might have been impressed by having the paper wet, which would explain the wrinkling, and held down over another printed page. But why? And who was "N. B." who wrote to Percy Shelley? More importantly, where were the Blood Islands of Corsica?

It was high time to call for some help. The room phone was inconveniently attached to the wall on the

other side of the bed. I took my letter around and settled in with my back against the headboard, feeling like
I'd aged a century or two, and placed my call to the
States. It was just prior to midnight here, which put
the time at close to 7:00 P.M. in New York. At least I
didn't have to worry about disturbing anyone at church
services.

Mr. Singh answered his private line right away.

"Blake here," I greeted him.

Mr. Singh responded as coolly as ever with, "I'm all
ears."

I grimaced, but I shouldn't have been surprised.
Mr. Singh was informing me that our phone line was
tapped, and it was a sure bet that our new friends from
Washington were keeping tabs on us. Singh continued,
"Mr. Riley wants to speak with you." There were some
clicks on the line, and then I heard the well-remembered
gravelly voice. "Blake? That you, boy?"

"Aye, aye, sir. Listen, I need—"

He cut me off. "No, you need to listen. I've heard
some very disturbing things about you lately from our
friends in the government. They tell me you're in a
great deal of trouble, and from what I've heard, you
should go and turn yourself in to the authorities right
away. And because of this, and I'm sorry as hell to say
it, but I need to let you go. For the good of the foundation."

"What?"

"I'm sorry, boy. But frankly, if even half the things
I've heard are true, then well, what can I say? Except
to tell you that I thought I knew you better, and that
I have to put the needs of Argo ahead of any individual. So you're fired."

Nick Riley's words hit me like a hammer. He'd warned me at the outset that I needed to keep Mr. Jonas and his government agents ignorant of my abilities, abilities that made me into Nick Riley's personal thief and smuggler, but I'd screwed up and let my criminal talents be revealed. Nicholas had to cut me loose so I wouldn't drag down the rest of the Argo Foundation with me.

I had a sudden lump in my throat that made it hard to speak. "I . . . understand. And I'm sorry too. I never meant to let you down."

"I know," Nick said. "Is there any last thing I can do for you personally?"

"I'd just like to say good-bye to someone."

"Surely. Who?"

"The librarian."

"I see," Nick rumbled softly. He'd obviously know I was up to something, and I could feel him weighing his options. "Certainly," he said at last. "Mr. Singh? Please give Blake the number. Good-bye, Jonathan."

I didn't reply; I couldn't trust my voice to hold up. I absently fumbled my pen from my pocket until I remembered I'd used the cartridge as an improvised escape tool, and then just cleared my mind to receive the string of numbers that Mr. Singh recited with all the emotion of a vending machine. When he finished, Mr. Singh said, "Blake?"

"Yeah?"

There was a pause. "May God's Sword protect you." Then the line went dead.

I unclenched my fist from the handset, unaware I'd been throttling the thing. Ever since Nicholas Riley plucked me out of the ashes of my former life, no matter what dark, dangerous place in the world he sent me, I always knew even though I was alone, I had Nick and the Argo Foundation behind me. Now that connection was cut, and I was like an old-fashioned deep-sea diver whose lifeline had been severed, leaving me in dark water and sinking fast.

I closed my eyes as I slowly shook my head. I'd come through blood and fire, and was now left utterly alone. Then, from some dark, sharp-edged corner of my soul, I felt a laugh well up. Rhea, Vanya, the Ombras, and all the rest who played a part in this tragedy had managed to make one critical error: They all had left me alive.

All at once, I knew what to do. I was going to use every skill, every ability, every down-and-dirty trick I had ever learned to make each and every single one of them pay for their mistake. And I was going to get Caitlin out of all this, even if I had to drag the rest of them down to hell with me to do it.

I made another call to the States using the number Mr. Singh had provided. I had to put all the pieces of the puzzle together, and to do that I needed information. And there was one woman in this world who could get it for me. The only problem was, she hated my guts.

The woman in question was Abigail Pennyworth, a British expatriate and a fellow member of the Argo Foundation. Abby was a creature like me, another of Nicholas Riley's collection of criminals. Abby was an artist, only her artistic talents lay in the area of document forgery, especially if you needed a paper artificially aged for apparent authenticity. Old Nick was the one who caught her in the act once, and he used that evidence to blackmail her into working for him. Her official title with Argo was librarian, which was about as accurate as my former title of field researcher. I also happened to know she had a fondness for classical poetry and a near photographic memory.

As the call was going through, I pictured Abby as I last saw her—a tall, slender woman with waves of wild red hair that never stayed constrained and luminescent green eyes that were magnified behind her round, black-rimmed goggle-like glasses. Her sense of fashion ran to thrift store chic for the colorblind. She and I were once assigned to perform a delicate bit of theft and forgery, which in this case meant stealing an unknown copy of a T. E. Lawrence manuscript from the unrightful owner and replacing it with a near-exact copy. The "near exact" being in the form of the almost microscopic Happy Face symbol Abby used in the dot of one i. For once, the job went off without a hitch, and Abby and I later celebrated with a night of good Scotch whiskey followed by bad judgment. Turned out that when we weren't committing crimes together, we got along like rabid cats and distempered dogs. When we broke up, I told her it was all my fault. It was the only time she ever agreed with me.

I heard her cautious "Hello?" from the phone. "Abby," I replied with forced cheerfulness. "It's Blake."

"Blake? Blake? Blake the seducer of innocent young maidens?"

"Couldn't be, I've never met any of the above. Listen, I need your help."

"Oh, he does, does he," she said with sly vexation

oozing in her voice. "Well, now, just what is it you need, and how much are you willing to pay for it, is the question."

"I need to know all the connections among Napoleon Bonaparte, Alexander the Great, and Lord Byron."

"Epilepsy," she responded quickly. "They all had it. Are we done now? Good-bye."

"Epilepsy? No, wait! Abby, damn it, I need you."

"Oh, sure, now he says such pretty things." She gave a theatrical sigh that could have blown air through the wires across the Atlantic. "I suppose it's all life and death, is it?"

"Yes."

"All right. But you have to tell me exactly what you're looking for. Right now, the only real connection I see is the one between you and Byron."

"What's that?"

"You're both 'Mad, Bad, and Dangerous to Know.'"

"Thanks. I think. Look, what I've got right now is a letter addressed to Percy Shelley, but the person who wrote it just signed his name as 'N. B.'"

"Noel Byron," Abby explained, then she laughed, never a pretty sound at its best. "His lordship used to say that his initials could have also stood for Napoleon Bonaparte. It was one of Byron's jokes."

"So there is a connection between Byron and Bonaparte?"

"It was more of a love-hate thing with Byron. Of course, the only person Byron really loved was Byron, but he was once a big fan of Napoleon's, and dedicated some poems to him. Then old Bony up and abdicated, and Byron turned on him like a spurned lover."

I looked at the letter again, noting the traces of

brownish ink under the six crucial words. "Is there any evidence that Byron could have been some kind of spy or something?"

"A spy? More like a revolutionary without a portfolio. His lordship was always getting himself mixed up with conspiracies and such."

"What about around 1822 or so? And is there any connection to Corsica?"

"Corsica? Hmm. Well, I know when Byron was in Italy he was involved with one group . . . what were they called? The Calamari?"

"Calamari? That's a fancy word for squid."

"No, wait. Carbonari! That's it! The Carbonari were a group that were all about meeting in secret and overthrowing something or other. Byron was thick as thieves with them. Of course, a lot of his lordship's history has been covered up."

"What do you mean?"

"Well, turns out Byron sent his journals and such to his friend Thomas Moore. Only Moore burned all Byron's memoirs later. Then there was Dr. Polidori, Byron's personal physician. After he passed on, Polidori's sister got all his written recollections about Byron. And what does she do with them? She burns them too, that's what. Curiouser and curiouser, eh? Makes one wonder what was being covered up."

"Yeah." My mind flew back to Madam Ombra's words: "Byron knew. And Shelley. That's why he had to die." "Abby, was there anything unusual in Percy Shelley's death?"

That caused her to snort. "Unusual? That bugger Percy's death was unusual before, during, and after the event."

"Like how?"

"Well, it's been said that Percy Shelley presaged his own death, but the boy was also prone to hallucinations. But in truth he survived actual attempts to assassinate him."

"Really?"

"Oh, yes. While he was in Italy, he was almost shot on two separate occasions."

"Shot? Who the hell would want to kill a poet?"

"Some say the British government. They weren't happy about his being a rabble-rouser and all. But the day he actually died, he was on his way back to his villa in his private yacht. A storm brewed up, the boat went down, and Shelley drowned off the coast of Italy."

"Sounds accidental."

"Except that when the boat was found, the side of it had been staved in. One theory is that Shelley's ship came under attack from local pirates who rammed his boat to board it, but it sank too fast."

"Wait. Shelley's boat was rammed during a storm? That doesn't sound likely."

"And yet, it was found staved in. Poor Shelley washed ashore a few days later. Byron and a few cronies later cremated Shelley's body on the beach in some kind of pagan ritual nonsense. As the legend goes, Shelley's heart was the only thing not consumed in the fire. Later, his heart was given to his wife, Mary Shelley; you know, the author of *Frankenstein*?"

"Yeah," I responded dryly. "I think I heard that once."

"Sorry, dear boy," Abby said mock-contritely. "Just being thorough. Anyway, sometime after Shelley washed up on the beach, they named the area where he drowned the Golfo dei Poeti in his posthumous honor. Is any of this helping?"

I was piling up more questions than answers. "So you're saying Percy Shelley could have been murdered?"

"Some people wouldn't have minded his shuffling off the mortal coil, and that's a fact."

I turned the aged letter over. "So how would something like this figure in," I asked, and then I read the poem out loud.

When I finished, I heard Abby faintly on the other end saying, "Wait . . . wait . . ." I had seen her do this trick before when she was searching her memory, her head back and her eyes staring up, darting from side to side as if reading something only she could see. Finally I heard her say, "'Endymion'!"

"What?"

"'Endymion.' It's a poem by Keats."

"Keats?"

"Yes. Shelley and Keats were good friends, but Byron didn't care for him at all." Abby's voice trailed off as she added, "Now, that's funny."

"What is?"

"When Percy Shelley's body washed up on the beach, they found him with a book of Keats's poetry in his pocket."

A cold shock ran through me, and I knew now and for a certainty that the letter I'd rescued from the Castle Joux was a vital key. A message in secret from Byron to Shelley; a letter that Shelley kept with him inside a book of Keats's poetry that he took with him down to a watery grave. A letter that was his own death warrant.

I was brought back to the here and now by Abby's voice. "You know, Blake, it's actually kind of nice to talk to you again," she said warmly. "I hate to admit it, but I've missed you. So how's the world been treating you lately?"

"Me? Uh, fine. Oh, I'm married now."

Abby's voice went flat. "Married? You?"

"Yeah. Look, I've got to go."

"Oh, you do that. You go. You go straight to—"

I hung the phone up on the wall, sorry I didn't part with Abby on better terms. But I still needed more information. I had enough history; what I wanted now was geography. I also needed to make certain no one else was going to see the Byron letter. I pulled myself off the bed, gritting my teeth against a groan as I forced my bruised body to my will. I picked up my letter, folded it carefully, and placed it in my shirt pocket over my heart, then went downstairs to the lobby. My friend the concierge was still on duty, and his long, droopy face lifted somewhat into the semblance of a smile. "Ah, monsieur. I was about to call your room. There are some difficulties with your *carte bancaire*."

I should have known Nick Riley would waste no time cutting me off from every aspect of the Argo Foundation. The foundation kept emergency accounts in banks in Switzerland, Singapore, and the Cayman Islands, so money was never a problem before. But now my fancy company credit card had been demoted to just another improvised weapon and burglary tool.

I put a bewildered smile on my face and produced cash, and in turn the concierge produced a real smile.

"*Merci,* monsieur, is there any other service required?" I requested a mailing envelope and addressed a letter to the Argo Foundation's New York address. I slipped the Byron letter inside and handed the concierge enough money to ship a bowling ball across the world in exchange for his promise to mail my letter at the first opportunity in the morning. I also purchased a pair of maps, one of France and the other of the European Union. We concluded our business and I was wished *bonsoir.*

I returned to my room and angled the table lampshade. I spread my map of France out on the table, then laid out my map of Europe. Squinting at the cartography, I wished I hadn't lost my pocket monocular/magnifier. I found the Golfo dei Poeti, on the western side of Italy, across from the island of Corsica. I turned to the map of France, folding it down until I was looking at only Corsica. The main island itself was bordered by smaller islands. I started at the eastern side, closest to Italy, and worked around clockwise. I was all the way on the western side of the island when I spotted them—the Iles Sanguinaires, the Islands of Blood. Right off the coast of Ajaccio, the birthplace of Napoleon Bonaparte.

Thoughts collided in my head, and my mind felt electrified as the connections hooked up: Napoleon's first stop upon returning from Egypt was home to Corsica.

I folded the maps up and stuffed them in my jacket's inner pocket. There was nothing more I could do at the moment, and I was completely exhausted. I decided to get what sleep I could. Wheels were already set in motion, and if I was right, I was destined for a rude awakening.

And I desperately wanted to stop thinking of what Caitlin could be going through right now.

CHAPTER TWENTY-FOUR

"Rise and shine, Blake."

Being awakened by an angry man holding a gun is not a novel experience for me. Still, it's an event one never really gets used to. I opened my eyes, squinting against a glow of early morning sunlight bleeding in between the cracks of the curtains, to see Sam Smith standing near the foot of my bed. He was dressed all in black, and his dark features blended with the shadows in the room, leaving his eyes as hard, glittering points of light that reflected the glint from the small stainless steel pistol he held rock steady in his hand.

"You told me back in Paris you didn't have a gun," I said.

"I lied."

"Now I know you're with the government. You planning to shoot me?"

"What I should do is knock you upside your head and leave you tied up. And I may get around to doing just that. But first, we have to have a little talk."

"May I get up?"

"Sure. Just do it real slow."

That last order was easy to comply with. My body felt as stiff as if it had been left to harden in concrete overnight. I wasn't planning to show any weakness in front of Smith, but I failed in my effort as sharp-edged jolts of pain shot through my chest when I pulled myself into a sitting position on the side of the bed. I had been expecting company ever since Mr. Singh warned me that our phone call was being monitored, and I'd elected to sleep in my clothes.

"What the hell happened to you?" Smith asked.

"People keep shooting me."

"That I can believe."

"What time is it?"

"After six. Why? You think you're going somewhere?"

I did, but I wasn't going to tell him that. The five hours' sleep I got should have done me some good, but at the moment I felt like I'd overslept a century or two and was feeling my age. I watched as Smith placed a small metal briefcase on the table with his left hand, all the while never taking his eyes or gun off me. He opened the case and I could make out the form of a laptop computer inside, just like the one Mr. Jonas used in New York during our meeting at the Metropolitan. Smith aimed the monitor toward me, tapped a button, and the device sprang to life. From the machine on the desk I heard the voice-from-the-grave sound of Mr. Jonas. "Good morning, Mr. Blake. You have a lot of explaining to do."

I stared at the square, Cyclopean eye of the laptop, knowing that everything I said was going to be recorded. And every utterance I made was going to be a step on a high wire with no safety net.

Sam Smith said, "Let me get the ball rolling. Where's Caitlin? Last you told me, you were going to go find her."

"I did. Only now she's on Vanya's private Greek island. At least she was when I saw her yesterday morning."

Jonas's voice from the machine said, "Start the story from Paris. Do not leave anything out."

The light in the room was starting to brighten as I recited the events that had brought me here, from the discovery of the map in the gilded eagle to the catacombs beneath the church of Val de Grâce, to the abduction to Vanya's island and his plan to recover the body of Alexander the Great, and Rhea's revelation of Vanya's plan for global genetic genocide, and up to the murderous events at the Château de Joux. I told the whole ugly truth. I just kept one tiny fact to myself.

When I finished, the room was silent for a moment, quiet enough to hear the sounds of a door down the hall opening and closing, and footsteps walking away. Ordinary sounds that belonged to an ordinary world, a world that was light-years from here.

The man on the other end of the machine finally asked, "Mr. Blake, have you heard any mention of Trieste, Italy, during this time?"

"Trieste? Wait; yes. It's where Joseph Fouché died."

Smith said, "Fouché? You mentioned him back in Paris. He was Napoleon's spymaster, right?"

"Right. Is that what you mean?"

"No," came the cold voice from the computer. "Trieste is the location of the International Center for Genetic Engineering and Biotechnology. Did Vanya or the Rhea woman ever mention that?"

"No. Why?"

"Because we have information that Vanya has been a sponsor for the institute. More to the point, almost a year ago several scientists from the institute supposedly died in a boating accident. Only no bodies were ever recovered. At the time of the event, Vanya's yacht was in the vicinity, and it promptly sailed back to his island after the scientists went missing. Have you seen any sign of these people?"

The laptop's screen lit up and displayed color photographs of three men and a woman in succession. After I saw the slideshow, I said, "I think I've seen the Asian woman and one of the men on the island, but I'm not certain."

The voice of Mr. Jonas said, "You said Rhea told you that Vanya has scientists who are, as she put it, prisoners on his island?"

"That's what she said. Only I can't say how reliable her information is. She did try to kill me, you know."

Sam Smith just shrugged at that thought as I continued, "I did see medical facilities down underground on the island, but I wasn't given a full tour." I felt a lump of ice coalesce in the pit of my stomach. "Are you saying that Rhea was telling me the truth about Vanya's biological terror plot?"

Jonas's voice from the laptop's speaker came into the room like a frozen wind. "Yes. And though I have serious doubts in regard to Vanya's scheme to successfully resurrect Alexander's genetic material, much less produce a viable living being, I have no such doubts about his capability to create a lethal genetically engineered virus. Our own Department of Defense has produced a report called the Pathogen Genome Project. In short, modern science gives us the ability to genetically manufacture specifically designed plagues on demand. We know Vanya has the resources and a fanatical following all around the world, and if he has indeed recruited people with the scientific knowledge, he could have everything he needs to start a twenty-first-century version of the Black Death. Only far, far worse."

"But Rhea, or Suzume Saito, or whatever her name is, also said she was a Japanese government agent. Was she telling me the truth about that?" I asked.

Mr. Jonas said, "I've just run her name through our database. Is this the woman?"

The computer screen changed again, and this time it showed a color photo of Rhea. In the picture she was younger and her hair was straight, with bangs, but there was no mistaking her beautiful features. "That's her," I said with certainty.

"Interesting," Jonas's voice mused from the machine. "Suzume Saito, according to our liaisons with the Japanese government, is listed as a former operative of their Public Security Investigation Agency, and that agency includes their foreign counterintelligence operations. They've issued a notice to the allied intelligence services stating that they wish to be advised of any sightings of her. But at the same time the Japanese have made it quite clear that they wouldn't complain if any other government happened to liquidate her. Ah."

Smith and I waited for Mr. Jonas to continue, and he resumed by saying, "Now this is most interesting.

It says here that Agent Saito's last assignment was in connection with the investigation into the Aum Shinrikyo nerve gas attack in the Tokyo subway. Therefore, I believe the fact of the matter is that the woman has defected and willingly joined Vanya's cause. As for you, Mr. Blake, just how long did you think you could deceive us?"

I put on my best poker face, the one I use on Nick Riley when I'm holding a busted flush. "What are you implying, Mr. Jonas?"

Smith coughed a rude noise. "Oh, please; you've got way too many twisted moves to be a mild-mannered antiques geek. And you sure as hell ain't one of us. So just where did you learn all your voodoo jujitsu anyway?"

I gave myself a moment; I was about to go marching blindfolded through a minefield. I kept my eyes on the floor as I said, "Okay. But you've got to promise one thing first."

There was a hesitation, then the voice from the machine said, "Go on."

"You've got to promise not to tell Nicholas Riley what I'm about to tell you."

"What's that?"

"That I'm a fraud."

"How so?"

I shrugged. "I'm a crook. A thief, to be exact. And I've been using the Argo Foundation as my cover for years now."

Smith asked, "What do you mean by cover?"

"Just what I said. While I was traveling around the world on Argo Foundation business, I was taking some opportunities to steal some of the antiquities we located for myself. My work at the foundation gave me a legit-looking cover. I'd just hate for Nick Riley to find out. The old man's been good to me, and if he knew I'd been risking the good name of Argo for my own use, it'd break his heart." If he actually had one, I added silently to myself.

I bowed my head while I let my audience ponder over my mixture of truth and fiction, the same set I used on Vanya, until Mr. Jonas said, "So you're a thief. That doesn't explain how you've managed to survive all this time. I've seen the video of you in Troyon's apartment. My associate there says he can vouch for the fact that you've had extensive combat training. There's also the fact that your personal background becomes more questionable the closer we examine it."

"Not to mention having a mean sucker punch," Smith added, stroking his goatee with one hand and keeping his gun held steady on me with the other.

"Well, I picked up most of my education while being involuntarily incarcerated."

"Incarcerated?" Mr. Jonas inquired. "Where?"

"Somewhere other than America, under a different name."

Smith asked quickly, "If you've been stealing all this time, how come you're not rich?"

"I'm a lousy gambler."

The voice from the machine asked, "So who are you?"

Enough was enough, I thought. I'd done my best to give Nick Riley and my fellow pirates at Argo a plausible out as my parting gift to them, but now it was time to put my own plan into action. I shook my head and said, "Forget me. Why aren't you guys sending a small army to invade Vanya's island?"

The frustration in Jonas's voice came through the computer loud and clear. "Because we lack the actual proof we need. There is no way the American government will sanction a military strike on foreign soil, even a privately owned island, based solely upon on the suppositions we have."

"I told you; Caitlin's still there."

"We don't know that for a fact," Smith said tightly. "Even if she is, that bastard Vanya could drop her in the Mediterranean Sea before anyone could get close enough. We know he's got a radar installation up and running, and from what you've told us, he's got his own private army and an underground bunker as well. Just how the hell are we supposed to get through all that before he has a chance to eliminate all the evidence? Including Caitlin and the missing scientists?"

"If they are even there at all," Mr. Jonas mused darkly.

I let the heavy mood sink in for a bit, then said, "Well, then. Looks like we have no choice."

The voice from the computer asked, "What do you mean?"

"You have to send me back to Vanya's island."

Everything stopped dead for a moment. Then Smith said, "Or I could save time and trouble and just shoot you here."

Mr. Jonas added, "Even if we did send you back, what makes you think you could survive after you arrived? According to what you've told us, Suzume Saito tried to kill you just last night."

It was time to play the card I'd held back up my sleeve. "Because I've got the one thing Vanya's been tearing up heaven and earth looking for; the one thing he wants above everything else."

"What?" asked Smith.

"I know the location of the tomb of Alexander the Great."

There was an absolute vacuum of silence in the wake of my announcement. The look on Smith's face was priceless until he clapped his jaw shut, then said, "Say what?"

Mr. Jonas chimed in with, "You mean to tell us you've actually located the tomb? Where every archeologist in the world has failed? You expect us to believe this? Do you have proof?"

"Yes, I do."

"Where?"

"Someplace safe," I replied, hoping that my greedy friend, the night concierge, didn't just forget to mail the envelope containing Byron's secret letter. "Besides," I continued, "I don't care if you believe me or not. The important thing is that I can get Vanya to believe me."

After a pause, Mr. Jonas said, "Even if we agree to send you back, just how do you propose to accomplish this? There's no way to approach the island unseen."

"No problem. I'm licensed and certified for both skydiving and scuba diving, and I've done a fair share of both at night. Just get me the gear and throw me out of an airplane close enough to the target, and I'll swim the rest of the way in."

Mr. Smith laughed softly as he shook his head. "Putting aside the fact that you're crazy, just why in the hell would you want us to send you back to a place that you're certain to die in?"

"Like I told you before, I'm going to get Caitlin out. Oh, and one more thing—I'm going to wreck Vanya's little island paradise."

"Oh?" Smith prompted.

"Yeah. He's made me mad."

From the computer I heard, "Mr. Smith? We need to confer privately." Smith nodded and reached over to turn the laptop screen away from me. He then gave me a baleful warning glance as he set his pistol next to the computer and started typing on the keyboard in quick, staccato bursts, all the while darting his eyes up at me at brief intervals. I tried to keep a calm exterior, but inside I was boiling over, counting every second that ticked away that I was kept from heading toward Caitlin. I was also planning my moves against Mr. Smith in the event they decided not to send me back to Vanya's island. My hand was scant inches away from the silenced pistol under my pillow, but I truly didn't want to risk a lethal injury against someone who was technically on the side of the angels. The problem was, he was ready for a fight with me, and I was suffering from the compounded effects of all the physical damage I'd been accumulating.

Finally, I saw Smith glance up from the keyboard and vent a grunt. "Too bad for you, boy. Looks like you're getting a free one-way trip to the Greek islands."

From the machine I heard, "Let me be very clear on this, Mr. Blake; you are going in entirely on your own. The United States government will completely deny any and all connection with you. As it is, we are having a very difficult time keeping the French authorities in the dark."

Smith added, "With everything that's been blowing up or burning down lately, they must be going nuts over the fact they don't know who to surrender to."

"So you understand your position?" Mr. Jonas asked.

"Yes. Completely."

"Very well. Now, our primary objective is to obtain evidence that Vanya is in possession of biological weapons and has kidnapped citizens of other countries against their will. If you can gather the proof we need and manage to escape from the island, head north to Corfu. We will have people monitoring the area. We will also be scanning all radio wavelengths, so if you can get ahold of a radio, just use the name 'Vanya' in your message, and we'll pick it up. Now, what will you need in the way of equipment?"

"Nothing like the stuff Caitlin was carrying. Vanya got a big laugh out of your little shooting pen and the sunglasses with the concealed knife blades. Then I had to watch that psychopath Rhea kill two people with your damn spy toys."

"We need to be able to track your movements," Jonas stated flatly. "Mr. Smith still has the wedding ring with transponder."

Smith grinned. "It's guaranteed to work down to two hundred feet underwater, in the event Vanya just drops you into the sea."

"Great. It doesn't have a self-destruct device or anything, does it?"

"I wish."

From the machine I heard, "We'll go ahead and

use your idea of a night parachute drop off shore. What will you need?"

I'd been thinking about my approach to the island already. "Just a parachute and a glow-in-the-dark altimeter. Waterproof flashlight. Diving mask and fins, with a snorkel if I can get one. And a good knife."

I noticed Smith had left his pistol on the table as he said, "I'd lend you my knife, but some jackass wrecked it using it for a pry bar. So that's it? You're just gonna waltz right in with that little bit of storebought gear?"

"Sure."

"What makes you think Vanya's troops aren't just going to shoot you out of the sky or blow you out of the water?"

In truth, the worst part was I was running a colossal bluff. I had no way of knowing if Lord Byron's letter had anything to do with the tomb of Alexander the Great. All I could do was hope that whatever was hidden in the Corsican watchtower was a secret I could use to convince Vanya to keep me alive long enough to find out, and thereby give me a chance to rescue Caitlin. But rather than admit any of this, I said to Smith, "I have it on good authority that the Sword of God is on my side."

Smith just stared at me for a long moment, and then said, "You don't need to say stuff like that to make me think you're crazy."

The voice from the computer said, "I'll begin the preparations. Good luck, Mr. Blake."

Smith shut the lid on the laptop and said, "Well, let's get going. I'd hate to be late for your funeral."

I casually pulled the silenced pistol out from under

my pillow and held it up. "Here. You might as well carry this."

Smith had his own gun out and pointed straight at my head before I finished speaking. "Jesus! Give a man some warning before you pull some shit like that!"

He came over and reached out with his left hand like he was about to grab an angry snake, then snatched the pistol from my hand. Shaking his head, he slipped his small pistol into his jacket, then twisted apart the silencer from the other gun and pocketed the pieces. "Any more stupid surprises?" he asked testily.

I just shook my head and gathered my small collection of personal gear from the nightstand. I was allowed to use the bathroom unaccompanied, and while I readied for the day I took note of my unshaven, beat-up and burnt-out features in a mirror. My wrists were scraped up from the iron manacles, but they'd stopped bleeding. I also checked out my injured chest. The two previous bruises had spread, and now I had an angry red welt on my upper chest from being shot the night before. It looked like my bruises were mating and giving birth to painful babies. I emerged to find Smith waiting impatiently by the door. When we made it to the lobby, I was stopped short by tantalizing scents. "I'm starved," I said. "How much time do we have?"

"It's going to take about five hours' driving to catch a plane. After that, you fly."

"Five hours? It took Rhea and me just over an hour to drive here from Geneva."

"We're not going to Geneva. We're going to Germany."

"Germany? Why?"

" 'Cause that's where the airplanes are."

Smith was being obstinate, but the fact remained that I had to wait all day anyway until the sun set over the Ionian Sea before I could chance sneaking back to Vanya's island. "Fine. But I want breakfast. I hate getting killed on an empty stomach."

"Don't worry about that, I've got you covered."

The first-floor restaurant of the nearby Hotel Le Soleil was another beautiful example of Old World design, clad in dark wood paneling from the floor to halfway up the chandeliered ceiling. Smith and I were greeted by a friendly, smiling blond woman of healthy proportions, and she escorted us to a table set between one of the tall windows that offered a view of the mountainside and an ornate piano that had to be a century old at least. Maybe it was because I was starving, but the croissants were the best I'd ever tasted, melting on the tongue. Smith ate his share with efficiency, making only one comment, about avoiding the cheese. "I hate the stuff," he explained shortly.

"Then what the hell are you doing in France? Is this some kind of punishment detail for you?"

"Could be worse," he said after a sip of coffee. "They could have sent me to England. Now let's get moving."

We left the hotel and walked into a cold, bright Alpine morning with the sunlight reflecting off the surrounding snow-covered mountains. The town of Pontarlier had been asleep when I'd arrived the night before, but was now alive with people and cars going about their business. I followed Smith down the street until he stopped in front of a diminutive two-door automobile that looked small even in the company of its European pint-sized brothers. I watched as Smith opened up the driver's-side door of the fire-engine-red

Renault Clio. "That's our ride?" I asked incredulously.

"Shut up and get in," Smith barked back, slamming the car door. I opened my side and eased myself in as Smith struggled to get my pistol and silencer out of his pants pockets and stashed back on the rear floorboards under a tan coat. The car was as claustrophobic as a coffin with one too many occupants. "Does this thing have stuff like ejector seats or hidden machine guns?"

"Shut up," Smith repeated.

As he fired up the tinny-sounding engine, I laughed, ruefully remembering the hot BMW sports car I recently drove. "Man, if you aren't the most unglamorous secret agent in the world."

Smith didn't reply as he drove us out of Pontarlier, and I took my last look at the town as I settled in for a long ride. But then he turned the car south, and as soon as we cleared the elderly, gray stone buildings, I caught a sight that stopped my breath: Starkly outlined against the vibrant blue sky, the Château de Joux loomed above.

Smith saw it too and said as he craned his neck, "So that's the place you busted out of?"

I merely nodded, wondering just what had transpired throughout the night in that foreboding mass of cold stone after my escape. Smith gave out a low, long whistle, then sped up as we cruised through La Cluse et Mijoux until the castle was lost from view. I closed my eyes and relaxed my body as I was rocked and swayed by the twisty mountain road. I tried to keep my mind away from thinking about Caitlin and let my thoughts wander into speculations about Corsica and the watchtower on the Islands of Blood.

In my half-aware state, I must have been humming aloud a fragment of an old, dimly remembered song. Out of the blue, Smith named the tune. "'All Along The Watchtower,'" he said. "That is one righteous song."

"Yeah. One of Bob Dylan's better ones."

"Dylan?" Smith snorted derisively. "It was Jimi who made that song."

"No argument here."

"What made you think of that?"

I didn't answer at once. "Seemed fitting for the occasion."

"Hmm. I know you're a thief; you calling me a joker?"

"Yeah. You're a laugh a minute."

Smith drove through the mountain pass in silence for a while, and then said, "Blake? Your taste in music notwithstanding, I still hate you, man. But I hope to God you know what the hell you're doing."

I could only nod in agreement.

CHAPTER TWENTY-FIVE

Smith and I didn't speak much as the hours unwound and the kilometers piled up, and I couldn't help noticing that he was looking worn out, his dark skin betrayed by a grayish cast. The weather also reflected his look as clouds started to converge overhead once we cleared the Jura Mountains. I figured he must have been on the go since his agency traced my call from Mijoux the night before. At one point I pulled out a cigarette, and Smith threatened to kill me if I lit up. I offered a compromise, saying if I could smoke it halfway I'd let him give me a savage beating. He didn't bother to respond, and I put my tobacco away. I got my chance to indulge when we had to pull over for petrol. My throat was still raw from breathing the burning remains of ancient paper from the fire in the library of the Château de Joux the night before, and as I crushed out my cigarette I caught a glimpse of Smith surreptitiously downing a pill when he thought I wasn't looking. I silently sympathized with him.

Throughout the drive, I saw Smith receive text messages on his phone. He never bothered to tell me what information he was getting. I was more concerned over the contraband in our car. We had at least two pistols between us that I was aware of. But other than a couple of toll stations, we had no interference along the way. After nearly four hours of driving through France, we came to the border with Germany at Metz toward Saarbrucken. The crossing was a nonevent as we cruised through the post indicated by the blue European Union flag. I tried to relax as we drove through the green northern European landscape, marshalling my strength and hoping Smith wouldn't fall asleep at the wheel despite his use of chemical stimulation.

Further down the tree-lined road, I spotted a sign as we shot past that read USAF MILITARY OPERATIONS AREA. Shortly after, I saw tall flagpoles planted along the streets, flying the United States Stars and Stripes. The road led to a gated security point where another set of flags flew—the USA's along with NATO's banner, anchored by a dark maroon pedestal that announced WELCOME TO RAMSTEIN AIR BASE. Smith wasn't kidding when he said Germany was where the airplanes were. The armed guards at the gate, dressed in camouflage fatigues and black berets that were completely offset by the blue-and-yellow-striped safety vests they wore, waved us over to a small blockhouse. A serious-looking young guard approached our little auto, and Smith handed him an ID. The guard spent a few moments glancing from the ID to Smith, then saluted, handed back the wallet, and spoke into his shoulder radio microphone as he waved Smith to continue. We were suddenly bracketed fore and aft by military

Humvees, complete with top-mounted machine guns. "I see we were expected," I said. "Where're we going?"

"You wanted a ride, you're gonna get a ride," was all Smith said in reply.

As we followed the military escort around the base, I noticed the solid, blocklike uniformity of the buildings, painted in shades of brown or beige. I was surprised by the number of civilian people and vehicles I saw along the way, their colors standing out in stark contrast to the drab, muted greens of the military. The route our miniature parade followed appeared to be circumnavigating the base, and I could see wooded hills in the distance as we approached the enormous concrete runways. My eyes were drawn to the behemoth aircraft, painted in camouflage or dusty olive drab, slumbering on the runways. Even at this distance, I could tell how monstrously huge they were, and it made me wonder all over again just how something so much larger than a whale can fly like a bird. I also wondered if one of these airborne titans was going to be my chariot.

Smith followed the lead vehicle to a hangar, smaller than most of its kind, that housed a twin-engine propeller job. I saw our escorts continue on their way as Smith pulled up beside the open cavernous maw of the structure. Smith and I pried ourselves out of the tiny Renault and stretched our limbs as two people approached from the hangar: a dark-haired male and a blond female, both in plain green flight suits. Smith retrieved his metal briefcase and approached the duo. "I'm Smith," he announced, and then said with a nod toward me, "And this here's the cargo. You can call him Blake."

The couple came and stood at a polite semblance of attention. I could see now that the man's face had dark, solid features that were belied by a ready smile. The woman was just flat-out beautiful, with blue eyes that graced a face already blessed with subtle perfection and full, promising lips. Looking at her almost distracted me from noticing that neither jumpsuit displayed any rank or insignia, just bare patches of Velcro where the symbols would normally appear. The woman spoke first, with a musically husky voice that was made for a blues piano. "Good afternoon, gentlemen. I'm Captain Arden. Since we're supposed to be informal on this trip, you can call me Nicole. This is Tech Sergeant Vega."

"Call me Don," her partner said as we shook hands all around.

"You've been briefed?" Smith asked of the pair.

Nicole nodded. "Affirmative. Don and I have been detailed to panty raids before."

"Panty raid" must have been some kind of military spy speak for "drop some poor bastard out of a plane over hostile territory" or some such. I looked up at the airplane in the hangar. "Is this our ride?" I asked.

Nicole smiled and looked over. Men would kill to have her look at them the way she gazed upon that airplane. "That's my baby," she said. "C-12 Huron. She's rigged for medical transport. And, of course, other things," she added slyly.

"Yeah," I replied. "I couldn't help but notice the air force insignia. I take it all the stealth aircraft were tied up?"

Nicole laughed. "We'll be flying so high no one's

going to notice. Plus, we're going to dogleg our approach, so we'll look like we're transiting east toward Turkey."

Don Vega asked, "How many HALO jumps you got under your belt?"

I knew the term, a military acronym for high altitude, low opening. "Would this be a good time to admit I have none?"

Vega's smile dropped off his face. "None?" He looked over to Smith. "What the hell is going on here?"

Smith shrugged. "Ask Blake. He's the one who said he could parachute."

"What's your rating?" Vega demanded.

"Well, officially I hold an A license—"

Vega was incredulous. "A? That's it? Twenty-five lousy jumps? You need at least two hundred jumps to qualify for a HALO."

I ignored the interruption. "I've actually made quite a few jumps that never made it into any log book. Most of them at night."

"I bet you have," Smith murmured.

"You ever done any high-altitude jumps?" Vega asked quickly. "Ever had to use a bailout bottle?"

"No."

Vega threw up his hands. "This is supposed to be a covert mission, not assisted suicide. I didn't sign up for this."

Nicole looked straight at Smith as she asked, "Is that it? Are we scrubbed?"

"Well, Blake?" Smith asked. "It's your call."

I had all eyes on me. "I'm going."

Vega just shook his head and muttered something

about "hypoxia" and "insanity" as he turned and walked into the hangar. Smith hefted his metal brief-case and followed Vega, saying, "I've got to make a call." I was left at the mouth of the hangar with Nicole Arden, who was staring at me with her electric-blue eyes. "You'll have to forgive the sergeant," she said with a matter-of-fact tone. "He's with Pararescue. He's used to saving people's lives, not helping them kill themselves."

"Point taken."

"I was just wondering whether you're brave, or just crazy," she said levelly.

"Let's just assume I'm enough of both to get by."

Nicole just nodded slowly. "I'm going to go and re-vise the flight plan," she said. "You better get with Ser-geant Vega. He'll do what he can to get you up to speed." She turned, but before she walked away, she added, "I just hope whatever it is you're going after is worth it."

I let the good captain walk out of earshot before I answered, "She is."

I walked into the hangar, toward the back wall. Smith had his laptop set up on a workbench and was busy typing away, probably writing my obituary. Ser-geant Vega stood near a covered tarpaulin laid out on the concrete floor. "You really going through with this?" he asked seriously.

"Yes."

He nodded like a man who'd received bad news he already expected. "Okay then," he said. "Let's see what we can do." He bent down and whipped the tarpaulin off like a magician before an audience, and I was amazed at what he made appear. Laid out with careful precision was an array of equipment that could cover every possible contingency on land, sea, or air.

I shook my head as I surveyed the sleek, compact parachute and the scuba tanks colored in flat black, arranged next to a set of climbing gear. There was so much stuff I almost overlooked the shortened M-16 commando assault rifle with the collapsible stock, but I was instantly drawn to one singular item on the mat. I picked up the knife and freed it from its sheath. It was a bowie-style blade, at least seven inches in length with a serrated section near the hilt that had wicked, sharklike cutting teeth. I hefted it once, twice; the balance was excellent and the edge felt razor-sharp as I lightly stropped it on the back on my hand. "Well, well, well," Smith said as he came to join us, "found another knife to break?"

"Okay already," I grumbled. "Just as soon as I get back, I'll replace that one of yours I busted up back in Paris. Crybaby."

"Easy bet to make since I highly doubt you'll be coming back, so pardon me if I don't hold my breath. I just updated Mr. Jonas on your lack of parachute qualifications."

"Oh?"

"Yeah. He said to throw you out of the plane anyway."

He handed me the silver wedding ring Caitlin had given me, the one I now knew contained a homing device. "This doesn't mean we're going steady, does it?"

"No," Smith replied easily. "It just means we'll know where to find your body." He then looked over the display of equipment and whistled. "Well, if you can't get the job done with all this G.I. Joe crap, then I don't know what to tell you."

"There is one thing I don't see," I said.

Vega frowned. "What?"

"Lunch. I'm starved."

It was Sergeant Vega to the rescue on that score, as he went and produced some military cuisine: bottled water and plastic packages marked MEAL, READY TO EAT, INDIVIDUAL, the armed services version of camping food. I'd been on enough wilderness treks with similar provisions to be impressed with the variety of foodstuffs each package contained, although I was warned to avoid the chili and beans entree since I was destined for a potential gut-wrenching high-altitude, low-pressure experience. I settled on a selection of pot roast and vegetables, and Smith and I prepared our repast with flameless chemical heaters while Vega explained that the military acronym for the food, MRE, actually stood for "Meals Rejected by Enemy," though Smith disagreed and said it stood for "Meals, Rarely Edible."

After lunch I started reviewing the equipment I'd be taking. The parachute and heavy-duty lighted altimeter were necessities, along with the small green bottle of pressurized pure oxygen, "Just to keep you alive long enough to make it down to the water and drown." Vega also informed me that the chute was called a HAPPS—High Altitude Precision Parachute System, otherwise known as the "stealth chute." As Vega drilled me on the chute's operating systems, I was relieved to see that everything was arranged like its civilian counterparts. Vega also insisted I use a computerized automatic opening device preset for four thousand feet, just in case I happened to forget how to pull a ripcord on the way down. I acquiesced, of course, but inside I knew I wouldn't trust my life to any gremlin-prone electronic devices.

After the parachute, I next had to decide what other gear I'd be lugging along. There was a forearm-mounted GPS device that would guide me to Vanya's island once I had control of the parachute, and as I've come to distrust anything more complicated than a paper clip I added a luminous wrist compass as well. My plan was to hit the water close to the island and swim in, so the underwater diving mask would be worn in place of the skydiving goggles. Swim fins and a waterproof flashlight came next, and I chose to take the small pony bottle of compressed air instead of the full-sized scuba tanks. Since I wasn't going to be diving at depth, I figured I'd get about twenty minutes of underwater time if I paced myself. With a helmet, jumpsuit, diving boots, and gloves, I'd be as ready as I could be.

As for all the rest of the gear, it would just slow me down, and I was planning to ditch all the equipment before I tried to contact Vanya anyway. And since every item was unmistakably military in origin, I didn't want to have to explain where I got it. I was most reluctant to discard the compact medical kit that even included a mini-defibrillator and drug box. It was a real luxury item, considering that my first-aid gear usually consisted of a bandanna, some safety pins, a pocketknife, and my lighter.

As Smith watched me finish my selections, he said, "That it? What about firepower? You want that silenced Glock back?"

"No," I answered. "The trick is going to be to get

in close enough to Vanya to talk to him. Gunfire makes for a lousy conversational opener." I held my new knife up. "Besides, I've got this."

"Just what, pray tell, are you gonna do with one little knife? There's an old saying about bringing one to a gunfight."

I really shouldn't have done what I did next. One of the first rules I ever learned was to never reveal your abilities until you actually have to use them. But I yielded to an instant impulse and whipped the knife out of its sheath and sent it flying over to a standing corkboard that held a map of the Mediterranean. The knife landed with a solid *thump* that rocked the board, almost knocking it over as it punched through the target down to the hilt.

Smith shot me a look as he walked over to the board, where he wrenched the knife free. "Great," he said sarcastically. "You can throw away your weapon and disarm yourself faster than anyone I know." Smith then looked at where the knife had landed, and then looked at me. "What were you aiming at?"

"Europe."

He shook his head and walked back to me, handing me the knife hilt-first. Vega walked up to the map and ran his finger along where the knife landed. "Just what do you have against Corsica?" he asked.

"Oh? Is that where it landed?" I asked innocently. I didn't look at Smith when I said this, and wondered how long it would take him to figure out that I had just literally pointed out my ultimate destination to him.

"Where'd you learn to do that trick?" Vega asked. I just shrugged. The quiet little man from Thailand who taught me to throw everything from knives to scissors and screwdrivers wouldn't appreciate being given public credit for my training. When he saw I wasn't going to answer his question, Vega said, "Well, let's see if you can learn any more tricks." The next hour was taken up with Sergeant Vega drilling me on the finer points of high-altitude jumping. He was a good instructor, only raising his voice when he had to yell over the jet turbine screams or basso profundo propeller moans of the arriving and departing airplanes outside on the flight line.

Finally, Nicole Arden returned, clipboard in hand. "Okay, listen up, people," she announced. She went to the map board as we gathered around. She spotted the gash on the map and turned a scornful eye on the rest of us, all of whom decided to look away, badly feigning ignorance. Nicole muttered something disparaging about "boys" under her breath, then said, "I've run the flight plan based on best possible speed, arriving at the drop zone at twenty-two hundred hours local time."

Twenty-two hundred hours translated to ten o'clock at night. Way too early if I was going to try and sneak onto the island when most would be asleep, but I didn't want to delay any longer than absolutely necessary. "Good," I said. "I want to get there as soon as possible."

"So I figured," Nicole said dryly. She took out a marker pen and traced lines on the map. "We'll head south, then traverse Italian airspace to give us an approach due east toward the target. At one hundred and fifty miles downrange I'll take us to twenty-four thousand feet. This will minimize your exposure to the altitude."

Vega took over. "We'll depressurize the cabin and have everyone use oxygen masks for thirty minutes prior to jump. This is the 'pre-breathing' stage to get all that nasty nitrogen out of your blood. At the two-minute warning, you'll switch to your bailout bottle for the descent. During this time, you need to tell me immediately if you're experiencing any headache, tunnel vision, tingling or numbness, faintness—in fact, anything out of the ordinary. I'll be monitoring you for signs of hypoxia or cyanosis. Also, at this altitude, you're gonna freeze your ass off during the descent. If all goes according to plan, I strongly recommend you deploy your chute at four thousand feet."

I did some quick calculation—at twenty thousand feet, I'd be free falling for approximately two whole minutes. That's a lifetime of worry, wondering if your damn parachute is going to open or not.

Nicole checked her watch and said, "You have just half an hour before takeoff. Let's get packed up and squared away."

Smith went back to his laptop on the workbench as Sergeant Vega attended to all the equipment I wasn't taking with me. I watched Captain Nicole walk away toward the plane, leaving me on my own. I made some final preparations, packing my wallet, passport, and other items into plastic bags and taping them water-tight. I was going to have to leave my shoes behind and wear the neoprene diving boots instead, but I kept the shoestrings, knowing how handy some strong, thin cord could be. I then cut off the sleeves and legs of my clothes; I'd need the extra mobility after exiting the water. If I managed to get that far.

I dressed in the black jumpsuit and shrugged into

the Kevlar-lined leather jacket. With nothing left to do but kill time, I headed for the mouth of the hangar. I lit one of my few remaining cigarettes while standing under a "No Smoking" sign and watched a large, four-engine turboprop plane coming in for a landing, its motors rumbling low as it glided down from the leaden sky. I wondered if it was bringing soldiers home. I hoped so.

I'd never been a soldier myself, not in the honorable, conventional sense, but I was made to be a damn good unconventional warrior and had the skills and experience to prove it. And I had no doubts that I was going off to fight for a cause that was just; Vanya and his psychopathic pet killer Rhea were monsters. Monsters that scared the hell out of me. And then I thought of Caitlin. My feelings for her were as surprising to me as they were strong, but I had no time to question myself. All I could do was see that Caitlin and I survived all this madness, and then we could see for ourselves what the future would bring. A poet once wrote that it was for the sake of a woman that a thousand ships were launched to war and a once-proud empire brought to ruin. All I had to do now was see to it that history got repeated.

CHAPTER TWENTY-SIX

I felt like I was dying by inches.

Prior to this, for roughly the first four hours after takeoff, I was left to my own devices. When we climbed aboard, I saw that the passenger section of the plane had been engineered to serve as an emergency medical transport. It was like being inside a low-ceilinged, tubular operating room. All the medical equipment was stowed away, leaving Spartan seating accommodations. Sergeant Vega went to the pilot's cabin with Captain Arden. Not that I blamed him; she was a lot better-looking than either Smith or me. As soon as we were airborne and leveled out, Smith unstrapped from his chair, unlocked a fold-down patient stretcher, then made his coat into a pillow and climbed on. "Wake me when it's time to throw your ass out," was the last thing he said to me.

So I stared out the portholes, looking down at the magnificent Alps as we traversed Switzerland and into Italy, and then watched as we flew south along the

Italian coastline. Eventually, we veered east, over some less impressive mountainous ranges, until finally we were over a blue Mediterranean Sea. All during this time I felt a gnawing in my gut as minute by minute I wondered and worried about Caitlin.

I felt the stomach-dropping sensation of our descent as Sergeant Vega appeared from the pilot's cabin. He put on a heavy oversuit, complete with a hood that he left slung back, and then came astern to Smith and me. He woke Smith up and then proceeded to dress me in my gear like a mother with a backwards child getting ready to play in the snow.

Vega said over the moan of the engines, "Now we're going to go on individual oxygen. Mr. Smith, put that coat on, strap in, and don't unbuckle until I say you can, got it?" Smith made no response other than an affirmative nod as he followed Vega's orders.

My world got smaller as Vega helped me put my diving mask and helmet on, then the oxygen mask that connected to an overhead pipeline. I felt a cold rush of oxygen in my mouth as the sound of my own breathing competed with the engines' noise. I gave Vega a thumbs-up, and he moved over to Smith and checked him as he put on his own air mask and goggles. Having made sure everyone was hooked up and ready, Vega took a seat opposite me. The cabin lights switched to red and my ears started popping.

I sat in my chair, hunched forward with the parachute pack on my back, and concentrated on relaxing, but I was constantly distracted by moving my jaw to clear my ears and trying to swallow in a throat gone dry. It was getting damn cold inside the fuselage. From time to time, Vega would flash a small penlight around my mouth and jaw, probably looking to see if I was still breathing as I hugged myself around my armored leather jacket. My problem was that while I was inhaling, it felt like I wasn't getting anything to breathe. I suddenly realized I was actually panting, and I felt hot pepper being sprinkled on my brain and pinpricks running up and down my body as my world got fuzzy and gray around the edges. But if I reported any of these symptoms to Vega, he'd scrub the mission, and I couldn't risk that for Caitlin's sake. All I could do was try to keep my failing body together and fight against the hypoxia, at least until I could get the hell out of the plane and get my parachute open.

I gathered my strength and tried to concentrate, sucking in the cold gas as tiny electric minnows swam across my vision. Finally, the bloodred lights flickered, and I saw Vega come toward me and disconnect my air hose from the ceiling line and then hook up the one from my portable oxygen bottle strapped to my left thigh. The lights flickered again and I was pushed against my seatbelt as the plane decelerated and the engine pitch dropped to a rumbling moan. Vega held up two fingers in front of my face. Two-minute warning to jump.

I felt a tinge of embryonic panic start to blossom. I felt like I was forgetting something critical, but I could not remember what it was. I watched Vega move back to the hatch and attach a safety line to the bulkhead. I shook my head in an attempt to clear my mind, but all it did was make me dizzy.

I tried to stand up, twice in fact, before I realized my seat belt was still attached. My neoprene-gloved fingers were as useless as wet clay, and I finally had to bang the heel of my palm on the belt release. I lurched up on legs that felt dead from the thighs down and half fell over to where Smith was sitting, glad I didn't fall flat on my face.

I pushed off from the back of his chair, but not before I saw the wide-eyed look in Smith's eyes. Smith was yelling something too, but I couldn't make out what he was trying to say as Vega, who was now hooded and gloved, undogged the hatch. Instantly, the moan of the turboprops magnified a thousandfold as a hurricane exploded into the cabin, sucking all the heat away in the blink of an eye.

Vega waved me to come to the hatch. I felt like I'd been dropped headfirst into an Arctic ice pond, but I stepped forward, one numbed stump of a leg at a time, until I made it to the hatch. I felt more than heard the shatterproof glass of my face mask crinkle as frost started to coat the edges of my vision. I saw through the opening a slash of angry red light cutting a curved horizontal swath through the inky blackness toward the wing of the plane, and then I felt a thump on my left shoulder as I fell out into space.

I was body slammed into a tumbling fall as the roar of the engines tore through my head, then faded fast as a million fiery pins stabbed every centimeter of my body. I was dimly aware that I was flailing like a man drowning in an icy lake. My jumpsuit was flapping and slapping me, as if it were desperately trying to remind me of where I was. A half-forgotten voice screamed in my head: "Position!"

I forced my arms and legs out and arched my body, fighting the urge to curl up into a frozen ball as I blinked to clear my eyes, only to find myself falling in total blackness. My hindbrain was yelling "Pull! Pull! Pull!" but my thoughts snapped to Sergeant Vega's warning words echoing in my mind: "Pull too early and you will *die*." I gritted my teeth and sucked in oxygen, forcing the animal panic to recede. The shot of pure adrenaline did me some good, and I felt like I was waking up out of a dream where I was falling. Only to find myself falling.

I looked to my altimeter; the green glowing arrow was spinning a countdown, and through the fog of my mask I saw I'd just crossed eighteen thousand feet. I was still higher than I'd ever jumped before. I checked my GPS unit on my right forearm and saw that I was over three miles off target, with the lighted indicator pointing behind me. I cut a pair of ninety-degree turns until I was all the way around, and saw a jagged constellation of stars laid out below me in a rough arrow shape—the lights of the island of Corfu.

Having a target in sight, coupled with the rapidly fading crush of freezing-cold air, gave me focus as I whipped through the night sky and angled my fall into a forward arc, cutting down the lateral distance between me and Vanya. I confess to one mad, joyous moment as I thought, I'm coming for you, you bastard!

I kept glancing between my altimeter and the lights of Corfu, watching them fade out at the upper corners one by one as I fell toward the sea like Icarus. At forty-five hundred feet, I popped the chute and felt the reassuring rapid slithering across my back as the parachute was drawn into the sky, followed by the *rumble-crack* sound as the harness grabbed me by the haunches and my head and spine were suddenly forced down toward my guts. Then, the blissful sensation of being carried through the night sky.

I looked up to see a sea of stars surrounding a sharp, black rectangle, as if someone had cut a hole in the sky. The lines felt right in my numbed hands as I fumbled for the steering toggles. A bright fat crescent of a moon was over my right shoulder, and ahead of me and slightly to my left, sitting on a vast plain of black water, I saw a tiny cluster of lights in the distance. I took a moment to pull the breathing mask off my face. It came off like it had grafted itself there, and I let it fall down my neck as I fumbled for the valve on the tank, choking it off.

I kept making minor corrections since the sea breeze would lift and toss me gently as I angled toward the lights, ruefully noting that all this would be a lot easier if I had the powered paraglider I used back in Afghanistan, but the engine noise would kind of defeat the purpose of a sneak attack. So I sailed on at the mercy of the wind. My GPS unit kept subtracting the distance, telling me I was on course with less than two miles to go.

Then I saw with a sickening shock that whoever preprogrammed that GPS unit was off about a mile or so. My still-fogged dive mask finally revealed that some of the lights I was aiming for were actually the running lights of Vanya's yacht, now looming up out of the darkness like a materializing whale. And I was an airborne cannonball coming right for it in slow motion.

I was too damn close—if I could see the ship, then anyone on the ship could see me. I yanked my steering toggles straight down to stall my forward momentum and accelerate my drop, but the sea breeze wasn't cooperating and I felt the wind rush and lift me. I went for my ultimate last-ditch maneuver and yanked the cutaway, jettisoning the parachute and dropping myself into space. The lines whipped away and I flailed my arms to keep myself on a feet-first dive into the open water.

It felt like it took forever, and when I finally broke the surface my legs rolled up and I was spun into a slamming, head-spinning backwards underwater somersault that kicked the air out of my lungs and felt like a concussion bomb went off in my head. To my altitude-chilled arms and legs the water felt boiling hot, but as the sea washed under my helmet and armored jacket, the shock of it felt like liquid ice. I fumbled in the disorienting blackness to stuff the mini scuba tank regulator in my mouth while my ears suffered the change in pressure, which felt like a pair of ice picks were shoved into my brain. I barely managed to jettison my parachute harness and wiggle the swim fins on over my neoprene boots, almost losing one in the process, when the surrounding water silently burst with light, like a momentary flash of lightning.

I kicked upward to the surface, breaking the choppy water just in time to see the swath of a searchlight from the yacht come scything back toward me. I waved myself down with my arms then kicked ahead with my rapidly numbing legs, biting down on my mouthpiece while mumbling unintelligible curses as I plowed through the sea. So much for the stealth approach, I thought, just as my throbbing ears picked up the magnified sound of speedboat engines.

I pumped my legs and fixed my eyes on the glowing wrist compass, the only point of light in my cold, oil-black world as I followed the needle northward. The rhythm of my movement helped me fight the chill and gave me focus. My high-altitude drop already felt like the memory of a delirium dream, and I briefly wondered how close I'd come to going unconscious up there. I shook off that thought and started kicking harder as the humming buzz of motorboats got louder in my head. I was in an underwater race for my life.

With a shock, I felt my forward-stretched hand contact a smooth wall that I barely avoided ramming my head into. I'd run straight into the bottom of the yacht. I stopped my breathing mid-breath, fighting the urge to pant as I trickled the air out of my lungs, forcing myself to minimize the bubbles I was sending to the surface. I slowly kicked downward, keeping one gloved hand on the hull and clamping down on my raging urge to breathe. I knew Vanya's troops had automatic rifles, and if he had those, then hand grenades were almost a certainty. I could be concussively blown out of the water in an instant if someone started dropping improvised depth charges into the sea. I cleared the keel of the hull, and then kicked for my life in the direction of the island as I sucked in life-giving draughts of air.

The pervasive engine sounds stayed in the background as I used my compass to change my course ten degrees east. I wanted to avoid the boat docks on the island. My legs were getting tired and feeling leaden as I lost track of the time. I was wondering how much longer I could continue to draw on my little air bottle when my hands plowed into a rough, rocky mass. I slowly kicked toward the surface, breaking water that was gently rolling waves. Through my face mask, the island was a blackened mass blotting out the stars, and behind me I saw the lights of the yacht and a pair of speedboats farther out, scouring the sea for me.

Keeping low in the water, I unloaded all my gear until I was left with my mask, flashlight, and knife. I half swam, half crawled with the gentle waves until I could pull myself ashore. I peeled off the face mask, getting the scent of salt water blended with a mixture of pine and olive tree as I scrambled up the rocks to the hard-packed soil of the island. The moon poured out light from a cloudless sky, bleaching the island bone white. I could clearly see the eastern walls of Vanya's compound across the way. The entire complex was darkened, giving it the appearance of an empty, abandoned fortress.

My jacket and jumpsuit clung to me like dead wet skin, cutting me off from the warm Mediterranean air, and I gritted my teeth to keep them from chattering as I hurried across the bare expanse. I spied a raised area of cover, and ran to a concrete pavilion, shaped like a miniature Acropolis. Stretched out below was an oblong, open-air amphitheater that brought to mind the gladiatorial arenas of Rome. It was Vanya's training ground that Caitlin had told me about. I didn't have the time for the view, however. I could hear footsteps approaching.

I eased back against a fluted pillar and readied my best close-quarter weapon—my flashlight. I slipped my thumb through the lanyard and felt for the light switch. I counted down the steps, feeling like my heartbeat was louder than the sound of approaching booted feet. Then I attacked.

I whipped my arm around and fired off a flash of light, revealing I had a single opponent as I charged. I heard a gasp and had a brief, flickering impression of a dark-skinned soldier, hands up to his face as if trying to wipe away the instant blindness. I gave him a hard, backhanded blow to the head with the butt of the flashlight then slipped in behind him, whipping my free arm around his throat as I released the flashlight and clapped my hand to his mouth. He lurched against me and we fell back together, slamming me between his body and the hard ground.

My chest felt like I'd been stabbed through with a blunt flagpole and I almost lost my grip with the shock of the pain, but I held on as Vanya's soldier flailed about and yelled against my gripping hand, trying to connect with me while fortunately forgetting the heavy rifle that slid back and forth across his chest as he struggled. His body finally melted into unconsciousness and I gratefully rolled him off of me.

I didn't have time to enjoy the respite from being crushed. The carotid hold I used is normally good for rendering an opponent unconscious for only a minute to a minute and a half. I quickly stripped off my neoprene gloves and dug through my wet pockets for the shoestrings that I'd brought with me. I tied the guard's hands behind him, then laced his boots together and fashioned an improvised gag by slicing a long swath from his camouflage shirt. He was just starting to moan and struggle against his bonds as I took up his AK-47 and did a quick search of his web belt. I found a hand-sized radio unit that I turned off before putting it into one of my own pockets. I didn't want to risk triggering an accidental transmission.

I scanned the moon-washed area around me and found it unoccupied. I slipped my knife back into its sheath that I wore on my calf under my jumpsuit and felt inordinately pleased with myself for neutralizing the guard while leaving him alive. All I had to do now was breach Vanya's defenses and get an audience with him. Without being killed, of course. The walls of Vanya's compound were unassailable with my present lack of equipment, but the hillside that the complex was attached to offered possibilities. I ran, not so fast as to risk twisting my ankle on the uneven terrain, until I reached the base of the hill. The mound was overgrown with low, twisted bushes and branches of scrubby pine trees. I checked the safety on my captured rifle, then slung it across my back. Grabbing the curled branches, I pulled myself up the hill.

The foliage had two virtues: it made fairly good handholds and they smelled nice. On the downside, the damn greenery seemed almost animated as it scratched at me and tangled me up almost every inch of the climb. The twisted growth seemed especially fond of grabbing my slung rifle, causing me to stop and free it. I climbed and crawled my way almost to the top of the mound, stopping short of the apex when I spotted Vanya's radar and radio antennas. I didn't know if I'd be tripping any alarms if I got any closer to them, so I moved along in a sideways progression, until I was looking down into Vanya's courtyard. From my vantage point and with the moonlight above, it was like looking into a giant-sized toy box with chess pieces arranged on the bottom. I could hear the rushing sound of the artificial waterfall that covered the entrance to the Roman-style baths in the cave below me.

Climbing up the covered hill was a chore; getting down was flat-out dangerous. Twice, clumps of branches uprooted in my hand, causing me to slip and slide as I grabbed for my life while sending showers of pebbles down ahead of me. Eventually, I reached solid ground at the corner where the wall of the complex mated with the hillside. I unslung my rifle, slipping the selector switch to single-shot fire as I peered around the courtyard. Except for the running waterfall, everything was still and silent, all the marble statues bearing mute witness to the night.

I straightened up and walked ahead. I'd fought my way here, to the very heart of the enemy camp, and now, everything depended on being able to actually talk to Vanya. I made my way to the marble table and Vanya's throne as unnoticed as a ghost in a graveyard. I saw the pedestal and statue of Alexander the Great, wearing the moon like a silvery laurel. A wicked inspiration took hold of me.

I got the transceiver I had taken from the guard and clicked it on. I hit the transmit button and announced, "Vanya, it's Blake. I've come to speak with you."

There was a hiss of static, and then I heard Vanya's voice. "Blake? Where are you?"

"Right here," I said, then tossed the radio away. Had the statue of Alexander been a genuine artifact, I'd never have dreamed of doing what I did next. As it was, I offered a silent apology to the artist as I crouched down for a clear field of fire, flipped the Kalashnikov assault rife to full automatic, and let rip a thunderous, trip-hammering rain of steel and lead that blasted the marble effigy into broken shards.

When the gun ran dry, I whipped it off my shoulder

and slammed it into the pedestal. With my already abused ears ringing, I took my place on Vanya's throne as the sound of running footsteps approached. I was blinded by a bath of light pouring in from numerous sources, and I held my hands up, more to ward my eyes than to signal surrender. As I heard the clicks and clacks of weapons being readied, I said to my unseen captors:

"Take me to your leader."

CHAPTER TWENTY-SEVEN

There was a rough, confused jumble of activity as unseen hands grabbed me and pulled me off of Vanya's throne. Steel handcuffs were ratcheted onto my wrists and I was shoved along with the crowd, like being carried along by the waves of a wild surf. I was prodded along by more than a few jabs from the metal fingers of rifle barrels until I was propelled into the main building and over to the elevators. It was crowded inside on the way down, with all the young soldiers forcing their way in, and when the doors opened up we all spilled out into the concrete bunker. I was marched down the hall and back to the conference room, where I was shoved down onto a chair. With the sound of the heavy metal door shutting me in, I was suddenly surprised to find myself alone.

The room was the same as when I last saw it, with the map of the Mediterranean displayed on the long wall. I eased my leather chair forward until I could rest my handcuffed hands on my lap below the oval, polished-wood table, and waited for my host to make his appearance, fully aware I was being watched the whole time.

Despite the chill I felt within my sodden clothes, I was slowly surrendering to the embrace of exhaustion and had to fight to keep my head from dropping on the table. Finally, I heard the far side door open, and Vanya made his entrance, with Rhea in his wake. Vanya was wearing a dark shirt and slacks, a change from his usual Greek philosopher garb, while Rhea was all in tight-fitting black, and when she took a step to the side, I saw she was wearing a holstered automatic pistol on her belt. What was striking about the pair were their disparate expressions: Vanya glowered, his anger clearly evident on his face, while Rhea looked at me with a smile reminiscent of a kid who'd found a live pony beneath her Christmas tree.

I cut to the point before anyone could suggest cutting my throat. "I've got what you want," I said, glad to hear my voice sounding steadier than I really was. "I know the location of Alexander's tomb."

Vanya leaned his hands on the end of the table, fixing me with a stare. "You're too late," he said in a voice laced with menace. "So do we."

I laughed. "No, you don't. Because if you did, you'd be on your way already. Or you'd at least have sent your pet assassin. I'm betting the Fouché documents you stole from Château de Joux weren't nearly as informative as you hoped."

Vanya tried to stare me down, but I had too many years of facing Nicholas Riley across a poker table to be bluffed. I just smiled and waited, until Vanya broke and said, "Tell me what you know, and I just may let you live."

"Let's put everything on the table, shall we," I said. I hadn't been idle while waiting for Vanya. I'd used the time to unlock the handcuffs with one of my safety pins that I'd converted into a lock pick while I was waiting for liftoff back at the air force base. I tossed the cuffs on the table along with the combat knife that his guards had overlooked in their haste to drag me down here. Vanya thrust himself backwards as if I'd thrown a pair of live snakes at him, slamming into Rhea in the process. While the two of them were off balance, I stood and held my hands up just in time to keep Rhea from shooting me. I said quickly, "Listen to me, I've got what you want, but because of you and that homicidal lunatic girlfriend of yours, I've been implicated in murders and a string of other crimes, and now my own government wants to send me back to prison. So the bottom line is, you took my life from me, and I want another one in return. I suggest a trade."

Rhea kept her small black pistol pointed at my face as she said, "If you know where the body of Alexander is, why didn't you go get it yourself?"

"Because you have Caitlin."

I got a sick feeling in my stomach when I saw the looks Vanya and Rhea traded at the mention of Caitlin's name. "She'd better be alive," I growled.

"She is," Rhea said quickly. Too quickly. "But you didn't answer the question."

I dropped my hands to my sides. Since Rhea didn't shoot, I said, "I have the location, but that's all I have. To actually get to the tomb and recover what's inside,

you need manpower and equipment. All I have is me.
So here's the deal: You let Caitlin go free and give
me ten million dollars for my trouble, and you get
the location of the final resting place of Alexander
of Macedonia. Oh, and there's one other thing I'll
need."

Vanya was stroking his beard, his eyes calculating.
"What's that?"

"The antidote for your Pandora plague. No point
in getting rich if you're not alive to spend it, right?"

Vanya's head slowly turned toward Rhea, anger
clouding his face. Rhea just gave a small shrug. "Blake
wasn't supposed to survive," she explained softly. "I
told him about Pandora to gain his trust."

Everything went quiet inside the conference room.
Vanya's eyes kept flickering to the knife on the table.
Finally, he slowly eased himself into the chair at the
head of the table, and I followed suit in mine. I kept
my hands in the open while Rhea stepped in and stood
behind her master, all the while still smiling at me like
I was a long-lost love returned.

Vanya said, "We could make you talk."

I flexed my scarred right hand. "Sure you could. But
that would take time, trust me, and in the meantime
I could send you off on wild-goose chases all across
the globe, knowing you couldn't kill me until you'd
checked out what I told you."

"How is it that you know the location of the tomb?"
Rhea asked. "How could you possibly know?"

"Especially since you killed everyone at the Château
de Joux and burned the library to cover your tracks?"
I said. "Good try, except for the fact that you bungled
the murder of Madame Ombra. She was still alive

when you left the dungeon. If you weren't in such a hurry to knife her to death, you might have learned what she told me."

"Just how did you manage to get out of the dungeon?" Rhea asked.

I tossed a contemptuous glace at the open handcuffs lying on the table. "Please; locks and I are old acquaintances. Which is another point. Alexander's tomb will doubtless be protected. As I've just proven by waltzing onto your little island retreat, I'm pretty good at getting past defenses. Also, since your Commander Vandervecken is no longer with you, I figure you'll need all the help you can get."

"Vandervecken," Vanya said flatly. "You killed him."

I didn't bother to reply. Vanya looked like he was trying to swallow broken glass, but Rhea's smile never wavered, and she kept her eyes on me as she bent down and whispered into Vanya's ear. Her words seemed contagious, because Vanya's face started to rise in a smile too, until he nodded once, then got up and left the room, but not before giving me a look like a hungry wolf spying a crippled goat.

When the armored door shut behind him with an airtight sound, Rhea walked over toward me, casually picking up the knife from the table. "I really am pleased to see you," she said in a languid tone.

"Oh? Run out of butterflies to pull the wings off of?"

She slowly walked around behind my chair, and then slung a slim hip onto the table as she leaned in close, gently waving the big knife blade like it was a fan. The shimmer of the blade was reflected in her obsidian eyes. "Let's have no more lies between us," she purred. "How did you get back to the island?"

"I used up a lot of money and cashed in a lot of favors. This was a one-way trip for me."

"But why come back at all? You should have known that we'd kill you."

"Like I said, you have Caitlin."

She gave a low, throaty laugh as she suddenly slipped the edge of the knife under my chin. "And you came back for her. How sweet. But you have already told me she's not really your wife."

"No. But she is a government agent, and it'd be stupid to kill her." I felt the sharp edge press in, and I pulled my head up. My voice was tight as I said, "And speaking of governments and agents, looks like you're out of a job too."

"What do you mean?" she asked quickly.

The razor's edge stayed in place and I could feel my pulse against the steel. "I used up one of my favors checking you out. You're not with the Japanese government anymore. Rumor has it they're not pleased with you."

I felt the edge turn up, and Rhea slowly scraped the knife against the skin of my throat, cutting a swath off my whiskers—a haunting reminder of the last time she held a blade to my neck. "So, no more lies indeed," she said as she laughed softly. "It's better this way, is it not?"

A bite of pain shot along my neck, and I saw Rhea pull the knife away. She reached a finger to my skin and came back bearing a bright drop of my blood. She kept her dark eyes locked onto mine as she took my blood with a flick of her tongue.

"That's not what they call a safe practice," I uttered through a strained throat.

"There's no fear here," Rhea said. "Everyone who comes to Vanya's island is examined by his doctors. You and that woman were medically screened before you were allowed to wake up."

"Why?"

"Vanya is a complete germophobe," she whispered conspiratorially. "No one is allowed near him without a thorough examination."

"What? Wait, if that were true, then why in the hell would he be developing a biological weapon? It doesn't make sense."

"It does for him. Death by infection is the most horrible thing Vanya can imagine. It is a measure of his true courage that he has chosen this to be his weapon against the world. Although he is almost obsessive the way he constantly checks on our medical containment facility."

"So it's all true? Vanya really does have biological weapons?"

Rhea suddenly tilted her head and put her hand up to her radio earpiece. Then she slid off the table and said to me, "Come. We have something to show you."

Rhea led me out into the bunker hallway and took me back to the room marked "L-13," the observation room where I first saw Ombra after his torture session. Rhea activated the door and as I entered I saw Vanya inside, bracketed by two of his soldiers along with a woman. She was a short, rounded Asian with her glossy black hair cut into straight bangs that almost came down to the black horn-rimmed glasses she wore. Her eyes were myopically minimized behind the thick lenses. She was dressed in a white lab coat and she wore an expression of hopelessness as if she were weighted down with lead. The wall-sized viewing glass was opaque, reflecting the overhead light like polished obsidian.

As Rhea shut the door behind us, Vanya said, "This is Dr. Song Meilun. Dr. Song has produced quite an interesting little formula for us, haven't you, Doctor? Tell us all about Pandora."

Dr. Song swallowed, as if forcing down a mouthful of hot coal, then she bobbed her head once and said, half mumbling, "It's a derivative of the Q fever, *Coxiella burnetii*. It's been genetically modified to enhance its virulence while retaining its infectivity and resistance to heat, pressure, and various antiseptic compounds. With recombinant reconstruction, we've shortened the incubation period to a projected average of twenty-four to forty-eight hours."

"And the mortality rate?" Vanya prompted sharply.

Dr. Song winced. "Possibly eighty percent. Possibly."

"Symptoms?" Vanya prompted.

"Infected vascular prostheses, aneurysms, osteomyelitis, pulmonary and cutaneous infection."

"In short," Vanya announced, "you bleed out through your pores. But we have the cure, don't we, Doctor?"

Song swallowed and nodded. "We've managed to produce oligonucleotides that will bind and inactivate the infection's biological agents. They act like a synthetic antibody and can be utilized as a prophylactic vaccine."

"Thank you, Doctor," Vanya said dismissively. Dr. Song looked up at Vanya, and then gave a quick bow as she hurried from the room, being trailed by one of Vanya's guards.

I have an eclectic collection of words and phrases I've memorized from languages all across the world. I know the words for "don't shoot" in several tongues. As Dr. Song passed by, I was certain I heard her mumbling in Mandarin the words that asked for forgiveness.

After the door was shut, I said, "So you've got the modern equivalent of the Black Death."

"And more importantly, the cure," Vanya said. "But there's one thing we have a shortage of."

"What's that?"

"Test subjects."

Vanya pressed a button on a nearby table, darkening the lights in the room. Suddenly the opaque wall that separated us from the medical lab cleared, and I saw a sight that stopped my breath like a punch in the throat.

Caitlin and Ombra were in the medical lab, the same one where I spoke with Ombra after he'd suffered through his torture session with Rhea. His face was bruised and drawn, and he was sitting up on the operating table, no longer strapped in. Caitlin was standing in front of him, and both were dressed in hospital-style gowns. As the glass wall cleared, they both turned their heads toward us. Caitlin's eyes narrowed like a cat spotting prey, until she saw me. Then her face lit like sunshine as she hurried toward me. From a speaker concealed somewhere in the viewing room, I heard her voice as she said, "Hello, Jonathan. How goes the Trojan War?"

I pushed past Rhea and put my left hand on the glass. Caitlin looked, and saw the wedding ring she had given me was back on my hand. She smiled and brought her own hand to mine, separated by the cold, thick wall. "Hi, honey. Are you all right?" I managed to say.

Her voice through the hidden speaker sounded far away. "We're fine. Although there've been no shortage of threats." Caitlin shot a look of pure poison over my shoulder. "That creature standing behind you told me you were dead."

"Well, that report was slightly exaggerated. Listen, I've come to get you out of here."

A look I'd walk through fire for welled up in Caitlin's eyes. "I knew you would," she said.

Before I could respond, Caitlin faded from view and I was left staring at a dark reflection of myself. I said to Vanya over my shoulder, "All right, damn it. You've made your point. Let her go, and I'll give you what you want."

Rhea's laughter gave me the answer I dreaded before Vanya said the words: "It's too late, Mr. Blake. Ten hours ago, she and Ombra were infected with Pandora. Now the question is, what will you give me for the cure?"

I had just enough sense left to know that the moment Vanya got the location of Alexander's tomb out of me I'd be demoted into one more disposable test subject. "What you want is on Corsica," I said. "But you'll need me to get it."

"Corsica?" Vanya said quickly. "Where? Where on Corsica?"

I turned my head, and whatever Vanya saw in my face made him take a step back. "Like I said, you'll need me to get it. We're going to be partners, remember? So where you go, I go."

I looked back to the oil-black mirror that separated

Caitlin from me. Behind me, I heard Vanya muttering quietly to Rhea while I studied my face in the reflection. The man before me displayed an expression of dark and dangerous promise, and I wanted this face to be the last thing on earth Vanya ever saw.

I was marched back under guard to the conference room and left there on my own. I shrugged out of my sodden leather jacket, and the combination of air-conditioning and evaporation along with my exhaustion gave me shuddering chills. I attempted a cure by raiding the liquor cabinet for a bottle of Napoleon brandy and taking a mouth-scalding pull that dropped like a burning bomb to my gut. At least it smoothed out the shakes somewhat while I worried about whether all my half-made and half-mad plans were going to unravel on me.

Almost two solitary hours went by and I was starting to feel like the Forgotten Prisoner of Castel-Mare when the hallway door finally opened to reveal Rhea, dressed just as she was before our flight to the Château de Joux and carrying her large black shoulder bag. "Come on," she said. "It's time to get going."

I peeled myself off the chair and grabbed my jacket. "Where to?"

"You did say Corsica, did you not?"

She didn't wait for a reply and I followed her down to the elevators. Once we were in the topside lobby we proceeded out the double front doors to a waiting electric Jeep. The sultry night air felt good as we rode the twisty seaside trail toward the helicopter pad, and though I was glad to get moving, I wasn't looking forward to another chopper flight. But I was far less happy when the Jeep pulled over next to the boat dock.

"What the hell are we doing here?" I asked.

Rhea said over her shoulder as she headed for a powerboat, "Going to Corsica."

That's when I looked over the water and out to sea, where the navigation lights of Vanya's yacht haloed the ship's sleek outline. "You're kidding," I said. "We're taking that tub all the way to Corsica? How the hell long is that going to take?"

"Longer if you just stand there."

We barely got aboard the powerboat when one of Vanya's troops at the helm cast off and fired up the engine. I fell onto one of the cushioned seats in the stern next to Rhea as the boat leapt forward and skipped across the low waves. As we approached the yacht, I saw another powerboat heading back toward the island at full speed. There wasn't much chance of conversation between the roar of the engine and the jaw-clapping slaps of the boat on the water, and I turned my attention to the yacht.

Even in the moonlight, the ship looked like a creature born for speed. From its sharp prow to its curved radar mast, it looked as smooth and sleek as a polished ivory shark. And although I'd been under the belly of this beast, I couldn't appreciate its sheer size until we angled toward the stern. Our pilot executed a fast bootleg turn, killing our speed, and then gently motored up to the lowered landing platform. From the aft view, I could see this seagoing creature was four decks tall and displayed the name of PHAETON flying under the flag of the Cayman Islands. Rhea tossed her bag up to a waiting soldier, and I followed her aboard. There were twin sets of stairs going up either side, and I climbed the port set after Rhea. She led me along the covered outside deck until we reached another set of stairs amidships and went up one more level, then into the ship. Once indoors, it was like we'd crossed over into a low-ceilinged luxury hotel, with soft indirect lighting overhead that gleamed off polished wood and marble-inlaid floors. Rhea took me around a corner to a set of double doors, and opened them up like a magician performing her best trick, snapping the lights on to reveal a stateroom that put almost every landlocked hotel I'd ever stayed in to shame. The suite was appointed with black lacquered wood and chrome accoutrements, surrounding a king-sized bed dressed in black silk on a room-sized Oriental rug. Taken at a glance the place brought the contrary phrase "samurai decadence" to mind. "You'll be staying here," Rhea announced. "There will be guards posted outside, of course."

"Of course."

I could feel more than hear enormous engines being unleashed below my feet as the ship lurched forward. That's when a wasp's sting spiked me on the back of my neck. I whipped around to face Rhea as the feeling of ice-cold water being poured directly on my brain took hold. Rhea's smiling face was bordered in a halo of wavering color as I launched myself toward her to take her down and out, only she wasn't there anymore, and the last thing I heard as solid blackness reared up and hit me was the sound of her laughter somewhere far off in the distance.

CHAPTER TWENTY-EIGHT

Aboard the Phaeton

The next thing I knew, I was miserably surprised to find myself alive. I was cold, chilled by the damp clothes I still wore, and nauseated by a gut that had been set afire. I opened my eyes and instantly shut them again as a spear of light shot into my head. I gritted my teeth and forced my body to rise, aided by the grip I found on the edge of the bed, and hauled myself up to a sitting position while ignoring the grinding pains in my chest. Shading my eyes, I guardedly looked around and saw I had been left on the floor of the neo-samurai stateroom. My head felt dizzy and I could feel the motion of the ship along with the subtle vibrations of the engines. Sunlight was pouring into the room from the partially curtained windows, far too bright to be coming from something as small as a common porthole. I went to check the time on my watch and found myself staring dumbly at my bare wrist. A cursory search yielded the fact that my pockets had been emptied as well. I'd been completely stripped of anything useful, including my self-made lock picks.

I gathered what was left of my strength and stood up on shaking legs, pushed off from the bed, and bounced along the wall to the doors. To my surprise, they were unlocked, and I leaned my head out into the hallway only to see a young, darkly handsome man dressed in a white uniform and cradling a shortened AK-47 standing guard in the rotunda down the hall. He motioned with the barrel of the assault rife, urging me back into the stateroom. As I shut the doors, I briefly wondered how many thousands of dollars worth of damage he could have done to the richly appointed hallway if he'd let rip with his machine gun.

Retreating back inside the room, I tried the only other set of doors, a pair of black lacquered ones adorned with gold-leaf inlays, and found a small but lavishly furnished bathroom, complete with a shower and tub. The only thing that ruined the view was the reflection in the triple mirror of a walking corpse. I'd seen drowning victims look better than I did at the moment. But as the bath was equipped with everything a guest might need, I wasted no time peeling off my clammy clothes and getting into the shower, pouring some cleansing liquid heat on my skin, and scouring the bitterness out of my mouth. When I felt halfway human, I reluctantly shut off the water and rubbed myself dry with the oversized towels. I grimaced at my face in the mirror as I saw the clean-shaven swath that Rhea had made on my neck with the combat knife, and since my hands weren't shaking quite so badly now I decided I might as well take the rest of my whiskers off.

Finally, I wrapped myself in a guest robe, let the

steam out into my cabin, and opened the curtains. I had a full-sized window view of a vast expanse of sea under a cloudless blue sky with sunlight sparkling off the waves as the ship arrowed across the water.

I heard the door to the stateroom open behind me as Rhea called out cheerfully, "Good morning. I heard you were awake."

I turned to look and almost did a double take. Rhea was wearing a sundress that was a riot of color, and had her long, glossy black hair down and free. The way she was smiling, she looked like a tourist having the time of her life.

"What are you doing here?"

She glided up to me, standing too close for comfort, and offered up a white bundle. "I've brought you some clothes. Please dress now. Vanya wants to speak with you."

I took the clothes from her and waited for her to back up and give me some space, but she just stood there, smiling at me. So I let the robe fall—damned if I was going to let her make me flinch—and put on the white shorts and short-sleeved shirt that looked like they could have been a British Navy tropical uniform. While I was buttoning the shirt, Rhea reached out and took my left hand in hers. She lifted my arm up until the wedding ring I wore reflected sunlight. "Why do you still wear this?" she asked. "That woman back on the island is not your wife. Are you actually married to someone else?"

"No."

"Ah. Well, then, you won't be needing it any-more." Rhea slipped her fingers up my hand, pulling the ring off while reaching over with her free hand to

open the sliding glass window. A buffet of warm salt
air and engine noise blew into the room and my ring
flew out of it, taking its electronic secret to a watery
grave. I kept my face in neutral as I wondered what
Smith would make of the ring's last signal.

As she slid the window shut, Rhea sighed as if in satisfaction and said, "Now, we need to go. Vanya does
not like to be kept waiting."

I followed her out of the stateroom and aft to the
rotunda. Mirrors inlaid with gold leaf gave the illu-
sion of depth as Rhea led me to a circular stairway,
where I also noticed that the ship had an elevator system installed. We went one deck down and Rhea took
me to another door aft, only this one looked as solid
as the hatch of a submarine. She spun the locking wheel
and pulled the hatch open, then she reached in and
pulled aside a thick white curtain. When I stepped
through, I saw that the bulkhead in this room was
heavily armored.

Rhea should have said "Open Sesame," because going inside was like walking into a story straight out
of the *Arabian Nights*. The large room was hourglass
shaped and dressed in silky curtains. Soft light emanating from chandeliers illuminated a sybaritic scene
that a Saudi prince would have envied. My bare feet
sank into a rich Oriental rug as my sense of smell was
allured by the scent of rich and exotic food, spiced with
a hint of incense. Low tables on either side held delicacies, and it took more willpower than I cared to admit
to not let my empty stomach lead me astray.

Vanya was ensconced on a divan of plush cushions, guarded on either side by a couple of his young
soldiers. Vanya himself was decked out in something

that looked like a cross between white silk pajamas and a naval admiral's uniform, while his guards wore the same white shirt and shorts arrangement that I did. It would have been a lot more aesthetic if they'd been carrying spears instead of automatic rifles. The last person in the room was an older man with dark, scarred features, standing off to the side with arms crossed and bearing a scowling expression. He was also in a white uniform, but one that declared him to be a ship's captain. He gave the impression that he'd be more at home among the Barbary pirates of old.

Vanya waved a greeting. "Ah, Blake. So, what do you think of my ship?"

"Caligula would have been envious. I need to know about Caitlin. This deal is off if she dies."

Rhea said, "It's been just over nine hours since we left. We should reach Corsica within forty hours overall."

"Forty hours! But Caitlin—"

"Will be past the virus's incubation period," Rhea finished. "She is young. She should be able to survive for some time after we arrive. But I don't think Ombra will make it. You could save her much earlier, you know."

"How?"

It was Vanya who answered. "You could tell us exactly where the tomb of Alexander is. Once we have verified the information, we could send the signal to give the cure to your Caitlin. And Ombra too, if you like, though I don't know why you'd want to save him."

I felt my jaw clench as if to keep the secret of the Blood Islands locked in my teeth. I was absolutely certain that once Vanya knew the location, I'd be tossed overboard to join my wedding ring down in the depths. Not trusting myself to speak, I just shook my head.

Vanya shrugged, as if the matter was of no great importance. "Regardless, Captain Tobias here will need to know where we should anchor the ship once we reach Corsica. We should be in the vicinity by early tomorrow evening. Also, I need to know exactly what resources we will need to recover Alexander's remains."

Rhea directed me to sit on the other side of a low oval table across from Vanya, and she settled in next to me. The table itself was covered in nautical charts and several color photographs I assumed were of the island of Corsica. They depicted a variety of locales, from dusty rose-colored Mediterranean towns to rugged mountains and forests to seaside scenes. Surveying the maps, I asked, "Where are we now?"

Captain Tobias answered in a rolling bass voice with a lilting accent, "We are on course for the Strait of Messina once we round Italy; six hours present speed."

My eyes traced our route from the Ionian Greek islands across to the southern tip of Italy and the narrow passage between the Italian peninsula and the island of Sicily. Once clear of the strait, the course would be northwest to Corsica. There was another chart on the table that displayed Corsica itself and the smaller islands surrounding it. Then a particular photograph caught my eye.

"What is it?" Rhea asked quickly. "What do you see?"

Mentally, I was kicking myself. While I was looking over the maps and photos on the table, Rhea was studying me—watching to see if I would give away a clue to our destination by making a reaction. The picture that arrested my interest was of a stone tower standing guard on a rocky shoreline. It looked like a giant-sized rook chess piece, and my heart skipped a beat as I wondered if this was the watchtower Lord Byron referred to in his letter to Percy Shelley.

I was glad to see my hand wasn't shaking as I reached across the photograph of the watchtower and tapped the map of the sea that separated Corsica from Italy. "Monte Cristo island," I said aloud.

Vanya leaned forward with greedy alacrity. "Monte Cristo? Is that the location?"

"No," I replied. "But that would have been fun, wouldn't it? It does make me wonder why Alexandre Dumas chose that particular island as the location for the hidden treasure in *The Count of Monte Cristo*."

Vanya was not amused. "Indeed," he said flatly as he settled back into his cushions. I examined the chart showing the Tyrrhenian Sea that separated Italy from Corsica, thinking about Lord Byron's letter, where he wrote that he could see Elba and Corsica from his seaside villa. Although he didn't know it at the time, old Byron was also looking straight at the place where his friend and fellow poet Percy Shelley was destined to drown. But all of this concerned the eastern side of Corsica. The Blood Islands, or the "Iles Sanguinaires," as the map proclaimed, were on the western side of the island, right next to Ajaccio, the birthplace of Napoleon Bonaparte. And again I wondered at the confluence of historical events.

I let my eye wander over the photographs, careful not to display particular interest. "Looks like lots of mountainous terrain here."

"Is this a concern?" Vanya inquired.

I shrugged. "I guess we won't know until we get there."

"We've been doing our homework," Rhea said. "Corsica is one of the largest islands in the Mediterranean Sea and covers over three thousand square miles. It's interesting to note that Corsica has over one hundred caves scattered throughout the island."

The last statement was a gambit designed to draw information out of me. "Really?" I said in my best politely bored voice. To move Vanya's attention away from the map and pictures, I asked, "So what resources do we have on this old tub of yours?"

It was Rhea who replied with, "We have twenty-eight able-bodied young men aboard. All have had military training. And we have enough armaments and explosives to overthrow a small government, if we had to."

Vanya stroked his white beard and said with a sly tone in his voice, "It would save considerable time if we knew what part of Corsica we should head toward. Time your Caitlin can't afford to lose."

I was trapped between the inescapable logic of Vanya's statement and my need to retain enough information to save my own life. Finally I said, "You can put into port at Ajaccio. That will be close enough."

Vanya's eyes lit up as he hissed, "Ajaccio! Of course! It was Napoleon's first destination after he fled from Egypt. But I'd have thought that was too obvious. Still, we'll anchor well off the coast. I don't want to be trapped in the harbor."

Rhea said, "We have a variety of small boats aboard. We can move our men to the island on those."

"What sort of defenses can we expect?" Vanya asked quickly.

I just shrugged like a gambler with a fifth ace up his sleeve and said, "I guess you'll just have to take me along to find out."

Vanya's eyes flashed, and then clouded over as he leaned back on his cushions. "Very well," he said, then to Rhea, "Take Blake back to his room."

Rhea and I stood and I let her lead me out of the suite while Vanya had a hurried and hushed discussion with Captain Tobias. Walking down in the marble-floored hallway of the rotunda, I saw another armed guard on duty, who nodded to Rhea as she escorted me to my room. "Try and get some rest," she advised with a cryptic smile. "I'm sure you'll need it."

Once back in my seagoing-samurai stateroom, I was glad to see an array of silver platters and carafes of food and drink waiting for me, fit for Arabian royalty. I wasted no time in refueling myself while I observed that the main difference between the forces of Good and Evil came down to the fact that in this particular case, Evil had much better accommodations.

The rest of the day was torture in slow motion, with every moment counting as a nail in Caitlin's coffin. At one point during the seemingly endless day I heard the engines slow and I felt waves of uneven turbulence sway the ship. I drew the curtains back and saw we were traversing the Strait of Messina. From my port-side window I watched as we sailed past the island of Sicily with the western sun backlighting the buildings and towns dotting the reddish rocky landscape and the ships and boats sailing to and from the harbors, until we cleared the last spur of land and picked up speed in the open sea.

Hours later, after I'd watched the sun sink into a

flaming red death, I heard the stateroom doors open and saw Rhea enter, leading a rolling chrome serving cart. She'd changed from her multicolored sundress into a red and gold kimono, but my eyes were drawn to the bottles she'd brought. "What are you doing here?" I inquired.

Rhea set the tray on one of the black lacquered tables. "This is my room," she said simply.

I went over and looked at the contents of the serving tray. "Jack Daniel's and Bacardi?"

"Yes. And Russian vodka, along with some cocaine from Peru or hashish from Turkey, if you'd prefer."

I also spotted my crushed box of cigarettes and my lighter lying next to a hash pipe and small silver spoon. "Isn't this kind of premature for a celebration?" I asked.

"This is our last night before we reach Corsica. We should take advantage of the time we have." Rhea picked up my lighter and took one of my flattened cigarettes from the box. She lit up and drew in, then passed the cigarette to me, all the while keeping her dark eyes aimed at my face. I took the offered cigarette and tasted her lips on the filter as she held up my lighter, displaying the side with the dragon design, and asked, "Does this hold a special meaning for you?"

"My lighter? Not really. Why do you ask?"

Rhea traced the etching as she said, "I was born in the Year of the Dragon."

I went to open the window. "Really? I'd have guessed some other creature entirely."

I heard her laugh as she asked, "So what would you prefer?"

I gazed out across a sea full of stars. "I'll take a Bacardi on ice and some privacy."

I heard the tinkling of ice and glass, and then the lights went low and soft as gentle music floated into the room. Rhea's jasmine scent heralded her arrival next to me as she handed me a glass and sat down on the divan beneath the window. She took my arm and guided me down beside her. "I'm staying here with you tonight," she said softly.

"Why?"

"Vanya thinks someone should keep an eye on you, so you don't get into any mischief. Besides, I'm the only woman on board. You should feel privileged."

I took a drag of smoke and chased it with the liquid fire of the rum. "I'll try to keep that in mind."

In the semidarkness, I watched as Rhea gracefully rose from the couch and walked around the large bed, letting the kimono fall from her body. She slid in between the covers and smiled at me, resting her head in her hand and letting her midnight-black hair spill over the pillows.

Despite the fact that I knew what a dangerous and ruthless creature she was, I could feel the electric thrill evoked by the presence of a desirable woman. I took a last draw of my cigarette and tossed it overboard, then finished my drink in one swallow. I shut the windows as the lights in the room flickered out and I considered that my choices of places to sleep boiled down to the carpeted deck or sharing the large bed with Rhea. Despite my better judgment, I chose the bed.

The silken sheets felt cool and slick, but the temperature rose fast when Rhea slid over to my side, wrapping herself around me, and laughing as she felt the shirt and shorts I'd kept on. "This could be our last night together," she whispered in a husky, bedroom voice.

She ran a finger down my face. Her fingertip felt rough, like the tongue of a cat—a reminder of all the deadly things her hands could do. She was a creature so much like myself, and like me—she wasn't born this way. Something in her past had changed her. I reached up and took her hand. "What happened?" I whispered.

She froze. "What do you mean?"

"What made you sell out your country to a man like Vanya?"

She pulled her hand away as if it had caught fire. "A man like Vanya? There has never been a man like Vanya in my life," she whispered fiercely.

Rhea raised herself up on one elbow, looking down at me. "As for the other so-called men I have known, my father abandoned my mother before I was born, leaving her in poverty. You don't know what it was like growing up a half-caste in Japan, the rejected daughter of a 'gaugin.' The next man in my life came to me when I turned eighteen and told me how I could serve my country and my people. That's when I became a whore for the government."

Her bitterness was palpable as she continued. "I was trained for other things, of course. But with my appearance, my superiors thought that I could serve my country best by seducing men, and in some cases women, and stealing their secrets from them. After all, it was not like they were asking a pure-blooded woman to commit such unclean acts, no? Then I discovered that one of the many men I had been sent to have sex with had given me a disease."

She must have felt my reaction, because she then said, "Oh, have no fear. I have long ago been cured. But not before my womb was destroyed. My unborn children were sacrificed for the greater good of my country. Then I met Vanya."

"That's when you joined him?"

"Oh, no. At first, he was just another assignment. I was to infiltrate his organization, join his religious movement, and do whatever was necessary to find out if he was involved in the sarin gas attack in Tokyo. So I did. But then, I discovered something wonderful."

"What?"

Her mood shifted like the wind; now she sounded almost happy as she murmured, "What one man of true vision can do. Vanya is going to change the world, and he has chosen me to make it all possible."

"How?"

Rhea laid her head down on my shoulder as she said, "Vanya has chosen me to bring the future leader of the world to life. His doctors have already harvested my womb and we have found suitable surrogate mothers to bear my future children. With all the benefits of science at Vanya's command, I will become the mother of a race of Alexanders. A family of them. And together we will reshape the world."

With a small sigh, she settled her head against my chest. I was left entwined with a mad, dangerous creature. I slowly turned my head toward the window, catching sight of a silver wedge of the moon as the ship sailed on, and wondered if I'd still be alive come morning.

CHAPTER TWENTY-NINE

Corsica

Much to my surprise, I woke up in sunlight.

Rhea was gone, leaving behind only her scent on the sheets and pillows. A quick survey of the room revealed she'd left my lighter on the drink tray, and I slipped it into my pocket. With nothing better to do, I used the shower and bathroom to my advantage. I briefly toyed with the idea of creating some improvised weapons and escape tools from the supplies I found, but decided that even if I wasn't under constant surveillance, Vanya and Rhea were on to me, and I doubted I'd be allowed to keep anything I could put together. When I emerged, I saw that the trays and cart had been removed and fresh food and drinks provided, including a blessed serving of coffee. I made use of my cushioned captivity by taking my abused body through some slow stretching exercises, probing for the limitations of my injuries. Then I had nothing to do but endure the agony of waiting.

Ultimately, when the sun was once again low on the horizon, I felt the ship's engines throttled back to a dull mutter, and a young soldier rudely opened my door and waved the barrel of his assault rifle around to indicate I should follow. He prodded me along the circular stairway up two decks, past what looked like a recreation area, until I was outdoors in the Mediterranean wind under a sky lit by a sinking sun that turned the clouds above into glowing embers. Vanya, wearing his white admiral's clothes, and Rhea, dressed in a form-fitting lightweight black diving suit, were already present on the observation deck, which rocked slightly from the low waves that swelled under the ship. Above and astern I saw the towering radio and radar arrays, while ahead I could see the smooth white roofs of the layered levels below and an arrowhead-shaped open deck area at the bow. That's where a pair of crewmen were assembling a tripod-mounted, belt-fed machine gun. I nodded down toward the armament preparations and asked, "Expecting company?"

Vanya raised his head from a mounted pair of powerful binoculars. "We have arrived," he announced. "Now, if you would be so good as to tell me where I can find the tomb?"

I pointed to the binoculars, and Vanya stepped away. I bent down and scanned the eastern horizon and the coastline of Corsica. I could see the raised mountainous terrain, vibrant green with patches of bare, bone-colored rock, and the ivory-and-rust-colored coastal towns, along with the rainbow-hued sails of pleasure boats in the water near the harbor. It took a few minutes to get my bearings, but I finally spotted a separate set of smaller islands bathed in the bloody dying light of the sun almost directly north of us. I zeroed in, getting the rhythm of the movement of the ship as I focused on the largest island and saw the watchtower crowning its crest. Vanya must have seen me smile. "What is it?"

I relinquished the binoculars. "Over there." I pointed. "The Iles Sanguinaires; the Blood Islands. That's the place you want."

Vanya grabbed at the binoculars greedily as I stepped aside. I let him find the view before I said, "So tell me—you're really going to destroy most of the people in the world?"

Vanya didn't reply. He just stared through the lenses. Finally, he stood up and turned to me, speaking in a calm and reasonable-sounding voice. "The world is a sick place, Mr. Blake. It's chaotic, and overcrowded, and filled with conflict and death and suffering. What this planet needs is unification and guidance. Only a true worldwide empire could bring about the peace and prosperity that would take our planet to a utopian future. And only another Alexander can bring the world what it needs and give it peace."

"Peace? You mean the peace of the grave? You're planning on wiping out most of the people on the planet."

"Yes," he replied calmly. "There must be a cleansing, the slate wiped clean. And out of all the blood and fire will come a world worth living in. When I resurrect the bloodline of Alexander I will create a dynasty that will unite the world as Alexander himself had intended. And I will be the father of that dynasty."

Vanya was no longer seeing me. He stood before me

bathed in the fiery glow of a dying sun and lost in his vision. I had a vision of my own just then as my mind raced through all the ways I could kill Vanya here and now. But it would have been my last act on earth, and if Vanya wasn't lying about his minions being ready to activate the plague upon his reported death, then I would also become the man who set off the Apocalypse.

My moment passed as Vanya said to the guard behind me, "Take Blake below."

"When are you going to signal your doctors to give Caitlin the cure?"

"When I have the body of Alexander in my possession. So you better be prepared to do your part. You'll be going over with Rhea and my men, just in case there's anything you've neglected to tell us about."

With a dismissive wave from Vanya and a gun-barrel poke in my kidney, I turned and went below to my cabin. Once alone I paced the stateroom, wondering if my cryptic clues about Corsica and watchtowers would be enough for Sam Smith to figure out Vanya's destination or that he at least had people shadowing the yacht. My one hope was to find a secret welcoming committee waiting for us at the watchtower.

When the last rays of the sun extinguished themselves in the sea, Rhea came to my room. She tossed a black diving suit on the bed. "Here, put this on. We're leaving now."

I did as I was told, pulling the suit on over my shirt and shorts. I could feel my lighter snug in my pocket. It was my only remaining tool. With any luck, I thought, I could at least add one more dent in its casing before someone killed me tonight. As I dressed, Rhea said in a wistful tone, "I'm sorry we didn't take advantage of last night. It could have been beautiful."

I had a brief, fleeting vision of me and Rhea, holding each other close with our hands wrapped around each other's throats. "It could have been something," I agreed.

I finished dressing in the thin, tropical diving suit. It wouldn't offer much in the way of protection against cold water, but at least I wouldn't sweat to death while wearing it. I left the black hood of the suit off and followed her out and toward the stern and then over to the starboard covered promenade. I heard the whine of powerful hydraulics and saw the side of the yacht open up like a slow-moving wing of a giant bird. Once Rhea and I made it to the rear, we descended two levels of stairs until we reached the stern boarding platform, where we joined a silent group of men dressed in form-fitting black and bearing packs and slung weapons. While Rhea was donning a pack of her own, I leaned over the rail and saw a small, twin-engine powerboat being lowered into the water from the underside of the ship's extended wing. Vanya had the ship on running lights only, and as my eyes adjusted to the starlit darkness, I saw that the stern platform was armed with a tripod-mounted machine gun along with a rack of shoulder-borne, rocket-propelled grenade launchers set up nearby. I heard muted engine sounds, humming low and bubbling in the water as the powerboats were piloted up to the docking ramp. Rhea tapped my shoulder and pointed to the one on the right. I climbed aboard the small seating area at the bow with Rhea and three of her men coming aboard and crowding the boat with me.

Without a signal given, the twin miniature power-boats motored off and curved toward the islands. Above us a sickle of moonlight cut through the inky black clouds that blotted the sky. Ahead toward the island, the lights of Corsica glowed like a bundle of stars had been compressed flat on the horizon, and triple-beat flashes were fired from a lighthouse like silent, rhythmic lightning.

I saw that our pilot, dressed in aquatic ninja wear like the rest of us, wore a pair of night-vision goggles as he steered across the gently rolling sea. Our two-boat flotilla quietly motored past a chain of tall-spined islands jutting out of the water like volcanoes, one of which was crowned by the lighthouse, until I could see a jagged, solid blackness rearing up ahead. We passed a chain of smaller outcroppings and then reached a black mountain washed in dark silver moonlight. The pilot cut the engines and came forward, grabbing a line and jumping into the water. Rhea and I followed suit overboard along with the three other soldiers, and I slogged through the cool, thigh-deep seawater up to the rocky shore.

While the water lapped on the edge of the landfall, I counted the soldiers assembling—there were twelve of us altogether. Rhea tapped my arm, and with the rest of the assault team I climbed up the rough, jagged side of the island. Taken at a glance, we looked like an army of giant black spiders attacking a monstrous anthill. The ragged, broken teeth of stone and clumps of tough vegetation provided hand- and footholds, but it was still a dangerous climb, and I was given sharp, painful reminders from my chest that my ribs hadn't had a chance to heal from their previous ordeals. I kept my concentration on the terrain, and was surprised when suddenly I found myself standing on a flattened ledge comprised of a man-made concrete walkway. The soldiers were unslinging their weapons and I wasn't given a chance to catch my breath as Rhea pushed me along the path that took a circular course up the hill.

As we neared the summit, I could see the massive, rounded turret of the watchtower at the apex. Rhea and I continued to walk uphill as Vanya's soldiers broke off and took up positions in the surrounding area. That's when I spotted the shadowy outline of a man lurking at the base of the tower. I felt a surge of relief when I heard the well-remembered voice of Sam Smith call out, "Blake? Is that you?"

But my relief was broken into a thousand bitter shards when Rhea replied warmly, "Hello, Sam. I hope we didn't keep you waiting long."

I watched with a feeling of numb paralysis as Rhea glided up to Sam Smith and they exchanged a warm embrace. I took a few faltering steps over to the watchtower and let its weathered walls keep me from falling over. Through the darkness I heard Smith say, "You sure took your damn time getting here, Blake."

"Sorry to inconvenience you, you traitorous bastard."

"Hey now, that's mighty rough talk from an admitted thief like you."

"Besides, Blake," Rhea said, "you really shouldn't be surprised. I told you there was a mole in Smith's agency. Sam was also kind enough to let me know all about that wedding ring locator you had. Now no one knows you're here but us."

"Actually," Smith said, "I prefer the term 'undercover entrepreneur.' But credit where credit is due, Blake; we couldn't have found this place without you."

My words seemed to boil up out of my burning gut. "Yeah. I led you right to it, didn't I?"

"Right to it, my ass," Smith countered. "I bet you thought you were being clever with that 'All Along the Watchtower' hint, didn't you? But did you know how many goddammed watchtowers there are on Corsica? Ninety-one! We had no clue which one was which until just a short time ago."

"Like I said, sorry for the inconvenience, et cetera."

"What have you found so far?" Rhea asked Smith.

"Come around the other side and I'll show you."

I let the Mediterranean Sea breeze blow away the cold sweat that welled out of me as I pushed off the wall and walked around the rocky ground behind Smith and Rhea. The tower was huge, easily over one hundred feet in circumference, and it loomed almost forty feet high. As I walked around the base of the tower, I was dimly aware of all the young gunmen who surrounded the area like ghosts haunting a castle. On the other side of the watchtower, I could see the mountainous mass of Corsica with its faint girdle of twinkling lights beyond. Smith said, "First of all, where we are right now is actually a peninsula, not an island. I was able to drive here, so we have to be careful not to attract the attention of the local police. But the real problem is this damn tower. Namely, there's no way to get inside from the ground level."

Smith shot a narrow flashlight beam over the stone face of the tower, revealing a rectangular doorway cut into the irregular stone mortar nearly twenty feet above our heads. "There must have been a ladder or stairs here once," Smith explained.

Rhea tilted her head back, examining the tower. "This is where the tomb is? It seems so . . . so obvious a place. Why wouldn't it have been discovered before now?"

As lonely as the windswept tower was, Rhea was right. But the words of Lord Byron's coded letter came back to me: "Blood-Islands-Corsica-Beneath-Watch-Tower." I said, almost despite myself, "What you're looking for is underneath the tower."

Smith looked up at the massive edifice, and then kicked at the rocky ground. "Underneath it? How're we supposed to get below this thing?"

"I guess we'll just have to cut through a wall," Rhea stated in a matter-of-fact tone. "The path may start within the tower."

I winced at the thought of the destruction of the centuries-old watchtower and said without thinking, "What, no one thought to bring a rope or something?"

I could hear the smile in Rhea's voice. "Well, it's a good thing we've brought along our very own tomb robber, isn't it?" She hissed out a command to her men, and as one of the soldiers came running up to her, Smith said to me, "You know what they call this place, don't you? It's called the Islands of Bloodthirsty Men. Kind of fits, don't it?"

"Come a little closer and we'll see if it's true."

Smith laughed quietly, but he did move a few paces away from me as he did so.

One of Rhea's soldiers did have a rope and grapnel hook arrangement, and for the next few minutes I watched as he tried time and again to throw the hook through the opening above. Finally, the hook held and Rhea said, "I'm going first." It was disheartening to see how she climbed up the rope with both speed and skill. As soon as she disappeared into the shadowed doorway, I heard her voice call out, "Send Blake."

I'd learned how to scale walls during my early Argo survival training, and it was a skill I'd employed on several occasions since, but I was painfully reminded how long ago that was. By the time I managed to reach the doorway my arms were burning from the strain and my ribs were splinters of agony, and I was grateful for the hand Rhea offered as I pushed myself over the transom with my trembling legs. I made it through the doorway, which was a short hallway through the six-foot-thick fortress walls, and then rolled out of the way and lay on my back, gasping for breath. In quick succession, four more black-garbed soldiers came through the opening. I was the only one who was breathing hard.

As Rhea and her men spread out, they waved flashlight beams in all directions. The room we were occupying was a rounded chamber with a low stone ceiling. There was a slight breeze that blew through with a low moan, coming from a hemispherical opening in the wall on the seaward side. I peeled myself off the cold stone floor and took a slow walk around the room. Along the wall was a set of stone stairs that twisted up to the next level and down to the floor below. Rhea led the way, sidestepping down the stairs as silently as a cat. A soldier behind me gave me an encouraging shove with a gunstock to let me know I was next in line.

As we descended to the chamber below, the air grew still and was saturated with a musty, graveyard taint. Rhea's flashlight cut around the room, revealing rounded, featureless stone-and-mortar walls. Her voice was oddly refracted by the room as she said, "If there was anything here once, it's gone now. So tell me, Blake—has your usefulness come to an end?" She was patently asking if there was any reason to keep me alive any longer. Fortunately for my limited life expectancy, Rhea was right on the mark when she called me a tomb robber. Treasures and secret hiding places went hand in hand all through history, and I'd seen more than a few hidden doors and passageways in my travels.

"Check the along the floor," I said. "There may be another level beneath this."

Rhea's voice dripped with derision. "You mean, you want us to look for a secret passage or something?"

"Secret passages have been around since the time of the ancient pyramids. Hell, in Japan, no one ever built a castle that didn't have at least one hidden escape route."

As the rest of Rhea's men joined us below, their lights found a bathtub-sized hole in the floor, but a quick check showed this led to a sealed chamber below. "A cistern," I explained. "It's where they stored their water supply. Keep looking."

It took less than a minute to see that there was no obvious way down. So I started to look for an unobvious one. I let Rhea and her men tap along the walls, knowing that to be a futile endeavor; no fortification builder would compromise the defensive thickness of the walls just to conceal a passage. The only other shape that intruded into the room was the curved stone stairway. I felt along the time-worn stone and found a rusted iron bar, like an oversized staple anchored to the side. I braced my leg against the wall and pulled, but the only thing that happened was that I felt like I almost popped a rib through my skin. I took a breath and instead gave the bar a shove, and felt a section of the wall as it moved a bit and scraped on the floor.

Rhea heard the sound and was over beside me in an instant. "Did you find it?" I just gave the wall another push and this time it gave way, exposing an inner set of stairs heading downward. "Fantastic!" Rhea said, and in her excitement she threw an arm around me and gave a squeeze that caught me on my injured side. I kept from venting a howl of pain as she turned to her men. "Castor, you take the lead, then I'll bring Blake as the rest of you follow."

The stone steps were steep and the passageway narrow, and then the passage gave way to a tunnel cut through the rock. I was at a disadvantage, as the soldier ahead of me was blocking the light of his flashlight and my own body cast a shadow from Rhea's light behind me. As the cave continued to twist and turn in a claustrophobic, angled path, Rhea spoke and gave words to my own growing fears. "This is wrong," she said. "There's no way anyone could have carried something as large as a sarcophagus down this tunnel."

I was poignantly aware of Rhea's penchant for stabbing people in the back as I replied, "Let's at least see where this leads."

Rhea said in a sweet-sounding half whisper, "Maybe we'll just find a good place for us to say good-bye to each other."

We continued our cramped, twisting, single-file descent. There were signs here and there where the dark gray granite had been artificially chipped away to widen the fissure. Finally, we reached an area that opened into a small cavern, and over the shoulder of the man in front of me I saw a black iron door had been bolted onto the rock, a door that reminded me of the one I saw at the underground torture chamber back in the Château de Joux. The man in front put his shoulder to the metal and grunted. "Locked," was all he said.

Rhea pulled me aside and I watched as another soldier unslung his pack and opened it up on the cavern floor, while a third soldier held a light overhead. I saw that the pack contained flat packages of explosive and other demolition tools. Rhea's boys worked with smooth efficiency as they took a small lump of C-4 and molded it along the edge of the door. One soldier placed a pencil-sized detonator cap into the explosive and then waved us back to the tunnel. We went back along far enough to be out of the line of fire, then I warded my ears with my hands as the soldier thumbed a radio detonator and unleashed a clap of compressed thunder.

The air was laced with the smell of spent explosives and hot iron, and before I could say anything the lead soldier ran to the doorway. I could see the iron door was bent and slightly ajar, and the soldier gave it a kick. Only then the door kicked back with a fiery explosive blast that dropped the man like a disjointed doll. Rhea tackled me and took me to the hard rock floor as the rest of her men opened fire over our heads, battering our eardrums with the staccato concussions of their silenced submachine guns, mixed with the crack of jacked bullets hitting rock and the drumbeat gongs of rounds slamming into the metal door. Then there was nothing but the ringing in my ears and the weight of Rhea across my back, pressing my splintered ribs into the stony ground.

I lifted my head up while the gunmen quickly dropped spent magazines from their assault rifles and slammed fresh ammunition in place. In the waving beams of the weapon-mounted flashlights, I saw the young man who had been blown back from the door sprawled on the ground, his chest a wet red ruin. One of the remaining three soldiers shot a light beam ahead, and through the doorway I saw a short-barreled shotgun affixed to a wooden frame tripod, now broken and askew. It was a death trap rigged to shoot anyone who came through the door. The lead soldier reached in and grabbed the weapon, roughly yanking it free from its cradle. I heard Rhea's soft whisper, spoken in Japanese, as she went to the man on the ground. She knelt down, stroking his face, but his sightless eyes showed he was beyond the reach of any earthly comfort.

Rhea stood up and her face in the reflected light was a hard mask of frozen anger. She held out her hand,

and the soldier with the shotgun handed it over to her with a short bow of obeisance. Rhea motioned for a light, and as she examined the gun I saw to my surprise that the rusty antique shotgun was of a type that wasn't manufactured until about a hundred years after Napoleon's time.

That's when a scent came to me, one that cut through the odors of burnt gunpowder and fresh blood. I could suddenly sense we were close to the sea; it was a sharp, tide-pool smell that came from farther down the cavern. Rhea caught the scent as well, and she gave her men hand signals to move past the door. Rhea pushed me ahead of her, and I walked into another chamber of the cavern, only this area looked like it'd been used as a refuse dump. Rusted cans and containers were heaped near flat piles of broken glass. But one stack caught my eye. "Hold it," I whispered.

Rhea didn't stop me as I carefully stepped among the trash until I came to a set of six rusty, rectangular metal boxes with handles built onto the tops. I selected the closest one to me, and held it up to catch a beam of light. It was an old German Army ammunition box of World War II vintage. I could clearly make out the winged eagle and swastika stamp on its battered side. The box was empty, but when a beam of light caught on the inside, I saw streaks of gold specks glitter back at me from the metal sides. "What is it?" Rhea hissed from behind me.

"Proof that this place has been visited since at least the last World War," I whispered back. "And evidently by the Nazis."

Rhea's strained voice was pure anger. "No!"

I turned and held the German ammo box up for her. "See? With something like this, you might as well have a sign that reads 'Hitler slept here.' "

"But if the Nazis found the hiding place of the tomb of Alexander, then why . . . ?"

I finished the thought for her. "Then why didn't Hitler announce it to the world? Who knows? But it's looking like this is a dead end." Literally, I thought.

Rhea's arm fell, splashing her light on the ground and casting her face into darkness. One of her men said, "The tunnel continues," in a voice that was devoid of hope. Finally, Rhea said, "Then let's see this through to the bitter end. Come, Blake."

We followed the intensifying smell of brackish seawater until the rough-hewn tunnel opened up again, this time into a cathedral-sized cavern. The flashlights waved around the enormous cavity until one cut across something that reflected back with a dull gleam. We all walked forward, spreading out as everyone's lights converged on a massive form that seemed to grow out of the ground.

The area ahead sloped downward and we could see the ground disappear into black water. At first glance, I saw what looked like a huge beached whale, colored dark green in the lights, lying half submerged near the rocky shore. As we drew closer, I could make out a rounded raised section on the top of the thing that glittered back as if it were a cyclopean eye. I felt an electric charge run down my spine as I heard myself say, "My God! It's a submarine!"

"What?" Rhea hissed. "How can that be?"

I started walking toward the craft, drawn as if by a magnet. "Look, there's the conning tower on top. I bet this ship is like the mini-subs that the British made during the Second World War."

"Mini-subs? But what's it doing down here?"

"Hell if I know," I answered. Heedless of the men with guns behind me, I ran around one side, sloshing into the cold water up to my knees. As the lights scoured the surface, I saw that the ship was resting in a metal cradle that had partially collapsed, leaving the vessel listing slightly to one side. The ship was nearly thirty feet long, but even as I marveled at the sight, my eyes were drawn to strange, anomalous features. What I first took for the conning tower was only three feet off the deck, just big enough for a man's head and shoulders, with rounded glass viewing portholes on all sides. A vicious-looking ram, like the head of a giant pike, crowned the bow and gave the ship the aspect of a beached narwhal. Along the spine of the ship, nearer the stern, was a row of teardrop-shaped metal barrels the size of oil drums. The plating of the armored leviathan was the color of ancient jade, except for the reinforced ram on the prow that was the rust-red shade of old blood.

Then a beam of light illuminated the side of the bow, and all the pieces of the puzzle locked into place. That's when I saw the single, stylized letter emblazoned on the greenish copper hull that stopped me dead in my tracks. "It can't be," I whispered.

"Can't be what?" Rhea demanded. "What are you talking about?"

I numbly pointed to the listing ghost ship as I uttered, "The submarine. It must be over two hundred years old. And if I'm not mistaken, Jules Verne has a lot of explaining to do."

"What? What the hell are you babbling about?"

My voice, echoing through the cavern, sounded strange to my ears. But nothing was as strange as the words that came out of me next:

"It's the *Nautilus*."

CHAPTER THIRTY

At this point in my life, I'd never seen anything as amazing as the scarred old hulk before me.

Years ago, the Argo Foundation sent me on an expedition to hunt for a sunken German U-boat off the coast of Argentina, to chase down some rumors that the submarine contained stolen Nazi treasures. Prior to departure, I spent some time in the foundation archives to study up on World War II–era submersible boats, but at one point I got distracted by the history of much older and far more interesting submarines. In between Bushnell's Revolutionary War–era *Turtle* and Hunley's Civil War attack submarine was Robert Fulton's *Nautilus*. I remember poring over Fulton's designs, burning up time I should have spent becoming familiar with U-boats. The *Nautilus* was an incredible invention for her time, and I remembered reading how Napoleon Bonaparte financed the building of the submarine, but then later gave up on the idea and cut Fulton's funding, even after Fulton demonstrated his ship's lethal abilities. And with that, the history of maritime warfare was set back, all because no one at the time could see the tremendous advantage of submarines as the future of naval warfare.

Now I found myself standing right next to one of the greatest inventions in the history of the world. I was so lost in the moment that I failed to notice Rhea had waded into the water and was standing right beside me, until I was dimly aware she had said something.

"What?"

Rhea waved her light across the side of the ship, exposing the green-hued corrosion that looked like frozen algae at the waterline. "I said, just what the hell are you talking about? And how did this thing get in here?"

I couldn't take my eyes off the ship. "Like I said, it's the *Nautilus,* one of the first submarines ever constructed." Rhea allowed me to take the flashlight from her hand, and I trained the beam on the bow, illuminating the stylized letter *N,* wreathed like a Roman emperor's seal. "Robert Fulton built one for Emperor Napoleon, but His Majesty wasn't impressed with the result. Or so he said at the time."

"But why would it be buried in here?"

I waved the light around the cavern, and spotted heavy, rusty iron chains that ran through metal rungs built into the rock ceiling. I traced the path of the chains and saw they ran from the wall across the flooded portion of the chamber to a giant spoked-wheel contraption that used suspended boulders for counterweights. "There," I said as I pointed out the chains, "that's how they did it. The whole seaward wall works like a medieval drawbridge. I'm betting the outside wall just looks like one big slab of stone, concealing the entrance to the underground harbor that used to be a sea cave."

"But who could have built such a thing?"

I laughed, and heard my voice echo across the chamber. "Napoleon's engineers were geniuses; hell, they built the Arc de Triomphe! Something like this would be a minor construction project for those guys." I turned the light back onto the *Nautilus*. Maybe, I thought, with any luck, Rhea would let me board the ship as a last request before she killed me.

"Rhea!" a voice came booming out of the darkness. "Rhea!"

She took her flashlight back and marched through the cold, black water toward the inner cavern, leaving me in pitch dark. I felt my legs getting chilled from the water, but couldn't leave without touching one of the most wonderful things I'd ever seen. I reached out my hand, feeling the cold, pitted surface of the marvelous, man-made machine. Then the spell was broken by the sound of Rhea's voice calling my name.

I sighed, and sloshed through the blackness and the water back to the granite shore. "Blake!" Her echoing voice held a mixture of triumph and urgency. I could see a cluster of lights ahead and above me—another offshoot of the cave. My eyes winced from the reflection cast by the beams, and I tried not to trip on the uneven rocky ground as I made my way toward the lights. Evidently I wasn't moving fast enough, as one of Rhea's men came down and grabbed me by my right arm and pulled me up the slope. I made better progress with the help of the light mounted on my guard's rifle, and then I saw what Rhea was shouting about.

Rhea, flanked by her two other guards, was standing behind an enormous, translucently glowing block, looking like a high priestess and her acolytes before a crystalline altar. Their flashlights illuminated the massive edifice, whose surface scattered their beams around the cavern in shards of flitting light. Rhea's hand caressed the glowing surface of the slab as she said in a voice gone soft, "This is it. We've found it. This is the sarcophagus of Alexander the Great. And it's ours!"

I almost lost my footing as the impact of her words hit me. I couldn't doubt the evidence before my own eyes: a sarcophagus made of glass, built by Ptolemy IX to hold the body of Alexander of Macedonia. The walls of the coffin were thick and massive, resembling giant frozen blocks of ice. I could see the edges of gilt metal built to frame the heavy walls of glass. As Rhea lovingly moved her light across the surface of the sarcophagus, I saw a blurred reflection from within, shaded in a deep blue—a blue the color of royalty.

And that's when I began to laugh.

I couldn't help myself. All of a sudden, connections started snapping in my brain like overloaded electric circuits:

The letter of Fouché, writing about the "American ship," no doubt the *Nautilus,* its voyage to Alexandria, and its return to its 'secret island harbor.'

The death of Percy Shelley, who had learned from Lord Byron the secret of the Corsican watchtower, and whose boat was rammed and sunk in the middle of a storm before he could explore the watchtower himself. No other ship in the world at the time could have attacked Shelley's boat during a storm. No other ship than a submarine like the *Nautilus*.

I thought of an exiled emperor who had escaped from the island of Elba, leaving by sea in such a way that no one saw him depart.

I thought of the words of Peter Weir, who spoke of a "ship in the shape of a wine cask and painted the color of the sea." A ship to rescue from exile one of the greatest military minds the world had ever known.

And I thought of the last wishes of an emperor regarding his final resting place.

I couldn't stop laughing. Not even when Rhea grabbed a gun from one of her men and pointed it straight at my head. "What is the matter with you?" she screamed.

I pointed my free hand toward the sarcophagus. "I can't help it. It's the greatest joke in the world!" I spat out.

Rhea ripped back the cocking bolt of the automatic rifle. "Blake," she hissed in warning.

I kept laughing as I pointed and said, "That's not Alexander in there!"

"What?" Rhea howled.

"It's goddammed Napoleon Bonaparte!"

Rhea's head snapped down toward the coffin and she peered inside through the translucent glass. The light reflecting off the top of the sarcophagus underlit her face as it slowly transformed into a mask of horror as she began to see what lay within.

I could barely contain my maniacal glee as I said,

"Napoleon said he wanted to be buried back home on Corsica. He also once said he wanted to be laid to rest in the tomb of Alexander. And the little bastard genius got his way after all. But, hey, look at the bright side."

Rhea stood frozen, as still as the glass coffin she stood over, as I said, "Maybe Vanya's scientists can still work it out for you. If you took Napoleon's genetic material and mixed it with yours, you could hatch out a lovely bunch of sawed-off little megalomaniacs!"

Rhea screamed.

That was my starting gun. I had to unleash my inner monster or die in my tracks. The gunman to my right didn't stand a chance as I whipped my arm free and slipped behind him, grabbing his head with both hands and exploding my pent-up fear into the controlled combination of force that broke his neck like an old stick and left him functionally dead before he hit the ground. I grabbed his rifle as his body dropped, and I raised the weapon, triggering a short stuttering burst that clattered off the rocks above Rhea and her men. I let myself fall in a rolling back somersault then got to my feet and moved in a crouching run back toward the *Nautilus,* the closest cover I had, while my path was lit by staccato strobes of red firelight and shots cracked off the stones around me. I took a final flat dive into the black water just past the prow of the submarine, all the while cursing myself for my instinctive inability to shoot directly at Rhea for fear of hitting the ancient sarcophagus.

I pushed out of the chilling water, spiting the briny, brackish stuff out of my mouth, and crouched behind the bow of the *Nautilus.* The ship was vibrating as dozens of rounds punched through the hull and rang like steel hammers hitting a giant gong. Then everything went quiet and black, and all I could hear was the ringing in my ears, which pulsed with the rapid beat of my heart. Until I heard a sound that froze me worse than the water I was drenched in as Rhea called out through the darkness in a childish, singsong voice, "Blake . . . Blake . . . Where are you . . . ?"

I didn't have to see to know that Rhea's men were inching toward me, creeping on soft-soled boots like spiders moving in for the kill. I was trapped in the dark with my mind racing to find a way out. Then my ringing ears heard a new sound coming from behind me—a soft, hissing noise. I was completely blind as I eased back in the water, keeping one hand on the grip of my gun and the other on the rough, pitted hull of the *Nautilus*. When I was chest-deep in the cold seawater, I felt my hand come under a soft cascade of what felt like coarse dry sand. But one sniff told me the stuff pouring from the top of the ship was explosive black gunpowder. Those teardrop-shaped casks lined on the deck of the ship must have been bombs that got punctured by gunfire and were now leaking explosives. I had a sudden, insane idea.

I'd never make it back to the tunnel entrance past Rhea and her two men, and even if I did I'd be stuck inside a narrow shooting gallery and shredded to pieces with automatic gunfire before I'd make it out. That left the massive stone seaward gate, currently held up in place by the drawbridge chains. I felt for the button that activated the flashlight mounted on the rifle barrel and shot a beam out, zeroing in on the old wooden drawbridge gears that linked the iron chains and counterweights to the outer gate. I slipped the fire selector to "single shot" and started hammering bullets into the wrapped chains, striking sparks and making ear-splitting whines with every hit. I was just in fear of running out of ammunition when the mechanical gate lift collapsed in on itself as if crushed by a giant unseen hand. I heard a metallic sound like a train clattering along its tracks boom out from overhead as the chains were pulled along their iron moorings.

I held the gun up and triggered my last few shots over in the general direction of Rhea and her men, just as a spoiler to keep their heads down, then I heard a whooshing splash, like a rogue wave hitting the shore, as the sea gate fell open. I dropped the gun, unzipped my suit, and clawed my cigarette lighter out of my shirt pocket. If I could ignite the falling black powder I'd get a blinding flash followed by a cloud of smoke that'd let me disappear like a stage magician, covering my escape to the mouth of the cave. I snapped a fire and my hand and face were slapped by a sudden flash of flame that then hissed and sputtered, engulfing the side of the *Nautilus*. I shoved the lighter back inside my suit as I took a breath laced with burnt powder and dove under the water, swimming as hard as I could while having that nightmare feeling of running and not getting anywhere. The water warped a cacophony of sound—surging tide noise peppered with muted ripping pops of automatic weapons—until the world turned bloodred through my eyelids and a piercing shriek tore through my ears.

I broke water and flipped around to look back, and

my body froze. Jets of flame shot from the *Nautilus,* lighting up the cave in strobing red glare while the ship screamed like a dying beast. A thought like a jolt of raw electricity shot through me as I realized that I'd set off a chain reaction in the ship's bomb supply.

I whipped back toward the mouth of the cave, attacking the water with frenzied slaps and kicks as the sea pushed against me. Until a stuttering concussion hammered my entire body and drove spikes through my ears as I was blown through the opening of the cave like being shot from a cannon.

Everything was roaring chaos until the sea spit me out, only to let me crash back down and be swallowed under again. I was flailing in the dark, until my hand collided with a hard mass. I grabbed and clawed for life until I was hugging the rocky shore.

I gripped as hard as I could, afraid the sea would pull me back under as I coughed and gasped for air. I heard a clattering chorus of falling rocks and managed to raise my head until I could see the black outline of the watchtower's mountainous crag looming above. I crawled the rest of the way out of the water and collapsed on the rocky shore while my head kept spinning and my body shivered uncontrollably. Then I heard someone call my name.

Of course, I thought to myself. After all I'd been through, I just crawled out of hell only to have one of Rhea's remaining men kill me. God help me, I actually started to laugh, far too exhausted to do anything else.

"Monsieur Blake?"

It was the French honorific that finally penetrated my brain. I forced myself to look up and saw a shadowy form in the darkness. The man was cradling an automatic rifle and was dressed all in black, but I also detected the odd outlines of a helmet and other gear that Rhea's ninjas didn't come equipped with. "Yes?" I croaked.

The man placed a hand up to his chest and said quietly to an unseen audience, *"Oui, c'est Blake."* In English, he asked me, "Can you walk?"

When I realized that this French-speaking storm trooper just might not have come to murder me, I made my tortured limbs hoist me up until I was on hands and feet, holding on to the side of the steep, rocky shore. "If you can call this walking," I answered.

The man took my arm, and between the two of us we managed to not let me slide back into the sea. I crawled more than climbed up the stony incline until I reached the summit and was allowed to collapse against the rounded stone side of the watchtower, where I slid into a sitting position as the balmy Mediterranean breeze cooled down my overheated body. Another commando came and knelt beside me, opening up a black pack. "I am a medic, monsieur," the man said. "Are you injured?" Then I heard another voice, a voice that chilled me to the bone.

"Goddamn, Blake," Smith said with obvious admiration. "You're just harder to kill than a cockroach, aren't you?"

I raised my head and saw Smith outlined against the dark sky with his long coat waving in the wind. It took me two breaths to say it, but I replied, "Come down here and we'll see if the same is true of you."

"Slow down, boy. You're a little behind the curve here. I've been on your side all along. Vanya's men here

are all dead. I called in the French 'Division Action.'"
Smith put a hand to the medic's shoulder and said,
"Give us a moment here."

The medic looked to me, and I nodded. As he moved
off, I said to Smith, "So we've been rescued by the
French?"

"And man, was it beautiful," Smith enthused. "They
came gliding in on parachutes like bats. I swear,
they shot every single one of Vanya's men before they
hit the ground. I take back everything I ever said about
the French. But I got to admit, it was a little nerve-
wracking, wondering if someone wasn't going to mistake me for a bad guy in the dark."

"Bad guy? But, you and Rhea . . . ?"

Smith came and hunkered down beside me. "Rhea
just thought she had her hooks into me. She and I came
across each other years ago during a joint mission. I
later let her think my loyalty was for sale. Unfortunately, she's not the trusting type, and I was never able
to get the evidence we needed through her. But what
the hell happened to you just now? One minute I'm
watching the French paratroopers clean up, and then
'boom!' The whole place shakes and there's a god-
awful fireball shooting out of the water."

I leaned my head back against the cold, rough stone,
seeing in my mind's eye the fiery death of the *Nautilus*. "All I wanted to do was get away," I heard myself
mumble.

Smith laughed as he said, "Like I said before, we
leave you on your own, and you'll blow up half of Europe. But man, I wish I could have gotten a better look
at your face when you thought I was a traitor. It must
have been priceless!"

"So you and your boss just played me for a sucker?"

"Name of the game, my man. If you knew I was involved with Rhea, you could have spilled the beans. But the real problem was that Rhea kept me in the dark about a lot of Vanya's operation. That's why we needed a man on the inside. Once Vanya took you in, we were hoping you'd get the goods on him." Smith looked around to be sure we were relatively alone then leaned in and whispered in my ear, "Now tell me quick: Did you get anything solid on any biological weapons?"

"It's worse than that—Caitlin's back on his island and he's infected her with his Pandora plague. Everything Rhea said about the genetic virus was true. Caitlin's being used as a test subject, and Vanya's got the only cure."

"You certain of this?" Smith asked with heat.

"Yes. And Vanya couldn't have missed hearing that big bang just now; he's got to be spooked."

"Damn!" Smith hissed. He pulled out a phone and then held the device straight overhead like he was firing off an invisible distress flare. He slipped the phone back into his coat and said softly, "There. I just sent a signal out. In less than an hour, U.S. troops will be storming Vanya's island." Before I could comment, Smith looked over my shoulder and said, "Uh-oh. Better let me do the talking."

Another armed, black-clad warrior appeared on my other side and knelt down next to me as Smith announced, "Blake, this here's Captain Reynard, French Special Operations. Captain, this is our man, Blake. He's the one who infiltrated this terrorist cell."

Captain Reynard's face was shaded in dark camouflage war paint and hidden under his helmet. With a precise voice born of experience, he said in softly accented English, "We've eliminated six enemy combatants. Are there any more down below?"

"I don't know," I said. "There were six of us down there altogether. Wait. One of them died from a booby trap."

Captain Reynard started to speak, but Smith cut him off. "Hey, give my man here a break. You saw the size of that explosion. Hell, it felt like an earthquake up here. It's a miracle Blake is still among the living."

Captain Reynard was undeterred. "Booby trap? What was it you found down there? My men have reported that it looks like a cave has collapsed under the waterline."

While Smith clamped down on my arm like he wanted to squeeze my throat shut by proxy, I leaned my head back against the watchtower, wondering how to answer the captain's questions without speaking of France's greatest general, an ancient glass sarcophagus, and two-hundred-year-old submarines. I was saved from this task when we all heard the roar of engine noise coming from down below the slope. Captain Reynard and Smith shot to their feet as I used the wall of the tower as a crutch to join them. From down at the waterline, twin stuttering spurts of fire lanced out toward the sea as one of Vanya's motorboats powered away like a seaborne rocket.

Captain Reynard's hand went up to the side of his helmet. "One of them got away," he reported. "And wounded one of my men."

We could still hear the boat, but all I could see under the cloud-mottled mass of stars were the ink-black outlines of the islands out to sea and the lone lighthouse beacon that blinked in the distance. I then spoke the last thing that I ever wanted to say: "Rhea."

Captain Reynard was quick to ask, "Who?"

"One of the leaders of the terrorist group," Smith said quickly. "Oh, Christ. If that really is her, and she makes it back to the yacht . . ."

"She swims like a seal," I said, remembering a long-ago conversation on a bridge over the Seine at midnight. If Rhea got back to Vanya and told him that military troops took out his men on the Iles Sanguinaires, and if his people back on his private island radioed that they were under attack, then Vanya could panic. If he did that, he could take the whole world with him.

Smith spoke with urgency. "Captain, you've got to attack that yacht."

Reynard's exasperation was palpable. "With what? If you and your government had been more precise with their information, we might have been prepared. As it is, I had to scramble my men for this operation. My orders were to secure this area, nothing more."

"But the leader of these terrorists is on that ship! You're letting them get away!"

Reynard held a pair of binoculars up to his eyes. "By the time we can muster a response, that yacht will be beyond our territorial waters. If we act then, we'll be committing an act of piracy." Reynard dropped his binoculars down from his face and said, as if to himself, "And we have not had such good luck with operations involving ships in the past."

I didn't know what Reynard was talking about at the last, but something he said caught my ear. At that point I knew, with a sinking certainty, what I had to do. "Well," I announced. "You heard the man, Smith. Let's get to it."

"Get to it? Get to what?"

I looked out beyond the midnight-black water as I said, "Piracy."

CHAPTER THIRTY-ONE

"You are going to die."

Smith uttered those words as he and I were standing on the wave-lapped, rocky shore talking quietly to each other while two of Reynard's men were hip-deep in the water, holding on to the remaining powerboat from Vanya's yacht. I was busy making certain I'd managed to conceal the paltry few devices that I'd scavenged. The tight-fitting diving suit didn't offer much in the way of hiding places. As I patted myself down, I came across a familiar lump and dug out my cigarette lighter. I handed it to Smith. "Here. Hang on to this for me."

"What's this? Your good-luck charm?"

My mind flashed back to the sight of the *Nautilus* as it was engulfed in flame. "No. But keep it for me anyway."

"Look, I told you I've got a helicopter and some of my own troops on standby. They could be here in minutes."

"And then Vanya would just blow them out of the sky. I told you, he's got machine guns, rocket launchers, and God knows what else on board. And if he feels he's in a trap, he could just send a signal that'd release a worldwide plague, if he hasn't already. But if I can take his own boat and reach the yacht, they may think I'm another one of the crew that got away and give me a chance to get aboard."

"So he can kill you then."

"Hopefully not before I can talk some sense into him. Besides, this may be Caitlin's only chance. Vanya's the only shot we have of finding the plague cure. If he gets word that your soldiers have stormed his island, he might start his apocalypse anyway."

"Then let me come with you, or at least take a damn gun!"

"Sorry. You're not dressed in the right uniform. And if I have a gun they might get unfriendly."

In exasperation, Smith turned toward Captain Reynard and called out to him. "You're sure there's nothing you can do?"

The captain shrugged. "My men and I are not officially here. Therefore, while there's nothing we can do, we certainly cannot stop you from committing whatever acts you intend out on the open sea."

"Would it help if I told you that the man on that yacht is harboring biological weapons of mass destruction?"

"Really," Reynard said with Gallic indifference. "Now, where have we heard Americans tell us that one before? Now, you gentlemen must hurry; my superiors cannot keep the local authorities away from this place forever."

As Smith mumbled invective under his breath, Reynard continued. "But may I say for myself that I hope you are successful." Then he added, *"Partout oú nécessité fait loi."*

"Yeah," grumbled Smith. *"Vive la France* to you, too." Smith consulted his phone. "Okay, according to satellite tracking, Vanya's ship is on a heading due south."

I waded out to the powerboat. "Got it. Keep an eye out."

"Yeah," he said bitterly. "Good luck with Operation Trojan Sea Horse."

I didn't reply as I pulled a diving hood over my head—taken from one of the dead men laid out in a neat row next to the ancient watchtower. I pulled myself aboard the boat with the grace of a wounded hippo. Reynard's men gave me a shove toward the open sea as I took over the controls. I checked astern to make sure I was clear and then fired up the engine. There was a hearty roar and the thing damn near bucked me off when I touched the throttle control. I got a better grip and fed the beast more fuel, and soon I was riding high in the water, flying through the night.

I gave the Islands of Bloody Men a wide berth, sighting on the lighthouse beacon until I was certain I was in deep water, and then I checked my heading and opened the boat up full throttle, skipping across the water like a flat-thrown stone while gritting my teeth against the pains lancing my side. I had the lights of Corsica on my port side, looking like a belt of stars, and the great, wide blackness of the open sea ahead. The thought didn't escape me that I was in all likelihood charging headlong to my death, but I knew this was the only way to try to save Caitlin's life. If I were riding a horse, I would have spurred it on.

The lighted compass on the panel led me south, but all I could see was an expanse of black under a waning moon that sailed overhead through the clouds. Vanya had his ship running without lights, and I was starting to worry that I'd miss it altogether, until I saw the wake of a ship cresting ahead and I followed in the path between the foaming waves. I was finally getting close enough to her stern that even without night-vision goggles, someone keeping a lookout would have spotted me. I braced myself to be ready to make some evasive maneuvers in case anyone opened fire, but with all the armaments I had seen on the ship, I knew I'd probably be blown to bits before I could turn and run.

Over the whine of my engines I heard the deep-throated roar of Vanya's *Phaeton*. I throttled back as I saw a light break out from the starboard side of the ship. The hull panel was lifting open like a single wing of a monstrous albatross. As I pulled up even with the stern of the yacht I waved to the shadowy figures inside the boat bay, then kept my head down as I piloted my motorboat alongside. Two men, dressed in the same form-fitting black wet suit I was, jumped aboard, one on my bow and the other in the narrow stern, and attached cables to the boat as I shut off the engine. Once hooked, an electric winch hoisted the boat slowly out of the water, and then metal arms retracted and brought the boat inside the hull of the yacht. I was busy keeping my head down and trying to look like I knew what I was doing as I hopped aboard, only to hear a voice I could never forget say to me, "Oh, Blake. Did you really think you could just walk in here without being noticed?"

Rhea's voice made me grit my teeth, then I tried to force a smile as I raised my head. She was cast in silhouette by the light streaming from behind her, and was flanked by gun-wielding guards on either side. I held my hands out in the universal sign of being unarmed. "I have a message for Vanya," I said as firmly as I could manage.

"He has one for you, too," Rhea replied as one of her men came up and viciously slammed the butt of his rifle into the small of my back. I crashed flat to the deck, sipping air through gritted teeth and praying my legs weren't paralyzed as Rhea's men grabbed me by each arm and dragged me along. There were some twists and turns along the way, and then I was dropped facedown on a plush Persian carpet. There was the sound of a heavy door clanking shut and the lights came on as Vanya said in a silky voice, "Well, well, well. If I believed in the mythological God that man created, I'd say he delivered my enemy to me."

I lifted my head up as one of Vanya's men tore my hood off. Vanya was holding court in his Harem Room, surrounded by guards who all looked like they were ready to shoot me to pieces just to please their master. But my eyes were drawn to the most dangerous creature in the room. Rhea stood beside Vanya, looking like a war-torn Valkyrie, with her hair a wild Medusa's nest and streaks of blood drying on her face. Her eyes were wide open and fixed on me, as frozen as the evil, gleeful smile on her face.

I kept my eyes on Rhea as Vanya said, "I can't

believe, after all you've done to me, that you came back here. Rhea told me that Alexander wasn't on Corsica. What could you possibly say to me that would prevent me from killing you now?"

I was just on the verge of delivering my planned speech when I was interrupted by a voice coming through a concealed speaker: "Vanya! Cronos Island is under attack! Our men are retreating to the bunkers!"

Vanya's face purpled with rage and his whole body began to shake as he raised his hand and pointed a finger at me like Zeus ready to unleash a lightning bolt. "Wait!" I yelled. "What I have to say can change everything!"

Vanya's men, their gun barrels trained on me, all looked from the corners of their eyes at their master, who was struggling between rage and reason, until he finally choked out, "What?"

I slowly rose from the floor, glad that my shaking limbs could still function. With my best sleight-of-hand maneuver, I slipped the pen-sized remote detonator out of my sleeve and held it up as I unzipped my wet suit to reveal the strips of plastic explosive I had removed from the backpack of one of Vanya's dead soldiers and taped to my chest. I flipped the safety cover off the detonator with my thumb and held the device up for all to see as I announced: "Surprise! Look who's the most dangerous guy in the room now!"

There was a collective inhaling of breath that could have sucked the air out of the room as Vanya and his men all fell back against the curtained walls in a futile effort to create distance between themselves and explosive oblivion. Except for Rhea, who stood as still as a marble statue all the while.

"New rules," I said to my captive audience. "Do as I say, and no one dies. Make a move I don't like, and I blow us all to hell."

Vanya sputtered his disbelief. "But . . . you'll die!"

"So what? You were going to kill me anyway. But if you listen to me, we can all make it out of here alive. The first thing you do is radio your people back on the island to give the cure to Caitlin. Now!"

There was stunned silence in the room. Until Rhea started to laugh.

All eyes were drawn to her as she said in a soft, yet certain voice, "Oh, no. Blake won't do it. He hasn't got the will."

I clutched the detonator tighter, but I could feel how Rhea's words were draining away my power over the situation. Vanya looked at her, and with a sinking sensation I saw the growing hope in his eyes.

"Poor Blake," Rhea said with a sad shake of her head. "To come all this way, only to fail now. But you should know this before you die: There is no plague vaccine back on Cronos Island. All there is in the whole world is right here on this ship. And by now there's no way to get the cure back to your precious Caitlin. She is going to die, drowning in her own blood. I wonder if her last thoughts will be of you?"

She really shouldn't have said that.

I could feel the rage rising up in me, shaking the hand that held the detonator and causing my old wound to tingle with nerve sparks. It had all boiled down to Rhea and me, facing off in a duel of will, and she was winning. I could see from the corners of my eyes how the soldiers were starting to brace themselves to go on the attack, and then I saw Vanya smiling. That's when I knew I had to do it.

I looked straight down the twin black wells of Rhea's soulless eyes as I said, "Sayonara."

Then I triggered the detonator.

CHAPTER THIRTY-TWO

No one was more surprised than I when nothing happened.

When my thumb hit the detonator button, everyone in the room fell back in a shouting tangle, with Vanya screaming loudest of all. Then there was a breathless moment when all was still, and there I was, standing across from the unmoving Rhea and waiting for the explosion that never arrived—it was like a flash of lightning that had no thunder to follow.

"What the . . . ?" I stuttered. I hit the button again, and all it did was go *click*. The detonator's little telltale light winked at me, telling me the device was active, but nothing happened.

I snapped the button several times in quick succession, and even shook the thing in the universal method of trying to coax defective electronics back to life, but as the detonator remained stubbornly impotent a sick feeling welled up in my guts. "Uh-oh," I said as I saw Vanya's men gather themselves up, with a growing rage replacing their fear. Rhea's laughter pealed forth like a bell, heralding my coming demise.

While I was snapping away at the detonator like a man with a nicotine fit and a defective cigarette lighter, I saw Vanya shakily rise from the cushions. His face was as white as his beard and his hand trembled as if with palsy as he uttered with growing intensity, "Kill him . . . kill him . . . kill him!"

One of his men raised his rifle, and my eyes zeroed in on the black, unblinking eye of the gun barrel, but Rhea slapped the weapon away and spat out the Japanese word for "idiot." "Don't shoot him now," she snapped. "You might set off the bomb."

I felt the slightest touch of hope, but it was crushed as Rhea then said, "Drag Blake outside and throw him overboard. When he's floated past the stern of the ship, then everyone can shoot him!"

Before I could make a move, two of the men rushed up and grabbed me by each arm, squeezing me out of the cabin to the outside deck, but not before I heard Rhea call out to me in a happy voice, "Sayonara!" I was slammed back against the guardrail, hard enough to make my cracked ribs stab me with pain, as I convulsively clutched the detonator one last time.

That's when the radio signal was finally able to reach all the plastic explosives I'd scavenged from the packs of Vanya's troops and packed inside the life vest locker on the powerboat. My plan all along was to try to get aboard the ship and bluff Vanya into thinking I was ready to blow myself up, but the C-4 taped to my chest was just a decoy. I'd placed the armed explosives inside the powerboat to use as a last-ditch attempt to sink the *Phaeton* if I had to. Only the radio signal couldn't penetrate the thick, armored walls of Vanya's inner sanctum, so I hadn't been able to connect. Until now.

It was as if a great white shark had swallowed a hand grenade. The concussive blast slammed the man nearest the stern into me as a gout of flame blew out of the side of the ship like a navy cannon firing a salvo. The guards and I hit the deck in a squeezing jumble and I was sandwiched in between the men. As the ship shuddered to a stop in the water I bucked off the man on my back and struck the other guard an incapacitating blow to the skull with the detonator I still gripped in my cramped right hand. I grabbed the railing and pulled myself up to face the other soldier, only to see a jagged protrusion that looked like a shark's fin jutting out of his back as he sprawled on the tilting deck; he'd unwittingly protected me from a deadly flying shard of shrapnel.

The *Phaeton* was a heaving sea beast in its death throes as I snatched up an automatic rifle and lurched for Vanya's chamber. I shoved the hatch open and caught a glimpse of Vanya, all tangled up with his personal guard and bunched in a corner of the stateroom. One of his guards saw me as well and I barely had time to slam the metal hatch shut before the man let rip with a thunderous metal-storm of gunfire. I held the hatch shut like I was gripping an oversized shield as bullets hammered into it, until I heard the sound of a scream that cut off as the weapons fire died out.

I held on to the hatch for a silent count of three, then risked a quick look inside. The ship rolled and pulled me off balance as I saw the lights inside flicker and then turn a bloody red as the emergency lighting took over. There was a cluster of bodies piled against each other in the far corner of the room. The low tables started to slide along the carpeting that was bunching up like slow waves toward the rear of the ship. The curtains had been ripped from the walls, exposing the freshly scarred bulkhead.

Whoever opened fire at me wasn't trained well enough to keep from shooting while inside a metal-plated chamber—all the bullets bounced and rico-cheted off the armored walls and turned Vanya's safe room into a concentrated killing zone.

I let gravity pull me inside and saw that Vanya's men, loyal to him to the last, had covered him with their own bodies and taken the brunt of the gunfire. But the center of the bloody nest was moving, and Vanya's head and arms broke free from the dead limbs that covered him. His eyes were wide and sightless, and he was muttering "Oh, God! Oh, God!" over and over.

I braced myself on the shifting deck and yelled through the metallic clamoring, "Vanya! The vaccine! Tell me where it is and I'll get you out of here!"

Vanya's head started twisting about as he pawed at the bodies entrapping him. "Blake!" he screamed. "Blake! I can't feel my legs! Oh God! Get me out, and I'll give you anything! Blake!"

I slung the rifle over my shoulder and went for him, only to see his eyes fix on a point over my shoulder and freeze. That's when it hit me—Rhea.

I spun around, grabbing for the rifle, and saw Rhea outlined within the forward hatch. She was holding a small metal case in her hand. The case was open, and I could see the red emergency lights glistening off glass within. Her hair was wild, like plumes of smoke, and she was laughing like a maniac in between singing with a childish voice, "I have the antidote."

I raised my rifle, but Rhea was waving the box of vaccine around and I didn't dare shoot. "It's the one and only one, Blake," Rhea shouted with evil glee. "You'll never find where the rest is hidden. Now, throw the gun away. Or do you want your Caitlin to die?"

I didn't even stop to think as I tossed the automatic rifle down the hatch behind me, hearing as it clattered along the deck until it made a splash. All too quickly, Rhea tossed the case toward me. I almost had to jump as my hand flashed to catch it, and for a heart-stopping moment, the case bounced in my grasping fingers twice before I got a grip. The ship gave another lurch and I lost my footing, sliding down against the tilting back wall. I snapped open the case and saw it contained a single hypodermic needle. And an empty niche where a vial of medicine should have been.

Vanya was shouting something, but I couldn't make out the words because a roaring hiss like a ruptured steam pipe filled the room just as the scorching heat from a flash of fire burst in from astern. I shielded my face and raised my eyes toward Rhea, who stood across the stateroom and above me, holding up the vial of vaccine that she'd slipped out of the case before she tossed it at me. With a look of absolute triumph on her wild features, she smashed the vial against the wall, leaving a smudge like wet blood under the hellish light.

I roared louder than the dying wails of the ship as I launched myself at Rhea, charging up the slanted deck only to have her leap at me. Rhea and I collided in midair and I barely managed to catch her hand, now grasping a redly gleaming knife blade. We crashed to the deck, rolling over and over until I slammed into the back wall with Rhea poised above me and the knife aimed at my throat. The room was slowly turning over and the wall I was pressed against started to become the floor while I grappled with Rhea's knife hand. She shifted her grip, grabbing the knife with both hands, and shoved her weight against it, slowly driving the point to my throat while I held on with my rapidly fading strength. "Goodbye, my dearest," she hissed between clenched teeth.

"Go to hell," I grunted as I shifted myself to the right, letting the knife slide into my shoulder. The pain sparked a surge of strength and I reached around her, holding her close to me until I could see nothing but the fire reflected in her obsidian eyes. I threw all of my weight into rolling the two of us over once; twice.

Then Rhea was falling through the open hatch that had now become a trapdoor. I caught a glimpse of her as she flailed in the air. Her scream of rage was cut off when she fell through a curtain of fire and splashed down into a bubbling red-lit cauldron of water that boiled up from the stern of the sinking ship.

"Blake!"

It was Vanya, screaming as the mass of dead men that entangled him started to slide and drag him to the back hatch as if they were following after Rhea. I realized I had one last chance the save something out of all this death and destruction.

In the flickering bloodred light, Vanya's eyes were mad with fear—the weight of his dead soldiers was pulling his flailing body along as gravity dragged them all through the doorway to hell. Vanya desperately reached for me and I reached back, but not to take his hand. His fear-driven grip damn near pulled my arm out of the socket, but ultimately his strength failed, and mine didn't, and with a final heave of the deck, Vanya fell screaming through the hatch as if the ship itself had swallowed him up.

I didn't have a moment to lose if I was going to try to save my life and Caitlin's. I forced myself to crawl up the sharply slanted deck until I reached the hatch to the outside. I jumped to the railing, seeing the whole world illuminated by the flickering fires of burning oil that floated on the sea. I climbed as fast as I could toward the bow while the *Phaeton* itself reared and bucked, trying to throw me off. I made it to the apex of the dying ship and launched myself out to the sea. When I hit the water I swam as hard as I could, attacking the waves as the suction of the sinking ship pulled at me, trying to drag me under with it to the depths. At that moment I thought of Caitlin, and I fought the sea like a demon escaping a watery hell.

With a final, gurgling bellow, the *Phaeton* slipped beneath the waves, leaving only its flaming blood in its wake. I was wondering how long it would take the sharks of the Mediterranean to zero in on the shipwreck, along with the blood I was leaking into the water, when I heard the shuddering roar of a pair of large helicopters approaching fast. I didn't have the breath to shout nor the strength to spare for waving, but I felt a flood of relief when one of the airborne craft took up a position above me and whipped the water with the force of its twin-bladed downdraft. I saw a blinking light that swayed to and fro as it floated down toward me, and just as my leaden arms and legs were threatening to quit, I reached up and grabbed the yoke of a rescue harness.

I slipped my arms through the harness and gave a feeble tug on the line, then surrendered all my efforts as I was carried upward against the helicopter blades' beating gale that slapped my body and pounded my ears. As I slowly spun on the line, I saw another large helicopter hovering nearby, shooting a searchlight beam that swept the sea.

I was finally hauled aboard like a sack of cargo and into a red-lit fuselage whose inner walls were lined by heavily armed soldiers. The man nearest the hatch wore a helmet with a night-vision set that made him look like an alien insect as he helped disentangle me from the rescue harness. The side panel was shoved closed and someone clamped a set of headphones over my tortured ears. With a fuzzy mechanical overtone, I heard Smith ask, "You still with us, Blake?"

Before I could reply, the helicopter lifted up and away, flattening me to the hard, vibrating deck. I felt a pair of arms pull me up and over to one of the jump seats bolted to the hull and saw it was Smith, his dark face shining under the red-hued light as he demanded, "What about the Pandora plague? Did Vanya get the signal out?"

I shook my head, praying I was right, then Smith grinned and said as he strapped in next to me, "Hot damn! Operation Trojan Sea Horse really worked!"

"Where're we going?" I shouted into my headphone microphone.

Smith jerked a thumb at the soldiers. "We're heading for Vanya's island with the marines. Navy SEAL teams have already gone in; we're the reinforcements. French air-sea rescue is going to pick up any survivors from Vanya's boat."

"Have your troops reached the laboratory section yet? Have they found Caitlin?"

Smith hesitated a beat, then said, "Last report was there was still heavy fighting."

I unzipped my suit. "Get me a medic."

"A medic?" Smith's eyes went to my shoulder. "Whoa. Looks like you got tagged."

One of the helicopter crew came over and reached for my shoulder, but I intercepted his hand. "Smith, call your ground troops and tell them to find Dr. Song at Vanya's complex. They need to locate her and keep her safe."

"Who's Dr. Song?"

"She's the woman who cooked up Vanya's plague virus for him. And she's the only one who can fix a cure. With this." I held up the hypodermic syringe I got from the box that Rhea threw at me after she removed the plague medicine.

Smith stared at the syringe. "What the hell is that?"

"Blood. More importantly, blood that I'm betting has already been inoculated with the cure for the Pandora plague."

"Blood? Where the hell did you get that?"

"It's Vanya's," I said. "I managed to stick him with the needle before he fell out of reach. He won't need it anymore."

Smith took the syringe like a man taking hold of a holy relic, and then I finally let my body collapse while the medic examined my shoulder. I was too tired, too injured to do anything more than lean back and shiver with cold and fatigue. All I could do now was pray.

CHAPTER THIRTY-THREE

New York

"What happened then?"

I was standing inside the private office of the Argo Foundation. I'd just flown back to the States from Germany on this day to meet with Nicholas Riley and Mr. Singh for the last time. The main offices of Argo reside in one of the classic brownstones on Manhattan's Upper West Side, but you could walk past here every day of your life and you'd never know the truly strange events that are recounted within these walls. Nick's personal office is a large room, the walls covered to capacity with venerable old books, and furnished with dark, aged mahogany so that the place resembles a private club from the turn of the last century. I'd lost track of all the time I spent within this room, either planning a new venture, or reading for knowledge for its own sake, usually while I recovered from the exhaustion and injuries of my most recent mission.

Nicholas Riley's rough voice brought me back to the

here and now, and I turned back to the table. Nick was holding court in his favorite high-backed chair, his tailored shirt unbuttoned and the sleeves rolled up, while Mr. Singh sat at his right hand, impeccable as ever. I was wearing donated military clothes and was looking forward to dressing as a civilian again. I went back to my own chair across the wide mahogany table, still moving like an arthritic old man due to my accumulated injuries, and resumed telling my tale. As per our long-standing practice, nothing was recorded or written down, but I've never known Nick Riley to forget anything.

"Even with a military attack helicopter, it took us hours to get back to Vanya's island," I said. "And when we did, the place looked like my worst trip to Baghdad—everything was all shot to pieces. The Navy SEAL teams had done their job all right, but when Vanya's soldiers felt they were finished, they all committed mass suicide. No doubt following the last wishes of their master."

"Mother of God," Nick rumbled softly.

I thought of all the young, serious men I had seen, and I deeply wished that Vanya was now being tormented in the hell he claimed he didn't believe in. "And thank God for Peter Weir," I said. "When everything was getting blown to pieces, he managed to gather up most of the involuntary workforce, including Dr. Song, and Vanya's collection of young women, and hide them out until the Navy SEALs broke through to the bunker."

"But what about Caitlin?"

"It was close. Too damn close. She was almost into

the final stages of the Pandora sickness, but Dr. Song was able to whip up a serum out of Vanya's blood sample, and she saved Caitlin's life." My mind went back to all the hours and days I spent pressed to the glass in the medical observation bay, watching Dr. Song and her team, dressed in decontamination suits that made them look like they were ready for outer space, work on a pale and unmoving Caitlin, and how I watched the medical monitor screens, counting every beat of her heart. "That tough old bastard Ombra pulled through too," I added. "But don't ask me how. Dr. Song kept saying how it was all touch and go for a while."

"What about the Pandora virus itself? Who's got their hands on that now?"

"The nice man from the government told me not to worry about it."

I recalled my last meeting with Sam Smith, which I'd had the day before. We were standing on a balcony outside the living quarters on Vanya's island, feeling the cool Mediterranean Sea night breeze gently blow away the sultry air. Once Caitlin and Ombra had been deemed noncontagious and on the mend, we were all moved to the guest quarters and had been living like hurricane survivors who'd been trapped in a luxury hotel. I was still carrying my arm around in a sling, courtesy of the marine medic who did a good job stitching up my shoulder, despite the fact he didn't look old enough to shave, and my chest felt like it was slowly petrifying as it healed. That night, I'd brought along a six-pack of Heineken and a couple of Cuban cigars that I'd liberated from Vanya's supplies during one of my foraging expeditions.

Smith was in the process of lighting my cigar when I noticed he was using a familiar item. "Isn't that mine?" I asked around puffs.

Smith held my battered Zippo up and looked at it as if noticing the etched dragon motif for the first time. "Is it? Well, so it is."

He obligingly returned my lighter when he finished igniting our cigars and I asked, "So where the hell have you been?"

"Hey, I've been busy. Cut me some slack."

I believed him. For the past three days I'd seen and heard helicopters flying in and out on a frequent basis. I was restricted to the upstairs quarters, along with the rest of the survivors, and there were heavily armed American soldiers guarding all the elevators.

"So how are your patients?" Smith inquired.

"Critical. They both say that if they have to eat my cooking much longer, it'll kill them."

Smith laughed. "No worries there. Matter of fact, we're shipping all of you out tomorrow. Speaking of which, have you seen Ombra around?"

I shrugged and took a drink of my beer in lieu of answering. As a matter of fact, I'd seen Mr. Ombra earlier that night. I was coming back with a load of supplies just as he was exiting the room he had next to Caitlin's and mine, dressed in tan military fatigues. We both stopped and stared at each other for a moment, and then Ombra nodded, as if in salute, and I returned in kind, then we both went our separate ways. As far as I was concerned, the war was over. Besides, no one appointed me to be anyone's guard.

"Well," Smith mused. "We're on an island. He can't wander too far off."

"What about Vanya's Pandora plague?" I asked.

Smith blew a cloud of smoke out toward the starry sky. "No worries there, and we can thank dear departed Vanya for that. The old boy went and outsmarted himself. My government geek squad got into his computer system and found a whole stash of pre-recorded speeches Vanya must have kept around to cover up any extended absences. We've been broadcasting them via satellite right on schedule. And with the news blackout covering up the sinking of the yacht, as far as the rest of the world knows, Vanya is still alive."

"But what about all his cult members who had plague devices?"

"We found that list too. Don't worry, we're taking care of business on that account."

"What's going to happen to them?"

"Don't ask," Smith said flatly.

"Were there any survivors from Vanya's yacht?"

"A few, and they're in custody. They won't be talking to anybody for quite a while yet. But Vanya went down with his ship."

"And Rhea?"

"No sign," Smith answered shortly. I had a short, sharp flashback of Rhea falling into the flaming guts of the ship, screaming like a demon as she went.

"So all's well that ends horribly for some?" I asked.

Smith took another puff and said, "Which brings me to my point. What do you say about joining my outfit full time? We make a hell of a team."

I damn near spit out a mouthful of beer. "Team? What team? All you did was keep me in the dark, when you weren't out-and-out lying to me, and then you let me get shot, stabbed, and beat half to death more times than I can count."

"Like I said, we're a good team."

I was in the process of recalling my colorful and invective-filled refusal to Smith as Nick Riley said, "But what about the cave under the Corsican watchtower? What the hell happened with that?"

I sighed. "According to Smith, the French authorities reported that the underwater cave opening completely collapsed, along with part of the tunnel that led from the watchtower down to the cave. As far as the French government is concerned, the whole operation was to stop a gang of international terrorists who had been using Corsica as a secret place to stash their explosives. From what I've heard, the news networks just reported a minor earthquake occurred on Corsica that coincided with the accidental sinking of a private boat out to sea."

"So everything you saw, the glass sarcophagus of Alexander the Great, Napoleon Bonaparte, and even the *Nautilus,* everything is lost?"

"Not lost," I protested. "I know exactly where they are. They're just buried under tons of rock."

"They wouldn't be if you hadn't blown up the damn cave!" Nick rasped.

"Not my fault. How was I to know that two-hundred-year-old bombs would still be dangerous?"

Mr. Singh turned a large book around on the table, orienting it toward me. It was the same book I had studied years ago when I was taking my crash course on the history of submarines. "Did the craft you saw look like this?" Singh inquired.

I looked at the design Robert Fulton had created for

his *Nautilus*. "Oh, yeah. Except when I saw the real thing, someone had added the reinforced ramming spur on the bow."

"According to history, Fulton's prototype submarine was dismantled when Napoleon chose not to finance it," Mr. Singh said.

I laughed. "Napoleon probably stiffed old Fulton, then had his own engineers construct the actual *Nautilus* using Fulton's designs. With improvements."

Mr. Singh nodded and pointed to a teardrop shape on Fulton's blueprint. "This was the mechanism Fulton designed to sink enemy ships. Not a conventional torpedo, as we know it today. This was a bomb designed to be towed from behind the submarine on a cable. When the submarine dove under an enemy warship and pulled the bomb into place under the hull, it was detonated by an electrical current along a wire. Ingenious for its time."

"Yeah. Not to mention really well made to stay potent after a couple of hundred years. Those damn things must have stayed airtight. But more importantly, who could have built such a thing as the *Nautilus* back then and kept it secret all these years?"

Mr. Singh displayed one of his rare, brief smiles as he turned the book back toward himself and flipped to another page. "It is interesting to note," he said, "that Robert Fulton died in 1815, before he could work on his new design. But there was also a confederate of his, an Englishman named Captain Robert Johnstone, who had worked with Fulton on his earlier submarine projects. According to historical records, Captain Johnstone was also a smuggler, a privateer, and a soldier of fortune."

"Sounds like he could have worked for Argo," I opined, with Nick grunting agreement.

"Indeed," Mr. Singh said as he consulted the book again. "In 1817, Captain Johnstone was arrested in England on charges of conspiracy. He was suspected of collaborating in a plot to rescue Napoleon Bonaparte from exile on Saint Helena Island. Specifically by planning to build a submarine for that very purpose."

"Damn," I breathed. "With all things considered, from the *Nautilus* to the secret underground harbor, you'd think Jules Verne must have come across this information somewhere. At least he got to live to tell his tale, unlike poor Percy Shelley. Madame Ombra told me that she and her organization were in the business of keeping secrets throughout the ages, but whoever Ombra's people are, I'm betting Verne was one of them."

Nick trained his sharp blue eyes on me like a pair of lasers. "Speaking of the cavern under the watchtower, you mentioned earlier that you found evidence that people had used the cave during the Second World War?"

"Yeah. That threw me for a bit. But between the shotgun booby trap and the German Army ammunition boxes, it's certain that someone had been down there up until the 1940s at least."

"German ammunition boxes, you said," Nick rumbled.

"Yeah."

Nick and Mr. Singh traded looks. "Rommel's treasure?" Mr. Singh asked aloud.

"I'd bet on it," Nick growled.

"Someone want to fill me in?" I inquired.

It was Mr. Singh who spoke. "It is said that during the Second World War, Rommel's Afrika Corps smuggled out a quantity of gold, silver, and jewels from North Africa and hid them in an underwater cave near Corsica. The treasure was purportedly carried inside metal ammunition boxes."

I saw in my mind's eye how the insides of those rusted old ammo boxes gleamed with traces of gold. "Oh. Well, if there was any treasure there, then someone cleaned it out long before I arrived."

"Which brings us back to the fact that for all of your efforts, you've got nothing to show for it. Not even one measly Chinese bronze vase," Nicholas grumbled. He stared out into space for a moment, and then said, "Was it truly Napoleon Bonaparte in that tomb?"

"I didn't get close enough to see myself. But Rhea sure as hell saw something that pushed her over the edge. And speaking of the sarcophagus, just what the hell did Napoleon do with the body of Alexander?"

"We may never know the truth of it," Nick growled softly. "Let's face it—if there's one thing we've all learned in this business, it's that there are Lies, Damned Lies, and History."

I nodded silent agreement, seeing in my mind's eye the secret library hidden away in the depths of the Château de Joux as it burned in the searing flames, and wondered how many long-buried secrets were lost in the ashes.

"And now," Nick mused, "all we've got to show for our troubles is one tattered old letter from Lord Byron."

"Do me a favor?" I asked. "Give Byron's letter to

Abby Pennyworth. She really helped me in getting this whole thing figured out. She deserves something."

"Great," Nick rasped sourly. "I give away the one artifact we recover, and I lose my best man in the bargain."

Nick's words brought me back to the finality of the moment. Too many people, especially government types, had seen what a dangerous creature I'd been made to be. There was no way Nick could afford to keep me with his band of pirates and still maintain the fictional innocent cover of the Argo Foundation. I watched Mr. Singh take the china teacups away from the table, the tea being yet another ritual of our meetings, and I thought of how much I would miss all of this as Nick Riley reached for the bottle of twenty-one-year-old Scotch, the traditional signal that our business was concluded and it was time for the toast.

But I had one last thing to do before I left. I reached down to the hardwood floor and picked up the plain black nylon bag I'd carried with me all the way from Vanya's island. I placed the bag carefully on the table as Nick poured drinks for himself and me and Mr. Singh returned with his teacup refilled. "What's that you got?" Nick asked.

"Something you may be interested in," I announced as I lifted the old rectangular wooden box out of the bag. "I found this while rummaging around Vanya's island. This is the Egyptian scroll I picked up when I was in the catacombs of Paris. From what I was told, this could actually be the books of magic that Septimius Severus placed inside the tomb of Alexander back around 200 AD. It may even be one of the legendary Books of Thoth."

Old Nick's eyes bulged underneath his shaggy brows as he slowly reached a hand across the table, but I slid the box back toward myself before he got there. "Of course, since you had to fire me, I guess that makes me an independent businessman now."

Nick had to try twice before he ground out the word "What?"

"So I guess the bottom line is, how much are you willing to pay me for it?"

I thought Nick was going to explode. And he did. With laughter. And while he roared, I saw a twitch of a smile from Mr. Singh, though it was almost concealed by his thick black beard.

When Nick finally wound down, he wiped away an imaginary tear from his guileless-appearing blue eyes. He leaned back and placed his hands on the equator of his belly and said to no one in particular, "It's always a bit sad when the children grow up." Then he graced me with his most gentle smile as he said flatly, "Let's talk."

In the end, I came out with more money than I expected, which was a complete reversal from my usual poker game losses I'd suffered at that very table over the years. We all said our farewells in the time-honored way of men, and I left as something welled up in the base of my throat—I was damned if I was going to be the only one to give an emotional display.

It was nearly ten o'clock at night when I walked out to the sidewalk, where a summoned cab awaited. I turned and took one long, last look at the fortress-like brownstone that was the one fixed point in the chaotic pattern of my second life. Then I turned away and settled into the backseat of the cab as one of Mr. Singh's countrymen expertly drove me to the busy, noisy streets of Midtown Manhattan. I looked out the window at all the people making their way along the crowded sidewalks. At that moment, I was content just knowing that every single one of them could just go about the everyday business of living, and they would never have to know about the imminent catastrophe that they'd just missed.

I let the taxi drop me off near Times Square and walked with the bustling crowds under the frantic, megalithic marquee lights up toward the Algonquin Hotel. I nodded to the doorman and said hello to the cat as I made my way through the wood-paneled lobby then headed up the stairs toward what I hoped to be my future. I quietly opened the door and went toward the bed in the darkened room. In the light that came through the window I saw Caitlin's golden hair spilling across the white pillow. I knelt beside her and let my eyes adjust until I could see her face. I'd spent a lot of time just watching her sleep back on Vanya's island. It was a sight I knew I'd never grow tired of.

She must have sensed my presence because she slowly stretched her arms above the covers and opened her lovely eyes a bit. "Hello, you," she said sleepily.

"Hi yourself. Hey, I've got money."

"That's good," she said with her secretive smile playing on her lips. "I certainly didn't marry you for your looks."

"Do you think your doctors would allow you to have a real drink with dinner tomorrow tonight?"

"Probably. Why?"

"I'm in the mood to buy you a really expensive martini."

A tomb now suffices him for whom the whole world was not sufficient.

—ALEXANDER OF MACEDONIA

Venice, Italy

I was standing outdoors in the wide space between two massive pillars, flanked and guarded by a saint armed with spear and shield atop the pillar on my left and a winged lion on my right as I looked over the crowded Piazza San Marco in Venice. I was hoping it would turn out to be a lousy place to commit a murder. Namely mine.

It was midmorning on a bright, hot, late-summer day and the plaza was alive with crowds of people and flights of pigeons among the beautiful façades with vaulted archways and columns crowned by marble statues. Ahead of me I could see the proud domes and elaborate spires of the Basilica of Saint Mark and the tall red-and-white clock tower pointing like a gigantic arrow toward heaven. Music from a string quartet wafted in the air, underscored by the sound of small motorboats in the waterway behind me.

There was too much motion and confusion to spot trouble coming, and I hoped that meant too many witnesses in the event that someone had lured me here just to drop me in a Venetian canal. I was an easy target, standing between the marble pillars like they were oversized gun sights. It was almost a relief when I heard the voice of Mr. Ombra say from close behind me, "Napoleon called the Piazza San Marco the 'Drawing Room of Europe.' It is easy still to see why."

I turned around, slowly, and saw Monsieur and Madame Ombra standing before me. They were both dressed in white—a casual suit for him and a long summer dress for her—and both wore wide-brimmed straw hats, looking for all the world like middle-aged tourists out for a stroll. I squinted against the glare of the sunlight dancing off the water behind them as I said, "Well, you're both looking much better than the last time I saw you."

Madame Ombra came up and took my hands in hers, kissing my cheeks in greeting. "It is with thanks to you that we are."

I looked to Mr. Ombra. "Just how did you get away from Vanya's island? You drove a certain government agent I know crazy when you disappeared."

Ombra waved the question away as if it held no importance as his wife said, "We are both just glad that you received our message and decided to meet with us."

"Let's just say my curiosity won out over sanity. So what do you want?"

Madame Ombra smiled as she said, "We truly wanted to thank you in person. We owe both of our lives to you. Also, we wish to pose a question to you."

"I have a question of my own," I said. "Who are you?"

The Ombras traded a look between themselves, one that held that subtle telepathy shared by lovers of many years. Then Madame Ombra replied, "The 'who' is immaterial, Mr. Blake. Over the long centuries, we have had many names, but always we have stayed in the shadows."

Mr. Ombra said, "The true history of the world will never be found in any book, Mr. Blake. For what you believe is history is nothing more than a thin tissue of lies and suppositions. The truth is far stranger. And we are the guardians of that truth."

"Truth? The truth about what?"

Madame Ombra said gently, "The truth of our struggles, for several hundred years, to shape and guide and, yes, to rule mankind. But always as the invisible power behind the thrones of the kings and queens of the world."

My head was spinning from the implications that poured from their words. "So, Napoleon Bonaparte was . . . one of you?"

"It is more fair to say that Emperor Bonaparte had the benefit of our guidance," Madame Ombra replied. "At least at first," she added with a slight, knowing smile.

"And so everything I saw—the treasure room in the Parisian catacombs, the *Nautilus*, Alexander's sarcophagus—they were all because of . . . you?"

The Ombras didn't answer. But the steady looks I received from them both made an eloquent though silent affirmative.

"You mean to tell me that your organization has been pulling the strings behind the scenes all throughout history with no one being the wiser?" I asked.

"Let me ask you this," Madame Ombra said in lieu of a reply. "With all that you personally learned about the fate of Napoleon and the island of Corsica, why is it that you have not told the world yourself?"

While I stood in the warm sunshine, surrounded by people who went about their business completely unaware of the fact that three individuals among them were discussing crimes and conspiracies of epic proportions, my memories ran through my head in a tangled, violent collage. Finally, I found the words to say, "From what I see, the people of France have their emperor on display in Paris. And on Corsica, a sick and tired old man who once accomplished great things got his wish for a final resting place. And if anyone ever found out how close we all came to a worldwide plague epidemic, it'd have caused a panic."

"Just so," Madame Ombra said like a teacher whose pupil came up with the right answer.

"And that, my friend," Mr. Ombra added, "is how secrets have always been kept. Our Benjamin Franklin said it best: 'History is written by the winners.'"

"Your Ben Franklin? What do you mean by that?"

I received only a pair of gentle smiles in response. "So why are you telling me all of this?" I asked.

The Ombras shared their secretive glance with one another again, and then Madame Ombra said, "We have grown old, Mr. Blake, and our people are now few in number. We bear the burden of keeping safe the true history of the world, and our work will never end. We need new people who can carry on with our task. Someone with intelligence and, shall we say, special skills? We need someone like you."

"Think of it, Mr. Blake," Mr. Ombra added earnestly. "You would be granted access to all of our knowledge; all of our records would be yours."

"I thought the library in Fort de Joux was destroyed?"

"No," Madame Ombra said serenely. "When our men arrived at the chateau, they discovered that the door to the archives room had been shut, I assume by you? The fire died out and much of the library was saved. But in truth, that was only one of our repositories. And a small one at that."

"But why keep these secrets for all these years?"

Madame Ombra said, "In our struggles to make a better world, we have had to be ruthless. If the true nature of our actions were to be made known, we would be judged as criminals, and worse."

Mr. Ombra said, in a voice gone soft, "All you have seen, Mr. Blake, is only the smallest thread in a very large tapestry. Join us, and you will become one of the very, very few to truly know the secret history of the world."

My head was swimming with the possibilities, and then just as quickly I started drowning in them as I remembered all the death and destruction that surrounded the Ombras like crows over a battlefield. I looked past the pair of them to the sparkling Adriatic Sea beyond and thought of an English poet who was killed, all because he learned of just one of the terrible secrets that Ombra was speaking of.

"No," I said at last. "Sorry. But the price is too high."

The Ombras both looked down, Madame Ombra whispering, "So. That is unfortunate."

I felt an old, familiar tinge of pending danger dance along my spine as I asked, "So what happens now?"

"Now," Madame Ombra said, "we part as friends, and sincerely hope we never meet again."

"We still owe you a debt for our lives," Mr. Ombra said, somewhat wistfully. "Tell me, do you intend to pursue the tomb of Alexander?"

"What? No. That was Vanya's quest, not mine. And anyway, I'm officially retired."

The two of them did it again, shared a silent communication between themselves, only this time it was like a pair of mischievous children who were up to something. "Have you had a chance to see the Piazza San Marco yet?" Mr. Ombra inquired casually.

"No."

"It's quite beautiful," Madame Ombra said. "It was fortunate that Napoleon spared the city of Venice when he conquered it in 1797. Although his ransom demands were quite severe. Napoleon was paid not only with gold and priceless artworks, but also in rare books and manuscripts. Still, you should be certain to see the Basilica of Saint Mark. It has a fascinating history, you see."

"Oh?"

Madame Ombra said, "Tell me, Mr. Blake; what do you know of the saints?"

"Enough to know that I'll never be one."

Beneath the rim of her hat, Madame Ombra's blue eyes were alight. "It is said that the body of Saint Mark was brought to Venice in secret in the year 828 AD, from a tomb in the place where he was martyred: Alexandria."

I felt the word catch in my throat as I said, "Alex-andria?"

"Yes," Mr. Ombra answered with a cryptic tone. "The body of the saint was taken from the very city that was also Alexander the Great's final resting place."

"It seems a strange coincidence, does it not?" Madame Ombra said to her husband, but for my benefit. "How so shortly after he conquered Venice, Napoleon sailed to Alexandria. One might wonder if he learned something from those archaic manuscripts he acquired. Such as the location of a certain tomb discovered by Venetian sailors hundreds of years before. The tomb would have been empty by the time Napoleon arrived in Alexandria, of course. But who is to say if that particular tomb had once contained the body of a saint, or that of a demigod?"

I slowly turned and looked back over the piazza to the domes and spires of the basilica in the distance. At first glance, it reminded me of the Chapel du Val de Grâce in Paris, but a closer look revealed how the French chapel was a poor pauper compared to the Byzantine majesty of the basilica. My mind was surrounded by bits and pieces of fact and speculation, blown around my head like leaves in the wind: Napoleon . . . Saint Mark . . . Alexander. "Wait," I said, not taking my eyes off the basilica domes. "Are you trying to tell me that the remains of Alexander the Great are actually inside . . ."

I stopped speaking as I belatedly realized that the Ombras had silently vanished from behind me. I was looking back toward the basilica, my mind churning over the possibilities, when I felt a warm hand take hold of my own.

"You mind telling me what that was all about?" Caitlin inquired.

Her presence took hold and brought me back to the here and now. She was standing next to me with her golden hair spilling to her shoulders and her lovely eyes shaded by her sunglasses. She was dressed in a brightly colored blouse and white shorts that revealed shapely legs, which were starting to show a healthy glow.

Caitlin continued by saying as if to a backwards child, "The Ombras. You know, that nice couple that almost killed you a time or two? Why did they want to meet with you? Don't get me wrong; I'm glad I didn't have to come to your rescue. It's far too nice a day to ruin it with bloodshed. But why did they want you to come all the way here?"

I shook my head. "They offered me the secrets of the world."

"Really?" Caitlin said dryly. "Was it anything like the offer Eve got from the snake?"

I laughed, feeling the spell of the Ombras' words dissipating. "Yeah. Only I didn't bite."

"Good," she said with finality. "Now, I seem to recall that we are supposed to be on a vacation and you promised me a gondola ride. Let's see if you can actually get on a boat and not sink it this time, shall we?"

Before I could answer, Caitlin stopped and said with a delicate eyebrow arched over the rim of her sunglasses, "Jonathan Blake, I'm starting to recognize that look you have right now, rare as it is. You're thinking of something."

I nodded. "Uh-huh."

"What?" she asked suspiciously.

I kept hold of her hand as I looked back over my shoulder.

"I think it's high time you and I went to church."